Down Stepney Way

Sally Worboyes

CORONET BOOKS

Hodder & Stoughton

First published in Great Britain in 1999 by Hodder and Stoughton
First published in paperback in 1999 by Hodder and Stoughton
A division of Hodder Headline PLC

A Coronet Paperback

10 9 8 7 6 5

A CIP catalogue record for this title is available
from the British Library

ISBN 0 340 72876 0

Printed and bound in Great Britain by
Mackays of Chatham plc, Chatham, Kent.

Hodder and Stoughton
A division of Hodder Headline PLC
338 Euston Road
London NW1 3BH

About the author

Sally Worboyes was born and grew up in Stepney with four brothers and a sister. She is married with three children and lives in Norfolk. She has had several plays broadcast on Radio Four, and adapted her play and novel *Wild Hops* as a musical, *The Hop-Pickers*.

Already an established saga writer, Sally Worboyes starts a brilliant new trilogy with *Down Stepney Way*, to which she brings some of the raw history of her own family background.

Also by Sally Worboyes

Wild Hops
Docker's Daughter
The Dinner Lady
Red Sequins
Keep on Dancing

For Mum
My thanks to Kirsty Fowkes and Jane Heller

Chapter One

1936

In the clear October morning, clusters of people from around the East End were gathering in Cable Street with one aim in mind — to stop the Blackshirts from marching through Stepney. Some were filling their pockets with stones from ready-made piles while others armed themselves with pieces of splintered wood and bottles. The sombre mood changed to one of unease when a local lad arrived, excited and out of breath, to announce that the march had begun. The Jewish Party and the Communists were joining forces to make it clear that the Fascists would *not* get through.

Oswald Mosley had originally planned to meet his legion at Royal Mint Street, march on to Aldgate, along Commercial Road and into Salmon Lane in Limehouse, where a big outdoor meeting was to be held, but the route had been changed. He was in fact leading the Blackshirts along the Highway by the docks towards Cable Street.

The police were out in force, there to see the procession through without trouble, but men, women and children were ready to rebel against authority and had come out to make their voices heard and to show their outrage. Along the route barricades had been built of beds, chairs, and anything else that the people could lay their hands on. Prepared for the worst, the Jewish Party had set up a first-aid post in Aldgate, near the Whitechapel library, and a team of cyclist messengers had been organised between main points and headquarters. Another team was ready to rally those still inside their homes and urge them to come out and help stop the march of the Fascists.

Suddenly another young messenger climbed onto a make-shift platform and yelled, 'They're coming! They're coming! The Blackshirts are coming!'

There was a roar of protest and then the brass band began to play. Soon the streets were filled with patriotic song: 'Rule, Britannia, Britannia rules the waves, Britons never never never Shall be slaves . . .'

Jessie Warner gripped her younger brothers' hands and pulled them through the seething mob. Pushing and dragging the boys, she wove her way through as best she could, cursing herself for taking this route home from the Tower of London.

'Is it a war, Jessie? Is it?' Stephen, the seven-year-old, was too frightened to cry.

'No, Stephen, but we shouldn't be here! There's going to be a fight!'

'Why, Jessie? Why are they going to fight? They're grown-ups . . .'

'Just don't let go of my hand,' she ordered.

'It's the Blackshirt march, Stephen!' screeched Alfie, fired up and doing his utmost to pull away from his sister. 'We can watch from a side road!'

'No! Keep moving!' Jessie kept a tight hold on both of them but the sudden jerking as thirteen-year-old Alfie stopped in his tracks caused her to lose her balance and twist her ankle. Her scream shot through the noise of the mob but was ignored. She limped across the pavement to sit on the windowsill of an old terraced house.

'You shouldn't have done that, Alfie,' said Jessie, wincing in pain. 'You could have brought the three of us down.'

Alfie wasn't listening; stretched to full height and craning his neck, he was desperate to get a view through the ever growing assembly. 'I'm gonna make my way up the Highway to watch 'em march!'

'You are not! You stay right where you are until this pain eases, then we'll go home, *together*.'

'Come out of your houses!' a young Jewish lad flew by, yelling at top voice. 'They're on their way. Come out and fight!' He was waving a red flag. 'The police are there as well! The police are coming!'

'It *is* a war, Jessie,' murmured Stephen, tears now rolling down his cheeks. 'They're going to blow us up. I want to go home.'

'We will, sweetheart. We will. Just give me a minute.' She pulled the silk scarf from her neck and tied it round her ankle.

'Ready now then, Jess?' asked Stephen, gripping her hand.

'Nearly.' Jessie removed her combs which had come loose, pulled her long wavy hair back and secured it. 'Now we'll go. We'll stop off at Grandfather's and—'

'The police are on horseback!' Alfie was beside himself. 'They've got batons and guns!'

Within seconds, stones and bottles were being thrown in the direction of the mounted police. Shouted insults followed. More stones. More bottles. The sound of breaking glass and yells of abuse were terrifying. 'Surrender!' yelled one man. 'They shall not pass! *They shall not pass!*' Others joined in with the chant and more groups arrived carrying banners. The noise reached a crescendo and Cable Street was packed with an army of civilians ripe for confrontation.

Alfie cheered loudly. 'They're pulling up railings and paving stones!' he said excitedly.

'We should go *now*, Jessie,' said Stephen, trying to be brave.

'Yes, we should.' Grabbing Alfie by the collar, Jessie hauled him away, defying the sickening pain shooting through her ankle.

3

Alfie half-heartedly struggled against her but deep down he, too, was frightened. The oncoming clatter of hooves on cobblestones and sound of breaking glass urged Jessie on and gave her the strength of two people. She pushed through the mob, her ears ringing with the roar of the protesters: 'Down with the Fascists! Fuck off to Germany! Sod off to Spain! Go and live in Italy! Get out of England!'

When the three of them reached their grandfather's house in Broom Court, Jessie was trembling. Stephen had stopped crying but the occasional sob still escaped as his mind filled with what he had seen and heard. Alfie was moody with himself because secretly he had wanted to leave the frightening scene. But he could always blame his big sister – it was she, after all, who had forced him away. Still, he was angry at missing an opportunity to throw stones at the police.

'It's not fair,' he grumbled. 'There were lots of kids there who were younger than me. I shouldn't 'ave took any notice of you, Jessie. If it wasn't for you hurting your ankle, I wouldn't 'ave come away.'

'Shut up, Alfie, and don't you *dare* cheek Grandmother Blake this time.' Instead of knocking respectfully on the door, as she would normally, Jessie found herself banging the knocker with some urgency. Grandmother Blake appeared looking very stern and disdainful.

'I'm sorry,' said Jessie, shrinking, 'we were in Cable Street and—'

'You've woken your grandfather,' came the terse reply. 'You shouldn't be knocking at all, never mind nearly smashing the door down. What do you want?'

'If we could just come in ... I've sprained my ankle and—'

'If you could walk from Cable Street to here, you can walk home. Let your mother see to you.' Her unyielding expression showed no sign of weakening as she began to close the door.

'I'm very thirsty,' said the brave Stephen, 'and Jessie's ankle is very, very swollen!'

Glancing dispassionately at Jessie's leg, Grandmother Blake raised her eyes and sighed. 'That's nothing. Tell your mother to put a cold flannel on it.'

'If we can just come into the passage for a tiny while,' pleaded Jessie. Her ankle was throbbing badly. 'I need to sit down on the stairs and if Stephen could have a glass of water—'

'No. Your grandfather's resting. He needs the quiet.' The door was slowly closing between them when Jessie heard the familiar quiet cough of her grandfather in the passage.

'That's all right,' came the softer voice of the man she loved. 'Let them come in for a minute.'

'Please yourself,' said Grandmother Blake, turning away. 'They can wait in the hall. I'll fetch a glass of water.'

'You shouldn't bang on the door like that,' said Willy, as his grandchildren filed in. 'What's the matter?' He looked from the boys to Jessie. 'Did someone hurt you?'

Alfie peered up at him. 'What's a Fascist?'

Quietly chuckling, Willy pulled on his braces. 'Someone who's not a Jew. Why?'

'There's a battle going on in Cable Street and—'

'Blackshirts and Reds,' sighed Willy, rolling his eyes. 'I might have guessed. Go on down into the scullery, you can wrap a wet cloth round that ankle, Jessie. I'll get Grandmother Blake to make a pot of weak tea to warm your bellies, then be off home.' Gazing into Jessie's frightened face he tried to comfort her with one of his infrequent smiles. 'Gang warfare, that's all it is. Give it a month and it'll be forgotten.'

'I'm sorry we didn't go straight home, Grandfather, but my ankle – I could hardly walk another step.'

'That's all right,' he said, 'you did the right thing, but don't stay too long. You know your grandmother likes her quiet.'

That was the last time Jessie saw her grandfather alive. A few weeks later, Willy returned from a day's work at his cobbler shop, sat down by the fire and slept his last sleep. He had told no one about the severe pains in his chest that had been troubling him of late.

Jessie took his death very badly, crying into her pillow nightly and asking the same question of God over and over. Why? Why him? Why was her grandfather dead when there were so many wicked people walking about in the streets?

Unlike Willy's other grandchildren, Jessie had been a regular visitor to 10 Broom Court since she was old enough to walk there on her own. Sometimes when she'd banged the iron knocker of the dark green door, one of her uncles would appear in the doorway, frowning. He'd put a finger to his lips and whisper in warning, 'Grandfather's in a mood.'

Shrugging, Jessie would slip past, along the narrow passageway and down the staircase to the basement where she knew he would be sitting in his armchair, looking into the glowing coals of the fire. Willy Blake had spent most of his leisure time thinking or reading. When he was absorbed in a book, Jessie would tiptoe across the room, lower herself into the other armchair by the fire and keep quiet until spoken to.

She loved the small, quiet room, with just the sound of the hissing coals, the rustle of a page as he turned it, and the breathing of his black mongrel dog, Peggy, who lay quietly at his feet. It was here that she discovered the reward of patience. When in the right mood, her grandfather would draw her into his private world, arousing her interest and curiosity. Then, he would tell her fascinating stories of times gone by. Other times, not one single word passed between them. He would end the visit by closing his book and giving her a nod or she would leave of her own accord, sensing his mood, and quietly pull the door shut behind her until she heard the brass catch drop.

When arrangements were being made for his funeral, Jessie was mortified to hear that even though she was sixteen, a working girl and the eldest of her brothers and sister, she was still considered too young to attend his funeral.

'It's not an occasion for young people, Jessie,' explained her mother, Rose. 'Stop fussing now and be more like your brothers and sister. They don't want to go.'

But Jessie did want to go, very much. There had been a special bond between her and her grandfather. She had inherited his Germanic looks, hair so blonde it was almost white and blue eyes, and was the only grandchild to have done so. She knew she was closer to him than any of the others.

On the day he was buried, Jessie stood with her arms woven through the black railings outside his house in Broom Court, watching with the neighbours as the hearse slowly pulled away. The sound of the horses' hooves echoing on the flagstones reminded her of the last day she saw him alive, the day of the Cable Street battle.

An occasional shake of the head and pursing of lips were the only movements from onlookers. To the people who lived in the courtyard, he was an ordinary man, of few words, who'd always return a smile and doff his hat or cap and who kept himself to himself. A silver-haired gentleman, no more, no less.

Jessie often thought about his last comforting words to her after the riot in Cable Street. *Give it a month and it'll be forgotten.* But he had been wrong. People were still talking about it. Communists were boasting that they had won the biggest fight in working-class history and the Blackshirts were angry because their march had been stopped. Insulting slogans against Jews were still appearing on walls in Jessie's neighbourhood.

Much to the family's dismay, Grandmother Blake soon married. Her new husband was a man with whom she had been having a secret affair. The grandchildren were told to call him Uncle. It was then that Jessie stopped going to the house. The mood there changed – the parties had begun. The piano in the best room, where Willy used to sit and play soft tunes, was used to accompany bawdy songs of the day, sung by the gathering of boozy friends. Laughter and ribald conversation filled the place, forcing out any trace of Willy's presence as master of the house.

On her last visit and before the new 'uncle' moved in, Jessie asked permission to tidy the locked cupboard to the left of the fireplace where her grandfather used to sit. It was his private cupboard and no one had been allowed to pry into it. Grandmother Blake grudgingly let her, though it was clear the contents of the cupboard didn't interest her much. Jessie hadn't got far in her search for something that would remind her of him when she found a small worn family album. She didn't recognise anyone in any of the faded photographs except for the one of her grandfather, which was loose and at the back of the album. Younger though he was, his eyes and high cheekbones placed him. He was standing with one hand resting on the hood of a large, old-fashioned pram, and in the pram, cramped together in a space for one, were two baby girls, sitting up and smiling.

Before closing the album, Jessie found, tucked inside its leather cover, a marriage certificate – between William Ernest Gunter and Ingrid Weiss. She held her breath and stared at it, knowing it was important but not understanding why. Then, for the first time in her life Jessie stole something. She stole the certificate and the loose photograph, stuffing them quickly into her boot, half afraid Grandmother Blake would burst in and catch her. For some reason she felt that the two were connected and that the piece of paper belonged to Willy, even though the surname wasn't the one she knew him by. The name of the woman he'd married, according to the certificate, was a mystery too, because it wasn't the name of her grandmother, or at least not the name of the person she had believed to be her grandmother. Was it possible that the cold, unfeeling woman known to her as Grandmother Blake was not kin after all? *She's Willy's daughter, all right,* is what Jessie had heard said about her own mother, Rose, but she couldn't remember anyone saying that she was the daughter of Grandmother Blake.

With the marriage certificate and photo safely hidden inside her ankle boot, Jessie left that special room for the last time. Heart pounding, she took the stairs two at a time, terrified that she might be found out. Once outside in the street, she made her way home to Stepney Green, and in the privacy of the bedroom she shared with her sister, Dolly, she pulled the crinkled document from her boot and read it again. William Ernest Gunter, occupation shoemaker. Her grandfather's Christian names were William Ernest and he had been a shoemaker but the surname was wrong. His name, so everyone had been led to believe, was Blake, and the woman thought to be his wife was hardly German, and her name was not Ingrid.

Jessie glanced around her bedroom for a secure place to hide her finds. She fixed on the air vent which had a metal cover. She climbed onto a chair and slipped both the certificate and photograph inside, safe in the knowledge that she could reach in and take it out whenever she wanted. Happier, she lay down on her bed, feeling as if she still had a very special part of her grandfather to herself. She wondered if Ingrid Gunter might still be his wife and her own real grandmother. She must have died – it seemed the only explanation. Jessie allowed herself a brief dream that the old woman was alive and lived nearby.

Jessie felt a mixture of hope and warmth at the thought. Maybe the strange feeling that had come and gone all through her life could now be explained. The feeling that something or someone was missing from her world. She decided then that somehow she would find out the truth and perhaps discover her real grandmother.

On Christmas Eve, following Willy's death, Jessie woke to the sound of her father, Robert, coughing in the passage. His footsteps on the lino had seemed to be part of her dream, but from the thin stream of light shining through the gap under the bedroom door she could make out her surroundings and was relieved to realise that she was in her room and out of the bad dream which had gripped her. Shadowy, evil men had been chasing her and her grandfather through dark woods. She had been having recurring nightmares since her grandfather died.

Safe and secure, she glanced at her sister Dolly, fast asleep in her bed a few feet away. Dolly, at the age of fifteen, slept as soundly as a baby. Alfie and little Stephen shared the bedroom next door and above them were the two attic rooms where the lodgers Mr and Mrs McCarthy lived.

Lying in her warm bed, with the sound of muted voices below, Jessie looked forward to the beginning of this special day, her seventeenth birthday. Hearing the mantel clock strike six, she did as she always did and drew her feather eiderdown round her, making the most of it. The room was freezing cold and condensation had iced on the inside of the window. She would wait until she heard the sound of the street door close behind her father as he went out into the frosty morning, on his way to the docks where he worked as a crane driver. Much as she wanted to see him before he went out, she knew he wouldn't have time to see her open her presents.

A few minutes after the street door closed behind him, she got up, wrapped her grey blanket round her and crept out of the room, only to find that her brother Alfie was in the passage, ready himself to creep downstairs.

'Where do you think you're going, Alfie?' said Jessie, all-knowing.

'To get a glass of water. I'm gasping.'

'Well, just you go back to bed and I'll fetch it up.' This wasn't the first time that Alfie had tried to creep downstairs on Christmas Eve before her.

'I can get it myself,' he barked. 'I'm not a cripple.'

Smiling at him, Jessie slowly shook her head. 'It won't work, you know. It's *my* birthday and you know that you're not allowed to go down before me. The same as none of us are allowed to go down before you on your birthday.'

'That was when we were kids,' he said. 'You're seventeen

now, and I'm nearly thirteen. I can't be bothered with all of that baby stuff.' He turned towards the staircase, but Jessie was too quick for him. She grabbed the corded waist of his pyjamas and would not let go.

'You're not too old for a clip round the ear,' she said. 'Now get back to bed and I'll bring you a glass of water up, and don't start arguing or you'll wake the lodgers. If they leave, Mum loses the rent and that means no pocket money for you and Stephen.'

'What do I care about pocket money? I'll be going to work soon.' He pulled away from her and slouched back to his room.

'Alfie, haven't you forgotten something?'

'No. Oh, yeah. Happy birthday,' he mumbled grudgingly.

She couldn't blame him, thought Jessie, going downstairs; it was, after all, Christmas Eve and as grown-up as Alfie liked to act, he was still a boy, especially at this time of year. More excited than little Stephen at times.

In the kitchen, after a birthday kiss and greeting from Rose, Jessie sat by the warm cooking range, her bare feet close to the glowing coals, and watched her mother lay the table. As well as the two best cups and saucers and small china plate of tea biscuits, Rose had spread the special lace-edged cloth the way she always did on her birthday and for some reason Jessie was reminded of the Christmas Eve morning when she was thirteen. Dolly had been given a new doll with arms and legs which were double-jointed, Alfie had got his train set and little Stephen, after months of pleading, was rewarded with something which was a strange request for a boy – a plain doll's house, made by their father, in which he'd placed quite a few of his lead soldiers.

Jessie had been given a red patent-leather box handbag and matching shoes, the first time she'd not been given a toy of some sort for Christmas. It was also the first time she had given Dolly one of her prize possessions. She gave her sister her bassinet pram for her new doll.

'I hope those boys are not going to come bounding down yet,' said Rose, breaking into her thoughts. 'There's a lot to do before I feed them.'

'I don't think they will.' Jessie's mind turned to her grandfather. She would miss the family visit made to him each year on Christmas morning, when he would be spruced up in his best clothes, with a small present for each of them piled up next to the fire. The few words that he repeated every year went through her mind. *It wasn't cheap so look after it.*

Gripped by a sudden need to touch and look at his photograph, she slipped out of the kitchen and went quietly to her bedroom. Standing on a chair, her hand inside the air vent, feeling for the secret document and photograph, she was appalled to find they had gone.

Rose's quiet voice behind her made her jump. 'I had a feeling you'd be digging around for those. You'd best come downstairs, Jessie.'

Jessie looked across to Dolly, worried.

'Don't fret about lazy bones,' said Rose. 'The house could fall in and she'd still sleep on. I dare say she's dreaming about Christmas time in the days of old.' Only one subject had interested the rebellious Dolly during her schooldays – the history of London from the time of the Romans who had named it Londinium. A casual reference to 'the twin-hilled City of the South ... girt about by fen and marshes' by her teacher had caught her imagination. From that day onwards, when she was no more than nine years old, Dolly had read and listened and questioned and bored to death even those who *were* interested in her chosen subject – and most were not.

Back in the kitchen, Rose, a little shaky, poured them both a cup of tea. 'I suppose your seventeenth birthday is as good a time as any to tell you a bit of home truth,' she said.

Ashamed, Jessie felt herself blush. 'I shouldn't have hidden Grandfather's things like that but, well, I wasn't sure what to do about them once I'd taken them and time just went on and—'

'It doesn't matter about that. I noticed that the metal cover on the air vent wasn't on properly. That's how I found your secret. The marriage certificate's safe now in my document box. Best we don't say anything to Dolly or the boys just yet.'

Flattered that her mother was speaking to her as an equal, Jessie rose to the occasion. 'I know you don't like me to be disrespectful but I've never really warmed to Grandmother Blake.'

'I know, but that's to be expected. She's not exactly put herself out for you, has she? She's not interested in any of my children, or me, for that matter, and I think you've worked out for yourself the reason why.' Rose sipped her tea, and waited.

'I'm not really sure, Mum, but I think I can guess.' Feeling as if she was treading on eggshells, Jessie went on, 'It was the name Gunter ... and, well, I did happen to see your birth certificate once and on that you're down as Gunter as well. Rose Maud Gunter. I wasn't spying, it's just that—'

'You were curious. You don't have to feel bad about it. I'd be disappointed if you didn't care less. Grandmother Blake is *not* my mother. What's more, and this you must keep to yourself, she and your grandfather were never married. He never married her because he never divorced his first wife – my real mother. You can work out what that makes my half-brothers and that's why we have to keep the skeleton locked in the cupboard. They don't know about it.'

Mystified by the casual way Rose was revealing family secrets to her, Jessie did her best to look and sound normal and to keep it going. 'So ... your real mother couldn't have married again either.'

'No.' Rose lowered her eyes. 'I really don't want to say much more than that, Jessie. It's enough that you've brought things to the surface. I *shall* tell you about it, but not now. Not today. Let's keep today a happy one. It's Christmas Eve and it's your birthday.' She looked at Jessie pensively. 'We'll keep the lid on it for now. It's a sad can of worms, I'm afraid.' Pulling herself out of her mood, Rose brightened. 'I've got a present for you which belonged to my mother. I was keeping it for your twenty-first when I thought I'd be ready to tell you everything about my past, but you may as well have it now. Now that you know.' Rose handed Jessie a small wrapped packet. 'It's a bit old-fashioned, so you don't *have* to wear it if you don't want to.' Wanting her daughter to open the present before Dolly or the boys came down, Rose urged her on, reminding Jessie that they had to make a start on the bird and plucking it in the back yard was out of the question. It had turned much colder in the night and the water barrel outside had a layer of ice on it. 'Look after it and keep it safe,' Rose went on. 'I'd like to think that you'll pass it on to your own daughter, one day.'

Untying the ribbon, Jessie slowly unwrapped the paper, savouring this time alone with her mother. She wasn't really expecting it to be anything more than something a bit special, but she was wrong. She could tell by the beautiful, small, red velvet box with domed lid that there was something really lovely inside.

Pushing open the lid with the tip of her thumb, she gazed at the delicate gold and pearl brooch. It wasn't a child's brooch, it was proper jewellery. For a second she thought her mother must have given her the wrong box.

'You clip it on to the collar or neckline of a dress,' Rose told her.

Touching the smooth reddish gold with the tip of her finger, Jessie couldn't find the right words to express herself. It was beautiful.

'My mother gave it to me when . . . when I was very young,' said Rose, casting her eyes down. 'She used to wear it all the time. That much I do remember. That and her sweet smell.' She drew a trembling breath and pushed back her shoulders. Composure was all-important to Rose. 'I've got something put by for Dolly as well. A locket. Apart from a ruby and diamond ring, those two pieces of jewellery were all my mother possessed.' Again, Jessie saw Rose summon her willpower as she quietly coughed and swallowed the lump in her throat. 'She was more of a plain woman than a fancy one when it came to dressing herself.'

Sorry now that she had caused painful memories to surface, Jessie remained quiet. Rose had always lived according to her own Victorian upbringing – that children should keep no secrets – yet here she was, confiding one to her daughter.

'I don't really understand,' Jessie murmured at last, longing to know more.

'You will in time.' Rose locked her fingers together and straightened. 'Now that you know about Granny Blake you'll understand why she's never shown any of you affection. Although to give her her due, she treated me much the same as her sons, more or less. Your grandfather made up for it when he could. I believe he loved me more than he loved my half-brothers, and he loved you, Jessie. He just wasn't very good at expressing himself.'

'He didn't have to show it. I knew.'

'Yes, I suppose you must have. You did spend a lot of time with him. I was pleased about that. It meant a lot to me.' Rose turned away then, saying, 'Maybe I'll be able to talk about my mother in years to come, Jess, but not yet ... and not so soon after your grandfather passing away. So, wear the brooch for high days and holy days and put it somewhere safe the rest of the time.' She added, 'You'll find that life will start changing from now on. Take it as it comes and ask me whatever you have to. I can't promise to answer all of your questions but I'll be disappointed if you go to others for answers.'

Jessie thought of the photograph that had been with the certificate. 'What about the photo of grandfather and the babies in the pram? Who were they?'

'I don't know. I expect it came loose in the album.' Rose turned her face away, hiding her guilt. 'I don't recognise it.' Quickly she changed the subject to the day's work and told Jessie she was to make the porridge while she herself got on with other things. 'No doubt those boys'll be down any minute,' she sighed, emptying her cup. 'I expect Dolly will sleep on until I drag her out of bed.'

Five minutes later she was busy with her chores, quieter than usual, but clearly the day would continue as normal, as if nothing had changed.

That night, before she turned off the gas mantle above her bed, Jessie wrote a few lines in her notebook: '24 December 1936 – Mum's told me a secret which I must keep from Dolly and the boys and it has to do with the mysterious marriage certificate. There are three million unemployed and we are very lucky that Dad has work. In November, Mum became the official owner of Grandfather's cobbler shop.'

It was a good Christmas, despite their recent bereavement. They all loved their presents and were allowed to stuff themselves full of chocolate, oranges and nuts, once they'd eaten their modest Christmas dinner. On 31 December, Jessie wrote in her diary: 'The most important things that happened this year were – on 20 January King George V died. On 10 December King Edward VIII abdicated from the throne. On 4 November William Ernest Gunter died.'

Very soon into the new year of 1937, the country saw a rise in trade and by the end of March Rose took on a cobbler full time. Jessie continued her employment in the offices of a soap factory in Hackney and Dolly started work as a waitress in a gentlemen's club, so small extra treats could be afforded.

The Warner family had been one of the luckier ones in the East End. Not only had Rose made a few pounds each week during the bad times but her husband, Robert, had always managed to get work in the docks, due to his size and hard-working nature. With so many unemployed, ordinary folk hadn't been able to afford to have their footwear soled and heeled but now that things were improving, Rose was considering selling new boots as well as repairing old ones. Spring brought a new feeling of hope to the working classes.

Sadly, though, the Jewish problem had rekindled and Fascist slogans were appearing on walls and hoardings again. No matter how many times the insulting remarks were scrubbed off the wall at the top of Jessie's turning, it did nothing to deter the culprits from slipping out after dark and re-chalking DOWN WITH THE JEWS!

Jessie, deep in thought, was trying to fathom the thinking behind it. The early evening May sunshine streamed in through the scullery window where she was sitting. She had also been remembering that dreadful day when she and the boys had walked innocently into the centre of the battle in Cable Street.

It wasn't just because Max, her boyfriend of two years, was Jewish that she was worried. Having seen the ugly mood of the anti-Facists as well as the menacing behaviour of Blackshirts, she was in fear of what might happen next. After Cable Street and all the publicity that followed, the Blackshirt movement had gone quiet, it was true, but during the past few months it had all started up again.

Shaking herself out of her sombre mood, Jessie got up and washed the pine table with soda water, cursing her sister Dolly for managing, yet again, to duck out of helping in the kitchen. Not that she wanted her around, with her endless chatter about Fred, her boyfriend. When she'd done the table, Jessie took off her apron and slipped into the parlour.

Dolly wasn't sewing the hem of her skirt as she had said but copying another poem from an ancient poetry book she'd found in a second-hand shop in Aldgate and which she would tell Fred she'd written herself – especially for him. She glanced up, her face full of innocence. She was wearing her best orange and black frock.

'If you think you're going to sneak out to see Fred, Dolly, you're out of luck.' Jessie glared at her sister.

Dolly turned a page of her book and sighed, as if she was sick of the sight of Jessie. Adding insult to injury, she then asked in her usual offhand way if she could borrow two shillings. 'It's

Friday, pay day, so I know you've got it, Jess. Fred's taking me to the pictures and paying for my seat but I need the bus fare there and back.'

Sometimes Dolly really did push her luck. The new frock she was wearing had cost her an entire week's wages and was one which Jessie had seen in the window of Pearls Fashions in Mile End Road and told Dolly about. Dolly knew full well that she'd set her heart on buying it and had got in first. That was Dolly.

'No, I won't lend you the money,' said Jessie. 'And what's more, you're not allowed to be by yourself with Fred till you're sixteen and that's nearly a year away.'

'If you tell on me,' said Dolly smugly, 'I'll tell on you. I saw what you were doing with Max on the doorstep last night. He had his hand up your skirt and you're not meant to be doing that, seventeen or not.'

'Your mouth needs to be washed with carbolic. Max isn't like your dirty boyfriends. He respects me.'

Closing her book with a snap, Dolly began to laugh. 'Miss High and Mighty. If you could only see yourself. Acting as if you're over twenty-one. You'll die a spinster, the way you go on. A stuffy, dried-up old maid.'

Hearing their parents coming down the stairs, Jessie bit her tongue. They were going to Hammersmith to visit some of Robert's family, the uppity Warners who had always believed that he had married beneath himself because Rose was a girl from the East End. Jessie was to look after the boys and see to it that Dolly didn't creep out. In truth she was glad that her sister was in a rebellious mood. She wanted her out of the house. Max was coming round.

Jessie leaned towards her sister and spoke in a quiet voice. 'I'm not lending you one penny.' She said this knowing full well that she would pay up, just to see the back of Dolly.

'Are you in there, girls?' Rose's voice drifted in from the passageway.

Dolly answered for them. 'Yes, Mum. I'm just about to do my sewing and Jessie's borrowing my poetry book for a read.' There was a sly smile on her face.

Popping her head round the door, Rose looked pleased. 'Good girls. See the boys go to bed at their proper time, Jessie, and you put away the dishes, Dolly. We'll be in later than usual. You can both stay up till ten o clock and listen to the wireless.'

'Thanks, Ma,' cooed Dolly, adding, 'If I clean all the windows inside and out tomorrow, would you treat me to half-a-crown? I thought I'd pop down to Riley's and buy some coconut ice, for all of us.'

'Take a shilling out of the lodgers' rent tin,' said Rose, straightening her hat, 'and learn a lesson from your reckless ways, spending all that money on a dress and leaving yourself with nothing. You should be ashamed of yourself. And don't think you'll get out of paying double keep next week, because you won't. You'll be just as hard up as you are now because you'll have your borrows to pay back as well. Bus fares to work and the like.' With that Rose disappeared and Robert looked round the door.

'If those boys play up you can send them to bed early, and no arguing, you two. I'll hear it from Alfie if a row breaks out.' He winked at his daughters and left.

Following him to the front door, Jessie asked her father if it would be all right for her to march with him the next day.

He rubbed his chin thoughtfully. 'Well, I don't think anyone else's daughters'll be on the dockers' march, but then not many are like my Jessie, are they? I didn't think it would take long before you took an interest in politics. All right. You can come.'

When they'd gone, Jessie turned her thoughts to Max. Dolly had been lying when she said she'd seen them on the doorstep. It wasn't possible to see the front step from any of the windows. She'd guessed right though, Max had put his hand up her skirt and not for the first time. Little did Dolly know that they'd gone much further than that.

'I heard you talking to Dad, Jessie. You needn't have crept to the front door to ask if you could go with him tomorrow. We all know you're his favourite and can wind him round your little finger. Dockers' march? What are you after then?'

'I'm not after anything. I feel like going on a march with lots of handsome dockers, that's all. Don't worry, I'll tell them I've got a young sister at home who can't wait for it.'

'Speak for yourself,' said Dolly tartly. 'Won't catch me with my knickers down.' She tilted her head to one side and recited, '"Jessie this and Jessie that and Jessie wouldn't pee on the new doormat." If Dad only knew what his beloved Jessie got up to with Max on the doorstep.'

'I don't s'pose for one minute that you've thought any more about our grandmother?' said Jessie, changing the subject which might have led to a scratching session. 'Our *real* grandmother. Because if you haven't, I think it's time you did.'

Dolly looked away, feigning interest in something she'd seen though the window. 'No, Jessie, I 'aven't. Mum's not bothered so why should I be? She's probably dead anyway.' She went back to her copying of other people's thoughts.

'You surprise me. Isn't history what you live and die for? Apart from boys.'

'My interest goes back one thousand seven hundred years, Jessie. You can keep this century and the one before it. I'm only—'

'Yeah, all right, Dolly. No lecture, thank you. As for our grandmother, you've known since February, your birthday, and you love the gold locket Mum gave you, which was *hers*. For all we know she might be living in poverty somewhere, all by herself, wondering if she's got any grandchildren, wondering what her own daughter looks like. She could be a lonely old—'

'Well, whoever she was and wherever she is, she can't be all that 'ard up – she had some nice jewellery so she must've had a few bob. That brooch you collared must be worth something.'

'Three bits of jewellery aren't exactly the crown jewels. For all we know, what she's given us might 'ave been all of her precious belongings.'

Dolly raised her eyes to the ceiling and sighed theatrically. 'I see poor lonely old women every day. You only 'ave to walk down Whitechapel. There are plenty of war widows to take pity on if that's what you want to do with your time. You should join the Salvation Army, the uniform'd suit you.'

Refusing to rise to her sister's bait, Jessie satisfied herself with the fact that Dolly would soon be out of the house and the boys in bed. She had stopped off and bought them a comic each on the way home from work, the *Eagle* and the *Dandy*, which she'd promised they could read by gaslight, ensuring that she and Max would be undisturbed in the sitting room.

Pouring herself a glass of water, Jessie thought about the next day and the real reason for wanting to go on the dockers' march. She wanted to have some time alone with her dad. She would ask him if her real grandmother was still alive and where she was living. He had always listened to her in the past when she had other questions and he'd always answered as best he could – they were close, which made Dolly jealous. Not that Robert showed favour but Dolly loved to be the centre of attention and resented her sister getting some of it.

Jessie opened the tiny iron fire door to the copper boiler and checked to see if the fire needed stoking. The weekend hock of bacon in the simmering water, according to Rose's instructions, had to be taken out at eight o'clock. She was relieved to see that most of the coals were bright orange since the coal bucket was low and the last thing she wanted was to have to go into the dark, damp coal cupboard to fill it. The heat from the boiler didn't do much for her complexion; it was hot enough to redden her pale cheeks and once that happened no amount of face powder would tone them down. She didn't want to look a sight when Max arrived.

She straightened, pushed the fire door shut with the tip of her shoe and went to the window, pressing one side of her face against the cool pane and then the other. Sudden loud banging on the front door startled her.

She hurried to open it. When she saw their neighbour, old Bob Jennings, on the doorstep Jessie knew instantly why he was there. His wife had been very ill, and Jessie guessed she had just passed away and the old man wanted Rose to lay her out. In Tanner Street, it was Rose Warner that people turned to when someone died.

Cap in hand, eyes red-rimmed and too distressed to speak, Bob's grief was all too evident. He and his wife had been married for sixty-two years.

'Mum's not in, Bob,' Jessie said gently.

'Oh,' was his choked reply, 'that's a pity. Do you know what time she'll be back?'

'About half past ten.' Jessie stood to one side and invited him into the passage but he raised a trembling hand.

'I must get back. She's on 'er own – not that she knows much about it.'

'Shall I tell Mum to come over once—'

'No,' he cut in. 'I dare say that'll be too late ... I don't know. What do you think, Jessie? Should I try and get one of the other neighbours?'

She squeezed his arm affectionately, telling him that her parents were walking to Stepney Green station and if she ran she would get to the station before they went through the barrier. Slowly nodding, the old man pushed a hand deep into his trouser pocket and pulled out a shilling, telling her to get a cab. For him to offer her a shilling out of his meagre earnings as warehouse porter meant that it was Rose Warner he wanted to see to his wife, and no one else. Jessie assured him it wasn't necessary to take a cab and that she would be able to catch them up.

Rapidly telling Dolly to see Max into the sitting room when he arrived, Jessie rushed out of the house and hurried through the back streets of Stepney Green, taking every short cut and forcing herself to remember the times when Bob's wife had been full of life. The couple had no children of their own and had made up for it by keeping open house where the children of neighbours were concerned.

Before she fell ill, Mrs Jennings would take in washing each week and sometimes Jessie, as a child, would help out by putting it through the mangle and folding it before carrying neatly ironed piles along the street to the owners. For this she sometimes received sixpence. Sixpence, a mug of cocoa and a biscuit.

As she neared the station, Jessie saw her parents chatting to friends outside the barrier, obviously in no great hurry. Relieved that she'd caught them, she hurried towards them. It was Robert who saw her first and he guessed immediately that something was wrong. His smile dissolved. His first thoughts were for Dolly, Alfie and Stephen.

'It's Betty Jennings,' said Jessie quickly. 'Bob came over . . .'

Rose understood at once. 'Oh dear, I'd better get back.'

'Bob's waiting for you,' said Jessie. 'He's really upset. You go on. I'll catch my breath and follow.'

Robert kissed the top of her head. 'We'll wait while you pull yourself together.'

Jessie shook her head, telling him that she would rather stop there for a minute or two. 'Five minutes, that's all, Dad.' She wanted to be by herself. Leaning against the brick wall of Stepney Green station, she waited until they had gone before she shed a tear. Covering her face, she tried to block out the echoing sound of people talking and laughing in the entrance to the station. Not all of them were there to catch a train; it was a meeting place. Ben the bookie, a familiar figure, small and skinny, was taking bets as usual, eyes darting everywhere, on the look-out for the local bobby.

'You all right, love?' Jessie looked up to see a tall, good-looking man with lovely green eyes smiling at her. 'You ain't asleep, are you?'

'I'm catching my breath if you must know.' Embarrassed, she pulled her handkerchief from her sleeve and blotted her face.

'That's funny, 'cos I'm catching mine as well,' he chuckled.

'Why, is someone chasing you?'

'The law. Some bugger pinched my cap so I pinched someone else's.' He flicked the peak of his cap and winked. 'Best quality as well.'

'I could tell by your voice that you was a tea leaf.'

'And I could tell by your face that you'd have lovely blue eyes – once you opened 'em. Fancy a drink?' He nodded towards the pub on the corner.

'No thanks.' She stepped away, not really wanting to turn down the offer. She would have loved to have had the courage to say yes and go with him, but it didn't seem right.

'I'm sure I know you from somewhere.' He took her arm, as bold as brass. 'What school did you go to?'

Easing her arm away, Jessie asked him the same question. 'Which school did *you* go to?'

'Be fair,' he grinned, flirting with her. 'I asked first.'

'Please yourself,' she said, feigning boredom.

'Cephas Street,' he confessed, shrugging.

'I might have guessed.' He was obviously a show-off and probably from a rough family if the school he'd attended was anything to go by; just another tall, good-looking charmer, she thought, turning away.

'Tom! What are you doing here?' A woman in her sixties, nicely rounded with a friendly face, was hurrying towards them. 'You promised me you'd help your dad get the dinner ready!'

'Give me a break, Mum. I was just helping this young lady.' The tone of his voice had changed and now he was touching her with anxious concern.

The woman rolled her eyes and turned to Jessie, her

face relaxing into a warm smile. 'Not in any trouble, are you, love?'

'No. I've just had some sad news, that's all.'

'I can see you've been shedding a tear or two. All right now, are we?'

'Yes, thank you,' she said.

'Where d'yer work then?' Tom asked her.

'Hackney soap factory – in the offices,' she said, and turned to walk away. She reproached herself for telling him where she worked and then questioned her reason for doing it.

'The name's Tom. What do they call you?'

'Everything under the sun!' she called back, smiling to herself. There was something about Tom and his good-natured mother that seemed familiar, but she couldn't put her finger on what it was. She hadn't met either of them before and yet she felt as if she might know them.

Tom was thinking the very same thing as he walked home with his mother Emmie.

'You were a bit shy with that one, Tom. Was it my imagination or were you blushing?' she asked, watching his expression.

'Course I wasn't blushing, Mother. She seemed all right, though, bit of a snob but there you go.' Tom shrugged.

'So, my son, a knight in shining armour. Whatever next?'

'Talk sense. I cheered her up a bit, that's all, Anyway, mind your own business, nosy cow.'

Emmie quietly laughed at his cheek, but he was right, when it came to her three lads, she did want to know all the ins and outs.

'Nice girl, though,' murmured Tom. 'She reminded me of someone.'

'Oh yeah?' Emmie wasn't really interested; Tom fell in and out of love more times than he had hot dinners.

'Didn't remind you of anyone then?' he asked.

'No, Tom, I can't say she did.'

'Same colour hair, I s'pose.'

'As?'

'Hannah.'

'There must be hundreds of natural blondes living in the East End, son.'

'I know, I know, she just reminds me of her, that's all.'

'If only Hannah was part of a decent family, the way that young lady likely is. At least Hannah's got you to look out for her. She values your friendship more than you realise.'

'Friendship? What are you on about? She's more like a sister than a mate.'

'That's true. Oh dear,' Emmie paused for a rest, 'my poor old pins. I've been on my feet all day long, serving snooty customers in Wickham's and then seeing to those poor sods down the home. I think I'm gonna 'ave to give up my charity work, Tom.'

'Oh yeah? Pull the other leg. Anyway, about Hannah . . .'

'What about her?' said Emmie, putting her weight on his strong arm and resuming her slow pace.

Tom looked at his mother sideways. 'You should have adopted her years ago. I doubt that Gerta the German would have cared, there's no love lost between mother and daughter there.'

Emmie didn't want to get into this topic, she'd kept a tight secret for many years and idle chitchat wasn't going to catch her out. 'Lumbago's a terrible thing, you know,' she said, changing the subject. 'One of my old ladies has got it real bad. I hope to God that when I go it'll be a quick death, a good strong heart attack while I'm in my bed. Let's hope our Johnnie'll do what he promises and get to be a millionaire, then I can have private nurses looking after me.'

'Johnnie,' chuckled Tom, 'my elder brother the entrepreneur. Anyway, be no need to pay out for a private nurse, will there? Not if you go quick, in your sleep.'

Johnnie's latest venture was to sell threepenny coupons outside Millwall, West Ham and Arsenal football grounds.

Emmie's youngest, Stanley, was a different kettle of fish, regular as clockwork and never missed a day's work down at the bell foundry. Tom, content with his earnings from the docks and a little bit on the side from his perks, didn't have the same ambitions as Johnnie. He was a romantic, through and through. Emmie hoped that when he did finally settle down, he would stay in the East End — which, as far as she was concerned, wasn't a bad place to be. Besides which, she would miss him if he left.

They reached the turning where they lived. Emmie couldn't wait to get inside her house and put her feet up. 'I'm gasping for a cup of tea, Tom,' she said.

'So am I. Let's hope Hannah's still there, with the kettle on the stove.' Tom pushed his hand through the letter box and pulled at the key-on-a-string. He opened the door and followed Emmie inside.

'Hello,' smiled Hannah as they came into the kitchen. 'I was just about to give up on you, Tom, and go home. Charlie's gone down to the pub, Emmie, he got fed up waiting too. Your dinner's in the oven.'

'Fed up with waiting? Do me a favour, he's casseroled the lamb chops instead of frying 'em just so that he could go down the pub. It's dominoes night. Trust my husband not to miss that.' Dropping into a kitchen chair, Emmie kicked off her shoes, glancing sideways at Hannah's face — at her swollen eye. 'Who did that to you?'

'It's not as bad as it looks. One of the Reds slapped me with the back of his hand, outside the Blackshirts' club, and caught me with his ring. I slipped out early before my mother got on the platform to give *another* of her long and well-rehearsed talks.'

Emmie chuckled gently. 'You've got to be more careful, Hannah. The chief librarian won't take kindly to you turning up for work looking like that. Don't forget, you're a public servant in a respectable place, you have to look the part. I take it no one there knows that you're a Blackshirt?'

'Don't call me that, Emmie. You know why I go. If I refuse my mother will get into one of her spiteful moods.'

'You've got to learn to stand up to her, love. She's just a silly, ignorant woman. Your father going off didn't help matters, but there we are.'

There was a silence from Hannah which was to be expected. Emmie had criticised Hannah's dad, Jack, and that was a mistake. His memory was all that the girl had to cling on to. Jack and Gerta had planned to emigrate to New Zealand when Hannah was just a baby but for some unknown reason, Jack had gone alone leaving Gerta, a German, with Hannah. If Jack had taken her with him, Hannah would be out there living the good life instead of having to put up with Bethnal Green and three miserable rooms above a tobacconist's shop. But she was a survivor and had learned very early in life that it was better to be servile where Gerta was concerned. Maybe Jack would come back for her one day. It was Hannah's dream that he would, a dream that had kept her going. He had loved her more than life itself and he was the one who took her to the zoo and carried her on his shoulders to Bethnal Green gardens and to the fairgrounds. In his letters to her, Jack always made a point of writing about New Zealand and how healthier the life was there, but the worst of it was, Gerta cut his address out of the letters so that Hannah couldn't write back.

Tom looked at Hannah's face and frowned. 'I've told you before, Hannah, it's your own fault getting involved with that lot.'

'I don't want to talk about it,' she said dismissively. 'Oh, and by the way, my mother was expecting to see you this evening, Tom. She had another newspaper clipping to show you about her hero Mosley. Because you didn't come round she got at me. You shouldn't tell her something and then not do it.'

'That eye looks like a monkey's arse,' he said, which brought a smile to both Hannah and Emmie's face. He handed his mother a cup of tea.

'She's determined to get you to join, Tom,' Hannah persisted.

'Over my dead body!' said Emmie. 'She'll have me to answer to soon if she goes on at him for much longer. You tell me, Hannah. You tell me if she does keep on at him, because as sure as I'm sitting here, he won't let on. I'll wring her skinny neck, so help me. A son of mine a Blackshirt? I don't think so! It's bad enough she's dragged *you* into it.' The Blackshirt movement was growing in the East End and Gerta Blake was an ardent member. She had forced poor Hannah to join up too, though Hannah had deep misgivings, Gerta, however, brooked no resistance.

'She's been trying to find a way to persuade Tom for years. She knows I warn him against it and that makes her angry.' There was a smile on the girl's face which gave Emmie hope; perhaps Hannah *was* beginning to fight back. 'Last week she managed to get him to herself in her room,' Hannah continued. 'Tom lit a cigarette just like I told him to. She hates the smell so she asked him to leave. My plan worked.' Her blue eyes could go from mournful to sparkling in a moment, swollen and bruised or not. She pushed her hand through her short curly blonde hair and laughed.

'If it hadn't, you would have eavesdropped and got caught,' said Tom, sipping his tea. He looked at Emmie. 'She's done that before. She gets me to leave the door ajar and raise my voice so she can hear what's going on but Gerta clocked it. Sharp as a razor.'

'Tom pretends to be deaf in one ear,' said Hannah. 'He used to do that at school when he was poking fun at the headmaster.'

'It's a wonder they didn't expel the little sod, he played truant enough times.' Emmie poured herself another cup of tea and listened to their banter. Hannah would be all right, she was growing up at last. Seventeen and only just beginning to think for herself. Gerta had been worse than just strict with the girl, never allowing her to read fashion journals or listen to what she wanted on the wireless.

'Gerta's a character, Hannah, I'll say that for 'er.' Finishing his tea, Tom stood up. 'A very strange woman.'

'She believes she's won you over, Tom, that she's got you interested.'

'She *thinks* she's won me over — there's a difference. You know I can't be bothered with all that palaver. Your mother bores the bloody life out of me. Mosley this and Mosley that. The bloke's trying to be another Mussolini. I see it every day, down the docks, men with nothing in their lives so they start preaching. If it's not politics it's religion. Bore you to death and know they're doing it but does it stop 'em? Hitler's Gerta's hero, silly cow. She ain't got a clue. How old is she? Forty-two? Forty-three? Yet to listen to 'er you'd think she'd turned fifty. I bet she's not had a man since your dad ran off.'

'Don't be disgusting, Tom!' said Emmie. 'You're not down the docks now, thank you.'

'Sorry, Mum.' He stretched and announced that he was going to have a wash and shave before his dinner and then go down to the pub to have a pint with his dad. 'I might have a bath by the fire when I get back — if the water's hot in the copper. I've been running about all day, some bugger nicked my cap.'

'Well, how comes you were wearing one when we came home?' asked Emmie.

'That was someone's else's. That's why I've been running. Silly bastard would 'ave called a copper as well if he'd seen one, all over a cap. That's all I needed, a pocket full of easy-come fountain pens and I get pinched for nicking a cap. I can hear my mates laughing now.'

Emmie stopped herself from chastising him; he was nineteen, after all, and in any case it would have been a waste of time. Her son had been stealing bits and bobs since he was six years old and no number of whippings had stopped him. 'I wonder what it's like in prison?' she murmured instead, trying a different tactic, hoping the thought of being locked up might at least make him think.

'I don't intend to find out. I'd jump on a ship to Australia if there was any danger of that.' He grinned and went into the scullery for his wash and brush up.

'My mother said something quite odd the other day.' Hannah had slipped into a reflective mood and sounded as if she was miles away. 'She asked me if Tom intended to marry me.'

'She did *what?*' laughed Tom. The scullery door opened and he stood grinning in the doorway, in his vest with his braces dangling. 'Whatever gave her that idea?'

'I don't dream about you either, Tom, but I don't find the idea that ridiculous.' Hannah couldn't help looking a little hurt at Tom's disbelief.

'But I'm your mate, Hannah! We've never been—'

'I'm not asking you to marry me! I'm just telling you what she said.'

'But we've never been like that together. She must have seen—'

'Oh, for God's sake! I only mentioned it because I thought she wanted to talk you into joining the party not the family,' Hannah said, exasperation in her voice.

'What did you tell her?'

'I said that I loved you but not in that way, and that you love me but not in that way.'

'Oh. So that's all right then.' He closed the door between them again.

'Fancy her asking a thing like that,' said Emmie, puzzled.

'She was in one of her tormenting moods, said that I would probably end up being a spinster in any case.'

'You should tell her that you've got dozens of men on the

end of string and that you plan to take 'em all back home, one at a time, to try 'em out. See what she makes of that.'

Hannah smiled. 'Maybe I will — one day. One thing's for certain, as much as I care about your daft son, I wouldn't want to be his wife.'

'Just as well!' called Tom, ''cos I think I might 'ave met the love of my life today. She wouldn't tell me her name but I know where she works.' There was the robust sound of splashing water from the scullery.

'Well, Tom,' Hannah called back, 'that's the first time I've heard you mention a girl without using an expletive to describe her qualities.'

'Cheeky cow! She reminded me of you, funnily enough. Don't know why. Same white wavy hair, that's all. Longer than yours, though. She's a bit of a toffee nose as well. Nice though, I liked her. Could be love at first sight.'

'Again?' said Emmie, stopping him before he got too carried away. 'I'm ready for my dinner and bed. It don't look like Tom's stopping in to play cards, Hannah love. Will you be going to the pub with him?'

'No. My eye's beginning to throb again. I'm not in the mood for cards anyway. I'll call round tomorrow after the dockers' march — it is tomorrow, isn't it, when Tom's marching?'

'I think so, child, yes. Try and keep away from the Blackshirts, there's a good girl. That eye'll get worse before it gets better.'

'The club's running down in any case, the numbers have steadily been falling. Only the strong Fascists are still members now, and those who've started romances and use the club to meet up, without wives and husbands realising what actually goes on there.'

'Yeah, but all it takes is just one well-planned speech from Mosely to get them all going again,' said Emmie, concerned. 'It's been quiet for a while so you can bet your life something's on the boil somewhere.'

Returning to the room, Tom put an arm round his mother's shoulders. 'Couldn't lend me five bob, could you, Mum?' He'd lost at cards again.

'Playing in your lunch break at the docks again,' grouched Emmie, reaching for her purse. 'You'll never learn, will you? And I want it back! You get away with blue murder.'

'Well, you will keep opening your purse, Emmie,' said Hannah. 'I'll see you tomorrow evening,' she added as she left.

'I put some money on a greyhound, Mum – a tip and a dead cert. I wanted to buy that new hat you've been going on about.'

'The trouble with you, Tom, is that you spend money before you've got it in your pocket. You'll end up in the debtor prison if you're not careful.'

'And you can fetch in a cake and a file. You'd love that, you know you would.'

'It's not funny, you've got to start acting more responsible, Tom.'

'I was unlucky, Mother, that's all. It should 'ave won!' Tom leaned forward and towel-rubbed his hair.

'What's tomorrow's dockers' march in aid of this time?' asked Emmie, pleased that he was at least accountable when it came to the union.

'More money, less hours, better conditions.' With that he went upstairs to put on a clean shirt and tie, leaving Emmie to think about what Gerta had said, about him marrying Hannah. What would happen when Tom did meet the right girl? How would Hannah fit into that little scene? The two of them had been as thick as thieves since they were very young.

Opening the door leading to the flat above the shop, Hannah did her utmost to be quiet. She had almost managed to creep past the door of Gerta's sitting room when she heard her moving about. Hoping her mother wasn't going to appear, Hannah tiptoed towards her bedroom. There was the sound of the doorknob slowly turning and then the telltale creaking of the door.

'Why must you creep about like a *fluchtling*! If I don't hear you come in, I smell you.' Gerta was standing in the doorway scowling at her.

'I wasn't creeping, I was going quietly, in case you were having a nap.'

Gerta narrowed her eyes. 'You went out looking like this? You didn't cover that eye? It isn't something to look at. Do you feel proud of it? Is that the reason? You want people to stop and ask what happened?' Her heavily accented voice was shrill and cross.

'The patch made it feel worse. I thought it best to let the air get to it and anyway I was only going round to play cards with Tom and I knew he wouldn't mind seeing me looking like this.'

'Tom? But he was supposed to be coming here, to see me.'

'He forgot.'

'Ha! *Ich glaube nicht.*' Gerta moved closer to Hannah and examined the eye. 'You said you were going to the market.'

'I changed my mind.' She tried to look forcefully at her mother and hide her longing to get to her room.

'Was that after or before you left the flat? Because if it was before, you lied to me then, and if it was after, you are lying now.'

'I had the pad on when I went out. It irritated so I took it off and then decided to go to Tom's instead.'

'You think I don't see through your lies?' sneered Gerta, her face too close for comfort. 'Why would you want him to see that ugly eye? He is a man. Doesn't it bother you? At your age I did something special with my hair. If I had been cursed with white hair I would have coloured it by now, and if my face looked like that, I would choose not to be seen by a man.' She leaned to one side and studied Hannah's blushing face. 'I don't recall you having a crush on a boy. Isn't that a little odd? You don't like men — is that it?'

'My eye's throbbing,' murmured Hannah. 'I'm going to have a wash and lie down.'

'*Wasche?* Ha! You spend time in there just *looking* at yourself. Or are you in the wash room scrubbing your body over and over? Because if that is so, let me remind you that it is God who may cleanse the soul. Soap and water will not do his work.'

Hannah knew that her mother was a bitter and twisted woman but she still couldn't brush off her spitefulness. All her self-doubts, ironed out by Tom or Emmie, returned within minutes of being back in her company. A few selected words from Gerta and Hannah withdrew, back into her shell.

'I don't feel hungry this evening so I won't have any supper. After my wash I'll go to bed and—'

'Haven't you forgotten something? Or do you want free food now as well as free service?'

'I haven't opened my pay packet yet,' said Hannah, her voice quivering. 'I've never once missed giving you my keep.'

'There is always a first time. I would like to think I could trust you but you have already turned into a liar. Cheating people is never far behind.'

Taking her pay packet from her handbag, Hannah opened the small manila envelope and withdrew a pound note. Hiding her contempt, she placed the money on the side table in the hallway.

'You can ill afford to pull faces, Hannah,' snapped Gerta, sweeping up the note. 'There is cold pork and red cabbage in the kitchen. Cucumber salad is in a side dish. If you don't eat it this evening it will save me bothering tomorrow.'

In her bedroom, Hannah vowed that soon she would find herself somewhere else to live, far away from her mother. Feeling very much alone, she switched on the bedside lamp, sat on the small wooden chair and tried to imagine herself in different surroundings, anywhere but in this silent, lonely room.

Chapter Two

On Sunday morning, to the sound of the church bells in the background, Jessie was enjoying her favourite hobby, helping out in the back yard, or garden as her dad preferred to call it. Leaving him to prune the climbing rose on the back wall, she snipped at the dead tulips and placed them in her basket. Her thoughts were on the handsome Tom whom she had met once again on the dockers' march. Worried that she had agreed to go on a date with him, she toyed with the idea of asking Max if he would mind. She had surprised herself by agreeing so readily to meet up with Tom but more surprising was her reaction at seeing him again — she had, without a shred of doubt, been more than pleased. Seeing him the very next day after their first meeting was certainly an odd coincidence, but even more strange was that she felt as if she had known him for a while — and from the way they had chatted, anyone could have been forgiven for thinking the same. Tom was the exact opposite of Max who was the quiet, serious type with a more gentle humour.

'I think we'll have a lovely show of roses this year, Jess,' said Robert, cutting through her thoughts.

'We always do, Dad. I've missed the tulips again. I wanted to press the petals but they've had it — all limp and falling apart.'

'Never mind, wait for the roses to come out in summer

and press those instead. So,' Robert wiped the sweat from his brow, 'what did you think of yesterday, Jessie? Your first dockers' march.'

'It was good, and I wasn't the only female there, was I? Some of the wives came out, and in good voice. I liked Tom. He seemed nice.'

'He's all right. Pass me that sack, Jess. I'll put the cuttings in there for now, till they've dried out, then we can have a small bonfire.'

Handing him the damp sack, Jessie probed a little further. 'You don't know much about him then?'

'Tom? No. But if first impressions are anything to go by, he's ... like I said, all right. But I wouldn't set my sights on him, Jess, he's not the settling down kind. If he was a sailor he'd have a girl in every port, I reckon.'

'It won't hurt to go out with him just the once, though, will it? You don't think Max would be upset if he found out?'

Robert drew breath and raised an eyebrow. 'I wouldn't like it if your mother had done that to me, but as you say, it will only be the once and you say it's a foursome so it can't do no harm. But best you don't mention it to Max for now.'

'I'll tell him afterwards – once a few weeks have gone by.' Jessie smiled broadly which did not go unnoticed by Robert. 'It's funny really,' she said, 'my meeting him a second time like that, within twenty-four hours. Does he work in your wharf?'

'He goes from one to another. Tall, strong lads like Tom will always get work.' Robert looked at his daughter sideways as he worked. 'How is Max these days? Haven't seen him to talk to for a while. Not going off the boil, is it?'

'Course not. He's worried about the Blackshirts though, spends more time at the Jewish Club, at meetings, discussing the troubles and that.' Jessie paused and then said lightly, 'So, you think that Tom's a bit of a wide boy then?'

'I never said that. He's a bit free-spirited, that's all.' Lighting his pipe, Robert went back to examine his climbing rose. 'I think that'll do for now. I don't know about you, Jess, but I'm ready for a nice cup of tea. Come on, we'll take a break.'

Following him in through the back door, she said, 'So you think it's all right, if I go on the foursome?'

'It's up to you, Jessie. I'm not going to interfere one way or another, you're old enough to make up your own mind. Just don't go two-timing Max, that's all I'm saying.'

He was right, thought Jessie, but then she had no intention of two-timing Max. She fancied a bit of fun, that was all, and Max at best wasn't full of joy. She loved him, or at least she supposed she did. Why else had they been courting for two years or so? And it wasn't surprising he was a bit serious these days, with the anti-Jewish undercurrents that were all around and seemed to be swelling. 'You won't say anything to Mum, will you?' she added as they arrived in the kitchen.

'Not until a few weeks have gone by,' he chuckled, echoing what she had said. 'Now let that be the end of it.'

Pleased that her dad had, in his own way, given her the thumbs up, Jessie felt more settled about it. She knew she could rely on him to make her feel right about things, he always did. She couldn't imagine life without him. She loved Rose just as much but they weren't as close as she and her dad were – and, on the other hand, there had been times when she envied the way Dolly and her mother chatted together, so that evened things up.

Washing her hands under the cold tap, Jessie found herself thinking about Tom again, wondering if he would behave himself when they were in the picture palace. Being a foursome made it feel less like a proper date and for that she admired Tom for suggesting it. Maybe he was just as shy about going out with her as she was with him? Perhaps he'd heard she was already courting. She remembered the way he and his mother, Emmie, got on so naturally and warmed to them both.

Once Emmie had seen her husband Charlie off to Brick Lane

that same Sunday morning, she enjoyed a quiet cup of tea by herself. Charlie wouldn't be back for hours. After he'd spent time rummaging through boxes of spare bits for his old crystal set collection, he would go on to Petticoat Lane where he'd meet up with his fellow wireless enthusiasts in their favourite pub. She wouldn't see him until three in the afternoon when he would want his Sunday roast, and that suited her fine. Emmie was ready for her favourite pastime – baking tarts and cakes for the week. She looked at the four wirelesses sitting on the sideboard and hoped Charlie wouldn't come back with more clutter.

Tom, still dreamy from his chance meeting with Jessie the day before on the dockers' march, drifted into the kitchen and sat down. Emmie listened as he poured out his heart for ten long minutes. He was in love again and waiting for her to say, 'Bring her home then, son' – though his brothers and dad would crucify him in front of the girl if he didn't leave a gap between her and his last girlfriend. Emmie had counted seven loves of his life so far this year and the month of May wasn't out yet. God help me through June, she thought, with its silvery moon.

She finished her tea, took her rolling pin from the drawer and went to work on the pastry she'd prepared for a steak and kidney for the next day's dinner. With her husband working in the fruit market and her three sons in full-time employment, the neighbours believed she was rich. She had always wanted strapping sons who would take after their father and that's what she'd got, but strapping sons have big appetites and hers ate her out of house and home. Tom continued to bend her ear, as she worked and she kept one ear open to his chatter.

'It's different this time, Mum. I've never met anyone like her.' Sitting in his father's old Lincolnshire chair, he reminded her of Charlie when she was first married to him. He and Tom were like two peas in a pod. 'She does work in the offices of the soap factory like she said, and as luck would have it, so does Ron's new girlfriend Sally. She knows Jess and likes her.'

Ron, Tom's best mate, was just as bad, in and out of love

all the time. 'I thought he was gonna marry the last one,' Emmie said innocently, having a dig at both lads.

'Changed his mind – just in the nick of time. She wasn't all the ticket,' Tom said firmly.

'Couldn't have been if she thought she could tie Ron down.'

'Jessie lives over Stepney Green, in one of the nice streets. Her old man's a crane driver – East India Docks. Probably earns twice as much as Dad. Nice bloke though, from an educated family over in Hammersmith. He reckons he's the black sheep.'

'Didn't take you long to find out the family history, did it? You might've done better chatting up the girl instead of her dad. What was she doing while the pair of you was chewing the fat?'

'Walking next to us, all quiet and thoughtful. I couldn't believe my luck when I saw 'er. I meet 'er by chance on Friday and then the next day she appears out of the blue in a bloody dockers' march, of all things. I was straight in, talking to her old man, putting my best foot forward.'

'How old is she?'

'Dunno. Seventeen, eighteen. What difference does it make?' He was challenging his mother to criticise this newfound angel of his. 'She is a cracker, though, ain't she? A natural blonde with lovely blue eyes.' His gaze was unfocused as he indulged his fantasy. Emmie had seen it all before. 'And she's clever with it ... Works in the manager's office ...'

'What's her father's name?' She wasn't really interested, concentrating more on rolling out her pastry. 'I might know the family.'

'Robert Warner. You won't know him. I told you, he's from Hammersmith way and if Jessie's anything to go by, her mother'll be from somewhere nice as well. Christ knows what they're doing in the East End.' His head still in the clouds, he didn't notice his mother's reaction to what he'd just said.

Emmie was stunned. She pulled up her kitchen chair and sat down heavily, dusting off her hands. Of all the girls that he could have met up with, it had to be Jessie Warner. There weren't many miles between Bethnal Green and Stepney Green, but it hadn't crossed her mind that their paths would cross and neither had it occurred to her that the girl at Stepney Green station could be the baby she had once held in her arms. It might have been funny if it didn't spell trouble.

Emmie took a deep breath and said sharply, 'Pretty blondes are ten a penny and you've hardly spoken two words to the girl.' Abruptly she stood up and poked the hot coals of the cooking range. 'Anyway, enough of this. I've the beds to make.'

'The beds? You're in the middle of making a pie!' Tom looked at her in surprise.

'I can finish it later. I think I might have one of my headaches coming on, I might lie down for a bit to save it getting worse. Cover everything with a clean tea towel for me, there's a good lad.' She wanted to be by herself. There was some serious thinking to do. She would have to be very careful how she handled this new situation. Very careful indeed. 'Did you arrange to see this blonde of yours again then?' she asked, dreading the answer.

'Yep. In a foursome. We're going to the pictures next week – that's if she turns up.'

Let's hope she doesn't, son, thought Emmie, let's hope she doesn't turn up.

Up in her bedroom she weighed up the pros and cons of paying Rose Warner a visit and then cursed Tom for spoiling her Sunday. She would now have to break their unspoken rule of years gone by and meet up with her old friend.

The following morning, after a restless night tossing and turning, Emmie decided that she would not put off until tomorrow what could be done today. Tom had, without knowing it, brought chickens home to roost.

When she had fed and seen the men off to work, Emmie

dressed in her pink and green flower-patterned frock with matching bolero and her favourite straw hat and left the house to visit her old friend, Rose Warner. Making a note to give her doorstep a going-over with red cardinal polish and her windows and paintwork a good spring clean, she closed the door behind her and enjoyed the May sunshine on her face.

Walking along by Charrington's brewery, she thought back to the days when she was employed there as a bottle filler. The smell of beer brought back those heady days when she and the other women had larks with the lads, way back, before the last war. Blushing at the thought of it, she nodded and showed a hand to the chaps in the loading bay and remembered Charlie as a young man, when he worked there.

Emmie and Rose went back a very long way and their parents had also been good friends in the past. If she was honest with herself, Emmie would have been the first to admit that she would much rather turn round and go home, but Rose had suffered terribly in the past and if she could save her from more heartache now, she would.

'You're as pretty as a picture today, Emmie,' Jim of Jim's Bird Cage Shop called from his shop doorway. 'Where you off to?' The man had always made her smile; short and skinny, always chirpy, he reminded her of the birds he sold. Just as well he couldn't sing like a canary, she thought, because if he could, he would have, right there and then.

'I'm making the most of the May sunshine, Jim, and with a bit of luck I'll manage to persuade a friend of mine out of her cobbler shop for five minutes. I fancy an afternoon cuppa in the tea rooms.'

'Well, ducks, if she's too busy, you can always take me!' Jim laughed heartily, still managing to keep his tiny, hand-rolled cigarette tucked in the corner of his mouth. 'What d'yer think of my new sign then? Painted that m'self.'

Emmie drew back and read aloud, '"Budgies boarded during your holidays." You've always boarded birds, Jim, 'aven't you?' She tried to get round having to pass comment on his sign-writing which was, to say the least, uneven. 'It's a bit early in the year – no one I know goes away till midsummer or hop-picking time.'

'Well, I thought a nice brightly painted sign would cheer people up. I found an old tin of yellow paint and mixed it with a bit of red. Work of art that.' He gazed at it with an air of satisfaction, puffing on his cigarette

'Well, it's bright, I'll give you that.' Emmie grinned at him.

'What about a nice yellow canary then, in a golden cage?' He waved a hand at the various cages hanging outside his shop. 'I could let you have that little brass one cheap. Look at the way it's gleaming in the sun. Just polished it. I'll throw the bird in for threepence, seeing as it's you.'

Once a tout always a tout, thought Emmie. From the time Jim could walk he had worked alongside his father selling his fine feathered friends, as he called them. Formerly the proud owner of a battered stall in Club Row, Bethnal Green, he was now his own boss with a successful little business, hardly a rich man but certainly better off than when his arse hung out of his trousers.

'I daren't, Jim. I would love that little cage and I would love my very own bird.'

'I'll 'ave a word with your Charlie when *he* next passes, tell him how you've been yearning after that little cage. A canary, was it?'

Laughing at him, Emmie wished him the best of luck and went on her way. Monday was her day off from Wickham's department store and usually the day when she would catch up on everything: washing, ironing, the lot. Not this Monday, though. This Monday she had other more important things to think about. Tom, with his good looks and an eye for a pretty girl, was more trouble than he could imagine.

Turning into Hayfields Passage, Stepney Green, Emmie

imagined herself in bygone days living in one of the grand Georgian houses which surrounded the old village green. Cherry trees, now in full bloom, surrounded the square where she and Charlie had gone one night when they'd had a few too many – before they were married. She liked to think that that was where her eldest son, Johnnie, was conceived. Under the cherry blossom trees.

Not many people could afford the luxury of living in these towering houses now, and those who could had moved on to pastures new. What a shame, thought Emmie, that it stopped being fashionable for the well-to-do to live in Stepney Green. When she was a nipper, running around in bare feet in the 1890s, she'd often helped her dad deliver flowers from Covent Garden to the very house she stood in front of now. She had loved sitting up on the cart beside him, sipping hot tea from a tin flask while he drove the old carthorses.

Pausing below the marble steps leading up to the oak and glass-panelled door of the Craft School, an elegant Queen Anne terraced mansion, she remembered the days when she would go in there with her dad. They had never been further than the entrance hall, but that had been enough. At that time, a very grand family lived there, with housemaids, a butler, and a cook-in-charge, a rounded woman with a permanent smile who wore a big white apron. Emmie remembered her well. She also remembered the freshly baked buns and biscuits the cook had pressed into her hands while her dad brought in the blooms.

How proud she and others in that neck of the woods had felt, having the gentry as neighbours. Sighing, she allowed herself an impossible dream – there but for fortune go you, me and the boys, Charlie. And a suite for Hannah.

At the Broadway, Emmie pushed open the familiar door to Rose's cobbler shop. She was pleased to see that Rose was there, placing small tins of black shoe polish on a shelf.

'Stuck in 'ere on a lovely spring day, Rose?'

The look of surprised delight on her friend's face as she

turned round was a tonic. 'Emmie Smith! Well, well, well. My goodness.' Rose shook her head, beaming. 'This is a surprise! You look so well, Emmie. Flourishing like the blossom.'

'You're looking well yourself, Rose. You 'aven't aged a day.' Emmie smiled affectionately.

'Come on out to the back. Cobbler George'll look after the shop for me.'

The old man, tapping nails into the sole of a boot in the corner of the shop, nodded and smiled. 'If you're putting the kettle on, Rose . . .'

The women made their way through to the back quietly laughing. Stepping carefully around piles of shoes, some waiting for repair and others ready for customers, Emmie nodded to the apprentice lad who was giving a pair of shoes a spit and polish. To one side of him was a neat row of boots and shoes he had already shone and to the other a pile awaiting attention. He looked tired, bored and gloomy.

'You won't be sorry, son,' said Emmie. 'It's a good trade to be in and what you're doing is all part of your training. You'll soon be elbowing Cobbler George out the way.'

'Right an' all,' said the old boy, chucking. 'Right an' all.' The fourteen-year-old apprentice didn't look so sure about it.

As they went into the little room at the back, Emmie said, 'Oh, I do love the smell of freshly cut leather and shoe polish, Rose. You've got plenty of work, by the look of things.'

'Sign of the times, Emmie. A bit more work for everyone, thank goodness. Let's hope it lasts right up and into the forties.' A familiar faraway look that Emmie had once teased her about swept across Rose's face. 'Let's just thank our blessings and not fear tomorrow. None of us knows what lies in store, do we? The shoes and boots that are coming through now are fit for repair but a year or so ago we were lucky if there was any heel or sole left on them to be mended. We did our best but the work took twice as long and we couldn't charge a penny more. But there, I suppose you had your fair share of having to make ends meet.' Rose filled the kettle as Emmie sat down at the scrubbed wood table.

'It wasn't a bed of flowers, no. But all my men are in work now so I mustn't grumble. I expect you're wondering why I've turned up like this, out of the blue?'

Rose lit the gas ring beneath the kettle. 'It's lovely to see you, that much I do know. You should pop in more often when you're out shopping. I expect you usually go down the Bethnal Green market but you must wander up here to the Broadway sometimes.'

'I don't, to be truthful. Don't have the time. It's a good twenty-minute walk from my place to your shop. Anyway I'm here now and I'm pleased to see you looking so well.'

Rose eased the lid off a biscuit tin. 'You're a sight for sore eyes, I must say. I was ready for a break and it's lovely to share it with you.'

'You couldn't swing a bloody cat in here, Rose,' said Emmie, looking around, 'now you've put a bit of furniture in. It must be lovely to have a little back room like this. You can shut yourself away for ten minutes. We all need to escape sometimes, don't we?'

'It does get hectic, I must admit. I sometimes wonder if I'm coming or going.' Rose looked through the doorway to check that the shop hadn't filled and then closed the door. She was genuinely pleased to see Emmie and it showed. The difference in their ages hadn't mattered all those years back and it didn't matter now that she was in her forties and Emmie in her fifties.

While she piled a plate with biscuits, the kettle boiled and Rose filled the pot, set out the cups and sat down opposite her friend. 'How are those sons of yours, Emmie? Still hanging on to your apron strings?'

'That they are, all three of the bleeders.'

'You've always mollycoddled them, don't deny it,' Rose chuckled quietly and poured out the tea. 'No wonder they're in no hurry to go.'

'What about your two lads and those girls of yours, Jessie and Dolly?'

'Much the same as ever,' said Rose, passing Emmie a cup of tea. 'Alfie's still a naughty boy, Stephen's as soft as ever, Dolly as lazy and for ever going on about the early days of London, and Jessie – well, she's turning into a very inquisitive young lady. Always questioning things. Questions, questions, questions.'

'And some you can't answer?'

'Some I'm not ready to answer. We never did need to say much to each other to get our message across, did we?'

'Which is how it should be. Who are Jessie's questions to do with?'

Rose shrugged, sipped her tea and then shrugged again. 'My mother. I don't want to have to think about all of that.'

'No, I don't expect you do. Jessie obviously takes after you. At her age and before it, you was full of bloody questions as well.'

'Was I? I can't say I remember.' A glazed expression crossed Rose's face. 'Jessie was very fond of her grandfather, and very upset when he died. She went through his things soon afterwards, looking for a keepsake. Found his marriage certificate, of all things. She'd hidden it well but I found it in the air vent in her bedroom. So I had to tell her that Grandmother Blake wasn't my real mother.'

'Perhaps it was for the best. Maybe you should have told your children before now, all of them. Keeping secrets for too long can cause a lot of problems – the webs we weave and all of that?'

'Maybe. I've told Dolly too now, about Grandmother Blake, nothing else, and she doesn't seem bothered. But like I say, my Jessie's the prying type, has to know everything. She'll want to find my mother next. She may well be led to an unmarked grave.'

'Now then, Rose, that's not like you. Your mother can't be

much more than seventy and that's no age. I take it you couldn't be persuaded to find out more about her?'

'No. As far as I'm concerned, she's gone from my life.' Rose's face showed no sign of emotion as she looked directly at her old friend. 'How's Charlie these days? Got plenty of work?'

Rose clearly wanted to change the subject, but, impatient to get to the point, Emmie answered in a tone to end that line of conversation. 'Charlie's all right. Still only a porter down Covent Garden but he's well known there and well liked. Earns an extra bob here and there.' Then, taking a deep breath and blowing caution to the wind, Emmie got to the heart of the matter. 'Rose, I'm afraid that something's cropped up, right out of the blue. I think we've got a little problem and to tell you the truth I don't know which way to go about solving it.'

'By "we" I take it you mean *us* – not you and Charlie.' Rose looked wary.

'I do. I suppose you guessed something was up the minute I walked in your shop.'

'Your face gives you away, Emmie. Out with it then. What have you got to tell me?'

'It's to do with Hannah.'

'I thought as much. Go on.' Rose was expressionless but she sat extremely still.

'My Tom's still as thick as thieves with her – mates though, not sweethearts.'

'She's gone away to New Zealand, hasn't she? That's what you've come to tell me.'

'No, Rose, she's still here, in Bethnal Green, and she's all right, all things considered. It's just that my Tom and your Jessie have—'

Rose cut her off with a laugh of disbelief. 'Your *Tom*? My *Jessie*? Don't be so daft, Emmie. Jessie's courting Max Cohen, Leo and Ginny's son from the shop next door. They plan to be engaged. Jessie doesn't even know Tom. She's hardly ever over your way and when she does go out it's usually with Max or . . .' Pressing her fingers against her lips, Rose closed her eyes. 'Please, Emmie, please don't tell me that she and Hannah have met up.'

'Pull yourself together, Rose! I didn't say that. Now for goodness' sake just listen to what I've got to say.' Emmie put her cup down forcefully.

'I'm sorry, Emmie, but deep down inside it's something I've always dreaded.'

'Jessie and *Tom* have met up. Don't ask me how it could have happened, it just has and he's walking around like a lovesick puppy.'

'Does he know?' Rose leaned forward anxiously.

'Not yet. But I'll have to tell him if he mentions her again, before things go too far and he wants to fetch Jessie home to show her off to his brothers. He's a good boy and he'll listen to me. I'll ask him not to see her and I shall tell him to keep it to himself. There's no risk of him telling Hannah, he's not like that. He'll be sworn to secrecy – as I've had to be all these years.'

A deep sigh escaped from Rose. 'Oh dear. Well, you have shaken me, Emmie. And there I was this morning, thinking how things were on the up. There's nothing to say that he won't go against your wishes. You know what they're like, young people these days. Tell them not to do something and they'll be all the more determined.'

'If I can't sway him, no one can. He can be a bit self-centred at times and there's not much I can do about that. We can't get inside our children, can we? We can't make them do what we think is right. We've got to let them make their mistakes and—'

'But this is too *serious*, Emmie. You mustn't allow him to make a mistake; but there, he'll see that, once you've told him, of course he will. At least I should hope so. Mind you, he used to be a little sod if my memory serves me right. Caused you to have sleepless nights many a time.'

'High-spirited, that's all.'

'Well, that's one way of putting it, I suppose.'

Emmie bristled. 'That's quite enough of that, Rose! Don't come the high and mighty, not with me. I know your beginnings, don't forget, and to give my son his due, he's no pansy. He has strong opinions about some things and I can't say that doesn't please me.' Emmie drew breath; this wasn't the way she wanted it to go. Softening her voice, she leaned closer to her friend. 'Neither of us'll come out in a very good light over this, Rose. He'll say we should have told Hannah much earlier on, and he'll have a point, but there, what's done is done, we have to think of a way round it.'

'He could cause so much trouble by meddling and not realise until it's too late.' Rose pursed her lips and shook her head. 'If you can't put a stop to Tom seeing Jessie then I shall have to do something. I'll find a way, even if I have to lie to her, say that I've heard things about Tom which aren't nice.'

'Well, you must do as you think best.' Emmie was disappointed. She had never thought that she would let someone threaten to defile her son's good name, especially not her old friend Rose Warner.

'Yes,' Rose went on, as if she was barely aware of Emmie's presence 'that's what I shall do. Tom won't know so it can't hurt him. There's no saying it'll work, Jessie has a mind of her own too, but we've got to try and put a stop to it now, before it gets out of hand.'

Straightening her hat, Emmie stood up. 'If I don't go now I'm afraid this will break into a row, Rose, and I don't want that. I don't think you're being very fair on my son, none of this is his fault.'

'Well, it's not mine, Emmie, and I'm sure my Jessie hasn't got thoughts on your Tom. Like I say, she's—'

'Courting Max Cohen,' Emmie finished angrily. 'Be warned, Rose, if we do try and keep our children apart, it might well have the opposite effect. Young people stand up for their rights more these days.'

'*Your* children might, Emmie, but mine wouldn't dare. I've brought Jessie up differently from that.'

'I wouldn't be so sure of yourself if I were you. You're living a cosy life now, and good luck to you, I say, but don't ever suppose that things'll drift on without trouble. Anything can happen to any one of us, at any time. Anyway, enough of all that. Once you've had time to take in what I've told you, you might want to hear what Hannah's been going through with that German bitch, Gerta. What she's still going through. The poor child's never had any friends except for Tom. The only children who were let into Gerta's home to play with Hannah came with their parents, Fascist party members or the like.' Emmie was deliberately laying it on, hoping to weaken her friend and touch the soft spot she remembered so well. 'Tom managed to cross Gerta's barrier,' she continued, 'but only because she sees him as useful, a potential Blackshirt, a steward.'

'Time's running on, Emmie,' said Rose, rising. 'I've a lot of work on. A great deal to do.' She locked her fingers. She was struggling to keep her composure. She didn't want to hear what a terrible time Hannah had had, and she certainly didn't want the word Blackshirt spoken in her shop. As far as she was concerned, there was nothing she could do now with regard to Hannah to make amends, it was too late for all of that, but Emmie was not easily stopped.

'Tom and I often laugh at Gerta. Whenever her hero, Mosley, is in Bethnal Green, Stepney or Shoreditch, she'll be there at the front, applauding him.'

'Well, let's hope that Tom and Hannah's friendship continues,' said Rose. 'We don't want to ruin something like that over a silly five-minute romance, do we?'

'Hannah and Tom's friendship is important, I'll grant you,' said Emmie, tight-lipped. 'He thinks the world of her.' She smiled at her friend once more and lowered her voice. 'She's turned out lovely, Rose. You can be very proud—'

The crockery jumped as Rose slammed her fist onto the

table. 'I have just *two* daughters, not three! Jessie and Dolly! And that's all! I *won't* have you stirring up the past. How could you, Emmie? Coming here and telling me all this. Just tell your son to keep away from my Jessie! Tell him she's promised to another man.' Rose took a deep breath to compose herself and then quietly asked Emmie to leave. 'Close the door behind you, there's a good friend. I need time in here on my own.'

'Drop me a line if you want,' said Emmie, choked. 'No one else will see the letter. I'll burn it once I've read it. You know my address.' With her head high, she walked through the shop, hoping this wouldn't be the last time.

She smiled at the young apprentice and then at Cobbler George in the corner, wondering if they had heard the heated conversation. She paused inside the shop door and was weighing up whether to go back and comfort Rose when a sudden rumpus outside startled her.

'Stinking Jews. Yids!' The sound of breaking glass followed.

Emmie shuddered. A lad no older than one of her own had thrown a brick through the grocery shop window next door. She threw open Rose's shop door and went outside, ready to give someone the sharp end of her tongue. She was pulled up short by the sight of Mr and Mrs Cohen standing helpless as one of the hooligans gripped the end of their egg stall and heaved it up, tipping the whole thing over and sending hundreds of eggs smashing to the ground.

'*Why?*' cried Mrs Cohen. 'Why are you doing this? We've always been here. You all know us. Ginny and Leo *Cohen!* Why? What have we done?'

'You're fucking *Jews*, ain't yer? Taking over our fucking shops and jobs! Get back to where you came from!' The last of the hooligans ran off, laughing.

'Come inside, Ginny, come in.' Mr Cohen, white as a sheet, was trembling. He turned to the bystanders, shocked and confused. What could he say?

'Bastards,' muttered an old man. 'Cowards. They want stringing up.'

'This is it then,' said another, 'they're back in business. It's started up again and this is just the beginning of more to come.'

'Beginning?' barked a third. 'Where've you bin 'iding out? You wanna walk along Whitechapel, see the windows that've been smashed there. Mosley's stirring things up again. Clever bastard. We might not 'ave 'ad the man's education but we know what he's up to!'

Emmie turned away. All she wanted was to be back in her kitchen having a drop of something in peace.

'Emmie! Come inside.' Rose's voice rang out above the gathering of angry people. It sounded like a headmistress issuing orders and it put Emmie's back up. First Rose had ordered her away and now she was ordering her back inside.

'I'm sorry but time's run on, Rose,' she said curtly. 'I should be elsewhere.'

Rose stepped towards Emmie and forced a smile. Squeezing her arm, she put her mouth to her ear and whispered an apology.

'There's no need,' said Emmie, drawing away. She had had enough.

'Don't let it all get churned up now, not after all this time, Emmie, please. Jessie will be deeply hurt if she finds out from someone else.'

'And so will Hannah. Perhaps you had best say something yourself before Jessie *does* hear it from other quarters. And maybe I should speak to Hannah. You can't keep this kind of thing bottled for ever. It's a sorry and sad thing if you can't speak straight to your own, Rose Warner.'

'But Emmie,' Rose gripped her friend's arm and Emmie could feel her trembling, 'we can't tell her, it wouldn't be fair or right, not after all this time. Think of my other children, Emmie.'

'I am, Rose, I am.'

'It's too late. Surely you can see that.'

'I shan't do anything, Rose,' Emmie said. 'The ball's in your court now. I've my own life to lead and three sons to think of.'

'We've got enough on our plates already,' said Rose, 'trouble coming in from outside.' She waved a hand at Mr Cohen's smashed window. 'We can't afford to cause grief between our own.'

'Bang on, Rose, and that's exactly why you should see to it that your own house is in order.' Emmie pulled her arm away. 'I shall tell my Tom in my own good time. I just thought you'd want to be aware that a storm may well be brewing. You can please yourself whether you act on it or not.' She turned and walked away, leaving Rose to stare after her.

It hadn't been easy but Emmie had done as she would be done by, and once the feeling of upset had gone, she would sleep easier for it. But the time between leaving Rose and clearing the dinner table that evening was very difficult. Trying to behave as if there was nothing playing on her mind had brought on a headache. While Charlie and the boys discussed boxing, Emmie mulled over how she might handle the problem of Tom, Hannah and Jessie. After much deliberation, she decided her only course of action was to tell Tom everything and persuade him not to see Jessie again.

Knowing that two of her sons and Charlie were going to listen to an important boxing match on the wireless, she pretended that her back was playing up and asked Tom to help her wash and wipe the dishes — he wasn't interested in boxing.

Rolling a cigarette, Tom compromised. 'I'm not wiping up and I'm definitely not wearing a pinny. I'll wash, you wipe.' Charlie, Stan and Johnnie left the kitchen very quickly, before they were roped into helping too.

Once they were by themselves, Emmie told her favourite son to sit down, she wanted to talk to him.

'Go on then,' he said, lighting his roll-up. 'I'm all ears. What's the matter?'

Nervously rearranging fruit in the bowl on the table, she began, 'It's about Jessie. Jessie Warner.'

'Oh yeah?' Tom's face brightened at the mention of Jessie's name.

'I know you won't want to hear this, Tom, but I shouldn't waste your time with that one. I heard something when I was down the market.' She was suddenly breaking the promise to herself to be truthful. In fact, she was being as bad as Rose Warner had planned to be, slandering an innocent.

'I don't *believe* this! You've been snooping around, checking up.' Tom shook his head defiantly. 'You go too far, Mother.'

'Her name cropped up, Tom, right out of the blue,' Emmie persisted. 'She's a do-gooder. Nice-to-everyone type, and she's broken many a heart. They say she leads the lads on and then drops them cold.'

'You don't know the first thing about Jessie. Gossip, that's all you know.' Tom pushed his chair back to leave but Emmie grabbed his wrist and looked him straight in the eye.

'Yes, I do. I know quite a bit more than I've let on and now it's time to put you in the picture, whether I want to or not. I admit I wasn't telling the truth about her just now. I did make it up, but still you mustn't see her again.' She leaned back and waited for his response. He said nothing, just raised an eyebrow and waited. 'I know the family,' she continued, 'and I know the family history and that's not because I'm a nosy old cow.'

'Go on then. What's wrong with the family?'

'Nothing. There's nothing wrong with her family, not really. As it happens, Jessie's mother is a very old friend of mine. I can't tell you what a bombshell you dropped when you told me the family name.'

'So what's the problem?' He was making it obvious that his patience was being stretched.

'It's to do with Hannah. With Hannah and with Jessie. I'm afraid that you're piggy in the middle on this one. It was a one in a million chance that you and Jessie should meet and become friends. Not so with Hannah, that wasn't fate, that was prearranged. I was keeping an eye out for her, even before you brought her home. This isn't easy for me, Tom, so don't you start shouting and swearing, just sit there and listen, and trust that I know what I'm talking about.'

'I'm all ears.' He smoked his cigarette, waiting.

'Hannah and Jessie are sisters.' The stunned silence from Tom was something Emmie had not experienced before. She wasn't surprised at his quiet laughter a moment later; in fact, she was relieved by it. This was more like her Tom.

'Tch. The things you come out with, Mother.'

'You'll have to drop the idea of seeing Jessie, son, unless you never see Hannah again, and for the life of me I can't see how that'll come about. I can't cut her off and as sure as I'm sitting here I won't cut you off.' Emmie had to make Tom understand the seriousness of the situation.

'Well, that's something, I s'pose,' he said, smiling and leaning back. 'But you can't expect me to believe Hannah and Jessie are . . . sisters.'

'It goes back, right back, to nineteen eighteen.'

'Oh, not the war, please.'

'Your dad fought alongside Robert Warner, Jessie and Hannah's dad, in northern France. Back here, me and Rose Blake, as she was known then, worked side by side at the sugar refinery. Rose and Robert were engaged at the time and if she hadn't fallen pregnant with the twins I think they'd have carried on with their plans to secure good positions before they married. Robert wanted to put a deposit down on a little semi in the suburbs and Rose wanted that too.'

'What did you just say?' Tom's voice sounded different, almost as if he really did have something stuck in his throat.

'Oh, for goodness sake, Tom. Listen and I won't have to repeat myself. Your dad fought alongside—'

'Not that!' His jaw clenched and he looked as if he was ready to hit someone. 'You know what I mean. You said *twins*.'

'That's right, son. Twins. Non-identical twins. Hannah and Jessie.' Giving time for it to soak in, Emmie went quiet.

'Oh, Mother,' he said, shaking his head. 'I hope you've got it wrong.' He glared at her and she just gazed back at him with a look in her eyes that said it all. No, she hadn't got it wrong.

'A shotgun wedding followed. Rose didn't carry well, which wasn't surprising, the young couple were living hand to mouth in one tiny room in a house which'd already been marked unfit to live in. Rose was a worker, scrubbed that room from top to bottom while Robert fixed and repaired windows, cupboards and doors, borrowing tools from your dad and using scraps of timber from the local yard.'

Tom eased himself forward, elbows on the table, and pushed his face close up to Emmie's. 'Are you really telling me that Hannah is Jessie's twin sister?'

'Robert was studying to be an architect,' Emmie carried on. 'He got work wherever he could, repairing and decorating, labouring backstage in the theatres, anything. In the end he had to give up his ambitions and get regular work down the docks. Eventually he went from being a labourer to a crane driver. So times got a bit easier for them but that was after they'd given up Hannah. Those times were very hard. You'd be surprised how much heartache people of our sort had to bear—'

'I'll get the violin out in a minute.' Tom's face was hard.

'You see, coming from a middle-class family, Robert had no skilled trade and unlike the rest of his kin, he wasn't cut out for the police force and had no intentions of joining the rank of city gentlemen. They was poor – too poor to support two babies and that was the simple truth of it. They had a hard choice to make and it nearly broke Rose's heart but in the end they decided one of the girls would have to be adopted. It would be best for both of 'em, the only way to give 'em both a decent future.'

Tom held up a hand to stop her. 'What has all of this got to do with my seeing Jessie?'

'You'll be bringing together twins who were parted before they were a year old.'

He slowly shook his head. 'Well, if it's true, Hannah'll be pleased as punch to find out that Gerta the witch isn't her mother.'

Emmie sighed sadly. 'No, son, it's not quite like that. What a lovely fairy story that would make. The parents don't want Hannah back, they don't want the girls to find out that they've been kept apart all these years, that one of them was given away. Things are not as cut and dried as you like to think.'

'Well, they're gonna find out. One way or another. I'll tell 'em if you don't.'

'As I said, things are never that easy. Jack Blake, the man Hannah believes is her father, is really her uncle, Rose's half-brother. Jack Blake and his wife – Gerta – couldn't have their own kids, and they was planning to emigrate to New Zealand. It seemed the perfect solution – to pass Hannah to her own flesh and blood and send her off to a new future in a new land.' Emmie shook her head. 'It didn't work out like that, though. Jack and Gerta had an almighty bust up and he went off to New Zealand without her.' She looked sharply at Tom. 'But she loves that man more than anyone. Don't you think that that bit of news on its own would destroy her? Finding out after all this time that Jack's not really her dad?'

Tom glared at her, his face taut. 'They gave Hannah away and no one, *no one*, saw fit to tell her once she was old enough? No one told her she'd been adopted or that she had a *twin* sister? That her father was really her uncle? It stinks, Mother. It . . . *stinks*.'

'Yes, it does, but it was their wish and with something like this you have to abide by those wishes.'

'Bollocks to that. What about Jessie's dad, Robert? He seems a decent enough bloke. Didn't he want to make arrangements to see Hannah?'

'That was the idea at the time, but Gerta soon put a stop to it. Once they'd handed over the baby, new rules started to crop up until Gerta had managed to banish Rose and Robert altogether. Rose accepted it for the sake of the girls and I promised to keep an eye out for Hannah. When you brought her home that day after you'd had a fight in the playground and wanted me to clean her up before she faced Gerta, I felt as if God was at work, and that's why I swept her up as if she was an Orphan Annie. You and your brothers thought she was a replacement for the daughter I never had and that was fine by me.'

'But you knew what Hannah was going through, living with that dried-up bitch,' said Tom angrily. 'You should have said something *years* ago, you should 'ave refused to be part of it. It's not right!'

'No, Tom, it's not. But I'm not stepping in and neither are you! Leave it be. Hannah's come through and no doubt she'll find herself a nice young feller and go off and get married. Then she can make her own family.'

'She's only *seventeen*.'

'And so is Jessie! But I s'pose you're going to say that's different.'

'*Hannah's* different,' Tom said. 'Never wears lipstick and powder. Dresses more like a boy than a girl. She won't be in any hurry to get married. Family of her own? Now *you're* trying to turn a grim tale into a fairy story.' Tom ground out his cigarette furiously.

'Hannah dresses the way she does because Gerta's been too bloody mean to ever allow the poor girl to spend money on a nice frock or lipsticks. You've seen the way Jessie presents herself. Put Hannah in the same clothes and make-up and she's even prettier than her twin! If Rose could have had her wish, she and Robert would have been able to raise both babies. It broke their hearts at the time and I *won't* see them go through any more grief! I won't! The secret is our burden too, and it must go with us to our graves.'

'Like hell it will,' Tom snapped.

'What's that supposed to mean?' said Emmie.

'It means that one of us is going to talk to Hannah – you can choose which one. And if I do start courting Jessie, I'll fetch her home to meet Dad and the boys. I'm not gonna add to things by keeping *her* hidden away.'

'And you don't think that's a bit thoughtless? A bit on the selfish side, to turn their lives upside down just because you've taken a fancy to Jessie?'

'No, I don't. You lot can't run our lives the way you ran your own.' Tom narrowed his eyes and glared at Emmie and she saw something she had never seen before. She saw loathing.

'I'm nineteen, not nine,' Tom went on. 'If I'd known earlier about Hannah, I would 'ave told her. As it is, you've put me right in the middle. You're just as bad as that German bitch she's had to put up with all these years.'

Emmie was deeply wounded, both by his words and by his anger. 'I'm gonna forget you said that, son. Let's put it down to reaction. You've had a bit of a shock and this is your way of—'

'Don't gimme all that toffee, Mother! I'm not a kid.' The expression on his face was unyielding, and Emmie could see that, right then, he despised her, that she was no longer his wonderful mum but an interfering old cow.

'I think you should sort out your loyalties, Tom.' Emmie moved towards the door; she needed to be by herself. It wasn't easy, being despised by her own son.

'And maybe you should sort out your loyalties,' Tom shot back. 'Stop trying to rule everyone's lives, and that includes Dad's. He's been under your thumb for too long.' He reached out for his tobacco tin. 'If you think you're gonna rule me as well, you're mistaken. If I want to see Jessie, I will. If I want to introduce her to Hannah, I will. It's my business now and if you don't like it, next time keep your secrets to yourself!'

Emmie felt sure this outburst wasn't coming out of the moment, but was an opinion of her that he must have held for some time. She wondered miserably if her other sons saw her in the same light; perhaps she had been living in cloud cuckoo land, all that fetching and carrying and baking . . . Maybe they'd all been taking the rise behind her back.

She turned to look at Tom, sitting at the kitchen table, his head nestled in his hands. 'Did you mean all of that?'

'Mum, please. Go and have a lie-down or something. I want to be by myself for a minute. You can stop worrying, I won't go on the foursome, I'll send a mate in my place, but that's not to say I'm leaving it there. I'll get Sally to put in a good word for me and keep Jessie sweet till I've decided what's for the best.'

Emmie felt a strong urge to go to him, to hold him close, but it wasn't the right time. She had seen him go from one courtship to another but this time he really did look like a man in love. Sod's law, she thought. Sod's law.

Chapter Three

When Sally Brown slipped Jessie a note from Tom in the factory canteen, her first reaction was to tear it up but she thought better of it. She didn't know Sally that well and she might report everything back to Tom. Why should she let the rotter believe he had got under her skin? Feigning airy indifference, Jessie pushed the note into her cardigan pocket to read again in private and went back to her office. She had gone like a lamb to the slaughter that night, turning up outside the Odeon, wearing her best clothes, waiting like an idiot in the drizzling rain. When Sally, Ron and a complete stranger arrived, she had wanted the ground to open up. The pathetic excuse given by Sally's boyfriend, Ron, was that Tom had sprained his ankle. In the note that Sally had given her, he'd written that he had put his back out playing football.

At her desk, Jessie took the envelope from her pocket and read it again before tearing it into small pieces and throwing it in the bin. Tom had had the gall to write that he would like to see her again, one day. She had taken a big risk going on that date behind Max's back; had he found out, she might well have lost him and deservedly so.

Preoccupied with her thoughts, she didn't hear the door open or Sally come into the office.

'What did he say?' Sally whispered from behind.

'Tell him to drop dead when you see him and say that I wouldn't go out with him if he was the last man alive and sound as if I mean it because I do,' snapped Jessie.

'I *knew* he wanted to see you. I knew it!'

'Well, you needn't sound so pleased, Sally, because I don't want to see him, so there won't be another foursome arranged, not with me there leastways.'

'Oh yeah, pull the other one,' teased Sally. 'You know you fancy going out with him.'

Jessie spun round to face her. 'I do mean it, actually. I'm only sorry I said yes in the first place. I am courting, you know.'

A loud, deliberate clearing of the throat came from behind the frosted glass partition; Jessie's boss, Mr Reed, was making it clear he didn't want Sally in there. 'You'd best go, I've got loads of work.'

'Miserable old sod. He needs a seeing to. I'll send Betty the bust from talcum powder round. *My* office manager never minds if one of the girls comes in for a quick natter.' Sally deliberately raised her voice. 'Anyone'd think we was in *prison!*'

'I'm trying to concentrate, Jessie. Would you please ask your friend to leave?' Mr Reed spoke in a quiet, controlled voice.

'I'll see you later and you can tell me exactly what was in that note,' chirped Sally. 'Tom's a right cracker and he's got it bad for you – lucky cow.' There was another, louder, clearing of the throat from behind the screen.

'She's just going, Mr Reed. Sorry about that.' Angry, Jessie waved Sally away and out of the office. If Tom really had thought anything of her, he wouldn't have stood her up. Sally was good fun but not very bright. She grinned at the impatient Jessie and hovered by the door.

'Can I ask you a question, Mr Reed?' said Sally in her best voice, the one she sometimes used when sitting on the switchboard in the post room.

'Very well. Just one.'

'Thanks. Well, we all know what's gonna happen on

the twelfth, don't we?' There was a touch of excitement in her voice.

'Get to the point, Sally.'

'Well, the point is, Mr Reed, I thought it would be nice if we could get up a charabanc and all go together to watch the procession from Buckingham Palace, after the coronation. They're 'aving street parties round our way but I'd much prefer to go to Buckingham Palace, wouldn't you, Mr Reed?'

'I shall be going, as a matter of fact, with my family.' His tone had changed, he sounded relaxed and friendly. 'My children are very excited about it. I'm pleased to see you take an interest in our current history.'

'Current 'istory?' Sally looked at Jessie and pulled a face. 'The King and Queen are getting crowned! Course I'm interested. Wouldn't miss it for the world.' This conversation between Mr Reed and Sally was being carried out through the frosted glass partition; neither of them could see the other. 'Them princesses are lucky cows, ain't they? Elizabeth and Margaret. You seen them frocks they wear, tch, all silk and satin and velvet. Still, there you go, they are royal, ain't they? They're bound to dress like that. I would if my dad was a king.'

Jessie was worried that Mr Reed would lose his patience with her. 'You'd best go now,' she whispered. 'I'm going with Mum, Dolly and the boys. You can come with us if you like.'

'It's unfortunate,' said Mr Reed reflectively from behind his screen, 'that the Duke of Windsor abdicated. A king of England, getting involved with an American divorcee. Scandalous. It'll be a blot on the history books I'm afraid.'

Sally smiled, a soppy expression on her face. 'Ah well ... he loves 'er, don't he? Must do. To give up a kingdom. Romantic, I think.'

'Mmm. That'll be all then, Sally,' said Mr Reed, ending the conversation with a tone of finality.

Sally looked at Jessie and curled her top lip in a comical fashion. 'Oh right, I'll be off then.' She turned to leave but was struck by another thought. 'I tell you what will be a blot on the 'istory books, Mr Reed.'

'What's that, Sally?'

'Old Blue Eyes the Duke being mates with Adolf Hitler. I mean, that Hitler's not a very nice man is he, all the trouble he keeps causing to the Jews and that. You wouldn't fink someone who was once King of England would be mates with someone like that.'

'We don't know that they're friends, Sally. People in high places often have to mix with others in high places. It's the way of things. 'Now, enough chat, Sally. Be on your way.'

'Oh right . . . if you say so, Mr Reed, if you say so. You bosses know best.' Sally backed out of the office, whispering, 'Fancy a coffee after work, Jess?'

Warming to Sally again, Jessie slowly shook her head, disappointed. 'Can't. Max is meeting me outside the gates.'

'Ne'er mind. Tomorrow, yeah?'

'All right. Tomorrow.'

Later, Jessie sat opposite Max, enjoying his treat of a cup of coffee and cake in Joe Lyons. He was unusually quiet, his dark eyes troubled and Jessie could tell there was something on his mind. There was no point in pressing it, he would tell her in his own good time. 'You do know that the Vicky park fair opens tonight, Max?' she said hopefully.

'It'll be there for two weeks, Jessie. We can go on Saturday,' Max replied in a flat voice.

'I thought it would be nice to go on the first night. It's where we first met,' she said, 'remember?'

'That was over two years ago,' he said dismissively.

'True.' Obviously sentimentality wasn't going to work, she thought.

'It was a nice idea.'

'But?' said Jessie, annoyed.

'But what?'

'But you don't want to go.' She waited for an answer.

It didn't come. 'You don't seem very happy, Max, bloody miserable, in fact. I know you're not one for smiling for nothing but you're giving me the blues as well.'

'I'm not very happy, Jessie, no. You seem chirpy enough, though.'

'Well, I would, wouldn't I? I'm sitting here with you, enjoying coffee and cake, and you know this is my favourite place ...'

'Times are bad,' he said, shaking his head, 'really bad.' Max didn't look up, just slowly stirred his coffee.

'I thought that trade had picked up. That your mum and dad's shop was doing quite well. Mum's shoe menders is up on last year.' Jessie tried to jolly him with her optimistic tone.

'I'm not talking about trade, although in a sense that has something to do with it. Blackshirts.' Max pushed his hands across his face and ran his fingers through his dark hair. 'It's getting worse. The more successful we Jews are, the more they see us as fair game.'

'It'll pass. Street warfare, that's all it is, at least that's what you've been saying over the past couple of years. They haven't been back since the egg smashing, have they?'

'No, but my parents are really frightened. It's why I wanted us to meet up now instead of later.' He looked at her earnestly.

Jessie couldn't remember ever having seen Max so serious and worried. 'Why? What's happening later?'

'There's a meeting at Harry Zeid's house, one of our members. We're keeping it quiet though.'

'Why? Why do you have to keep it a secret?' She didn't like the sound of it.

'Well, whenever we've met at the club just recently, things have gone wrong. Hymie comes with good information as to where the Blackshirts are going to hold a meeting or which hoarding they plan to stick their posters on, and it doesn't happen. We go to the venues – and nothing. We check the hoarding, ready to tear down the propaganda – nothing. Then we hear that meetings were held elsewhere and we see the bloody posters on hoardings we didn't know about.'

'There's a spy in the camp,' she said, teasing him. She couldn't help feeling this was all nothing serious, just boys enjoying their games, pretending it was all real.

'It's no laughing matter,' Max said, frowning. 'Anyway, there'll be just a dozen of us. If it happens again, that narrows the odds of finding out who it is. We can't rely on Communists or the Labour Party or the Liberals. If we're to avoid a repeat of what's happening in Germany and what happened in Austria, we've got to be more organised. The Jewish Party needs to change and become more disciplined. East End Jews have been singled out deliberately. The press focuses on the Fascism against Jews in the East End which keeps attention off other towns, where it's probably just as bad. More publicity means more trouble here, in Whitechapel. The Blackshirts are being seen as heroes, and the pack grows by the day.'

'And because of that, we can't go to the fair, kind sir?' she said, trying to lighten things.

'I wouldn't have gone in any case, not with the mood as it is. The thugs are out there hungry for blood. Jewish blood.'

'Show them you don't care. Brazen it out.' Jessie sipped her coffee, while Max stared at her with concern in his eyes.

'But I do care, Jessie. I care about my parents, my aunts and uncles . . . Grandpa . . .'

'Now you *are* being daft. Remember Cable Street? Just about everyone came out against the Fascists. A policeman even surrendered to your lot and Mosley was turned back, the march cancelled. You *won* that demonstration, and there'll never be another as well-planned. Come on, Max, you remember, everyone came forward against them, it was a triumph. The streets were packed with people doing whatever they could to stop Mosley getting through. Dockers, shopkeepers, housewives, kids even.'

'But that show's over, Jessie. You can't do something like that a second time. We Jews are passive by nature—'

'Until you're under threat! Even I remember the bricks and coshes, Max. Your lot are just as bad if not worse than the Blackshirts when push comes to shove.' Easing off one shoe, Jessie stroked his calf with her toe. 'Don't go to the meeting tonight. Let's go back to your house and play a nice record on the gramophone. We can turn the lights down low, lie on the sofa . . .'

Smiling at her, Max shook his head. 'I can't. I promised.' By the look in his big, soft brown eyes, she thought she might just win him over.

'Please. Just this once. Miss the meeting for me just this one time. I want to show you how much I love you. I'm wearing your favourite . . .' she waited for him to finish the sentence.

'Perfume?' He was beginning to weaken.

'Nooo . . .'

'Stockings?'

'Close, Max. Very close.'

'Well, the meeting's not until eight . . .' He reached across the small table and squeezed her hand. 'And as it happens my parents are out. We'll have the place to ourselves.'

Outside, Jessie impulsively guided him towards Violet Alley, where it was dark except for the dim street lamp. She slid her hands across his broad shoulders and caressed his neck, her soft blue eyes gazing into his. 'Do you love me, Max?'

'Of course I do. I've said so, haven't I?' He nuzzled her neck and murmured, 'It's a waste of my time telling you, Jessie, if you don't believe me.'

She smiled, moved closer and kissed him on the mouth. She would shake him out of his dour mood. Kissing him with passion, she slipped her hand inside his jacket, pulled at his shirt, then eased both her hands inside onto the warm flesh of his back. Within seconds Max's hands were everywhere, his breathing heavy and hot. Once aroused, Max never wasted time.

Lifting her skirt above her waist, he pulled the loose leg of her silk knickers to one side and pushed himself deep into her soft, fleshy crevice.

'Oh God, darling . . . you're adorable,' he moaned, his voice deep and husky. 'Who needs music . . .' He kissed her again and before she could answer he was affording himself protection against fatherhood. Thrusting himself back inside, as if there wasn't a second to lose, he quickly reached the heights of his passion. Once again she was left wondering if this was all there was to lovemaking. The earth did not move for her the way it did for Max.

Coming out of Violet Alley, arms round each other, they bumped into one of Max's friends and before she knew it, Jessie was being guided back into the coffee house, with his comrade in tow. There she listened patiently to Max and David for more than an hour until she was bored to death with their conversation. 'Well,' she said at last, 'it's all been very interesting, but I'm going to leave you to it, boys.'

'I'm sorry, I'm sorry.' Max splayed his hands. 'Not another political word, I promise.'

'You can't blame us, Jessie,' said David, nudging his loose glasses up and back into place, 'and we're not the only ones, you know. Quite a few of our friends are going to Spain to fight for what we see as the struggle against Fascism.'

'Pity they don't stop *here* and fight against it, then you and Max wouldn't be so concerned about being outnumbered by Blackshirts, David.' Jessie leaned over the table, smiled at him and then tapped his wristwatch. 'You've been going on about Spain for twenty minutes. Before that it was Hungary, and before that, Berlin.'

'Well,' said David, 'these are very worrying times, Jessie. Very worrying.'

'Yes, well, the debate's over for me. I'm going home. You can go on reasoning for and against joining or not joining the group leaving for Spain. If you want to link up with the International

Brigade in the revolutionary fight against the Fascists in Madrid, *do it.*' She pulled on her blue felt hat and pushed up the brim. 'But if you ask me, I don't think that either of you will leave England — but talk it over for another couple of hours, why don't you?' Leaving Max to his companion she stalked out of the coffee shop.

By the autumn, Max and David had still gone no further than London, other than in their dreams, but Jessie had to admit that more and more Fascist and anti-Fascist slogans were appearing in the streets, and Max had been right about one thing — the mood was worsening. People huddled in clusters, talking earnestly, their discussions sombre as the days got shorter and the nights colder.

Pushing the key into the lock of the front door after a refreshing walk home from work, Jessie wondered if her earlier damp mood had been brought on by some of the men at work going on about the atrocities abroad. As far as she was concerned, it would do more good if the British people focused more on the good things that were being reported on the wireless and in the newspapers. Industry was soaring and factories were booming with the demand for electrical appliances. Chain stores such as Boots and Marks and Spencer were opening dozens of new branches, and hire purchase was making things affordable to working-class families such as hers and Max's.

Inside the house, the familiar sounds of Stephen and Alfie playing Lotto and Rose moving around in the kitchen eased some of the tension Jessie felt, though she couldn't get rid of her nagging worry about her brother, Alfie.

Just recently, when tidying the boys' bedroom, she had discovered a packet of Woodbines and two cigarette stubs under Alfie's bed. Inside the cigarette packet was half-a-crown and to her horror she also found a sheath knife. She knew that Alfie had been hanging around with older lads of fifteen and she'd heard him using very bad language once or twice. More worrying than the smoking or the foul swearing was where the money was coming from to buy the cigarettes. If Alfie'd been dipping into Rose's shop till, as Jessie suspected, it would really shake her. She'd always had a tendency to think that her children were above serious wrongdoing. And what of the knife? Where had he got that from?

Going to her room, Jessie promised herself that she would at least mention the smoking when the time was right. Relaxing on her bed, she thought about Max and wondered if he would ever pop the question and if so whether she would accept. Lately he seemed to talk about nothing but politics or money. He was now working for a small accountancy firm and was never happier than when faced with columns of figures and difficult calculations.

She loved Max no less than when they first started to go out together and she still found everything about him attractive – the way he dressed, his sometimes dry sense of humour, his handsome face and thick black hair. Why then did she still not melt the way he did when they were locked together in passion? Max would never know it, but apart from enjoying his kisses, she really did the rest to please him; she got her pleasure from that. But did other girls do it for the same reason?

She was deep in thought as to how she might broach the subject with Sally when the bedroom door opened. She was surprised to see young Stephen in the doorway. He was tearful and pathetic. His lips and cheeks had been reddened with one of Dolly's lipsticks and their mother's hairnet was on his head. Worse still, he was wearing nothing but a brassiere and a pair of Dolly's crepe knickers. She heard laughter from the boys' bedroom, not just from Alfie but from Dolly too.

'They ... made ... me ...' He could hardly get the words out and he was shivering with cold. Jessie was off the bed and beside him in a flash, pulling him close and telling him to take no notice of them. Slamming the door shut she leaned on it so they couldn't come in.

'Take everything off, Stephen. Take off the knickers and rip them up. That'll teach Dolly a lesson. They're her best ones.'

Stephen just stood there, quietly sobbing and shaking his head. 'They'll ... tell ... everyone.'

Jessie knelt in front of him and looked into his face, smiling. 'No they won't, sweetheart, because I know things about Dolly – and Alfie too.' She pulled off the hairnet and wrapped her grey blanket round him, covering his skinny white body. 'They've got nothing up here, Stephen,' she tapped the side of her head. 'Their skulls are filled with cold porridge and hard-boiled eggs.'

A smile spread across his tear-stained face. 'That's why Dolly's always farting. Hard-boiled eggs do that to you. So do porridge oats.'

'Well, there you are then,' she laughed. 'They're full of wind.'

'They need a dose of syrup of figs.'

'Or caster oil?' said Jessie, egging him on.

'Or both?' He threw back his head and laughed. 'Let's give them both.'

'Yeah, let's do that,' she said, clasping his shoulders. 'Let's give it to them on Sunday. They won't 'ave a clue what they're scoffing when they eat trifle at tea time on Sunday.'

'Yes! Yes!' He jumped up and down, his eyes bright and shining again. 'And I'll get to the lavatory before they do. I'll lock myself in and before I come out I'll hide every bit of bottom newspaper up my jumper.' If only the other two would give Stephen half a chance, thought Jessie, he'd brighten up their days with his sense of humour. 'And it won't just be their vest bottoms that'll be yellow,' he added, giggling.

'Shush, Stephen, keep your voice down. They'll hear you and—'

A short sharp rap on the door stopped her mid-sentence. Jessie knew it was her father because he was the only one who knocked on the bedroom door.

'What's going on in there?'

'Nothing, Dad. It's just me and Stephen having a giggle.' Knowing he'd want to come in, and seeing the frightened look on her brother's face, she told her father she was in her underwear and that Stephen was taking the mickey out of her bloomers.

'Well, keep your voices down, your mother's listening to the wireless.' There was a pause but they knew he was still out there. 'Stephen, the lads have arranged a game of street football for tomorrow afternoon, after school. Why don't—'

'Good idea, Dad!' he called back, quick off the mark. 'I'll score a goal and show 'em.' Both Jessie and Stephen had to cover their mouths to stop him from realising that they were taking the rise.

'That's the ticket, son. That's the ticket.' Robert went downstairs a happier man.

Stephen stood in front of Jessie, bending both arms and flexing muscles which were as flat as fried eggs. She dropped onto her bed and buried her face in the pillow. Taking a sly glance at what he was up to next, Jessie roared with laughter – he was playing to his audience of one, striding around the room mimicking the strong man who broke out of chains outside the Tower of London. In that moment, Jessie knew that it didn't matter about him dressing up or being a skinny waif; one day her Stephen would be in the limelight, on stage, accepting rapturous applause with all the confidence in the world.

Sunday soon came round. Stephen had reminded Jessie three times what they were going to do with the syrup of figs. Making her way to the kitchen and looking forward to turning a boring sweet into something else, Jessie overheard her parents talking and was thankful that Stephen wasn't with her.

'Well, if you hadn't mollycoddled him from the start, Rose, he might well be out there now, with the other kids.'

'Oh, stop going on about it, Robert. If the truth be known it's only your own pride that bothers you. You always wanted he-men for sons.'

'Don't be silly. I just wish he was more like Alfie, that's all.'

That rankled, and before Jessie could stop herself, she was in there, surprising them with her sudden arrival. 'I don't think you'd say that if you knew what I found under Alfie's bed.'

They turned and looked at her, waiting.

'He's been smoking. I found a packet of Woodbines when I pulled his comics out from underneath.'

Instead of anger she saw her father's expression relax and then turn into a smile before he burst out laughing. 'So that's where he keeps 'em – the crafty little bastard.'

'Robert!' Rose slammed down the tea towel and stood with hands on hips. 'You just *swore*.' She spoke as if she truly couldn't believe it. 'And in front of our Jessie *and* on a Sunday!' Jessie wondered which her mother felt most protective towards, her or Sunday.

'I never swore,' he said, a touch defensive. 'The word's in the dictionary, Rose.'

'That's right, and with a clear definition, so now tell me that Alfie's a bastard.'

Jessie could hardly believe her ears; never, not once in her entire life had she heard either of them use that word. Twice in one day was unthinkable.

'I came to make the trifles,' she murmured, reminding them that she was there. 'I asked Stephen if he'd give me a hand, if that's all right.' They noticed her nervousness and did their best to relax back into a Sunday mood.

'Of course it's all right,' said Rose, 'and if you don't want to do it this week, Jessie, ask Dad to help Stephen. It won't be the first time he's made the trifles for me.' She eyed Robert, daring him to say that their younger son should be anywhere but in the kitchen – the woman's place.

'Twice. I've made the trifles twice, Rose. Once when you were laid up with tonsillitis and once when you were in bed nursing your baby.' He looked at Jessie and winked. 'Our little

Alfie. She gave me a strapping son — a ten-pound baby boy. I cooked the roast that day as well. I was so proud, I would've baked a cake if your mother had wanted it.'

Jessie glanced at Rose to see that she was blushing and was obviously flattered.

'Oh, go on up for your nap,' she said, giving Robert a warm smile. 'I'll be there shortly.'

'So what about Alfie smoking?' Jessie was puzzled by their indifference, she'd expected them to go through the roof.

Robert stepped towards the kitchen door and squeezed her shoulder. 'Boys will be boys, Jessie. But don't you worry, we know all about it, we've got a card up our sleeve. We'll offer him one of his own Woodbines and get him to smoke a whole one in front of us. I guarantee he'll be sick afterwards and won't be able to look at another one, let alone put it to his lips.'

When Jessie was alone with her mother, she decided to take the opportunity to ask her a question that had been on her mind for some time. She had been too wary of her mother's displeasure to ask before but over the last few months her curiosity had grown so much she could barely contain it. It was time to take the plunge and ask. 'Mum,' she said hesitantly, hoping her mother's good mood would last, 'why did Grandfather change his and your name?'

Rose slowly turned round, her smile gone and a haunted look on her face. 'Why do you ask that, Jessie, and right out of the blue? You are a strange girl.'

'Because I don't understand it. It keeps on coming back into my mind. There must be a simple explanation.'

'It's not a puzzle. I expect it was just something he did to please Granny Blake, used her name instead of his own because he already had a wife. I don't know and to be honest I wish you'd stop thinking about my parents.' Rose closed her eyes and sighed and Jessie could see the pain on her mother's face.

'I'm sorry, I shouldn't have asked.' Jessie moved towards her mother but Rose put up a hand to stop her.

'I don't really know why he changed his name, Jessie, but I can see you're not going to rest until you know as much as I do.' She turned her face away. 'Tomorrow. I'll tell you tomorrow, when we're by ourselves. Now let's leave it at that.' She walked out of the kitchen, leaving Jessie frustrated and wondering why her mother always put off telling her things.

'We gonna make the trifles then?'

She spun around to find that Stephen was in the doorway. His innocent, smiling face warmed her.

'Come here, funny face.' She held out her arms and he wrapped his skinny self round her waist. Hugging him, she kissed the top of his head. 'I love you, do you know that?'

'I love you too, Jess,' he said, adding, 'Did you find the syrup of figs?'

'No, but I found the caster oil.' She reached for custard powder and a packet of jelly. 'But we mustn't go too heavy, Stephen, just a drop in each of their glass dishes. Enough to teach them a lesson, that's all. It won't happen straightaway, you know. It takes hours to work, overnight even.'

'Not if you put twice as much in.'

'No, I'm not doing that. You'll have to be patient. You'll get your own back, don't worry,' she said, tousling his hair.

'If it hasn't worked by the time I go to bed I won't be able to sleep.'

'Stop trying to blackmail me. Anyway, you'll probably be gassed in the night by Alfie farting – that'll send you off.'

The following morning, Jessie woke out of a strange dream and knew there was something she had to remember. It came in a flash and she was out of bed and on her way downstairs in no time, wrapped in her favourite grey blanket.

'You're up early, Jessie. Your dad's only just left for work. Did the front door closing wake you?' asked Rose.

'No. I didn't hear him go.'

'Well, since you're down you might as well have a cup of

tea, there's one in the pot. And here, put these on your feet. They're your dad's old ones. You'll catch pneumonia walking about barefoot.'

'I woke up thinking about you this morning,' said Jessie, pulling on the thick hand-knitted socks. 'I was wondering what it must have been like all these years, not seeing or knowing where your own mum was. Did you ever try to find her?'

'I hardly knew my mother, you're making too much of it.' Rose joined Jessie at the table. 'It doesn't bother Dolly so why does it bother you so much?'

'I don't know. I just feel as if a part of our family is missing, that's all. I can't help it. I can't stop my mind from thinking about it.' Jessie considered. 'Maybe it's because Max's family, his heritage, is so important to him.'

'A part of our family missing? And you think that's because you never knew your grandmother?'

'It must be, mustn't it? Why else would I feel like this? Dolly's different from me, she can shrug things off. I can't help the way I am. I've tried to be more like her. God knows why.'

'All right, Jessie, I'll tell you all there is to know since I've promised and that'll be the end of it.'

Rose related everything in a passive voice, as if she was reeling off someone else's life story. She had been eight years old when she was put into a children's home, and she hadn't seen her mother since but could remember her. Her father had appeared at the home one day and taken her away to live with him and the strange woman she was to look upon as her new mother – Grandmother Blake. Her half-brothers were born over the next five years and although she got on with them, she never really felt she was as much a part of the family as they were.

Willy had dismissed any questions Rose had asked about her real mother until she stopped bothering to ask, and all she could remember about those times was that Willy had stopped smiling and laughing the way he used to. She could vaguely remember the house they'd once lived in but had no idea where it was.

Only when she described her tiny bedroom did Rose show any emotion, and even then she covered it well.

She went on to say that her real mother had spoken with an accent, which she realised now had been German. That much she could remember. She knew that her mother had been born in Germany and that her father, Willy, was half Polish, half German, but unlike her mother he had been born and bred in England, and that was why he didn't have a German or Polish accent.

'So there you have it,' said Rose, ending her story, though for Jessie it was only the beginning. 'Not such a mystery after all, is it, Jess? And not all that interesting. I should have your wash-down now, the water in the copper's just about the right temperature. Thank goodness we'll soon be on electricity, and with a bit of luck, by this time next year, your dad will have converted the back room into a bathroom. Isn't *that* something to look forward to?'

Rose went about her work, preparing breakfast and packed lunches as usual. In the scullery, Jessie filled the big blue and white jug with water from the copper and poured it into the china bowl, her mind on her grandfather and why he had changed his name.

'There must have been another reason for him to change his name,' she said to herself but loud enough to catch her mother's ear. 'It couldn't have been just to please Grandmother Blake surely.'

'Maybe it was all down to the war,' said Rose from the kitchen. 'Several Germans living over here then did the same thing. Your great-grandfather's shoe mender shop was burned down because he was a German. He opened another one later, once the war was over, which is the one we've got now. He was a clever man.' Rose's voice took on a worried tone. 'He always warned that it wasn't finished and that there'd be another break-out in the thirties or forties . . .'

'People at work are saying they can see another war coming.

They say Hitler won't lie down,' Jessie said, coming back into the kitchen.

'It's a wonder no one's shot that man in the back,' said Rose sharply, 'the amount of degradation he's causing to people he thinks inferior. I dread to think what those poor Jews and gypsies are going through in Austria. I don't know where it will all end. This Blackshirt business should have died out by now but it hasn't. Hitler's probably behind that as well, making chums with Mosley who's too slow to see he's being used. If I had my way we'd move out of the East End tomorrow, to the countryside, away from all the troubles.'

'Where there's no work,' said Jessie.

'Where there's no work,' agreed Rose.

'Did Grandfather fight in the war? He never spoke about it.'

'No. They needed people like him back here. He was the finest bootmaker around. Many Home Guards wore boots that your grandfather or his apprentice made. It's a pity none of my half-brothers wanted to learn the trade. I think that's why I took an interest in the shop, if truth be known. But I don't understand why people, women as well as men, are joining the Blackshirts, Jessie. I suppose they're frightened that unemployment will get worse again. They've had enough of having to watch their children go hungry and cold in the past. Now that things are better they want it to stay that way.'

Dolly stormed into the kitchen. 'There must have been something wrong with that trifle you made, Jessie. I had to get up in the night and use the chamber pot. I bet Stephen never washed his hands before helping you!'

'Yes he did. I hope you've emptied and washed the pot if you 'ave used it. I never heard you go out to the back yard.'

'Well, you wouldn't, Jessie, would you? Fast asleep and snoring while I was out there with a torch, freezing to death!' Dolly, looking rather paler than usual, turned to Rose. 'Her and Stephen put something in my trifle, I know they did, to get back at me.'

'Back at you for what, Dolly?' asked Jessie, smiling. She knew her sister would never openly admit what she and Alfie had done to Stephen. 'I don't know what you're going on about. I thought the trifle was smashing.'

'It was very good', said Rose. 'I expect you ate too much and too quickly, Dolly.'

Stephen and Alfie appeared next, and Alfie, too, looked a sorry sight. His face was bright red with embarrassment; he had his bed sheet rolled into a ball. 'This is for washing,' he said. 'I shit the bed.'

'Alfie!' Rose was taken aback more by his language than the state of his bedding. 'Don't you dare use that word again, my lad!'

'It wasn't my fault that it happened.' His pride really had taken a bashing. 'I thought it was a fart—'

'That's enough!' snapped Rose. 'We haven't even had breakfast yet!'

Jessie winked at Stephen who hid a grin.

'What shall I do with it then?' Alfie asked, backing away.

'Oh, put it outside in the yard, in the tin bath, and turn the tap on it.' His face went from bright red to off-white and Rose wondered if both he and Dolly were going down with something. 'Once you've done that,' she said, 'go on back to bed. You can have the day off school.'

'I don't want the day off, just the afternoon. I'm playing in the football match in the morning and—'

'You go for the day or not at all,' said Rose, 'and no more of your bargaining. Go back to bed or get washed and dressed. Suit yourself.' She sat down, shaking her head. 'I'm beginning to wish none of you had grown up, it was easier when you were small. Now you've all got minds of your own.'

'Ah, but we are still children at heart, Mum,' said Jessie. 'We've just got bigger, that's all.'

'Mmm,' murmured Rose, unconvinced.

'I haven't got bigger,' said Stephen. 'I'm under average – nurse at school said so.' The remark warmed Rose. She held out an arm to him and Stephen was in there like a shot, on her lap and cuddling up, gazing longingly at his thumb.

'Don't you dare,' said Rose. 'You might be under average but you're not a baby.'

Later that day, after work, Jessie slipped into her bedroom and lay on her bed, thrilled by what she had found out during her extended lunch break. Mr Reed had asked her if there was anything preying on her mind as she seemed preoccupied. His question surprised her, he almost had her feeling like an equal.

In actual fact his concern was for himself. Jessie was a good and reliable employee and he was worried about losing her. He had been wondering if she was toying with the idea of taking a position elsewhere. When she explained that she wanted to find her real grandmother but wasn't sure how to go about it, he became interested and she was surprised to discover that for some years he had been researching his own family line. He now had a family tree going right back to the seventeenth century and was not going to stop there. Mr Reed told her to go to Somerset House in the City and explained in detail how to go about tracing her grandmother in the records.

Jessie had thanked him from the bottom of her heart and Mr Reed had clearly been moved by her sincerity. He suggested she make a start by taking an extended lunch break which she could make up on another day. She did as he suggested and having followed to the letter the advice he had given her, she found what she was looking for at Somerset House. An entry in the records. Her grandmother was alive and living not so far away, by Victoria Park.

In her room, brushing her long wavy hair, Jessie was going over the fabricated story she would tell her parents as to where she was going this evening, when Dolly appeared.

'Mum needs a hand with the washing up, Jessie – if you

can pull yourself away from that mirror. I would help but I'm off to the Sally Army.'

Turning to look at Dolly, Jessie grinned at her. 'Pull the other leg. Sally Army? You?'

'They're meeting up outside the Salmon and Ball pub, on the corner of Cambridge Heath Road, and—'

'I know where it is, Dolly. Since when were you interested in the Salvation Army?'

'I'm not. It's one of the band players I'm interested in, a tall, dark, handsome musician,' she said, admiring herself in the mirrored wardrobe. 'He plays the tuba. It's why he joined the corps, so he could be part of a band. He wants to be a professional and one day play with the big bands.'

'So you're going to join up,' said Jessie, smiling, 'wear the uniform and do all that goes with it, are you?'

'If I have to. It's what musicians' girlfriends do. He's broke, of course, like all performers before they get their big break. He's a road sweeper at the moment and loves his old work horse – that's why he took the job. If he's not playing his tuba he's in old man Lipka's stable, brushing down that old mare. He'll have a stallion of his own one day and canter along country lanes.'

'And Fred?' Jessie wondered what had become of Dolly's old boyfriend.

'Too childish and he's got no ambition. He'll be a foundry worker all his life. Where's your rose-red lipstick?' Dolly rummaged through the side drawer of the dressing table.

'And Mum's pleased, is she – that you're showing an interest?'

'Course she is, she reckons that you should join as well, said it would be right down your street. I didn't agree. I said you'd take it all too seriously.'

'Really? And what did she say to that?'

'Never uttered a word, went straight into her quiet mood. She knows I'm right.'

'I would sooner you didn't use my lipsticks, Dolly,' said Jessie, watching her sister stroke her best one across her lips.

'Don't be selfish. I don't mind if you borrow mine. I've said so.' She hadn't, but there was no point in arguing with her, she would only insist she had.

'Yours are too bright and too cheap. You go out with well-shaped lips and come home with a big red smudge.'

'Do I now? Well, we can't all afford the best, can we, Jessie?'

'You could if you bought one or two good ones and made 'em last.'

'Said the old woman to the girl. I'm gonna have to have a word with Max, you need a good bit of the other to bring you alive.'

Jessie smiled to herself. Dolly believed she was a virgin.

Her mother's footsteps sounded on the stairs, and a moment after Dolly left the bedroom, Rose appeared in the doorway.

'You needn't help in the kitchen, Jessie,' she said. 'I'm making Alfie do the drying for a change, a punishment for being cheeky at school. They sent a note home.'

'That's good, because I'm going out soon, to the Whitechapel Art Gallery to listen to a talk on the designer, William Morris.' Jessie extended her lie, saying that after the talk there was to be a demonstration on weaving, embroidery, and tapestry.

'I s'pose Dolly's told you where *she*'s off to.' Rose was obviously relieved to think that her wayward daughter was showing signs of reforming. William Booth, the founder of the Salvation Army in the mid-eighteen hundreds, was Rose's hero. She'd often recited one of his lines: 'Some men's ambition is art, some men's ambition is fame, some men's ambition is gold. My ambition is the souls of men.'

'Maybe she's turning over a new leaf at last,' said Jessie.

'Oh, I shouldn't be so lofty about her. She's a bit strong-willed but in your own way you're no different, Jessie. I just wish she wouldn't wear so much lipstick and powder. I see that

Vaseline's no longer the mode, she's using mascara and eyebrow pencil now. What time does the lecture begin?'

'Seven o'clock sharp. I'd best get my skates on. I'll jump on the bus and—'

'So,' she looked directly at Jessie, 'you're not being like your sister and secretly meeting a new boyfriend.'

Jessie knew she was referring to Tom. Even though it had been months since Jessie had seen him last, and then been stood up, she still thought about him. Rose, who must have been told the story by Robert, sometimes mentioned 'a new boyfriend' with a strange look in her eye as though she was trying to catch Jessie out. This wasn't the first time that her mother had probed her about him.

'I wouldn't two-time Max.' Another lie. In truth she was beginning to tire of Max's sombre moods and their joyless dates. The girls at work always seemed to be going out and having fun and she was jealous. The truth hit home one day when Sally cracked one of her jokes and the sound of her own laughter made Jessie realise how little she had done that lately. She couldn't remember exactly when she and Max had stopped laughing together.

'Well, don't hang around afterwards,' said Rose, her voice cutting through Jessie's thoughts. 'You know what it's like out there at the moment.'

'We're not Jewish, Mum,' she said, fed up with hearing about it. 'It's those poor sods who're trembling in their boots.'

'Oh, I don't know so much. One of the lads along the road got a terrible beating from a group of Jewish lads – and just for chalking on the wall.'

'I can't say I'm surprised. You must 'ave seen what they write.'

'All the same, that's no reason to break his nose.'

'I don't know any more,' murmured Jessie. 'The more I hear about it, the more confused I get.' She swung her legs off the bed and slipped on her shoes. 'Anyway, I'll be all right, don't worry.'

'The chap on the wireless said that the fog was going to get worse tonight, pea soup time again. Remember to take a torch just in case and take your smog scarf or you'll be sneezing black tonight.'

When Rose had gone, Jessie clenched her hands and gritted her teeth. Why oh why did her mother say the same thing every time she went out in the evening when winter was on its way? Surely she realised that anyone would want to wrap up against the bitter weather.

On her way out, Jessie looked in on Robert, reading his newspaper in the parlour. 'I won't be late home, Dad,' she said. 'Keep the fire burning.'

'Ah, Jessie. I wanted to have a quiet word.'

'Oh. Must it be now?'

'I've been thinking,' he said, his brow furrowed, 'about you and Max.' He locked his fingers together and sucked on his teeth, something he was inclined to do when giving his children advice. 'I think it might be best if you weren't seen out together for a while.'

Jessie couldn't believe her ears. He was the last person she thought would say that. 'But if we all stop mixing with our Jewish friends in public, that'd mean Mosley was winning surely.'

'I'm not saying you shouldn't see him, just don't go walking out together till things calm down. Max can come round here sometimes and you go to his house. The nights are drawing in and you don't know who'll be lurking in alleyways armed with coshes, and in the present mood girls like you will be tarred with the same brush, in a manner of speaking. I'm not saying this just because Max is Jewish — he's a Red as well.'

'No he's *not*. Max might go on about it but a Communist? He's not that political, Dad. What made you think that?'

'It's what they're saying down the docks, Jessie, about the majority of the Jews, that they've united with the Communists for strength. Be careful, that's all I'm saying, and get Max to stay in the background for a while.' Robert turned back to his paper.

On her way to the bus stop, Jessie had to admit that her father had a point. There was an atmosphere of pending trouble. She'd passed four pubs on her way and although they were lit up, there wasn't much noise of talking or singing coming from them and she hadn't heard anyone playing the piano. And it wasn't just the men who were standing on street corners in groups, everyone seemed to be out that evening, street walkers, tram and bus drivers, conductors, cabbies. It was as if the East End was a place waiting for something to happen. Expecting it.

Crossing the Mile End Road she saw several more groups of people standing around, so she paused for a moment to properly observe what was going on. Couples were strolling hand in hand, small groups of men, small groups of women, all going in the same direction – towards the People's Palace.

There were no placards or patriotic flags, so it couldn't be a demonstration. Since she was going that way, catching a bus which would take her from the Mile End, down Grove Road and on to Victoria Park, Jessie slowed down. There was a different and strange mood in the air. A mood of defence rather than attack, of intrigue rather than fear, and it all seemed calm and controlled as more people arrived from side streets. A clock above a pawnbroker's showed it had just turned seven.

Debating whether to go on walking with the crowd or wait at the stop for her bus, Jessie caught a glimpse of a figure she thought she recognized. It was Tom. Unlike other couples who were enjoying each other's company, he didn't have his arm round the girl he was walking with and he wasn't holding her hand; they were simply strolling along together. Throwing back his head and laughing, Tom glanced behind him at another couple who were enjoying a quip and in that split second his and Jessie's eyes met.

His first reaction was disbelief, but then, with some hesitation, he waved her over. Surprising herself, Jessie made her way through the crowds towards him. As she drew near, a cloud of concern swept across his face as he looked from the girl beside him to Jessie.

'Hello, Jessie,' he said, greeting her as if they were old chums. 'This is my friend Hannah. Hannah, this is the girl I was telling you about. The one I met outside Stepney Green station in the summer.'

'Late spring,' said Jessie, correcting him, 'after you'd just pinched someone's cap.' She smiled to suit her mood. She felt very pleased to see him and ready to put him firmly in his place.

'I'm glad to meet you.' Hannah held out her hand, which came as a surprise. East End girls didn't shake hands, but Jessie responded as if it was the most natural thing in the world.

'Tom stopped talking about you,' said Hannah, smiling, 'so I presumed it had fizzled out.'

'There was nothing to fizzle, Hannah. Tom's manners aren't as good as yours. He stood me up. Sent someone else in his place – on a date, a foursome. A gentleman he is not!'

With a knowing smile, Hannah glanced at Tom and shook her head. 'You coward.'

'Coward?' said Jessie, unsure if she'd just been insulted. 'What makes you say that?'

'Tom believed it was love at first sight – you must have scared the life out of him.'

'All right, Hannah. That's enough,' said Tom, taking command.

'Why don't you walk with us?' Hannah glanced over Jessie's shoulder. 'Or are you with someone?'

'No. I'm by myself and just happened to be passing. What's going on?' Jessie looked at the crowds.

'You mean you don't know? And you really were just passing?'

'I'm on my way to somewhere else, to see a relative. Is it a demonstration?' Jessie sensed Tom's eyes burning into her and could feel herself blushing.

'I suppose you could say it's a demonstration, yes,' said Hannah, who was only too pleased to fill Jessie in on the details. It had been rumoured that Oswald Mosley would speak at the People's Palace, he would explain what his intentions were and had always been, and tell the Jewish community that he was not out for their blood as some of the press would have them believe. 'It's just another bit of Fascist propaganda to gain more members,' said Hannah.

'Come on, Hannah,' urged Tom. 'If we don't get moving we'll end up at the back of the crowd.'

'Tom thought it would be nice to go for a stroll on this crisp October evening, and I thought he meant just that. We were going to walk all the way to the Tower and have a drink in his favourite pub. I put on my best red hat for the occasion.'

Jessie was quite struck with Hannah; she seemed very natural and Jessie felt easy in her company. Glancing at her not-so-fashionable grey coat, Jessie saw that she was wearing a small clip-on brooch very similar to the one that Rose had given to her.

At the People's Palace, Jessie and Hannah chatted on while Tom kept himself to himself, looking around, hoping to catch a glimpse of the infamous Mosley. He was surprised at the number of people who had turned out. Hannah suddenly let out a low, despairing groan. 'Of course *she* would be here. I should have known. She said she was going to see a friend – she doesn't have friends, she has comrades.'

'Who?' asked Jessie.

'My mother. Her over there, in black. She tells people she wears that colour because she is still in mourning for my father – who is not dead.' There was a pause as Jessie tried to take in her strange remark. 'She is so conniving,' Hannah went on. 'She didn't tell me about Mosley coming because she wanted Tom to be here and knew I would try and stop him. But Tom is the one being tricked here.'

Tom scowled. 'Shut up for five minutes, Hannah. You can talk some things to death, you know.'

Quietly laughing at him she said, 'Mosley's not going to be here, she just wanted you to come and listen to one of his lapdogs. She tricked you.'

'And how would you know that?'

'Because, Tom, it would have made front-page news.'

'You're wrong there. Why do you think this many have turned out? Because there are no police around, that's why. He kept it a secret from the press. Let it be known by word of mouth.'

Again Hannah laughed at him. 'I told you it was more propaganda.' She pulled his jacket sleeve. 'Come on, we'll make our way to the Tower through the back streets. I don't want to get involved in this.'

'Don't be a silly girl, Hannah. It's a free country, we'll walk where we want. I want to take *this* route to the Tower and have a drink in my favourite pub on the way.'

'We can do that on the way back! They'll be gone by then. Please, Tom, I'm sick to death of listening to them. I know that's who it will be on the platform, one of Mosley's puppets.'

'According to some of the newspapers,' said Tom, distracted, 'Mosley's not as anti-Semitic as you've had me believe. He wants a great future for Britain, that's all.'

'Ah. So she finally got through to you then?' Hannah sighed. 'I knew she would, in the end.'

'Like I said, some of the news reports—'

'From *some* of the newspapers,' Jessie chimed in, to remind them she was there. 'It depends which newspaper you read.'

'You tricked me into coming out for this walk,' said Hannah. 'Why, Tom? Why do you need me by your side?'

'I never tricked you. I fancied a walk to the Tower and, yes, Gerta did mention this was scheduled and I thought I might find it interesting. So, yeah, I'm blacking my nose. Nothing wrong with that, is there? Hannah? Oh, for Christ's sake. *Now* what?' Hannah was staring past him at the platform.

'I was wrong, Tom.' She had spotted the banner, the

bodyguards and the man. Mosley *was* making a brief appearance. 'You will see the man in the flesh after all.'

Before either Tom or Jessie could get a good view of him, Mosley was off the platform again and into his chauffeur-driven limousine which was standing by with its engine running. All they saw of the man was the back of his head as the car sped away.

'Well, you could hardly call that an appearance.' Hannah was laughing again. 'He was here long enough for his publicity agents to take photographs of him with the crowd. Now can we go?'

'Be quiet for five minutes, Hannah,' Tom said, irritated. The rapturous applause mixed with catcalls and whistling was deafening as one of Mosley's men stepped up onto the platform to give a speech, his henchmen surrounding him.

'Come on, Tom, we can cut through the back doubles to Commercial Road.' Hannah looked and sounded nervous. 'We'll make our way to the Tower from there, or make our way back home. There's going to be trouble this evening, I can smell it in the air.'

'Don't talk daft. You go back if you're that worried. I want to have a butchers at the man. Take Jessie with you ...' He rubbed his chin thoughtfully and then pushed his hand through his hair, worried. 'No, on second thoughts, didn't you say you were going somewhere else, Jess?'

'Yes. I am, when I'm good and ready. Don't worry, I won't be hanging around here for much longer. This is not my idea of an evening out.'

'If you're really this interested, Tom,' said Hannah, 'I promise to let you know another time when Mosley actually is going to give a talk. I promise. This is not a good time.' Hannah's anxiety began to make Jessie feel edgy too.

'I want to stay and listen to the speech, that's all. Just listen to what this man's got to say. I'm not gullible, if I think he's talking a load of rot, I'll say so.' Tom grinned and winked at Jessie. 'Free speech. Mine. He should admire that.'

Resigned, Hannah linked arms with him. 'It'll look better if we appear to be a friendly threesome just passing by. Take his other arm, Jessie.'

Jessie did so, for the fun of it and to annoy him, but Tom wasn't annoyed, his sideways glance at her showed his interest in her. Squeezing her hand, he said, 'Stop worrying, you've got a bodyguard.'

'I can't stay long,' said Jessie, warming to him. 'I've got a date.'

Tom laughed quietly. 'So you said, with a relative. An old grandma?' He couldn't have known how right he was.

'Not one Communist,' murmured Hannah, studying the crowd for familiar faces. 'This spells trouble. They must have gathered elsewhere, ready to make a grand entrance. I wonder which route they'll take.'

'Stop *worrying*,' said Tom.

'Well, I'm going home. I don't think you should hang around either, Jessie, I really don't.' Hannah turned to leave but Tom was too quick for her and grabbed her round her waist.

'You're not going anywhere. I need you to tell me who's who.' With his arm firmly gripping her, Tom pleaded, 'Ten minutes, that's all, then you can go.'

The man on the platform began to speak and Tom lifted himself to full height and listened intently while Hannah continually looked around for the first sign of trouble.

'Soon the others will come,' she murmured, 'like small opposing armies. The Reds, the Jews and an army of Blackshirts, dressed to intimidate. Those already here are mostly sight-seers and people like you, Tom, on the brink of joining up.'

Jessie looked from Tom's serious, attentive face to the speaker who was dressed in a light-coloured suit, with black shirt and black tie. Tall, broad and erect, he was an attraction for the women, and there were several young women in the crowd. Mosley's men, like himself, had become heroes and heart-throbs to some as Rudolph Valentino and Clark Gable had to others, and this speaker was on good form:

'Sir Oswald Mosley counts it a privilege to live in an age when England demands that great things shall be done! A privilege to be of the generation which learns to say what we can give instead of what can we take! For thus our generation learns there are greater things than slothful ease; greater things than safety; more terrible things than death.

'Hold high the head of England; lift strong the voice of Empire! Let us to Europe and to the world proclaim that the heart of this great people is undaunted and invincible. This flag still challenges the winds of destiny! This flame still burns! This glory shall not die. The soul of Empire is alive, and England again dares to be great!'

'Oh yeah?' The voice of an old East Ender filled the calculated silence. 'Once you've kicked out the Jews and anyone not pretty enough to be at your party!' This brought laughter.

'Sir, anti-Semitism was never our policy! We never attacked the Jews as a people. We never attack any man on account of race or religion, and we never shall. From the very outset we have preserved the principle of no racial or religious persecution. The fact that Jews enjoy an excessive influence in British—'

'So what do you want then?' yelled another. 'What is it you're getting at? 'Cos I'm blowed if I understand your fancy talk. Speak as you find, sir. I'm a plain man. So give me some plain talk – if you can.'

'I will do my best, sir. Firstly, Blackshirts were hired for one reason and one reason only, to protect meetings from Communists and the Jews who attacked our Olympia meeting and have often been responsible for groundless assaults upon our members—'

'Yeah, yeah, we know all that! We wanna know why you're 'ere and what you want. What d'you want to do for this country and for us? What're you about, sir?'

'A fair question. We ask those who join us to march

with us in a great and hazardous adventure. We ask them to dedicate their lives to building in this country a movement of the modern age, which by its British expression shall transcend, as often before in our history, every precursor of the continent in conception and in constructive achievement. We ask—'

'Waffle!' yelled one of the crowd. 'The man was asking for answers, not claptrap. Tell us what's needed and what you intend to do!' There were both favourable and unfavourable responses from the crowd. Hannah felt sure there were people planted among the crowd to provoke conflict.

'What d'yer want the British people to do? And tell us why we should do it!' shouted a younger man.

'We must strive to continue to reduce unemployment figures! Improve economic conditions and social conditions! Deter a party controlled by Communists! Communism destroys all honour and trust among men, even within its own party.' The speaker paused for a few seconds to allow that thought to soak into the people's minds.

'The tactics are always the same,' said Hannah. 'I've seen this act so many times it makes my stomach turn. It's a well-planned speech.'

Jessie leaned forward and whispered in her ear, 'Are *you* a Blackshirt, Hannah?'

She whispered back, 'Yes. I have a tyrant for a mother. She forced me to join. Talk to Tom. Do what you can to persuade him to leave here now, before the trouble starts.'

Jessie studied Tom's face, he was hanging on every word the man was saying so what could she possibly do to make him leave? She would wait five minutes more and then slip away. She had, after all, another more important meeting to attend. She was going to find her grandmother. Her thoughts drifted away from the immediate scene as the speaker's voice rang out into the October evening.

'Many of the typically English characters among the Communists have come over to us. And for good reason, one being that the Blackshirt movement is the only guarantee of free speech in Britain—'

'Never mind about free speech! Tell us 'ow you aim to reduce unemployment so we can have some grub on the table! Because that's why most of us are giving you our time of day! You gonna ship out all the foreigners back to their own countries and make this a British Britain? 'Cos if you are, and you're prepared to say so in public, I'll wear the uniform of the Blackshirt! Enough's enough!

'The foreigners are getting all the fucking work! The Jews eat chicken while our families are making do on bread and fucking lard!'

'Come on, Tom,' Hannah pulled at his sleeve. 'He's finished, he's just given the stewards a nod. The seed's been planted and now they'll leave the crowd angry.'

'He's not going anywhere before he answers my questions – let's see if he'll admit that Mosley's an ally of Hitler.'

'He won't answer, he'll just smile. He's waiting for someone like you to take the bait, I've seen it all before.'

Jessie saw that an army of men were approaching, silently marching, with not one banner or flag to be seen. She nudged Hannah and nodded in their direction.

'I knew it. It's the Communists!' She jerked her hand from Tom's arm, turning quickly to look behind her, and sure enough another lot from the other direction was coming their way. 'And now we have the Jews,' she said.

Jessie thought about Max and the mood he and his friends had been in lately. They could very easily be part of the mob striding towards them. Jessie realised they were sandwiched between Communists and Jews who no doubt believed that all those gathered here were ardent Fascists.

'This is very organised,' murmured Hannah. 'They've got together over this one and no doubt there will be other small splinter groups coming too. Let's hope that the Blackshirts do turn up or we might well be the target here.' She stepped backwards, a very frightened look on her face. 'Tom. We have to get away from here. *Now*.'

'He's gone – the speaker's bloody well legged it!' Tom was furious. 'I've never seen anyone move so quick!'

'That's because he's seen there's going to be trouble!' snapped Hannah. 'He's no different from any other human being, Tom, except that just like his teacher, Mosley, he's an excellent showman.'

'Mosley's always been for his country though, Hannah, he never changed his spots on that issue. I've been doing my homework.'

'Listening to my mother, you mean. She's *hypnotised* you.'

'Nuts! I can work things out for myself. What that speaker had to say made sense. I—'

A milk bottle flew through the air and just missed Tom's head. Within seconds there were more sounds of smashing glass and shouts of abuse as well as screams from the women present, and both the Communists and the Jews were storming towards them.

'Where is the army of Blackshirts to protect us now?' said Hannah. 'I told you, this was a calculated plan to show the Reds and the Jews in a very bad light. The press will have a field day.'

Above the noise of the crowd came the voice of a young Jewish man who was no more than a couple of feet away. 'Bastard Blackshirts!' Turning to confront him, Tom was met by a heavy fist which sent him reeling backwards and down onto the pavement, bleeding and shocked.

His immediate response was to scream at the girls to run, but they were too stunned to move. Forcing himself to his knees, the blood pouring from his mouth, he shouted, 'Run, Jessie, run!'

Too terrified to react, she just stood there as if in a daze. It was Hannah who reached out and grabbed her arm, wrenching her away and yelling at her to run fast. Her heart pounding as if it would burst, Jessie felt the same fear as she had in Cable Street with her brothers.

They pushed and shoved their way through the angry fighting crowds. They sped through the back streets, under arches and through alleyways. They ran until they had to stop. Leaning on the wall of a local school, not one word passed between them until their breathing became more normal and their hearts stopped thumping as if they would burst.

'I have such a stitch in my side, Jessie,' gasped Hannah.

'Me too.'

'We needn't have run this far, we could have walked once we were out of danger.'

'No. I wasn't going to stop running until I had to. Where do you live, Hannah? Is it far from here?'

'No. A five-minute walk, if that.' Hannah pressed her hand to her side and doubled forward. 'My mother won't be in so you can come back if you would like to.'

Jessie took long, slow breaths of air. 'I would love a cup of tea . . . after a glass of water.'

'Me too. Come on. We can walk now.' Hannah held out her hands. They were trembling. 'I've seen what can happen when there's a clash. People will be hurt and I wouldn't be surprised if someone isn't killed. Did you see any police there?'

'No.'

'Precisely. No Blackshirts. No police. This time they even managed to outsmart the law.'

'Who?'

'The Union of Fascists.'

Safe in the flat in Hannah's small kitchen, Jessie took in her surroundings. It was all so clinical, cream and light-green paint, everything scrubbed and not one ornament around to collect dust. Everything had its place, in a cupboard or behind closed doors. This was not a homely kitchen and Jessie couldn't imagine cakes being baked here, ever.

'I hope Tom's all right,' said Hannah, pouring boiling water into the teapot. 'The people who'd gone to listen were totally outnumbered. Most of them were just ordinary folk, not there for the politics but simply to sightsee and catch a glimpse of Mosley. They were being used like pawns in a chess game. Maybe now Tom will drop any thoughts of joining the Blackshirts and my mother's work will have been a waste of time. She's been trying for years to get him to join up, telling him that it's not the Blackshirts who cause the trouble.'

'Well, he's hardly going to drop it now, is he, Hannah? You said yourself that the Blackshirts didn't turn out, so he'll blame the other factions.' Jessie took a steaming cup of tea gratefully.

'Yes,' Hannah sipped her tea, 'you're right, and the more I tell him the way it really was, the more he'll argue with me. He can be single-minded at times and I'm only a *female*, what do *I* know about anything?'

'More than anyone at that gathering, by the sound of it,' said Jessie, checking her watch. 'I have to go. I'd love to stay longer and find out more about ... well, about everything.'

'Meaning Tom?'

Jessie couldn't help smiling. 'Are you a mind-reader as well, Hannah?'

'I knew what *you* were thinking,' she said, triumphant. 'Jessie, why don't we meet up sometime for a coffee, or a drink?'

'Good idea, let's do that. I work at the soap factory, in the offices. Give me a pen and paper and I'll write down the phone number. Ask for the wages department, my boss shouldn't mind one call coming in for me.'

'Do you really mean it?' said Hannah, a touch of disbelief in her voice.

'Of course I do. Why shouldn't I?' The girls looked into each other's light blue eyes and a sense of familiarity swept through them both.

'I don't usually make friends this easily,' smiled Hannah.

'Well, it's high time you did.' Jessie leaned back and held her gaze. 'I like you, Hannah. I like you a lot.'

Chapter Four

Jessie tried to push all thoughts of the frightening attack from her mind but she felt that the People's Palace would never be the same again. Stepping down from the bus at Victoria Park, she shuddered against the cold mist in the air which enhanced the aroma of smouldering wood from a garden fire somewhere nearby.

It was eight thirty and the rising full moon broke the darkness, casting shadows behind the trees and catching small leaves as they floated down, adding to the carpet of rust-coloured foliage, not yet raked from the park. Crisp leaves on the wide pavement rustled under her footsteps as she peered at street doors, trying to make out the numbers. Somewhere along this road lived her grandmother.

Her steps slowed as she began to lose her confidence. A voice deep inside her told her that this mission could go badly wrong. Maybe Ingrid Gunter preferred to forget the past, like her daughter Rose. She might find this visit intrusive and upsetting.

Jessie found herself in front of wide steps leading to the front door of the house she was looking for. Without thinking, she brushed her fingers across the face of a rundown, life-size statue of a lion, one of a pair, sitting either side of the dilapidated wrought-iron entrance gate which had not been closed for several years. Wedged into the earth with its hinges rusting away, it was ready for the rubbish dump. The building itself had been neglected too and was in need of restoration and repair; paint was peeling and there were cracks in the plaster on the lower half of the façade.

Taking a brave, deep breath, Jessie climbed the steps and pulled on the old-fashioned brass bell. Twelve tenants were registered as residents here, some single, some married and some with children, and Jessie felt sure that one of them must be in. The wait seemed like an eternity.

The boy who eventually struggled to open the heavy door was a ten-year-old who looked as if he could do with a good bath and a hot dinner. He peered up at Jessie and narrowed his eyes as if he was seeing light for the first time.

'I'm looking for a Mrs Gunter,' said Jessie, hesitant. 'She's quite old and—'

'The owd German tart that lives dahn the airy?' The boy closed one eye and curled his top lip.

'Well, that might be her ... unless there's another old lady here, living on her own.'

'Nar, there ain't.' He sniffed and wiped his runny nose with the back of his hand and rubbed it down the side of his oversized trousers. 'You want the old gal in the pit. She ain't a witch, is she?'

'I don't think so,' said Jessie, half smiling. 'Why do you ask?'

'Dunno.' He lifted one leg off the floor and broke wind. 'Go dahn an' bang on the door. The bell don't work and she's a bit mutt and jeff.' He slammed the door in her face and shouted from behind it, 'Now fuck off!'

Jessie went down the worn steps that led to the basement flat, half expecting a mouse to run across her feet. Some litter had blown or been thrown into the airy but other than that it was all quite clean. Bracing herself, she knocked on the door and waited. The door opened before she had time to think about changing her mind. It opened soundlessly, no eerie creaking, no stale dank smell, no dark passage, no bent, witch-like old woman. Instead she looked into the fresh and intelligent face of someone she almost recognised. Ingrid Gunter had similar features to Rose and the same searching eyes.

'Yes? What do you want?' Although to the point, Ingrid had a soft, quiet voice and Jessie could detect the German inflection. She stood erect, her chin pushed forward, her eyes alert and not full of misery as Jessie had imagined. Her silver hair was pulled back into a neat bun and her clothes, dark and simple, had no creases. The lace-edged collar on her grey dress was snow-white and Jessie could smell the faint aroma of lavender. The woman didn't look as if she belonged in a basement flat in Hackney but in a thatched cottage in the country surrounded by orchards and rose gardens.

'I'm Jessie,' she said, smiling nervously. 'Jessie Warner.' She looked into her grandmother's face and saw her changing expression. 'I don't suppose the name means anything—'

'It means nothing to me.' Jessie was sure Ingrid Gunter knew exactly who she was, she had answered too quickly. 'You have the wrong house.' Ingrid stepped back and began to close the door but Jessie put the flat of her hand against it.

'Please, let me come in. I can tell that you know who I am. I won't stay long and I won't ask too many questions, I promise. Just give me a few minutes of your time, that's all I want.'

The old woman looked at her with a piercing gaze. 'Did she *die*? Is that why you've come? To tell me she's dead?'

'No. My mother doesn't know anything about this, no one knows. I did it of my own accord. I wanted to find you.'

'Why?'

'I don't know.' Jessie waited as the seconds ticked by and the old woman decided whether or not to let her in.

'And *nobody* knows you are here?'

'Nobody. Cross my heart.'

Ingrid's tension seemed to dissolve. She nodded and stood

to one side. 'Go through.' She possessed a quiet dignity. 'All the way to the end of the corridor and into the sitting room.'

In the small, comfortable room, Jessie at once felt easy. Memories of her grandfather washed over her. There was a dark, polished, carved sideboard, a small feather-cushioned settee and two old, comfortable-looking armchairs. There was nothing modern in the room except for a Clarice Cliff tea set and an orange, red and black vase filled with fresh flowers. A few patchwork cushions were scattered on the settee and there was a new cream Bakelite wireless under the wall lights which had lovely pale green and cranberry glass shades.

A small coal fire burned in the fireplace, and on the black iron trivet sat a kettle of water, from which steam was wisping out of the spout. The apartment, unlike Jessie's home, had already been wired for electricity, yet Ingrid Gunter still used the fire to boil the kettle. The walls had old-fashioned fading wallpaper on which hung some framed photographs and a collection of miniature paintings. The scent of beeswax polish reminded Jessie of home and there was a delicious smell of baking coming from the kitchen.

'Please, take a seat.' Ingrid waited until Jessie lowered herself into an armchair before she herself sat down in the chair opposite. 'You are young and will want to ask questions. I am old and will not want to answer them. Say what you have come to say and then you must go.'

Her forthright manner reminded Jessie of Dolly. 'I found out where you were living, through the records office.'

'Why? Why should you want to find me? I am not a part of your mother's family now or your life so why should you come here?'

'You're my grandmother.'

'Ha. It could be said.' She picked up a polished brass poker and prodded the glowing coals in the fire. 'I suppose your curiosity was aroused when your grandfather died. Something was said and you latched on to it. Too young to be wise. It must have been fun to discover you had a grandmother who had been kept in the dark. It gave you something to do. Dig up a bit of the past. Well, I hope your thirst for intrigue has been quenched. I'm not dead. What will you do now for a pastime?'

Whether she meant to or not, she was fuelling Jessie's passion, she wanted to know more. 'How did you know he'd died?'

Her grandmother paused, as though wondering how much she should reveal. Then she said slowly, 'The authorities. He was still my husband, according to the law. As far as I was concerned he died years ago.' There was a short pause as the clock ticked loudly. 'What if I tell you that I don't like callers?'

'I'm not a caller, I'm your flesh and blood. Did you have any more children?'

'No.' She turned away from Jessie's searching eyes and gazed at the floor. 'No. The love a mother has for her child is almost too much. Once is enough.' She went quiet again. 'My brother had beautiful children and now he has beautiful grandchildren. I see them often. They are my family.'

'That cake in the oven smells lovely,' said Jessie. It sounded cheeky but she was actually trying to remind Ingrid of it because there was a slight smell of burning coming from the kitchen.

'Yes. The cake.' The old woman pulled herself up from the armchair and went into the small kitchen. 'Would you prefer tea to coffee?'

'I don't mind,' Jessie called back, surprised at the offer.

'Perhaps you wouldn't mind giving me a hand.' A second invitation, and from someone who didn't want to spend much time with her.

'The cake did not burn. I've left the oven door just open. In a moment, perhaps you would lift it out for me while I grind the coffee beans.'

Jessie glanced around the small, neat kitchen. Everything was in its place, pretty cups and saucers were displayed on a small kitchen dresser and on the white enamel surface, in a corner, sat two of everything from a plain blue dinner service — her everyday crockery. One set for herself and one set should she have a visitor. There were lace curtains at the kitchen window and across the back door which opened on to the garden. The floor was covered with bright blue linoleum with small red squares.

Jessie watched fascinated as the graceful woman spooned coffee beans into her iron grinder. 'I don't think I've tasted real coffee, we always have Camp. I'm not sure about Joe Lyons, the coffee there does taste different but—'

'I doubt that Joe Lyons has time to grind the beans himself but I'm sure he would use good coffee and charge for it.'

Jessie lifted the fruit cake out of the oven and placed it on the draining board to cool. 'This looks delicious.'

'The sugar bowl is in that cupboard. It's dark brown sugar, you may not like it but I don't use white.'

'I love dark brown sugar, we always have it at Christmas time. Mum lets us scoop out the flesh from an orange and fill it with sugar. Once it's been sitting for a week she lets us eat some of it, before we chop up the peel for the puddings.'

Ingrid spooned ground coffee into her percolator. 'I suppose you will boast to your mother that you have found out about me and where I live.'

'Not if you don't want me to.'

'If *I* don't want? Since when did what *I* want matter? How much do you know about Mr Gunter and myself?'

'That he left you and it made him sad, that my grandfather, who I loved *very much*, was besotted by *her* until he realised his mistake and missed someone. You.'

'You seem to have known him well. Did you despise him for what he did to me?'

'No. I could never despise him, we were quite close.'

'You must have been special to have managed that. Here,' she handed Jessie an oven glove, 'bring in the kettle of boiled water from off the fire — and try not to scald yourself.'

Obeying her instructions, Jessie carried on talking, raising her voice a little. 'He never mentioned you or said anything about what had happened, but once I found out, after he died, I realised he must have sometimes been thinking about you when I was there.'

'And how could you know what he was thinking?' she said, taking the kettle from Jessie. 'You would have to be very smart to have seen inside Mr Gunter's mind.'

'I was the only one in the family who sat with him. Sometimes we'd talk but mostly we'd sit and be quiet. He would have told me to go home if he hadn't wanted me there. He was like that.'

Ingrid asked Jessie to carry the tray, laden with coffee and warm cake, into the sitting room. 'From what age did you visit him?'

'Always, right from when I was a scruffy urchin.' Jessie set the tray down on the small occasional table and watched as her grandmother cut two slices of cake.

'I doubt you were ever scruffy or an urchin.'

'Do you know what he mostly ate?' said Jessie, enjoying the memory. 'Slices of sharp cooking apple, a piece of cheese—'

'And raw onion,' the old woman finished for her. 'I can't pretend that I'm not pleased now that I've got over the shock of seeing you on my doorstep but don't take my hospitality to mean that I want you to come and go when it takes your fancy.'

'I wouldn't do that. My parents taught us to have good manners, not that Dolly or Alfie always practise it but at least they *know* when they're being bad-mannered. Grandfather wouldn't have stood for my coming and going either.'

Ingrid tensed at another mention of him. 'We'll drink our coffee and eat cake together and then I would like you to leave. Meanwhile I would prefer it if there was no further talk of that man. Willy Gunter has much to answer for. He did wrong and God would not have forgiven him – and he will have known that, which is why he had the worried look you refer to.'

'I didn't say worried, I said sad.'

'He had his Maker to face and I don't envy his last few minutes before death. He knew he had wronged me. I was a good, hard-working, faithful wife, and doting mother. I did not deserve what he gave me in return, the pain and the loneliness, the worst kind of suffering for someone who has lost her family. It's not good to love too deeply. Once, he did love me, yes, but not after he met the Gypsy whore. You shouldn't make excuses for him or try to justify what he did. Leave me something at least. I was the victim so I may curse him. Hating is easier than loving.'

Jessie sipped her coffee and found the silence strange; it was as if everything had been said and yet there were so many things to discover about her grandmother. She wanted to ask about Rose and what she was like as a small child, but that would have to wait until another visit.

'You should eat the cake while it's still quite warm, that way you will taste the fruit.'

'Mum always makes us wait until it's cooled down. She says it's not good for the digestion if—'

'That's because she's had English housewives to listen to instead of her own mother, and for that you may thank your beloved grandfather.'

'I know it's not much help now,' Jessie broke off a small piece of her cake, 'but I'm sure he regretted what he'd done and I know he wasn't happy with Grandmother Blake. He wasn't in his grave five minutes before she had another man move in.'

'He got what he deserved. When he left me I had no money and a child to bring up. He changed his name so that I could not trace him. I had no choice but to put my daughter into the orphans' home. I could have found him if I wanted, but I would not beg, I would never beg. I managed by myself, scrubbing thick grease from kitchen floors, always with the thought that I would one day get back my little girl. Then I discovered he'd taken her away from the home and I gave up. He had taken everything. When he took my child he left me with nothing.'

'I thought he changed his name because of the resentment in the East End – against Germans,' murmured Jessie, ashamed of what she was hearing.

'So that was his story? Ah well, it made my life easier not having to worry about my child's welfare. I trusted the Romany to look after her.' She raised her eyes and looked straight at Jessie. 'Was she a good mother?'

'Mum was fed and clothed, but I don't think she was loved. She grew up thinking that her real mother didn't want her.'

'Well, well. Aren't you a glowing light. I will sleep much better knowing that. What I could never understand ... is why your mother repeated what had happened to herself. She gave away your sister. Times were hard for her, of course they were, but—'

'She never gave away my sister! Dolly lives with us. She's always lived with us. Mum wouldn't give one of us away. Who told you that?'

Ingrid's eyes clouded over and her face showed her remorse. 'My brother has been bringing me tales for years, he doesn't live far from where you are and thinks it his duty to bring me news. As usual he got it wrong and I apologise.' She looked very uncomfortable. 'I'm weary now, you have tired me with your questions.'

'It's time I was getting back home anyway, they forecast fog, and there's been a lot of trouble round our way between gangs.'

Rising, Ingrid shook her head. 'Mosley is a foolish man who is causing trouble which could have a devastating affect on this country.'

At the front door, she said, 'Please try to understand that I am better off being left in peace. I've put the past behind me. Don't tell your mother that you came. As far as I am concerned I have no family and that is how I prefer it.'

Jessie found that very hard to believe. 'Surely you'd like to see your only daughter again. She'd come, I know she would, once I explained what—'

'After thirty-three years? I don't think so. You are young and fanciful and I'm sorry to dash your romantic notions. Had she have wanted to, like you, she could have tracked me down a very long time ago.' Ingrid looked up at the sky and frowned. 'I think the forecast is right. Be home before that blanket of fog begins to fall.'

Jessie didn't want to leave things there, it seemed too final. 'How come you know so much about us if you weren't interested?'

'My brother keeps me informed whether I like it or not.' She nodded her goodbye and the expression on her face forbade Jessie to ask anything else. Then Ingrid smiled weakly and closed the door.

Jessie leaned against the wall to collect her thoughts. Her grandmother had not shed one tear. Did she really not care? Jessie didn't believe it.

The sound of a man's voice from inside startled her. 'You were very hard on her, Ingrid! Too hard. She is just an innocent child!' It must be Ingrid Gunter's brother; he had presumably decided to keep out of the way until she left.

'I don't want to *hear* it!' Jessie flinched at the misery in Ingrid's voice. 'You hated my husband for what he did to me, so hate his offspring . . . *and* his offspring's children! That girl is nothing to us. *Nothing!* We must forget she ever came!' Ingrid's voice dropped to a pitiful tone. 'We must forget. I've lived without them, I will die without them.'

There was a quiet moment and then Ingrid spoke again. She sounded like a different woman. 'He did love me, you know . . .'

'I know, Ingrid, I know. Try to remember the good times.'

'My only child, Wilhelm, my only baby. We could have brought her up, we could have managed between us. Do you see what happened? She repeated the actions of her own mother. Do you see, Wilhelm? Do you *see*?'

'Shush. You have my family, Ingrid. My children adore you, you know they do. You have a family with us. We'll forget she ever came.'

Jessie arrived home exhausted and ready for her bed; too much had happened in one day. Hoping her parents were too involved with a programme on the wireless to start asking questions about the William Morris exhibition, Jessie went into the house very quietly. She'd had enough for one day and wasn't in the mood for trumping up a pack of lies about the Whitechapel Art Gallery and the exhibition. It would be much easier to deal with it in the morning over breakfast when everyone was in too much of a hurry to show interest.

Creeping along the passage, Jessie was surprised to hear laughter and conversation coming from the sitting room and recognised the voice of one of her uncles, her father's brother – the family orator. The family bore. She also recognised another uncle and an aunt. The Warners had paid a surprise visit.

Since Dolly was out and the boys were asleep in bed, she would have to go in for a few minutes and make polite conversation – it would be expected. Jessie knew the form. She ran the usual questions through in her mind: how was life treating her; had she received promotion at work yet; was there an engagement in the air; which author was she reading these days ...

Slipping quietly into the sitting room, she sat on a low stool, thankful that they were engrossed, or at least pretending to be interested in what her dad had to say. Glancing at the detached expressions on their faces, Jessie felt sorry for her parents; the Warners had never been interested in their lives or what happened at the docks.

Her eyes rested on Rose, who was sitting in the upright green velvet chair doing her best to look the part expected of her. Jessie longed to tell her where she had been and who she had found; she wanted her to know that she looked just like her own mother and she wanted to hold her very close and tell her what a lovely woman Ingrid Gunter was, a lovely old lady with as much pride as her daughter.

Sensing Jessie's eyes on her, Rose looked across at her, a puzzled expression on her face, her eyes full of questions. It was as if she knew what Jessie was thinking and where she had been.

'So I'll be testing it tomorrow,' Robert's voice broke through Jessie's thoughts. 'I don't think my crane'll take it and I've said as much, but I'll do it.'

'Testing what, Dad?' said Jessie.

'My crane. They think they know best. Extra load? It's asking for trouble, but that's the way it's going now. They want us to do more work in less time, Jessie.'

'You can refuse though, can't you?'

'Refuse? I should think not. There are too many men ready to slip into my driving seat. No. I'll do as I'm told and we'll just have to see who's right.' He tapped his pipe on the edge of the black iron grate in the fireplace and smiled at her. Turning to Rose he winked. 'If anything should go wrong, I just want red roses and don't go in black.' Polite laughter greeted this and Jessie excused herself, saying she had to be up extra early in the morning.

Closing the door behind her and allowing a long relieved sigh to escape, she was surprised to see Stephen sitting on the stairs, elbows resting on knees, hands under chin. Her heart went out to him – he looked lonely. 'Stephen? You should be asleep by now. What's the matter?' She sat down with him and kissed the top of his head. 'Who's upset you this time?'

'No one. There's nothing the matter.'

'Yes there is. I can tell. Come on, silly, out with it.'

'They keep taking the mickey out of me at school, calling me names.' He stared out, as if he was in a world of his own. 'Now I've been put at the back of the class and it's worse.'

'What kind of names?'

'Daffadown Dilly, Simple Simon, Silly Boy Blue . . .'

'But you're not simple, Stephen, far from it. You're much cleverer than Alfie and he's older than you. Come to that, you've got more up top than Dolly.'

'I know that. She lives in the past and never finks about the future. Mum said so.'

'Lives for the minute, more like. Well then what is it? Are you being lazy at school? Not learning your tables or spellings? Is that what it is?'

'No. I can't see what's written on the blackboard and now I've been put at the back with the dunce so it's worse.'

'Ah well, it sounds like you might need specs.'

'No! That'll make things worse. More names. I'd rather drown myself then wear those things, or cut my throat on Dad's razor, or put my head in the gas oven. Or—'

'Yeah, all right, you've made your point.' She tried not to laugh at him and tousled his hair, keeping a serious tone to her voice. 'Well, we'll just have to get Mum to have a quiet word with your teacher. Then she'll move you down the front and no one need know why you've been put there. Now stop fretting over that and listen. I've got a secret that I shouldn't tell.'

'A real secret or somefing and nothing?'

'A real secret and you're not to tell a soul. Promise me you won't.'

'God's honour,' he said.

'Come on then, into my room. I take it Alfie's asleep in bed.'

'No. He's gone out. Through the bedroom window. He'll get killed if Mum or Dad finds out. He's put stuff under the quilt to make it look like he's under the covers, asleep.'

'Oh God. Don't you ever think of copying Alfie, will you?

He's heading for trouble, make no mistake. Do you know where he's gone?'

'Yep.' Pleased with himself Stephen bounced up the stairs and into the girls' bedroom and lay on Jessie's bed, hands behind his head, skinny legs crossed. 'He's gone to chalk words on a wall with his mates.'

Her heart sank. 'What words?' As if she didn't know.

'Down with the Jews. 'Im and his mates are getting sixpence each for doing it, a man's paying 'em. Don't know who he is though. Fancy getting a tanner for chalking on the wall. It's the same man who gave Alfie a knife to look after.'

A wave of dread shot through Jessie. My God, she thought, it's as if we're all leading double lives.

'It's all right, Jess, isn't it . . . about the knife?'

'Course it is. I dare say Alfie bought it with his ill-gotten cash but fobbed you off with that story about a man. Unless there's more that you're not telling me?'

'Not really,' he said, sorry to disappoint her – and himself.

'Good. I tell you what, Stephen, on Friday, pay day, I'll give you sixpence for not chalking on the wall. And don't ever mention this to Max – about Alfie. He'd be really hurt.'

'You won't tell Dad, will you? Alfie'd kill me. So would his mates.'

Jessie smiled. 'No, sweetheart, I won't tell, but let me know when he's going again and I'll follow him, pretend I just happened to be out for a walk, then I'll clip him round the ear and his friends too.'

'But you won't call a copper?'

'No, I won't do that. No need. I've a feeling Alfie will draw their attention soon enough. Now then, wait till you hear this. Grandmother Blake is not our real grandmother.'

'So?'

'Oh. It doesn't bother you then?'

'No. She don't like me anyway. Never smiles or anything.'

'Fair enough. So what about our real grandmother? What if

I told you that that's where I've been. What if I told you that I've found where she lives and Mum doesn't even know that and what's more Mum doesn't even know if she's alive but I do. She's really nice. A proper granny.'

'What, with a silver bun and that?'

'Yep. With silvery-grey hair and soft blue eyes, just like Mum's.'

'Did she give you any presents to bring back?'

'No. She's a granny not a fairy godmother. She lives really close to Victoria Park, near the boating lake.'

'Has she got her own boat?' Stephen asked.

'Tch, she's not rich, Stephen, she's—'

'Poor?'

'No! She's just *normal*. Like us.'

'The kids at school say we're rich 'cos Mum's got a shop and Dad's got a job.'

'Well, I suppose we are, compared to most. Not rich, but not poor. Do you want to come with me next time, to see her?' Jessie looked at him eagerly.

'Dunno.' He looked doubtful.

'Oh, right. I'll take Alfie instead.'

That decided him. 'All right then, I'll come. When we going? Tomorrow?'

'No. In a few weeks' time.'

'A few weeks! That's ages away. Why did you tell me now? Now I'll have to wait. I can't wait all that time.'

'In *two* weeks then. We'll give her time to get over the shock of this visit. She didn't know who I was at first, she lives on her own but her brother visits. Just think, Stephen, she's our mum's mum, her *real* mum. Don't you think it's good that we've found her?'

'Dunno.'

Pulling her pillow from under his head, Jessie playfully hit him with it. 'You don't know nuffink, do you?'

'Nope.'

Within seconds Jessie and Stephen were thoroughly enjoying a hardened pillow fight, laughing and shrieking as each of them received blows. The childish fun banished Jessie's worries. Tomorrow was another day and another day meant facing up to all the troubles going on around them, but for now, all that was forgotten and she was happy. Very happy.

Arriving at her desk the next morning five minutes early and still in a good mood, Jessie found Mr Reed keen to know how she had got on in her search. She had hardly had time to take off her coat when he was firing questions at her.

'It's a very long story, Mr Reed,' she chuckled, 'but to cut it short, I went to the address and I found my long lost grandmother.'

'Wonderful, Jessie!' he exclaimed, excited. 'Wonderful! I wish I'd been there to see it. Do you think they'll get together now?'

'I don't know, we'll just have to wait and see.'

Chuffed that he had been of help, Mr Reed got carried away, telling her all about his own family history. 'It's a passion, I suppose. Once you make a start, you just have to go on and on. I wouldn't be the least bit surprised if you're not back there soon, Jessie, digging further into the secrets of your family.' He shook his head at the wonder of it. 'Fascinating . . .'

Thankfully, she managed to change the subject at an appropriate pause. A memo, which Jessie had seen on her way into the building, was her excuse. It was pinned to the notice board and had been signed by all three directors. The wording was careful but the message was clear: anyone discovered to have any involvement with the Blackshirt movement risked losing their job. There were quite a few Jewish people working in the factory and in the offices, not to mention the sales reps.

Mr Reed didn't have an opinion, but then, as he openly admitted, he wasn't the least bit interested in politics. 'Each to their own,' he said, 'each to their own.'

'There was trouble again last night, outside the People's Palace,' said Jessie, remembering the ugly scene.

'Exactly my point. Religion and politics, the cause of all ill.'

On her way home from work, smiling to herself, Jessie imagined Mr Reed taking his family on a tour of the Tower of London and behaving like a guide. The smile faded from her face when she saw yet another insult to Jews chalked on the wall at the top of the turning. It was time to have a word with Alfie about this man who had been paying him money to do his dirty work and giving him knives to look after.

Searching through her handbag for her door key, she hadn't noticed anything out of the ordinary and it wasn't until she pushed the key into the lock that Jessie realised the Venetian blinds were down. She stared at the windows and felt strangely aware of being watched. She turned round and saw one of the neighbours opposite, leaning against her front door, arms folded and looking very sad. She caught Jessie's eyes and lowered her head.

Crossing the cobblestone road, Jessie asked what had happened and why there was an eerie silence in the street. 'Our blinds are down, Mrs Adams, and your front room curtains are drawn. What's happened?'

The woman couldn't answer; she turned away and went into her house, leaving Jessie to find out for herself. Looking back at the drawn blinds of her house, she knew that something was wrong at home, that something very bad had happened. Walking slowly across the street she knocked on her front door instead of using her key, as a fear stronger than anything she had experienced rose from the pit of her stomach.

It was Dolly who answered the door, Dolly with a red, tear-stained face who stared at Jessie as if she was a stranger and then spoke in a monotone.

'Dad's been killed.'

Jessie stood paralysed, staring back at her sister, waiting.

Waiting for her to smile and say it was only a joke. But it wasn't April Fool's Day and not even Dolly would make such a joke. Jessie opened her mouth to say something but no words came. At last she spoke her sister's name. 'Dolly?'

'Dad's been killed,' she repeated. The house was still and silent, with no sign of movement. 'He's dead, Jessie. Daddy's dead.' She turned and drifted along the passage, away from her, as if she was only a dream.

Jessie went inside and lowered herself onto the fourth stair and sat gazing out at nothing, Dolly's words floating through her mind. *'He's dead, Jessie. Dad's been killed. He's dead, Jessie.'*

The crane. The heavy load.

Her face got colder and tighter by the second as a strange wailing sound rose from deep within her, growing louder and louder until she was screaming. 'No-ooooo! No! No! No!' She punched the stairs over and over and it didn't hurt; she couldn't feel a thing as she went on punching and screaming and punching, until she finally exhausted herself.

Raising her head, she stared at the front door. It hadn't closed properly. She would wait and see for herself whether he came home from work or not, see if Dolly was right. Soon he would come in, smiling and winking at her. She didn't move, just sat, silent and staring.

Nobody came. Nobody touched her. Through her flood of tears she could see the lodgers, standing on the stairs above her, watching. They never moved. They never said a word.

As if in a dream, she walked down to the basement and looked for her mother in the kitchen. She wasn't there. She glanced out of the window into the back garden and there was Rose, wearing the same dress she'd had on that morning and hanging out the washing. Jessie's mother was hanging washing on the line. Her mother was hanging washing on the line and her dad was dead.

Chapter Five

On the morning after the tragedy, the house had an exceptionally tranquil atmosphere. Rose had been up all night and the girls had been drifting about since the crack of dawn. When Dolly had slipped into bed beside Jessie during the night, she had welcomed it. Neither of them had said a word, they just huddled together as if it was the most natural thing in the world.

All three of them coasted silently through the house as if they were in church and slowly got themselves ready to face their first day without Robert. The boys, who had been crying on and off all night, were fast asleep, exhausted.

Rose, pale and red-eyed, made the porridge as usual but none of them ate a morsel, as if eating food was too normal. Several pots of tea had been brewed and this they did drink, sipping endless cups in silence. None of them mentioned Robert or the accident and when Jessie arrived at work, she could hardly remember having walked to the bus stop or getting on the bus. She had simply arrived here.

As she went into the building, one of the men from the loading bay met her on the stairs. His eyes were downcast as he murmured, 'Never mind, Jessie. We'll all rally round. All of us.'

It was those few kind words which brought reality and

she felt herself go icy-cold again. As he moved past her, she turned to him and whispered, 'Rally round?' Had more time gone by than she'd realised? Wasn't it just yesterday that it had happened. 'My dad?' she murmured, looking into his face. 'You know about that?'

'Bad news travels fast, love. We're all deeply shocked. I never, not in a thousand years, would have expected you to come in today. You didn't have to, you know.'

Nodding and smiling weakly, she backed away up the staircase. George was about the same age as Robert and she thought how like her dad he was. She hadn't noticed before. 'I might go home, George. I don't know.'

'Well, you just get the word through to me and I'll see to it that one of our drivers takes you. One of the women can go with you as well, for the company. You're not on your own with this one, Jessie, we're all behind you.'

'Does everyone know?' she asked, her voice sounding as if it was coming from somewhere else.

'If they don't yet, they will soon. There's a piece in the early editions. There'll be more before the day's out. I should think all the papers will cover it, Jessie, it's an outrage.' He doffed his cap and walked away, shoulders hunched.

The sincerity in his voice and his kind words had touched Jessie but not enough to draw tears. She hadn't cried since Dolly had first told her. Maybe other people were absorbing the grief and anger instead of her. She didn't feel angry. She didn't feel anything. Just numb. It wasn't a bad feeling. It wasn't really a feeling at all.

In the office she was mystified to see a small gathering round Mr Reed's desk. Was it his birthday and he hadn't told her? The conversation stopped the moment she stepped into the room and they all looked at her. A quiet word from Mr Reed and they began to leave, nodding and squeezing her arm as they went.

Once they'd gone, her boss walked slowly towards her, his

arms reaching out. 'You shouldn't have come in, Jessie.' He laid a hand on her shoulders, put a finger under her chin and smiled fondly at her. 'We'll see you get home. Would you like to go back in a cab with your friend Sally? Or shall I arrange for Mr Brady's chauffeur to take you home in the company car?'

'That'd be something, wouldn't it?' she said. 'Me in a Bentley.'

'OK. I'll see to it, and Sally can go with you.'

'I was only joking, Mr Reed. Why would they chauffeur *me* around. Anyway, George Brown from the loading bay said he'd get someone to take me in one of the vans.'

'If that's what you'd prefer, Jessie.'

'It doesn't really matter. I wasn't expecting to go home. Today's our busy day. All the dockets and wages—'

'Van or Bentley,' he spoke in a fatherly fashion, 'or a cab. You choose.'

The thought of her and Sally in a chauffeur-driven car should have made Jessie smile, but it didn't. 'The Bentley,' she said, shrugging.

'The Bentley it is. But first things first. Sit yourself down and I'll ring through to the kitchen for a breakfast tray. Would you like tea or coffee?'

'Coffee. Nothing to eat.'

The crashing of the door as Sally barged in startled them both. She had a newspaper in one hand and she was crying. 'Jess! They said you'd come in! I'm sorry, Jessie. I'm so sorry! It's terrible. It's the worst thing I've ever known!'

Jessie took the newspaper from her hand. It had been folded back to a page showing a news flash: DOCKER TRAPPED INSIDE RAGING INFERNO AS CRANE PLUNGES INTO THE THAMES.

'Silly thing. That wasn't my dad. That's not what happened to him. This is someone else. They overloaded his crane and—'

'But it mentions him by name, Jessie. That's *terrible* if they've made a mistake. Is your dad alive then?'

'No. He was killed yesterday. Dolly told me ...' She suddenly felt very sick. White stars were shooting through her head. 'I don't know. Do you think so? I don't know. We went to bed.' The feeling of nausea was overwhelming. 'Mr Reed?' The flashing white stars surged forward until everything was flashing white and then it went black.

Jessie didn't really appreciate the ride in the chauffeur-driven Bentley; she was fully conscious but it was as if she was drifting through time. She'd asked Sally not to go with her. She just wanted to be by herself until she was with her family. All she wanted was her mother, her sister, and her brothers.

The boys and Dolly were at home but Jessie was horrified to see that the sitting room was crammed with people, mostly men, her father's work mates from the docks, some of whom had witnessed the horror. Her uncles were also there as well as Grandmother Blake. Jessie thought of the scene in the sitting room the night before it happened, when they didn't show the least bit of interest in what her dad was saying. Jessie had never much liked them; now she felt that they were partly responsible. If they had listened, had reacted, had told him not to be a fool, maybe he would have paid attention and would be in his favourite chair now instead of in the morgue.

The more his smiling face as he explained about the heavy load and the crane came to mind, the more she believed that he had been waiting for his brothers to tell him not to drive it. But neither of them had, and they probably had no idea that he had been hoping for an excuse not to risk his life.

Jessie looked from them to officials from the National Workers Movement, who were having a quiet word with her mother. The conversation was low and their expressions serious. Jessie overheard one of them insist that it was management's fault and those responsible would be brought to justice and made to answer. Compensation was mentioned but Rose broke into tears at that point and the conversation stopped.

Dolly was earnestly telling a young reporter how she had

always wanted to be a writer herself, how she loved to read poems and early history. Sadly for her, he wasn't interested. All he wanted was a quote from a distressed member of the family.

'I bet no one around this way knows that Chaucer used to live in Aldgate,' Dolly told him, 'and that his dad owned twenty-four shops in Whitechapel. I don't expect you knew that either.'

'No, I didn't. How fascinating, Miss Warner. Now, about your father's accident—'

'Whitchapel was no more than a village then of course, same as Stepney and Bethnal Green—'

'It must have been a terrible shock,' he said, his pencil poised over his notebook. 'What were your first thoughts when you heard about it?'

'A shock? Oh no, it's an everyday occurrence round these parts. Men go crashing into the Thames every day. Of course it was a shock! I've told two reporters that already! We don't really want to keep on being reminded! It only happened *yesterday*.'

'Well, it's my job to let the public know ... and it will help your mother—'

'No it won't. It can't bring Dad back and that's the only help she wants.' Dolly went quiet and glanced around her. 'I think everyone should go now.'

'Of course, I understand how you must feel, but if I could just ask you one question. What do you think of the London Dock Management now?'

Dolly looked sideways at him and sighed heavily. 'I don't think about 'em, never have done.'

'Ah.' There was a glimmer of hope from the reporter, 'So you've always been against your father working in the docks, worried for his safety, cranes being somewhat antiquated.'

'No. I love the docks. Dad used to take us there sometimes to see the ships. The London docks are not that old, you know.' Now she was side-tracking to annoy him. 'St Katherine's was only built a hundred and fifty years ago. It was the Romans who started it really, they built Londinium on the banks of the River Thames and—'

'I, er, I see another young lady's arrived. Would she be your sister, Jessie?'

'Yeah, that's our Jess. She looks too upset to talk to you though.' Leaving the journalist to himself and without a quote, Dolly went over to Jessie and squeezed her arm. 'You all right?'

'Not really. I'm going up to our room. Can you cope with this lot?'

'I'm about to throw 'em all out.'

'No, you mustn't do that, Doll, as much as I'd love you to. You'll embarrass Mum.'

'She doesn't want them here, Jess. Look at her face, she's drained. Don't worry,' she whispered, 'I'll be as polite as I can.'

In the quiet of her room, Jessie lay on her bed and brought her dad's face to mind. His kind face and brown wavy hair, the way he was relaxed and smiling when he joked that if the worst should happen they were to send red roses and not go in black. The worst had happened, and Jessie could not take it in. How could he be dead? She thought about red roses. Imagined her bedroom full of them, deep red and scented. 'Don't go away, Dad,' she whispered. 'Stay with us.' She turned on her side, curled up her knees, hugged her pillow and cried herself to sleep.

Both Jessie and Dolly had been given a week off work with pay and the boys a week off school to allow them to mourn their father. When Robert's body was brought back to the house in the coffin, the atmosphere seemed to change and each of them found they were pleased to have him back and looking so peaceful, as if he was asleep. Fortunately, Robert hadn't been badly burned. Some of the newspapers had exaggerated the story or jumped the gun before proper press releases had been given out. The engine of the crane had been overstrained and a fire had been the result, but the neck of the crane had given way under the heavy load before the flames really took hold, plunging into the River Thames, where Robert died from drowning, not from burns or fumes.

On the eve of the funeral, relatives and friends arrived to see him for the last time before the coffin was closed for ever. Jessie was fetching and carrying sandwiches from the kitchen when she overheard one of her father's friends having a quiet word with Rose. Intrigued by the secretive tone of his voice, she listened outside the door.

'No, Rose, it's nothing to do with the compensation, I promise. I've something else to tell you.' The family friend sounded as if he was about to make a confession. 'It's about Robert.'

'Not now, Bert. Later,' said Rose, tired. 'Wait until everything's settled down a bit. I don't want to talk about the wrongdoing of the dock board for the time being. Maybe later when—'

'It's not about that, Rose. It's more private ... personal. Robert asked me to pass on a message to you if anything went wrong. I don't really think he believed anything would go wrong but, just in case it did, he wanted me to ... well, to say ...'

'Come on then, Bert, out with it. I must give Jessie a hand upstairs. What was the message?'

'He said I was to ask you to, well, to ... to bring the girls together and not to leave it for too long. I know what he meant, Rose, because he told me all about it, way back. It's not for me to offer an opinion, I'm just passing on his wishes.'

'I see. Thanks for telling me, Bert, and for keeping it to yourself. I'll give it some serious thought and I'd appreciate it if you could push it from your mind.'

'I will, Rose, don't you worry. As far as I'm concerned,

what he told me will go with him to his grave and with me to mine.'

They continued to speak in a whisper. Jessie slowly backed away, running the words through her mind. Think seriously about bringing the girls together? What had he meant by it?

Upstairs, Jessie was glad to see that Max had turned up. She hadn't given him much thought but he was a comforting sight and when he put his arm round her she realised just how much she needed him, needed that deep feeling of trust, warmth and loyalty.

That night, once everyone had gone and Rose was resting on her bed, Jessie and Max sat on the front step and talked in a way they had not done before, mostly about their childhood and their parents. When he pushed his hand through her hair and said he loved her, she started to cry.

'That's it, Jess,' he said. 'Let all the grief out, cry away the sadness, because one day you will smile and be happy again, I promise you. My Jessie will laugh again.' He kissed the tip of her nose and brushed strands of loose hair from her face. 'I'll always be here for you. Always.'

'I know you will, Max.'

Taking her hand he suggested they go for a slow walk, there was something he wanted to show her, something that might cheer her up a little.

Strolling along the Broadway, Jessie confided to Max what she'd overhead that day, the message from her dad delivered by one of his best friends. Max shrugged it off, saying that people got very emotional and sometimes carried away when there was a death in the family. He suggested she forget it. Jessie went on to tell him about her visit to her real grandmother. The accident had happened the very next morning so she hadn't had the chance or the inclination to talk to anyone about it. Other than Stephen and Mr Reed, no one else knew.

Max was pleased for her but in his usual, sensible way, he advised that she be very careful about mentioning it to Rose.

He told her to let it lie for a couple of weeks and although Jessie said she agreed with him, she had already decided that she would bring them together as soon as she could, before her grandmother died and it was too late. She had learned a very important lesson from her dad's death, *his* lesson, which he'd often repeated: put off nothing till the morrow if it can be done the day.

'Well, here we are,' said Max, stopping outside a small pawnbroker and jewellery shop. 'This is it what I wanted you to see.' He pointed to the jewellery display in the window. 'Can you see that tray in the corner, between the grid . . .'

'The ring tray? The diamond ring tray?'

'Engagement ring tray, Jessie. Look at the ring third from the left, top row. The solitaire.'

'Yeah, I'm looking.'

'Well, that's the one I've been paying off for. I was keeping it a surprise. Your dad knew about it, he was the only one I told.' Max placed his hand on Jessie's face and looked into her blue eyes. 'Will you be my fiancée, Jessie Warner?'

'Max, would you have been paying off on that beautiful ring if you thought for one minute that I would say no?'

'You do like it then.'

'Like it?' She looked from him to the ring, the sparkling diamond ring. 'It's beautiful. Of all the others, that's the one I would have chosen. I love it.'

'It's not the biggest though.'

'It is to me.' She wrapped her arms round him. 'I'm really, really pleased you told Dad. I feel as if he's here, giving his blessing. He thought a lot of you.'

Choked, Max lowered his eyes. 'I know.'

'It will be all right, won't it? Tomorrow. The funeral. Me and Mum and Dolly . . . and the boys. We'll get through tomorrow, won't we?'

'You'll get through it, Jessie. People always do. One way

or another.' Max gave her another long, comforting hug and they walked slowly home together.

And indeed they did get through it. The procession, the church, the heartrending service. When the guests had returned to the cars to make the short journey from the church back to the house, Rose, Jessie, and Dolly and the boys were left by Robert's grave to say their private goodbyes. Holding a beautiful wreath of red roses, they carefully lowered it onto the coffin and prayed together. Opening her eyes after saying a few silent words to her dad, Jessie glanced up to see that Rose's attention was elsewhere and that her face showed uncertainty. She was peering at a woman standing beneath an overgrown tree who was looking over at them.

Jessie looked from the strange woman to Rose and whispered, 'Who is she, Mum?'

'No one to concern ourselves over. You and Dolly take your brothers and see if your uncles have sorted out who's to go back to the house in which cars, there's good girls. I just want a few minutes by myself.'

Pressing a single rose in her hand, Jessie brought it to her lips and then dropped it into the grave. 'Goodbye, Dad,' she murmured and walked away, arm in arm with Dolly, towards the cemetery gates.

Rose moved towards the woman. She felt she should know her, there was something familiar about her. Something *very* familiar. She quickened her pace, hardly able to believe her eyes. She hadn't seen Gerta in a very, very long time. Why she should turn up at Robert's funeral was beyond her.

'I trust the service went well,' said Gerta when Rose came up to her. 'I was sorry to read about the tragedy. It was quite shocking.'

'Thank you'. Rose managed a tight smile. 'If I had known you were here I would have asked you to join us. How are you?'

'Struggling. But I'm used to it. Your brother, Jack, has

much to answer for. He left me a broken woman.' Gerta showed no sign of compassion. 'Why do you not ask about Hannah? About her welfare? Or have you completely wiped that daughter from your mind?'

'Of course I haven't. I think about you both. Don't forget it was *you* who insisted that Robert and I should have nothing to do with her, Gerta. Don't tell me you've changed your mind after all this time.' Rose felt her stomach turn. Was Gerta here to cause trouble?

'I am here for one reason and one reason only. To remind you that your late husband had five children, not four. I would like you to set the record straight, with your solicitor.' There was a chilling smile on Gerta's face.

How she has changed, thought Rose. 'Why would I want to do that, Gerta?'

'I doubt you would want to do it, but needs be.'

'Needs be? Get to the point, please. I've guests to attend to.'

'All I want is fair play. According to the newspapers you're likely to get a handsome sum in compensation for the way Robert died. I want my share. I'll settle for fifty per cent of your claim since I took on fifty per cent of your responsibilities those years back.' Gerta glanced over Rose's shoulder and saw that Jessie was by the gates, watching them. 'Maybe I should beckon Hannah's twin to come over so we might explain.'

'No. I've heard what you have to say and yes, I will speak to my solicitor if the claim is successful. But I warn you, these things take time, and I want your word that you will keep the secret.'

'I have nothing to gain by giving it away, though the loss to you would be heavy. Twins should never be parted and yours would not forgive you for it. Your daughter is on her way over. She looks very much like Hannah, doesn't she? Except for the way she presents herself to the public. I would have expected you to see that your girls would dress more plainly. It looks as if I am about to meet her. What would you like me to say? Who shall I pretend to be?' Gerta's cold eyes were livened with something like amusement.

Rose spun round. Jessie was too close for comfort. 'I'll be in touch as soon as I can,' said Rose, wanting to leave.

'Good. Because if you don't, you'll have the newspapers to deal with and you can be sure that the picture they paint of you won't be a pretty one.' The evil smile was back.

'If you talk to a reporter I'll see to it that you get nothing. I don't care about other people and what they think of me, I'm only concerned for my children. Robert and I did what we thought was for the best at the time. Now I see that we were wrong. Keep away from my family, Gerta, I warn you.'

'How can I do that when I have one of them in my loving care?'

Turning on her heels, Rose strode towards Jessie, linked arms with her and walked her out of the church grounds.

'Who is she?' asked Jessie. 'What did she want?'

'Never mind. We shan't be seeing her again. Let's get this funeral over and out of the way. I've had enough of people and false pleasantries. All I want is to be at home with my children by my side, and no one else.'

Later, when the last of the visitors had left the house, Rose, the boys, and Jessie enjoyed a cool glass of lemonade in the kitchen, exhausted from having to talk to so many people. Taking them all by surprise, Dolly appeared, made up to the nines. She'd taken off her smart funeral suit, put on one of her bright frocks and was wearing more make-up than usual. Her eyebrows had been pencilled black, her face powder was heavy and her rouge almost as bright as her lipstick. To top it all, her light auburn hair was brushed out and lacquered stiff. Even the boys were shocked into silence.

'And where do you think you're going, looking like that?' There was a slight tremble to Rose's voice, whether from the trauma of the day or the sight of Dolly, it was difficult to say.

'I'm meeting all my mates at the Tavern,' she said. 'It's free drinks! They want to cheer me up, they've arranged a whip-round. A shilling from each of them to pay for my drinks. There's gonna be about a dozen girls from work there, we might even go back to Ivy's house for a bit of a do. Her mum and dad said we could.'

'Well, you can just go and wash that muck off your face and take off that dress.' Rose's voice was unbelievably calm. 'We're in mourning for your father, in case you've forgotten.'

'I know, but we don't have to sit around and be miserable. Eileen at work is Catholic and they always sing and dance after a funeral. They're doing this for me. *Especially* for me!'

'Dolly, I can understand if you need to be with your friends for an hour,' said Rose, 'but you are not to go out looking like that. You know how your father felt about heavy make-up — and Eileen's family do things differently from us.'

'But Dad's not here to see me, is he? So he can't get into a temper over how I look. I can wear what I want now that Dad's not around.' She dabbed a little Evening in Paris scent behind her ears. 'I'll be sixteen soon, don't forget.' Having shocked them into silence yet again, Dolly flounced out of the room, telling them not to wait up. The slamming of the street door sent a shudder through them all.

Gripping the back of a chair, Rose used every bit of willpower not to break down. Her face showed her torment. Torment and fear. There were four children to bring through and she had to do it by herself.

Jessie beckoned her brothers away, into the passage, where she gave them a hug and told them to read their comics, on their beds, until she went up. They both started to cry, and it seemed to Jessie that her world, their world, was falling apart. The loud banging at the door snapped her out of her silence. 'Up you go, boys. I'll just see who that is.'

Jessie opened the front door to find her friend Sally on the step, holding a lovely bouquet of bright flowers, orange, red and yellow dahlias. 'These are from me, Ron and Tom. Tom suggested it. He thought they might cheer you up a bit.'

Jessie didn't know what to make of it. *Tom* had suggested they send some flowers? 'That's really kind, Sally, but you shouldn't have come out on such a damp night. Do you want to come in for a minute? We can go in my bedroom, Mum's not really up to seeing anyone.'

'I'm not surprised. I wasn't expecting to be asked in, Jess, I only came to deliver the flowers and say how sorry we all are.' She pushed the bouquet into Jessie's arms. 'And Tom sends his best wishes and love.'

Confused by the word love, Jessie waved Sally into the passage. 'My bedroom's the first door on the left, after the second small flight of stairs. Wait in there for me. I'll be up in a minute.'

Taking the flowers downstairs into the kitchen, she saw that the boys hadn't gone up to bed but were huddled close to Rose, Stephen by her side and Alfie on her favourite padded footstool, snuggled up, with his head on her lap.

'I was just saying to the boys that a day out would do us all the world of good. We could go to Chessington Zoo. What do you think, Jessie?' Rose's voice was thin and strained. 'It would brighten us all up.'

Moved by the small family scene, Jessie nodded and said she thought it was a lovely idea. Then she excused herself and went to her room, wondering if her mother would be able to pull herself through the next few weeks. She had always relied on their dad for companionship in the same way that he had relied on her. Now Rose was alone.

'I'm really pleased you came round, Sally,' said Jessie. 'How's everyone at work?'

'As if you care,' Sally said, eyeing her friend. 'You don't have to pretend with me, Jess. We're mates.' She pulled an envelope from her pocket. 'Tom asked me to give you this card and say how sorry he was about everything.'

Jessie took the envelope and put it in her drawer. 'I thought he might have been with the other dockers, outside the gates. The hearse stopped at the docks especially so they could say their goodbyes. I looked out for him, but he wasn't there.'

'Well, he wouldn't be, would he? He's still in the London.'

Jessie's eyes widened. 'The London Hospital?'

'Yep. Broken bones and a few stitches here and there. Luckily that handsome face of 'is wasn't marked — except for a busted lip and black eye. He's been in there for a week, Jessie. I thought you knew.'

'The attack at the People's Palace. I haven't given it a thought. I was there . . .'

'I know, he told me. He knows you got away safely though, Hannah told him.' Sally went quiet and thoughtful. 'I don't know what to make of this Hannah, they seem really close. I can't help thinking that they're sweethearts. Tom insists she's more like a sister but I'm not sure. What did you make of it?'

'I liked her,' Jessie said, her mind still on Tom. 'I should go and visit him . . .'

'Ron reckons that Tom's gonna join the Blackshirts over that night. Get his own back.'

Jessie ignored that. 'How long's he in for?'

'Another week or so. Would have been out tomorrow but the bone specialist was worried about his fractured arm. I won't go into the gory details but they might 'ave to break and reset it again in a couple of days' time. You must have read about it in the local.'

'No . . . I've not been in the mood to read about people trying to kill each other. I'll go and see him.'

'What's your boyfriend gonna think about that, Jess? You visiting a handsome feller in bed? Won't Max be jealous?'

'No. Max isn't like that. Besides, we're getting engaged. He's paying off for a ring.'

'Oh, right. So you're not interested in Tom then?'

'Not in the way you think. I suppose he sees me the same as he does Hannah – a friend.'

'If you say so, Jess. If you say so.' There was a wry smile on Sally's face.

Jessie's first day back at work after the tragedy wasn't as difficult as she had imagined. Once those who knew her had inquired about her and her family's welfare, life in the offices and the factory continued as normal – busy.

Making a snap decision to go and see Tom after work, Jessie wished away the butterflies which were playing havoc with her stomach. She felt nervous about seeing him again, as if she was doing something wrong. Sally's question as to whether Max would be jealous had touched a chord and worried her, so to avoid unnecessary upset she decided she wouldn't tell Max about the visit. What the head doesn't know the heart can't grieve over.

At the hospital, by Tom's bedside, in the long, clinical, hospital ward, Jessie searched for the right words and felt a complete fool. Seeing him lying there, bruised but as handsome as ever, she also felt shy. 'I'm sorry I haven't brought anything. The shops were closed by the time I left work and—'

'That's all right, Jessie,' he said, pulling himself up into a sitting position and wincing in pain. 'Mother sees that my cupboards are full – look at that fruit bowl. She fusses around as if I'm a six-year-old.'

'Are you an only child then?'

He raised an eyebrow. 'Hardly. So, Jessie Warner, you've pardoned me then, at last.'

'Pardoned you? I'm still waiting for an apology! Standing me up was one thing, but sending some poor sod to do your dirty work ... And as for your messages, sprained ankle? Hurt your back? You sure it wasn't a sprained wrist?' Jessie sat down by the bed.

'Good,' said Tom, straightening his pillow, 'that's that out of the way. You gonna ask how I am then?'

'I can see how you are. They'll be turning you out in a couple of days.'

'I wish. It's the nurses. They're doing their best to keep me here for as long as they can. They love me.'

'I bet they do.'

'Anyway, never mind me, how's your mum?'

'Not too bad. Oh, and thanks for the flowers – and the card. I appreciated that. Does it hurt?'

'Course it hurts ...' he placed a hand on hers, 'knowing you'll walk out of here soon and I won't see you again.'

She withdrew her hand. 'Why did you do that to me, Tom? Being stood up in front of Sally was really embarrassing.'

'I had my reasons. Anyway, I sent a good-looking bloke, someone who'd treat you like a lady. He was all right, wasn't he? Treated you with respect?'

'Tch. Respect. It was meant to be a date not an appointment. Anyhow, that's all behind us now. I must be mad coming in to see you but there you are. I'll probably kick myself for it.'

'No you won't. And I'm glad you came, I've not stopped thinking about that night when I could have been with you at the Odeon, sitting in the back seat. I'm sorry for what happened but I had no choice – I *thought* I had no choice.' Glancing past Jessie, his expression turned serious. Hannah was approaching.

Jessie followed his gaze. 'Ah ... I'd best be going, mustn't play gooseberry twice. Besides, I'm meeting my chap.'

'Oh, right, yeah, mustn't keep *him* waiting. Mind how you go, Jessie.'

'You as well, Tom.' She smiled at him.

'Tom, you look so much better,' exclaimed Hannah. 'I can't believe it. Your cheeks are *glowing* with health. Doesn't he look fine, Jessie?'

'He's all right. You can have him all to yourself now.' Jessie stood up as if to leave.

'I don't want him all to myself, thanks very much,' she smiled, 'so you needn't go on my account.' She looked at Jessie and showed sympathy. 'I was sorry to hear about your father. Very sorry. I wanted to come and see you but I don't know where you live.'

'Thanks.' Jessie was grateful for the simple, natural and sincere sympathy Hannah offered. 'It was a shock and none of us are over it yet. It's gonna take a very long time to get back to normal. It did cross my mind to call on you, as it happens, but I don't think I went outside our house all of last week, except to run down to the shop.'

'Well, you know where I live and you may knock on the door whenever you want. If my mother should answer, take no notice of her manner, she's not the friendliest of people.' Hannah looked from Jessie to Tom. 'He hasn't stopped mooning over you, you know.' She grinned and gave him a peck on the cheek. 'I said you would see her again.'

'Jessie's trying to leave, Hannah.' Tom was uneasy at the way the girls were getting on, they were a little too close for comfort. 'She's late for her date. I don't want her boyfriend coming in and breaking my other arm.'

'Pay him no attention, Jessie. You take the chair and I'll sit on the edge of his bed. Matron has just gone off duty and—'

'Hannah, she's got to go.' Tom sank his head into his pillow. 'I'm in a hospital bed, not a deck chair on the beach, enjoying the sun and air. I'm supposed to be resting. One of you go, for Christ's sake. Two of you at once is one too many.'

'You make us sound like a matching pair.' Jessie turned to Hannah. 'He doesn't exactly give out gentle hints, does he? I hope the nurses do what you want them to, Tom. 'Bye, Hannah.' Head down, she walked slowly away without turning back.

'Jessie!' Tom called after her. 'Thanks for coming! I'll return the visit once I'm out of here.' His shout was met with shushing from other visitors and hospital staff.

Jessie had to admit that she'd wanted to see him again, if only to find out why he had stood her up, though she was still none the wiser. This had been the third time she'd seen him and each time she had been left with a desire to see him again. Stupid cow, she thought. Stupid blind fool! Lost in her thoughts, she collided with a visitor.

'I'm so sorry,' she apologised. She began to perspire, inwardly blaming the heating system, it was very hot in the hospital. 'It was my fault and I'm really sorry.' She helped the woman pick up the bag of oranges which had scattered. 'I should have been looking—'

'That's all right, love, no harm done. But you should slow down a bit ... Jessie Warner. You'll get to wherever you're going a lot quicker if you do. What's my Tom done to upset you then?'

Jessie stared at her. She looked vaguely familiar but she couldn't place her.

'Don't recognise me, do you?' smiled Emmie. 'We met outside Stepney Green station. I'm Tom's mother.' She squeezed Jessie's arm. 'My condolences over the terrible tragedy. I was very, very sorry to read about it.'

'Thank you,' said Jessie, backing away. 'I came in to see Tom because I was there when it happened, at the People's Palace. I met up with him and Hannah and ... well ... I just wanted to come and see how he was.' Blushing, Jessie hurried away, anxious to be outside in the cool, fresh air and away from all of them.

'Poor kid,' said Emmie, pulling up a chair next to Tom's bed, 'losing her dad at such a fragile age. It doesn't bear thinking about.'

'It was good of her to come and see me,' said Tom, wishing Jessie hadn't left. 'I never expected that. I'll drop her a line while I'm in here,' he said, rubbing his chin. 'It'll kill a bit of time.'

Emmie checked the fruit in his bowl. 'I wonder how she knew you was in hospital.'

'Sally told her.'

'Oh, right. I thought perhaps you'd written her a letter or something.'

Ignoring that, he turned to Hannah. 'She never believes a word I say, I may as well talk to the brick wall.'

'She's a friendly girl, isn't she?' said Hannah to Emmie. 'I met her that evening when Tom was beaten up. We got on really well. She came back with me for a cup of tea. I feel as if I've known her all my life.'

There was a moment's silence as Emmie and Tom exchanged worried glances.

'Move your chair, Hannah,' said Emmie, inching hers closer to his bed. 'My bloody feet are killing me. I'm going to ease off my shoes.'

Tom rolled his eyes. 'Don't mind me. Make yourself at home. I can handle pain without the need for a bit of sympathy.'

'Go on,' said Emmie, enjoying herself. 'I would never 'ave guessed it.' She pushed her face close to his and examined his eye. 'That's coming along nicely. Have you opened your bowels today?'

'Bloody hell,' he moaned. 'If you ever embarrass me while Jessie's here . . .'

'Oh, she's coming again then?'

'I never said that, what I meant was, don't embarrass me in front of . . . strangers.'

'Oh dear. So she's a stranger now?'

'I don't think so, Emmie,' said Hannah, enjoying the banter between mother and son. 'You should have seen the way he brightened up when Jessie was here. You know what I think? That she was a little jealous of my coming during her cosy visit. She's as mad about him as he is about her. This time I think Tom was right about fate playing a hand.'

Emmie ignored that. She could act her way through this hospital visit but deep down she was very worried. The twins had met up sooner than she imagined. She wanted Hannah to go so she could find out from Tom what exactly was going on.

'Look at him,' chuckled Hannah. 'Doesn't he look like the dog who just let the bone go?'

'Listen, Hannah. I am in a bit of pain as it happens, my arm's throbbing and I'm tired—'

'She'll be back, Tom, stop sulking. Anyhow, I only came in to give you my good news. I'm looking for a flat,' she said, looking very pleased with herself.

'Good for you,' said Emmie. 'It's just about the right time for you make a move, but don't go rushing into anything. Let me have a look before you take one on, you don't want to make a mistake and have to go running back home to your mother, not once you've flown the nest.'

'Of course I'll want you and Tom to see it first. I'm going to take my time. I want two spacious rooms with plenty of light and it must be sunny and with a view. A beautiful view of a garden or a lake.'

'Around this way? You'll be lucky,' laughed Tom.

'Maybe not around this way, Tom. Maybe in Essex, Walthamstow. The chief librarian was telling me that his daughter found a small self-contained flat there which is very reasonable and has its own tiny garden. He thinks there's another one up for rent which is just a fifteen-minute walk from the railway station.'

Emmie couldn't remember seeing Hannah looking so radiant, she really was beginning to bloom at last. 'I can't say I know too much about the place, love, but one of our cleaners at work has a daughter who's marrying someone from

Walthamstow, as it happens. I'll get a bit more information from her if you like.'

'You see. Twice in one week — fate?'

'Can't see you living in the country, Hannah,' said Tom.

'Walthamstow's hardly the country, son,' Emmie answered for her, 'but it's out of the East End. Just don't bite off more than you can chew, Hannah, and take things one step at a time.'

'Don't worry, I will.' She leaned forward and kissed Tom on the cheek. 'Get Sally to write down Jessie's address for me. I would like to call on her. I think she wants to be friends as much as I do.'

Once she'd gone, Tom and Emmie looked at each other and cleared their throats. 'See what I mean, Mother? The pair of them met by accident and got on like a house on fire. Who's gonna be the one to break the news?'

'Well, I can't break a promise. I don't really see what I can do about it. I haven't got an idea in my head over this one.'

'Hannah hasn't stopped talking about her since they met,' he said.

'That's no surprise. You can't even count Hannah's friends on two fingers. She's bound to latch on to someone like Jessie, even if they wasn't twins.'

'My thoughts entirely, Mother,' he said, throwing her an accusing look.

On her way home, Emmie found herself thinking about the unhappy time, way back, when Jessie and Hannah were parted. Full of self-reproach, she wished things had been different. On reflection, she felt she might have done more at the time to help Rose and Robert to keep both babies. But she was younger then, she hadn't learned to deal with life the way she did later. She had gained power to the elbow with time and would speak out when right was right and wrong was wrong. No more than a couple of years back, she could have taken the reins and laid down the law, telling Rose what she must do and seeing that she did it. Not any more, though. She was feeling her age.

The thirty-minute walk home from the hospital tired her. The house was very quiet when she let herself in. She hung up her coat and hat and went into the kitchen. On the old pine table the flour was ready, the peeled and sliced apples marinating in brown sugar and cloves. Catching sight of her reflection in the small mirror above the butler sink she peered more closely at her face. She hadn't always looked like everyone's mother. She'd once had an hourglass figure and took pride in her looks, her good looks. She'd had the best head of hair in her time, thick, long, curly red hair. Her hazel eyes had been bright and clear. Now they were dull, with deep lines spreading outwards. In days gone by, she would have taken the time to put on make-up, brush and style her hair; she was fifty-six years old and she could have been taken for seventy. She pulled the lapel of her blouse forward and smelt her body. Instead of Lily of the Valley talcum powder, there was a tinge of perspiration mixed with the scent of Lifebuoy soap.

'What *have* you done, Em? Where's that lovely slim woman you once were?' She lowered herself into her chair, knowing exactly what she'd done; she'd given up what she once was in order to be the best mother and the wife of all wives. She'd been doing that for so long that she hadn't noticed the change or when it had come about. 'Emmie,' she murmured, 'Emmie, where are you?' She swept the back of her hand across her face and brushed away her tears.

The light of the moon shining through the kitchen window warmed her. It was as if a familiar old friend had come out to comfort her, a familiar and reliable friend who returned as regularly as clockwork, season after season.

Without thinking she reached out and took an apple from the fruit bowl, a lovely crisp, green and red apple with a nice smell. She bit into it and the juice ran down the corner of her mouth. When she was a nipper the only time she ate an apple was when she'd pinched one off the back of a market stall, way back when she wore no socks in the summer and second-hand boots in the winter. Through all of those hard times she couldn't remember being miserable. She'd come from a big happy family who made the most of everything. Emmie wondered right then if she would ever get back that 'couldn't care less' feeling.

The house seemed so quiet. Johnnie and Stanley were out and her husband, Charlie, had gone to bed. But Emmie enjoyed the time by herself. In the silence she could hear the call of an owl in the distance and thinking of nothing in particular she began to hum the tune of a song she used to sing along to at the local music hall, when she was no more than fifteen or sixteen. Before she realised it, she was quietly singing:

All the girls in our town ... they lead a happy life,
Except for just the serious one, who wants to be a wife.
A wife she shall be ...
According to who she goes with;
Along with a certain naval boy,
Who gave her a little bundle of joy;
A wife she shall be ...

As memories of those heady days came flooding back, she thought about her satin pouch containing her lipstick and powder, tucked away in one of her cupboards. Maybe she would bring it out of the dark, maybe she would put on her favourite rose-red hat and navy coat, maybe she would go down the local and join her sons for a drink. She was beginning to feel a little more like she had in the old days, when she would sit with the women in their corner of the local and start them off in song.

One hour later, Emmie was on the sofa with her feet up. She had remembered that she'd promised to take Tom a piece of that apple pie in the morning, on her way to work, and Johnnie and Stanley would be looking forward to a piece as well, after their bread and cheese supper. A couple of beers always gave them an appetite. She drank in the lovely smell of baking pies coming from the kitchen, sank her head into a feather cushion and closed her eyes for ten minutes. Her friend Rose would be all right. She'd get used to being a widow . . . in time. They would all get used to the idea that there would now only be a space where Robert used to be. Robert Warner, a kind and gentle man as well as a good husband and father. Emmie could hear her Charlie snoring from above and for once in her life she welcomed the sound.

Chapter Six

During the months that followed, the Warner family pulled together and did their best to get on with their lives. Dolly's strange reaction to her father's sudden death continued for a couple of weeks – she went out every night, dressed to kill. Fifteen- and sixteen-year-old lads were continually knocking on the door until she herself began to tire of it. Wisely, Rose said nothing to her daughter and waited for it all to fade away.

Christmas came and went with as little fuss as necessary. Rose just wanted to get it over with. On New Year's Eve, she flatly refused to share it with anyone except her children. She didn't want to have to see out that year with people trying to cheer her up and neither did she want to reminisce. When she woke on New Year's Day, she saw that it had snowed heavily in the night and would have been happy if it had gone on snowing until it reached halfway up their front door, blocking out the world.

In February there was more upheaval in the house as at last the electricity was put in. When the workmen had gone, all of them took delight in running around the house playing with the switches, thrilled by the instant and much brighter lights. For Rose's birthday in early March, Jessie and Dolly clubbed together and bought her a small bedside lamp from the Co-op, and as a really special treat, Jessie coerced Dolly into agreeing to paying off weekly for a small one-bar electric fire for Rose's bedroom.

The case of negligence over Robert's death dragged on, but the family solicitor was hopeful that the claim for compensation would soon result in a substantial sum being paid to Rose and the children.

Slowly Rose tried to pick up the broken pieces of her life and get back into her old routine of running the cobbler shop as well as the household. But her heart wasn't in it and she became quiet and subdued. Jessie found it difficult sometimes not to be sharp with her, but Max was a tower of strength, giving her advice, calming her when she was angry, lighting her up when she was down. He reckoned that by the following month, July, he would have paid for the engagement ring in full and it would be in its proper place, on the third finger of Jessie's left hand.

Alfie still had the occasional secret smoke and continued to slip out through his bedroom window when he was supposed to be turning in, but there had been no more sign of the knife under his bed. Stephen was still withdrawn but both Rose and Jessie agreed that he was gradually getting back to his old self. He still clung to Rose, and Jessie often discovered them enjoying a cuddle in the big armchair in the sitting room. Whether it was right for Stephen or not, Jessie wasn't sure, but to see them getting so much comfort from each other warmed her heart.

There had been a change in tenants and now, living at the top of the house, was a young Scottish couple, newly married. They, like the tenants before them, kept themselves to themselves and were always polite and friendly when they paid their rent. Since the tragedy, Dolly had had several jobs. She hadn't returned to the gentlemen's club where she'd been a waitress, even though they'd given her a week's leave with pay after Robert's accident. From the gentlemen's club she'd gone to a handbag factory in Leman Street and then on to waitressing in coffee houses and tea rooms; back to the handbag factory, on to a shoe factory and then finally to a toy factory in the Roman Road, Bow, where she had just met with a minor accident. A spring on one of the clockwork toys she had been assembling had skittered out and caught her eye. Walking around the house like an invalid, with the injured eye bandaged, she looked a sorry sight. Only Alfie had been brave enough to poke fun at her, which had been met by a thump on the shoulder. She was now on her bed nursing her eyes and sulking.

In the kitchen, impatient for the iron to heat, Jessie turned the gas flame higher; she was about to press her favourite dress to wear that evening. Leaning on the kitchen wall, she thought how easier things would be once the compensation came through. Her mother would be able to go shopping for modern electrical appliances, and an iron was at the top of the list.

Jessie wrapped a linen pad round the handle and lifted the iron off the gas flame, licked her finger and checked the heat and then pressed away the creases from the green, red and black patterned skirt of her frock. Max was taking her to the steak and chip restaurant at London Bridge.

'Watch your brothers out there for me, would you, Jess?' said Rose from the doorway. 'They're messing around with the hose pipe. I don't mind them playing with it so long as they've got their bathing trunks on but I don't want them annoying the neighbours again. They squirted water over Mr Brody's son, Rodney, yesterday and he wasn't amused. He'd been working so hard out there in the yard, mucking out that filthy chicken run. That lad's a saint – he loves those chickens.'

'I know. Stephen told me.' Jessie tried not to smile. Little did Rose know that she and Rodney chatted over the garden fence from time to time and she knew that he hated the birds and the run; more than anything he hated the smell. He did it for the weekly payment of a shilling and nothing else.

'I'm going to the Broadway to do a bit of shopping,' Rose went on, a little preoccupied. 'Get Dolly to peel the vegetables for me. Bad eye or not, she should be able to manage that.'

'I'd rather she stayed where she is, to tell the truth,' said

Jessie. 'Her face is as long as a kite and she's in a rotten mood. Max is coming round so he can peel the spuds.'

'I shouldn't think so. Men don't like to do kitchen chores.'

'Max is different, the men in his family muck in. I suppose that's got something to do with them being Jewish – I don't know. They're different from us.'

'I'm not saying it's a bad thing, Jess. All I'm saying is that you don't want to give him the wrong impression, that you won't make a good housewife. That's all I was thinking.' She picked up her handbag and left.

The fact that Rose hadn't taken her shopping bag or her basket didn't surprise Jessie. Her mother had been surreptitious of late and she had a feeling it had something to do with the strange woman at the cemetery. Whenever she broached the subject, Rose dismissed it, but this morning she seemed particularly worried and agitated. She hadn't even mentioned popping into the cobbler shop to check on how the Saturday help was coping. Saturday was now Rose's day off as well as Sunday; since Robert's death she had wanted to be at home when her boys were there.

Once Rose had left the house, Jessie tapped on the yard window to draw her brothers' attention and beckoned them in. Knowing Rose would be out nearly all afternoon and Dolly would more than likely sleep through most of the day, she wanted to spend some time with Max in the house without there always being one or the other of them coming or going. Alfie came to the kitchen to see what Jessie wanted. He stood in the doorway, tall and skinny, dripping water.

'How would you and Stephen like to go to the pictures this afternoon? They're showing a Mickey Mouse film at the Foresters. *Steamboat Willie*. Plus a cowboy film.'

'What, you gonna treat us?'

'Yeah, I'll treat you, Alfie. I would treat you more if I thought you was a good boy.'

'I'm not a boy, Jessie. I'll be going to work next year.'

'I know, but that doesn't make you a man either. You know that Dad knew about your smoking, don't you? He promised Mum that you were only experimenting and it would soon stop.'

'I only 'ave one now and then!'

'Yes, but one thing can lead to another and another and—'

'So you want us to go out,' said Alfie, stopping her flow, 'so you and Max can do it in the living room.'

'Do what in the living room?' Jessie couldn't believe that he meant what he was saying.

'A do. You know, up against the wall.'

'Alfie! That's disgusting! Me and Max wouldn't dream of such a thing!'

'Oh,' he said, disappointed. 'Dolly said you did it all the time.'

'Did she now? Well, Dolly doesn't know what she's talking about, and neither do you. If you realised what you'd just said—'

'I know what it means! I'm not a kid any more, Jess.'

'Oh, silly me! I forgot. You're a young man soon to be leaving school. Maybe you'd rather not go to the pictures with your *kid* brother.'

'I don't mind looking after him,' he said, sniffing.

'Nope, you're right. You are too old for all of that.'

'I *said*, I don't mind!'

'Well, if you're *really* sure, Alfie. Oh, and Mum left a bob on the table for fish and chips for the pair of you.'

'Blimey. Two treats in one day.' Alfie grinned.

'You know it wouldn't hurt you to offer to help in the shop on Saturdays. Mum works there all week and she only takes Saturday off so she can catch up here and go shopping. She has to pay someone to cover for her and Saturday's one of the busiest days.'

'Would she pay me?'

'Tch. I expect she'll let you earn some pocket money. Go on. Get out of my sight and tell Stephen to dry himself properly. Oh, and Alfie,' Jessie called as Alfie scampered off.

'What now? I can't do everything, you know.'

'A neighbour had a word with me the other day. I'm not saying who it was, because I promised I wouldn't. You've been seen chalking Fascist slogans on walls and you know that's wrong. Wrong *and* dangerous. If Mum gets to hear, you'll cop it, not to mention what Max'll think of you if he finds out. He'd be really hurt.'

Avoiding her probing look, Alfie turned away. 'I wasn't gonna do it no more anyway,' he muttered. 'I forgot that Max is Jewish.'

'And what about Max's mum and dad? Mr and Mrs Cohen? How would you like them to find out that you're one of the bully boys? They've had a brick through their window, don't forget.'

'I didn't *know* they were Jewish! I only did it for the tanner. I couldn't care less about anything else.'

'Good. Now come here and give me a cuddle. You're not too old for a hug – and neither am I.'

'I'm not cuddling you!' There was a telltale crack in his voice and he was pressing his lips tightly together.

'You're not gonna cry, are you? It's all right, Max doesn't know about the chalking, if that's what you're upset about. Alfie?'

'I miss my dad,' he said, screwing up his face, desperate to hold back tears. 'I want to see him again, Jessie, just one more time, that's all, so I can say things to 'im.'

Her own eyes filled and Jessie pulled him close and stroked his back. 'You *can* see him, whenever you want, Alfie. You can look at his photograph or just keep on remembering the good times together. It will help, Alfie. I do it all the time. I tell you what, in a couple of days' time, you and me are going to have a little talk. I've got something very special to tell you. Something which'll change all of our lives for the better. Especially Mum's.'

'Tell me now, Jess, tell me now,' he said, his head burrowed into her neck. 'Is it to do with Dad?'

'No, sweetheart, it's not. But you'll like it, I know you will.' Jessie led him to a chair, sat him down and held his hands. 'It's a long, complicated story and I'm not going into it all right now, but I will tell you this and you must promise not to go on at me until I've the time to explain it properly. Granny Blake isn't our real grandmother.'

Wiping his face with the back of his hand, he sniffed again. 'I've never liked the old cow anyway.'

'She's all right really. It's just that we're not blood relatives so she couldn't take to Mum nor us the way she might have. Anyway, we may have lost our dad, Alfie, but we're going to gain a grandmother and Mum will have her own mum back again, after nearly a lifetime of being without her. Last year, just before Dad was killed, the very day before, I found our real gran. Mum doesn't know and she might be cross with me for going behind her back, so you mustn't say anything. Promise you won't.'

He nodded and wiped away the last tear with his sleeve. 'What's she like? Where does she live? Why hasn't she come to see us?'

'I knew you'd do this to me. Just accept that better times are to come and leave it at that. Promise me you won't mention it again until I bring it up. Promise.'

'So long as you don't leave it for months and months.'

'Oh, I won't do that. I'll pluck up the courage soon and tell her.'

'I'll keep the secret then. I won't even say anything to Stephen – or Dolly.'

It was the wrong time to tell him that she had already told Stephen. 'Good.' He was out of the chair in a flash and away, happier than Jessie had seen him in a while. That little talk had done her the world of good too. It seemed to her that Ingrid Gunter, a real grandmother, would be a way of helping to heal the painful wound the family had suffered when they lost her father.

When she had the house to herself, apart from Dolly hiding away upstairs, Jessie washed and brushed her hair, put on some make-up and the freshly ironed frock and waited for Max. She didn't have to wait long. Unfortunately, though, he wasn't in the same frame of mind as she was. He'd arrived once again in one of his heavy moods. She thought she'd win him round with a kiss and a cuddle, but she was wrong. She had got him in the parlour, on the sofa, but she hadn't got him going — hot sunny day or not.

'It's true,' Max said, preoccupied, 'the BUF did weaken but—'

'The what? What are you talking about, Max?'

'The BUF.' He looked surprised, as if he was seeing her for the first time. 'You don't know what BUF stands for?'

'No. I can guess though. Blackshirts — United — Fascists?' She was making it clear that she couldn't really care less what it stood for.

'British Union of Fascists,' he said, shaking his head despairingly.

'I'm sick of trying to work them all out. What, for instance, does CPGB stand for?'

'Communist Party of Great Britain.'

'ILP?'

'Independent Labour Party, now replaced by the Socialist League.'

Jessie racked her brain but couldn't think of any more.

Max reeled them off for her. 'NUWM — National Unemployed Workers Movement. UAB — Unemployment Assistance Board. PLP — Parliamentary Labour Party. TUC — Trade Union—'

'ILU?' she said, interrupting his flow.

'There isn't one.'

'Yes there is.'

'No there isn't.'

'Think about it, Max. I L U?'

He shrugged, splayed his hands. 'Sorry, Jess, but there isn't.'

'I Love You.'

'Oh, and I thought for the minute you were really interested in what I was saying. Anyway, my party is easy for you to remember – I'm a Socialist. Coming back to you, is it?'

'Ah, but are you so sure about that, Max?'

'Of course I'm sure about it. I've always voted Labour. My family vote Labour. My grandparents—'

'Dad was worried that you might have become a Communist.'

'That's crazy, Jessie. Your dad was pulling your leg.'

'No he wasn't. It's what he'd heard down the docks. That your lot were joining with the Communists against Mosley and his Blackshirts. In fact he wanted us to stop walking out together for a while, until things calmed down.'

'Exactly. Which is why the Fascists put that about. The docks have always been a good grapevine, your dad should have known better than to be taken in by propaganda.' His expression as he looked at Jessie changed. 'I'm sorry. I didn't mean that.' He pushed his hands through his hair. 'It's getting to everyone. My sister said something similar, as it happens. She thought that we should ease off seeing each other for a while. Of course I said we—'

'Which sister?' Jessie asked.

'Moira.'

'I thought as much, she doesn't like me. She's never been keen on us going out together. She wants you to marry a nice Jewish girl. Nathan looked down on me and now she does as well. First of all she was just a bit unfriendly, now she's cold. Deliberately cold.'

'No she isn't, Jessie, you're overreacting. Moira and Nathan are not like that. My sister, like Nathan, just doesn't happen to believe in mixed religion marriages, that's all. If you were just a friend, she'd be different. Besides, what can you expect? She's bound to be concerned given all the anti-Jewish slogans that keep appearing.'

'That isn't my fault, Max.' All this talk about Moira and Nathan not believing in mixed marriages was news to Jessie. She hadn't actually thought much about Max's sister or her husband and she hardly saw the couple; when she did, Moira's snobbery drove her mad. 'What will she say when we get engaged, I wonder.'

'She's already said it. She thinks it's a mistake. She's been giving me lectures ever since I mentioned it.' Max's expression was wry.

'Oh, so you've told her our secret, that's nice. I've not even mentioned it to Mum, but Moira has to be told, mustn't leave Moira out of it.' Jessie knew she was sounding childish but she couldn't help it.

'I was just paving the way. I thought that by letting her in on it first, she might see things differently, but she didn't. She was shocked, in fact.'

'Moira was shocked? Tch. Oh dear.' Jessie was getting more and more upset, and she was infuriated that Max seemed oblivious of how he was making her feel. 'Well, maybe we should call the whole thing off then.'

'Don't be silly. I think the two of you should sit down and talk about it. She's got nothing against you personally, Jessie, she likes you. She likes you a lot, but . . .'

'But what, Max? What are you trying to say?'

'I'm not *trying* to say anything, I couldn't care less one way or the other, but she and my mother think—'

'Oh, *right*, so there's been a family discussion.'

'Let me finish. She and my mother wondered if you might like to think about converting. They would be willing to help with your Bible studies and—'

'Stop it, Max. You know full well that we're Church of

England. If Mum heard you saying such a thing she'd be offended and hurt.' Jessie went quiet and waited to hear his reaction but there wasn't one. Not one word.

'All right,' she said finally, 'I'll sit down with your mum and your sister and we'll talk about it. They can talk Judaism to me and I'll listen, but they've got to do the same and listen to *hear* what I have to say about Christianity.'

'Would you do that?'

'I've just said I would.'

He slipped off his chair and down onto his knees, laying his head in her lap. 'I love you so much, Jessie. I've been worried because I knew there would be a problem and I was frightened.' He eased her down onto the floor, onto the rag mat in front of the fireplace. 'I don't want religion to come between us, Jess.' He looked up at her with those doleful brown eyes. 'It won't, will it?'

'I hope not, Max. To be honest, I've not really thought about it. I've not considered what *my* family and friends might think about my marrying a Jew — it's not exactly an everyday occurrence, is it?' She kissed his puzzled expression away and then kissed him as she'd never kissed before. It was different this time because she was angry and her anger caused her to feel more passionate.

'I take it,' said Max, his voice husky, 'that your mother's not likely to come back and—'

'Catch you with your trousers down?' Jessie laughed quietly. 'Wouldn't that be something?'

Rose tapped lightly on Emmie's front door, hoping that her friend would be alone. If Hannah was there, she would turn round and go back home before her daughter saw her.

Emmie opened the door. 'Gracious me,' she said in surprise, 'you're the last one I thought it would be, Rose. What a turn-up for the books,' she smiled, '*you* slumming in Bethnal Green.'

'Don't be ridiculous, Emmie. Slumming indeed. Am I to stand on your doorstep then?'

Laughing, Emmie waved her in. 'I was only joking. It's lovely to see you at my door, I must say. Come in and take the weight off your feet.'

Rose followed Emmie through into the kitchen. 'You keep the place as nice as ever, Em. What lovely bright walls — very cheerful.'

'Your timing could have been disastrous, Rose,' she said, placing the kettle on the gas stove. 'It can't have been less than fifteen minutes since Hannah was here. Lucky for us, it was one of her flying visits. She's gone to view some lodgings — a one-bedroom flat.'

'It did cross my mind once I was at your front door but—'

'Well, there's no spilt milk to cry over, is there? She's gone. To be honest I don't really think she's that serious about moving away, it's enough for her to have the vision of one day escaping from Gerta. She's viewing places out of her reach and then reports back how lovely or how unsuitable they are. She's having a smashing time of it. God love her.' Emmie slipped one of her headache pills into her mouth and washed it down with a glass of water. 'You're lucky to have caught me in, Rose. I'm usually at Wickham's of a Saturday and if it hadn't been for my migraine attack earlier on, I wouldn't be here now.'

'I should have realised that as well,' murmured Rose.

Leaving the kettle to come to the boil, Emmie and Rose went into the front room where a small coal fire burned in the polished brass grate. 'You look as if you could do with a break yourself, Rose, you've lost a bit of weight. A holiday by the sea would do you the world of good.'

'I've too many things on my mind to think about that yet, Emmie, which is one of the reasons I'm here. It's to do with Gerta. She turned up at the funeral.' The sound of the whistling kettle filled the house.

Ignoring the high-pitched noise, Emmie's eyes narrowed as she stared disbelievingly at her friend. 'Gerta? At the funeral? No. You must 'ave been mistaken, Rose, surely.'

Rose waved a hand towards the kitchen. 'See to the kettle, Emmie.'

'Gracious me, I hope she didn't go to your house as well.'

'No. She was at the cemetery, hiding in the shadows, under a tree, waiting to get my attention. Emmie, please. That whistling is going right through my head.'

Emmie went into the kitchen, set the tray and returned to the sitting room, forgetting to put any biscuits out. 'The tea needs to brew for a couple of minutes,' she said, sitting opposite her friend. 'I can't for the life of me think why she would have turned up, Rose. Surely you're not going to tell me it was from compassion.'

'No. Greed. She wants a share of any compensation that's paid to me and the children, and she wants power of attorney over Hannah's finances. She has no understanding of the way these things work. I confided in my solicitor that there was another child to be considered and that's slowed things down even more. I don't think she believes me. It's why I came to see you, Emmie. I need someone to talk to. I'm at my wits' end in case Gerta shows up at my door.'

'Well, I never did,' said Emmie, shocked.

'I haven't seen her for nigh on sixteen years and, my goodness me, how she's changed.' Rose shook her head. 'She seemed such a decent woman all those years back. Quiet and reserved. She accused me of neglect, implying that once my brother had deserted her and gone back to New Zealand, we should have sent money to support Hannah. I know full well that Jack was sending her an allowance and still is. We may not write to each other much but we do keep in touch.'

'Well, it doesn't surprise me. The woman's a cold, conniving bitch. So what will you do about this? I know what I'd like to do.'

'I agreed to sort something out for the sake of Hannah but I feel as if I'm being blackmailed and I don't like it. It's a horrible feeling, and I can't shift it from the pit of my stomach.'

'You must be careful, Rose. You'll be making a rod for your back. That woman will always have something over you. I think you know what my advice would be.'

'I *can't* tell Jessie. How can I after all this time? I had to go outside, into the back yard, when Gerta chose which of my twin girls she would take. It nearly killed me. I don't want all of that dragged up again.' Rose shuddered. 'Goodness knows what it would do to the girls, never mind my other children.'

'It is blackmail,' said Emmie, pouring out the tea, 'and that's a criminal offence. I hope you told her so.'

'I don't know what I said in the end, to be honest. All I wanted was to get away from her. I do believe there is a streak of evil in the woman. She's within her rights to ask for compensation for Hannah, she is Robert's child and I know it's what he would want, but how do I go about it without Hannah knowing where the money's come from?'

'We can get round that, Rose. Gerta won't go to the authorities – she wouldn't have a leg to stand on. Your brother's been sending an allowance for her and officially Hannah was adopted, so I can't see—'

'That's just it,' Rose cut in. 'She wasn't legally adopted. We just put her into their care. Don't forget, it was fif-teen years ago. There were fewer regulations then. If Gerta's not satisfied, she could really go to town and likely get more than she deserves in any case. All she has to do is say that we dumped a baby on her doorstep and she took pity on it.'

'No, Rose, you're worrying too much. I'm sure if we sit here long enough and look at all the options we'll find a way through this.' Emmie felt sure there must be a way.

'I feel very uncomfortable with her having the upper hand like this. She can do what she likes, whenever she likes. She's very bitter about my brother leaving her and blames us, blames all of his family, for messing up her life.'

'Poppycock. She messed up Hannah's life, more like. She's got no feelings for that poor girl, Rose. None. I'm sorry if you don't want to hear it, but it's the truth.'

Rose let out a deep sigh. 'I've let Hannah down badly, haven't I?'

'Never mind that now. We have to think of the present and what's for the best.'

Sipping their tea, neither said a word for a while. There was nothing uncomfortable about it, no embarrassment, they were just two friends mulling over a shared problem.

Glancing out of the window, Rose saw that there was some pink and white blossom on the trees in Emmie's back garden. 'Sometimes I can see a light at the end of the tunnel, Emmie. Sometimes,' whispered Rose, distracted.

'Of course you can, now that the winter and those harsh March winds are behind us. We all need the sunshine. You'll pick up and have the strength of two to deal with that woman, I'm sure of it.'

'I hope so. I don't seem to have the heart to go into the shop and deal with the business any more. I've lost interest in cooking and I've still got Robert's clothes to sort out. They're hanging in his wardrobe and sitting on his shelves, as if he was still there.'

'Well, I can't help you with the shop, Rose, but I can see that Robert's clothes go to a very good cause. I've done it before, more than once. My neighbours rely on me for that sort of thing, and you can imagine what it's like down at the old people's home. Always someone popping off. Why don't I sort it all out for you on Monday? You go into the shop as usual while I'm at your house packing things away. It's got to be done and it's best that you're not there. It won't take me more than a few hours.' Emmie poured them some more tea. 'To tell you the truth, Rose, I'm very pleased that you came to me for advice.'

'I wish I'd come sooner,' was her tired reply.

'Never mind. What we've got to do now is get you back on the road again, because if Robert can see you, from wherever he is, that's what he'd want to see – you on your feet again, getting stronger by the day. Then we'll get you out there socialising again as well. I wouldn't mind getting out of the house myself, now and then. Wouldn't it be lovely if we were to join Sister Esther's sewing circle at Bromley-by-Bow. We always said we would one day, didn't we? You remember, way back, when the war was on?'

'Dear Emmie,' said Rose, drying her eyes, 'you do have a way of bringing back the good memories. We did have our dreams, didn't we?'

'We did that, and who knows where it might lead us? That space above your cobbler shop would make lovely needlework rooms. The light coming in through those big windows would be a joy to work by. I wouldn't mind betting those rooms are full of junk which should have been thrown out years ago.'

Quietly laughing, Rose agreed. 'They always said that you had second sight. How you could know what those rooms look like I've no idea.'

'Just imagine it, Rose,' said Emmie, carried away, 'a dozen of us women up there using the finest of fabrics to make up lovely evening gowns and day frocks.'

Rose smiled at the thought of it. Her friend was dreaming but, yes, Rose had to admit to herself that it was a lovely vision and Emmie was right, the rooms should be put to a good use and so should her wayward daughter, Dolly. The one thing she'd been very good at when she was at school was needlework. Yes, Dolly could sew a fine seam and had made quite a few of her own clothes, without a pattern. It was food for thought.

'So,' said Emmie, bringing them both back to reality, 'Gerta. The sooner we get started on her, the better. She's a touch scared of me, if the truth be known. I'll challenge her to go public about Hannah and Jessie and I'll defy her to try and squeeze a penny more out of you than your other children will have. We'll keep it all nice and fair and then a bit later on, once the finances have been dealt with, you and I will have a talk as to what move we make next — with regard to Hannah and Jessie.'

'Not that again, Emmie, please. The girls mustn't meet up.'

Rose was wishing for the impossible. Where Hannah and Jessie were concerned, thought Emmie, there was a hand much stronger than theirs at work. Emmie had a feeling Rose feared losing Jessie's love if she ever discovered what had happened. She toyed with the idea of telling Rose that the girls had already met up but decided that her friend had enough on her plate for the time being; the wretched woman looked as if she had all the troubles of the world on her shoulders. As for Jessie and Tom, their destiny was anyone's guess.

Jessie had enjoyed a long soak in the bath while the house was quiet. Max had gone to a meeting with the promise that he would be back later to take her out for supper at London Bridge, as arranged. Pouring the last remains of water out of the tin bath and into the outside drain, Jessie looked sadly at Robert's vegetable patch. The new season's potatoes he'd planted in early autumn were ready for pulling and the broad bean plants looked in good shape. Strolling to the back wall, she checked the climbing roses. They were already in bud and would hopefully be flowering before the pink japonica and orange burgeris had finished flowering.

Robert had loved his garden and spent several hours out there, working his tiny bit of land, which Rose still referred to as the back yard. Between the small shrubs Jessie saw that the weeds were taking hold.

Against the side of the brick lavatory was the wooden trough which Robert had made and in which he would normally have planted trailing lobelia and a mix of other flowers. This summer they would not have the pleasure of his display. Hooking the tin bath onto its place on the back wall, Jessie heard someone knocking on the front door and her heart sank. She was enjoying her solitude.

With a towel wrapped round her freshly washed hair, she opened the door a little and peered through the gap, astonished to see her grandmother Ingrid Gunter standing on the doorstep.

'May I come inside?' she said matter of factly. Jessie nodded and opened the door properly. 'You seem very shocked to see me. You think me too old to catch a bus or pay you a visit?'

'Mum's not in – no one's here except me and Dolly and she's asleep.' Swallowing, she was caught with an irritating cough.

'Show me where the kitchen is,' said Ingrid. 'You need a glass of water.'

Leading the way, Jessie went downstairs, still coughing. She sipped some cool water. 'It's a bit of a jolt, seeing you here,' she finally managed to say. After all her plans to visit Ingrid, now here she was.

'Well, you could offer me a chair. Maybe a cup of tea?'

'Of course, I'm sorry.' Jessie pulled a chair out from under the pine table. 'I'll put the kettle on, Mum should be back soon.' She felt herself go rigid. 'She doesn't even know that I went to see you.'

'You kept your promise. That makes me very happy. So, we have trust between us. Very important.' Ingrid looked around the kitchen. 'I like it here, there is a something about it that reminds me of the house I shared with your grandfather before he ran off. We had a back-to-back, two up, two down, it was smaller than this house, but yes, it had a similar feel. I was very sorry to have to give it up.'

'Mum could come in any minute,' said Jessie, nervous of what would happen if she did.

'I hope she does. After your visit, I thought about it, thought about what you said. It's time we met. I read about the tragedy and bided my time. Two shocks close together might have been too much for your mother to take. How is she?'

'Sad for most of the time but pushing on. We're all pushing on, not much choice really.'

'No. Sometimes one doesn't have a choice. I hear footsteps on the stairs. Someone is creeping about.'

'That'll be my sister, Dolly. She's been in bed all day with a sore eye.' Jessie glanced anxiously towards the door.

'Ah. And now she is in for a surprise. Why don't you go and speak to her in private? She may react against me if—'

'Why?' Dolly appeared in the doorway. 'Who are you?'

'I'm your grandmother,' said Ingrid smoothly. 'I was keeping myself to myself but your sister came in search of me and turned my world upside down. Why don't you join us? Jessie is going to pour us some tea when she gets round to it.'

'Oh. So you're not dead then?'

'Should I be?'

'You might as well have been.' Dolly pulled off the lid of the biscuit tin. 'We've never seen hide nor hair of you. Where 'ave you been all this time? Why haven't you come round before now? Grandmothers do that, you know. They bring presents at Christmas and birthdays.'

'Don't mind her,' said Jessie, giving her sister a black look. 'She's in a bad mood because she can't go out tonight. Well, she could but she won't, not with that bandage wrapped round her head.'

'I couldn't care less about the *bandage*. I can't wash my hair!'

The sound of the street door opening and slamming shut startled Ingrid. The girls were used to it. The boys had arrived.

'This'll test you, *Grandma*,' said Dolly. 'They'll fire hundreds of questions.'

Ingrid wasn't ruffled by Dolly. 'Then don't tell them who I am. Say I'm an old friend of your grandfather's.'

The boys rushed into the kitchen and raced to the biscuit tin. They seemed happy enough.

'Good film, was it?' asked Jessie.

'Champion. Is there any cake left?'

'There is, Stephen, but you can't have any yet, not until you remember your manners. We have a visitor, in case you hadn't noticed.'

Munching a chocolate biscuit, Alfie peered at Ingrid and gave a quick nod. 'Hello.'

'I'm very well, thank you. And you are?'

'Alfie.'

Ingrid held out her hand. Bemused, Alfie shook it. 'I am Mrs Gunter. A very old friend of the family. How do you do.'

'I'm all right. What country d'yer come from?'

'I was born in Germany but spent most of my life here, in England.'

Alfie regarded her for a moment then said, 'Oh. Come on, Stephen. They're playing Tin Can Tommy. Be back in an hour!'

Grabbing a couple of biscuits, Stephen followed his brother out of the kitchen and bounded up the stairs behind him. Then came the loud slamming of the street door as the boys ran outside.

'Well, that just leaves my daughter to be faced,' said Ingrid. 'I think it might be better if you girls were to go up to your rooms once she arrives. I have some explaining to do after all these years and so does she.'

'Don't you think I should say something first?' said Jessie, worried.

'That is entirely up to you but I wouldn't recommend it. You needn't worry. What I have to say will not make her angry, she may even forgive an old woman for not having more willpower when she was younger and stronger than she is now.'

'Well,' said Dolly bluntly, 'you don't have time to argue the toss. That's her coming in now.'

'Ah.' Ingrid breathed in, straightened, and then pushed her shoulders back.

'This doesn't feel right,' said Dolly uneasily. 'I don't think this is a very good idea. It's making my eye throb.' Ingrid found herself smiling at Dolly.

When Rose walked into the kitchen she was met with silence. She glanced at Ingrid and then at Jessie. 'What's going on?' she said, puzzled.

'Hello, Rose.' Ingrid's voice was quiet but there was no sign of worry on her face. 'I hope you don't mind but I asked the girls if they would be so kind as to leave us alone when you arrived.'

Rose stiffened and took a step backwards and then another until she felt the kitchen wall behind her and could lean against it. Beckoning to Dolly, Jessie slipped out of the kitchen. As quiet as lambs they went upstairs, hardly daring to breathe. They heard the kitchen door close.

'This doesn't feel right, Jessie,' said Dolly again.

'I know. We didn't have much choice though, did we? We couldn't throw her out. Should we listen on the stairs? What do you think?'

'Not me. I'm going up to our room. I don't want to take the blame for this. This is all your fault. You should have kept your nose out of it.' Dolly slowly climbed the stairs. 'It's too quiet down there. This is the calm before the storm. I'm going under the bed covers . . .' Her words trailed off as she made her escape.

'Thanks, Dolly. Thanks very much.'

Creeping back down the stairs, careful to avoid the creaky ones, Jessie trod carefully towards the kitchen door and listened. It was quiet. Too quiet. Neither of them was saying anything. She put her ear very close to the door in case they were whispering. Nothing. She decided to go in.

'Have you seen today's paper, Mum? I can't find it any-where.' This seemed an appropriate excuse.

'It's in the parlour,' said Rose distractedly, 'where it usually is.'

'Speaking of newspapers,' said Ingrid, 'what did it feel like having your name spread across the pages?' She seemed to be suggesting that that was how she knew where her estranged daughter lived.

'We got used to it,' said Jessie. 'One article was much the same as another. The nice thing about it was that they made Dad out as a hero. He would have had a laugh at that. Max says the publicity will help our compensation case.' Jessie looked from Rose to Ingrid. 'So. Am I in the black books then?' Neither of them said a word. 'Oh, come on, this is silly. You're together now so you may as well—'

'Mind your manners, Jessie, please,' snapped Rose.

'Manners? We're family, not strangers.' She turned to Ingrid, trying her best to make light of it. 'All we need is your mother as well. Still, for all we know, she may well be in this room with us, in spirit.'

'If you are talking about the afterworld, she is not there. My mother is still alive. Ninety-six and going strong. She lives in Düsseldorf. I went to visit her a year ago with my brother and his wife and she was in good spirits. We went by boat and train, and two trams – three if you count the tram at this end.'

Still Rose remained silent.

'Would you like another cup of tea ... Grandma?' said Jessie, chancing her luck.

'Thank you, no. Please call me Ingrid. I'm not used to such a grand title.'

'I'll try.'

The silence stretched, until finally Rose broke it.

'It's a pity you never met Robert. Just like Jessie, he wanted to know more about you, and why you had to put me into a home.' Her cold tone covered the hurt and confusion she felt at being confronted without warning by her long-vanished mother. Jessie meant well but she could have no idea of the conflicting emotions that were bubbling up inside Rose.

'And you? Weren't you curious? Didn't you want to find out why I had to do it? Maybe you were too ashamed of your father to face me.' Ingrid's voice was gentle and soothing.

'Or maybe I was waiting for you to find out more about me?' said Rose.

'I knew all there was to know about you. My brother gave me regular reports, he fancies himself as a detective. From the very day I placed you in the home, he kept check. I had every intention of getting you back once I had found somewhere for us to live, somewhere decent. A place that would not only provide a roof over our heads but give me employment as well. I was searching for a position as resident housemaid in one of the big houses or boarding schools.' It seemed that once Ingrid opened up, there was no stopping her. 'I found just the right place, but by then it was too late. Your father had you under his wing.'

'You could have come to see me!' Rose's hurt was fast changing to resentment.

'It would have confused you. Madam Blake had taken over my role and you seemed to be well cared for. I once saw you leave the house with them, a hand in each of theirs. They took you to the park and I followed to watch you on the swings. Mr Gunter was pushing you and you were laughing. I took that to mean that you were happy. I, on the other hand, was not. I walked away and vowed that I would not interfere. Decades later, a persistent granddaughter turns up for a cup of coffee.'

'I might have guessed she would go in search of you,' said Rose. There was the merest hint of a smile on her face but it faded within seconds. 'I suppose it couldn't have been a happy time for you either.'

'No, it wasn't, but I've not been miserable all of my life. I have some good friends, a nice home, a lovely family, my brother's family. Some of my old friends have passed on – Emmie Smith's mother, for instance. That did upset me very

much. She was an old and loyal friend, before and after Madam
Blake came on the scene. Her daughter Emmie takes after her;
she, too, is a good family woman and she has done well by both
you and me. I see her from time to time and she keeps me up
to date.'

There was another frosty silence. Jessie knew she should
leave but she wanted desperately to stay and find out more.

'Well now, isn't Emmie the dark horse,' said Rose tightly.

Ingrid pulled herself up from the chair. 'Now that you
know where I live, maybe you will come to see me, once in
a while. I hope, I very much hope you can find it in your heart
to forgive me.'

'I don't know where you live.' Rose spoke as if she didn't
care one way or the other.

'Ask your inquisitive daughter. Maybe she will bring you
with her on her next visit.' With that, Ingrid gave a graceful
nod and waited for Jessie to show her out of the house, leaving
Rose to herself.

'How long has all this been going on, Jessie?' asked Rose
when her daughter returned.

Jessie related the story from the beginning and ended by
telling her mother that Ingrid, underneath her resentment,
had been sad and lonely and upset by her visit and that she
doubted she would ever forgive Mr Gunter, as she called him,
for betraying her so badly. Rose listened patiently, looking
thoughtful and a little sorry.

'Well, some of this is news to me, Jessie, and I must say I do
feel some shame at what your grandfather did to her. I can hardly
believe it, but then Grandmother Blake is a very strong-willed
woman, not to say very beautiful when she was younger.'

'It was brave of her to come,' said Jessie, rubbing her hair
with the towel. She realized it had been ridiculous to think there
would a fairytale reunion between her mother and grandmother.
There was too much pain involved – but she hoped time would
soften it.

'Was it? I don't know. I'm a bit thunderstruck, to tell the truth. I had no idea that she'd been keeping watch from afar – and for so long.'

'She gets a bit muddled, though. When I went to see her she blamed herself for you giving away a daughter. As if you'd do a thing like that. I hope I don't get muddled when I'm her age.'

This off-the-cuff remark struck like lightning. Rose held her breath, wondering what would come next.

'I told her that Dolly lived with us. Then she blamed her brother for getting his facts wrong. She went all quiet after that.'

Relieved and thankful that her mother had not revealed anything, Rose asked Jessie where she lived.

'Over by Victoria Park. I'll write the address down and leave it on the dresser.' Pulling her hair back, Jessie pushed in a comb. 'Do you think you might visit her then?'

'I don't know. It's been a bit of a shock, one way and another.'

'Yes, but will you go?'

'*Yes*, Jessie. I will go. When I'm good and ready.' Rose refused to say another word on the subject.

Chapter Seven

When the day came for Jessie to go and see Max's mother and sister, there was a worried knot inside her stomach. Why had she agreed to this farce? She had no intention of changing religion and her original reason for saying she would go was to find out exactly what was on Moira's mind. As far as Jessie was concerned, Moira was at the bottom of this sudden problem which had little to do with her being a Christian and Max a Jew. Moira's sights were set higher for her brother.

Turning into the street where Max lived, Jessie braced herself for a confrontation and hoped that she was wrong and that they *were* thinking of her and Max's welfare and whether they would be able to adjust to the trials and tribulations of a mixed marriage, as Max had said. She rang the doorbell and was disappointed that it was 28-year-old Moira who answered the door and not her mother. Jessie liked Mrs Cohen, they had always got on from the time she was small and used to pop in to what was then her grandfather's shoe menders, to help polish boots.

'You're early, Jessie. I've only just got here,' said Moira brightly. 'Come in, come in.' Jessie checked her wristwatch; it was five to ten in the morning, she was just five minutes early.

With her hair set and lacquered, her make-up perfect, Moira looked glamorous next to Jessie, who had her hair tied back and apart from a smear of lipstick was wearing no make-up. Gliding through the passage and into the small back room where Max's parents spent most of their time, Moira pulled out a chair from under the small gate-leg table. In her bright orange and green frock and chiffon neckerchief, she looked as if she was ready to go to the theatre, but this was nothing unusual because she always looked smart and dressy.

Since it was Saturday Jessie was wearing slacks and a puff-sleeved blouse; she shouldn't have felt too casually dressed for the occasion, but she did. Before sitting down, she made a quick check of her nails to make sure her clear varnish hadn't chipped. Her confidence had begun to wane.

'I'm sorry if I'm too early, Moira. I must have walked too quickly,' she said. 'I meant to get here on the dot.'

'Not to worry, darling. I'll put the kettle on, but if you don't mind my passing on a bit of friendly advice, it's better to arrive five minutes late than five minutes early. I don't mind, of course, but you never know how your hostess might react. Some people might think it impolite.'

Settling herself in the newly decorated room, Jessie admired the pale pink and green flowery wallpaper. 'It's very quiet, Moira,' she said. 'Where's your mum?'

'My mother's had to go and see Auntie Becky,' she said. 'Auntie Becky gets headaches when she feels like it and has us all running round after her.'

Glancing at the spread on the table, Jessie thought it didn't look as if Moira had just arrived. A try was set with two bone china cups and saucers and there were smoked salmon bagels on a plate. Jessie could smell cigarette smoke in the air and more than one had been smoked if the glass and chrome ashtray was anything to go by. Neither Max nor his parents were smokers.

'My father's at the synagogue, Jessie, before you ask. He spends most of Saturday there.' Scooping up the ashtray, she went through into the adjoining kitchen and tipped the evidence into a small cream pedal bin. Jessie knew Moira's secret. They all knew Moira's secret and she knew they all knew but liked to pretend that she didn't know they all knew. That was Moira.

She put the kettle on and came back into the room.

'And Max is keeping out of the way while you and I argue religion' said Jessie.

'I hope that isn't what my brother said, Jessie. He knows I wouldn't dream of such a thing. Arguing over religion? I don't think so.'

'I was only joking, Moira, trying to lighten things, before we start discussing it.'

'Oh?' Moira raised an inquiring eyebrow.

'I'm sure God must have had a sense of humour. He would have had to, wouldn't he, if he really *can* see each and every one of us every second of the day – and what we get up to.'

'Yes, dear, if you say so, although I don't think your priest would think much of—'

'Vicar. Catholics have priests. We have vicars.'

'Of course, of course,' she said, shrugging it off in typical Moira style. She never admitted she was wrong.

'I wonder what Jesus would have made of Mosley and his little army of Blackshirts. I suppose in a way the Fascists could be seen in the same light as the Roman army. They wanted to change the world as well.' Moira's confidence and self-possession always made Jessie react by showing off – she couldn't help it.

Moira frowned. 'We don't mention that name in this house.'

Jessie wasn't sure if she was referring to Mosley or Jesus. 'Sorry. I wasn't thinking. How's your hubby then?' she said, trying to warm her future sister-in-law.

'Nathan is very well, thank you. He's just been promoted, as a matter of fact. Area manager. We're very pleased. Very proud. The company he works for are enjoying a boom year.'

'That's nice. It couldn't have been much fun for him, going round knocking on people's doors, trying to get blood out of a stone. The tally man's not that popular round this way. Not when it comes to paying out.'

'Nathan wasn't a tally man, dear,' said Moira. 'He was a debt collector. But you're right, he's much happier and far more suited to an office. He had to do the street rounds first – ground work. It's company policy to begin at the grass roots. Now he's got a beautiful desk to sit behind. Antique. He's very keen on antiques.' Moira got up to get the kettle. 'Personally I prefer Art and Craft. Our flat in Stamford Hill looks very different from this house. Not that my parents have antiques, of course. What do you think of the decorating? Nathan paid good decorators to come in once the house was wired for electricity. Does your house still have gas lighting, dear?'

'No, not any more.' Jessie bristled under Moira's air of superiority.

'That's nice. So . . .' Moira poured boiling water from the kettle into the coffee pot. 'I hear that you want to marry into our family, Jessie. Is that right?'

'I thought that was why you wanted to see me. I thought you knew that Max has been paying off for an engagement ring. His idea, not mine. He'd like us to get married early next year, which is why I don't think our little talk about my changing religion will have much point. It takes years of studying and practice, from what I've heard.'

'You surprise me, Jessie.' Moira sat down and placed a cup of tea in front of Jessie. 'Help yourself to milk and sugar. The milk is fresh.'

'Why do I surprise you?'

'Well,' Moira laid the flat of her hand against her breast, 'you know what they're like.' She flapped her hand. 'Men and their hearts. My brother was always one for the girls but I would have expected him to have grown out of that if he did have marriage on his mind. Seriously on his mind, that is.'

'So you don't think he has then? Grown out of it?' Jessie said, frowning.

'No, darling, I don't. He thinks the world of you, sure, but Max, settling down? I don't think so. Not for a few years in any case.'

This conversation was not what Jessie had been expecting. 'But if he's not ready for marriage why would he be buying me a diamond engagement ring?'

'Zircon, dear. I'm sure it's a lovely dress ring. Beautiful. But a diamond? Max isn't earning a fortune — yet.'

'It is a diamond, Moira. He pointed it out to me and said it was a diamond. He's not a liar, your brother. You must know that.'

Moira shrugged and lowered her eyelids. 'So he has dreams bigger than his wallet. Most young men do these days. In many ways Max is immature, although I wouldn't want him to know I said that. I worship the ground he walks on. He's a prince among men as far as I'm concerned. But then, I'm family.'

Determined not to be put down, Jessie straightened and looked her in the eye. 'He's been paying off for the ring for months and I don't think he's a prince among men, he's just an ordinary feller who I happen to love. And he's not immature, far from it.' Now it was Jessie's turn to sound smug, 'You can trust me on that one.' Seeing Moira's expression change from complacent superiority to discomfort was worth putting up with all her condescension.

'Of course,' said Moira, recovering herself, 'you should know best.'

'I feel bad now,' said Jessie, play-acting, 'telling you about the ring. I thought you knew.' She playfully pointed a finger. 'You crafty cow, Moira, you wormed it out of me.'

'I didn't exactly have to *prise* it out of you, Jessie. You must be very careful about bragging.'

'Anyway,' said Jessie, biting her tongue, 'what *did* you want to talk to me about? Max said it was to discuss Judaism and Christianity.' She looked into Moira's face. 'What's this all about?'

'Goodness, you have changed. You mustn't be so harsh, but then, poor darling, you have been through a very difficult time. If I may give you another little bit of advice,' she leaned forward and pulled a strange face, 'don't get bitter. It would be such a shame. You're a lovely girl.' She leaned back again and smiled benignly. 'I just wanted us to have a little chat, that's all. We never seem to see each other, and yes,' she said, lighting a cigarette, 'I have been concerned about the differences in Max's life and yours. Most of our friends are Yiddish. Everything we do is Yiddish. It's very unusual for a Jew and a Christian to become sweethearts, very unusual. We're a tight-knit community. Family and friends don't like it if one of us marries out.' She leaned forward again, resting an elbow on the table and admiring her red nail varnish.

'You're a sweetheart, Jessie, and we think the world of you, don't get me wrong. But marriage?' She reached out and opened a drawer in the table. 'Here, let me show you something.' She withdrew a few photographs. 'This one is of Cousin Harry's bar mitzvah, taken last year. I'm sure Max told you about it. This is the world you would be marrying into. We Cohens are a very traditional family. Now, can you see yourself fitting into that scene? You, with your lovely blonde hair, blue eyes and pale skin, you would stand out like a sore thumb. You see what I mean?'

This was like Hitler in reverse. 'You're saying that I wouldn't fit in because of my appearance?'

'Now you're being silly. Of course I'm not saying that. All I'm saying is that you should think seriously about it. Would you be happy? Or a fish out of water?'

Jessie studied the photograph and could see what she was getting at. 'I wouldn't *have* to go to bar mitzvahs,' she said, shrugging, 'although if I saw Max wearing a skull cap, I must admit I might laugh until I got used to it.'

'You *would*?'

'Yes, Moira, I probably would. I'm sorry if it offends you.'

'You know what I think? I think you should come to a Friday night Sabbath. Take supper with us next Friday.'

'When Max will wear a skull cap.'

Moira bowed her head, smiling. 'When Max will wear a skull cap.'

'You want me to laugh at him. In front of everyone.'

'You're sharper than you make out, Jessie, even if you are wrong. As if I would want you to laugh at my brother.' She placed a red painted fingernail on the photograph and tapped it. 'I think he looks charming.'

'Is that Max?' said Jessie, seeing him in a different light.

'Of course it is. You don't recognise him?'

'The girl next to him, the redhead, is she one of your cousins?'

'No, darling.' Moira quietly chuckled. 'No, that's Sadie and Bernard Marcovitch's daughter. The Marcovitches are very close family friends. Max has known Sarah for as long as I can remember. They practically grew up together. I would have thought he'd have mentioned her. Everyone said they would get married. Look at this picture.' She showed Jessie another and then another and another. 'Look at the two of them in this one. Dancing the Charleston as if there weren't any troubles in this crazy world of ours. Look, here's another.'

The next photograph was Moira's trump card and Jessie reacted exactly as she had hoped. It was a picture of Max kissing the very attractive redhead on the mouth, and it shocked Jessie. Shocked her to the core. It was a very recent photograph.

'Such a beautiful girl,' said Moira. 'You see what I mean? They fall at his feet, but this one he likes. As you can tell. Isn't that a lovely gown?'

'So this is what Max gets up to behind my back. Well, if that's how you lot behave, to be honest with you, Moira, I wouldn't want to marry into your family. Not for all the money in China.' Suddenly filled with rage, Jessie snatched the kissing photograph and ripped it to bits. 'Show that to Max.

Tell him that's what I think of him — and of you for going behind his back.'

Half running, Jessie left the house and made her way home, too shocked and too angry to cry. Max had been leading a double life, laughing and dancing and kissing other girls. She thought about the gifts that he'd bought for her; she would collect them together, pack them all into a shopping bag and throw them at him.

Stopping to draw breath, Jessie leaned on a lamppost, unable to believe what she had seen and what she had heard. Of course she knew about the family celebrations to which she hadn't been invited; she had understood at the time. She had never expected Max to attend a family christening with her or go to church for midnight mass on Christmas Eve or be there for the carol service, but she hadn't expected him to be trifling with other women at his family functions.

Slamming the front door shut, Jessie ran upstairs to her bedroom and banged around, opening and shutting drawers and cupboards until she'd found the gifts Max had given her. She would show him what she thought of his womanising.

She sat on the edge of her bed and remembered her lovely engagement ring, sparkling in the window. She looked at her naked finger and felt like weeping. Feeling desperately alone, she realised just how badly she missed her dad. She so wanted to hear his comforting voice telling her that it would all sort itself out and that she had overreacted to a jealous sister. She wanted her dad to tell her that Max wasn't a ladies' man but a good, loyal boyfriend, compassionate and understanding. She looked at the presents, half in, half out of the shopping bag. She glanced at his love letters on the dressing table tied with ribbon. Had they been full of romantic fantasies instead of genuine love? Then the photograph came back to her again and her anger returned. She *would* take them back. She had every right to be angry and every right to let him know that she was angry.

Grabbing the bag, she rushed downstairs and out of the

house, slamming the door behind her. She wanted her mother, Dolly, and the boys to know that she was upset and angry. She would tell them all about it later.

Rose called her name from the sitting room window and Jessie glanced up. Dolly was there too. Ignoring them both, Jessie strode off back to Max's house.

'All right, Jessie love?' A neighbour was scrubbing her doorstep. 'You look as if you've lost half-a-crown and found a penny!'

Jessie ran on, weaving and shoving her way through shoppers and those out for a Saturday browse on a sunny June day.

This time it was Max who answered the door.

'Here, you can have these back,' she snapped. 'I don't want them! Give them to the girl in the photograph. The one you were kissing! You cheat! You liar!' Furious, she threw the bag at his feet and turned away, forcing herself not to run. She would keep some dignity at least.

She had expected and hoped to hear Max calling after her, but he didn't. By the time she reached home, Jessie was more upset than angry. Finding Rose waiting for her, she burst into tears.

'What's going on Jessie? Dolly saw you rush out earlier. What's happened?'

'Max. That's what's happened! Good old trustworthy Max.'

'I thought it might have been. You've had a lovers' tiff. Come on. Come in the kitchen and tell me all about it. What's he done?'

It wasn't until she had a cup of tea in front of her that Jessie finally poured out her troubles. 'All that Max said was that his sister wanted me to go round there to discuss religion. To see if I could be persuaded to change.'

'To Jewish,' said Rose, knowingly.

'But that's *not* what it was about.' She explained what Moira had done and then waited for her mother's angry reaction.

'And that's all?' said Rose. 'That's what this is about? A photograph?'

'It was enough. Moira was trying to tell me something, something that Max couldn't bring himself to admit. I don't fit into the family. I'd be the odd man out.'

'I can't say I'm that surprised, Jessie,' said Rose quietly. 'Your dad was a bit concerned that you might have married and then had regrets. As nice as Max and his family are, they do things differently from us. I'm fond of his parents, you know I am, we've been friends for years. I couldn't have wished for nicer people to work next door to, but they have different ways to us. No better, no worse, just different.'

'But I thought you were all for it. Suddenly everyone thinks it's wrong. This is the first time it's come up. Why, all of a sudden, are me and Max not suited? Has something happened that I don't know about?' Jessie looked wretched.

'No, of course not.'

'It's all this Blackshirt business,' said Jessie. 'That's what's doing it. We're all turning against each other. We were never like this before. Did you ever know Stepney people to be like this?'

'You and Max are from different backgrounds, that's all. Very different backgrounds. I expect his sister was just letting you know what lay in store, that it wouldn't be easy for either of you.' Rose paused and then shook her head. 'Showing you a photo of Max with another woman wasn't the way to go about it. That was very hurtful.'

'I hate her for that. I do. I *hate* her. Once Max drags the truth out of her, he'll be livid. When he does come round to apologise for Moira — which should be any time now — will you let him come up to my bedroom, just this once?' Jessie pleaded, hoping her mother would understand how important this was.

'Did he say he was coming round?' asked Rose.

'No. But he will once he knows what's happened. He looked really hurt when I threw his gifts back at him. So will it be all right then? If he comes into my bedroom? I'll leave the door open, if it bothers you.'

'You can go into the sitting room, Jessie. I'll make sure no one disturbs you. That way you can have the door shut and there'll be no risk of the boys hearing your private conversation. Your bedroom's not the place, it wouldn't be right. Once you've made up, things might get out of hand. I trust Max with you, we've always trusted him to behave properly but—'

'You don't want us doing things we shouldn't.'

'I'm not saying that you would—'

'We already have, that's what makes it worse,' Jessie blurted impulsively.

The look of shock on Rose's face brought Jessie to her senses. What was she doing? Why had she said it? There was no stopping now, she would have to go on. 'We have been courting for two years, Mum, and we did plan to marry.'

It hadn't crossed Rose's mind that her seventeen-year-old daughter might have already tasted the forbidden fruits. 'I hope you're not saying that you've let him go all the way?'

Jessie could feel her cheeks burning. 'Well, no ... not all the way.' If there was a time to lie, thought Jessie, this was it.

'Gracious me,' said Rose, pressing a hand against her bosom and taking a deep breath. 'Thank goodness your father isn't here to listen to this.' She stood up and turned her back on Jessie. 'I think you'd best go to your room now, Jessie.'

'We've been going out together for two years! Didn't you and Dad ever think that we might have ... well ... you know?'

'Please, Jessie. I don't like this kind of talk. You should know that.'

'You're not being fair! I've seen your marriage certificate and I know that you were pregnant with me before you and Dad got married. That never bothered me so why should Max and me have to wait?'

There was a pause, while Rose collected herself. 'We'll talk about it another time.' She had no intention of doing so. It had been distressing enough to hear her daughter speak so casually about her own guilty secret, her and Robert's secret. The last thing she wanted was to have her own past picked over as some sort of point of comparison.

Later, in her room, Jessie started to cry. Soon Max would come round and make her feel better, she felt sure of it. Then she would apologise to her mother who was far too strait-laced to discuss sex with anyone, even her own daughter. She had shocked Rose and now she would have to lie her way out of it and try and get things back to where they were before she made that damning confession. She would say that she was still a virgin.

After several nights of crying herself to sleep, Jessie realised that Max wasn't going to appear, he wouldn't be coming round to say that Moira was wrong and that it had all been something out of nothing. Jessie hadn't realised just how much she would miss his friendly face and comforting ways. It was as if a part of herself had been taken away.

Dolly, Alfie and Stephen were being kind to her, which made it worse. Rose knew what Jessie was going through but was helpless to do anything about it; her daughter was going to have to be brave and face facts. Max, for whatever reason, was not going to run to her and she would have to go back and apologise for her behaviour if all was to be saved.

Eventually, Jessie decided she had to stop crying. It wasn't fair. Passing her mother's bedroom, she had seen Rose sitting on the edge of the big double bed holding a pair of her father's pyjamas which she had kept back. There had been other things, too, to remind them – a letter through the post addressed to him, one of his socks turning up in the wash or under the bed.

Going into the sitting room, she found Rose sewing a patchwork cushion. 'I'm going to make a pot of tea, Mum. Do you want a cup?'

Rose looked up at her and nodded. 'That would be nice. What time is it?'

Glancing at the hall clock, Jessie told her it was half past four. 'Shall I call the boys in for a wash before tea? They're in the street playing football.'

'No, leave them for a while,' said Rose. 'Stephen's fulfilling your dad's wishes at last, we don't want to spoil that. Give them another half-hour.' She laid down her sewing and rubbed her eyes. 'I've given myself a headache with this tiny stitchwork. Pull the curtains across, would you, Jess? I'll stop in here for twenty minutes or so. I expect it'll pass once I've sipped a warm drink and closed my eyes.'

Back in her own bedroom, sitting on her bed and drinking her cup of tea, Jessie ran it all through her mind again: Moira; the photos; their talk. Perhaps her pride had made her see things in a worse light than intended. But she had thought about it every night and arrived at the same conclusion. It was over, and while Moira's methods had been underhand, she was right about the reasons. That hadn't stopped Jessie from missing Max. They had been seeing each other for so long that he really had become an important part of her life. She likened it to losing her dad. She was grieving for two men who had meant everything.

Sally had been a godsend. It was her shoulder that Jessie had cried on in the office, she who had patiently listened to the story about Moira over and over again; she who had many times heard how all Jessie's plans for a future with Max would now come to nothing.

The one thing that had struck Jessie was something that Sally had said in the canteen the day before, on Friday: 'Jess, you do realise that not once, through all of this, have you mentioned the word love.' And she'd been right. They had gone on to discuss love and what love actually was. Sally had said, 'You just *know*, Jess. There's no other way of describing it.'

Their tête-à-tête in the canteen had been the reason why Jessie had at last come out of herself. She had hidden herself away almost every evening since she and Max had split up. Now she was back in her room again, drinking her tea alone, but for a different reason — she *wanted* to be by herself. It was as simple as that.

With her pillows propped behind her, Jessie listened to the children in the street. The boys were playing football and the girls were enjoying a game of skipping. She could hear their chant and it took her back to when she had done the very same thing out there in that same street. Lighter inside, she sang along with them:

> All come in together,
> Never mind the weather,
> When the wind begins to blow,
> We'll all go out together ...'

'Jess? Are you asleep in there?' Rose sounded timid by comparison to the woman she had once been. A wave of guilt swept over Jessie. She slipped her legs off the bed and sat up, determined to turn over a new leaf, for the sake of herself and everyone around her. She pushed her hand through her long unbrushed hair and braced herself, ready to be the person she was before she broke up with Max.

'Jessie? Your friend's downstairs. Shall I ask her to come in or would you rather I made an excuse? It's Sally from work.'

'Sally?' Jess was off the bed in a flash and opening her door. 'I'll come down,' she said, smiling.

'Oh, that's better, Jessie. Much better. You have bucked up. The boys are just in and the table's laid with sandwiches and some cake. If your friend wants to come in and—'

Jessie placed her hands on Rose's shoulders. 'Mum, it's over. I'm not going to mope around any more so you can stop worrying about me. Next week, we'll go to see a show, a really good, old-fashioned variety show. Something for all of us.'

'That would be a tonic, Jessie, I must say.' There was a genuine smile on Rose's face too.

'Good. I'll have my tea later. Will it be all right if Sally comes into my room for a short while?' Rose had never encouraged any of her children to have friends in, especially not in the bedrooms.

'I should think so. There's a bottle of lemonade downstairs, Sally might be thirsty after her walk. It's very hot and dry out there.'

Jessie went downstairs to greet her friend, feeling much lighter inside. Maybe she would go out with Sally for a drink that evening.

'Blimey, Jessikins,' exclaimed Sally, 'you look a right two and eight. I think it's time you went to the hairdressers', you need a style and set. Still, not much we can do about that now except to sweep it all up on top and put some lacquer on. Hurry up, we're going out.'

'I haven't got any lacquer, Sally. I don't use it. It's like glue.'

'I'm sure it is, but who cares so long as it does the trick. You'll have to do something with it, and you could put a bit of lipstick on.'

'Where are we going?' Jessie's spirits began to rise. Sally always cheered her up.

'Anywhere. I don't care. After our little chat yesterday, I thought it was time you had an outing. Can I come in then? Or you gonna leave me standing on the doorstep like a stray cat?'

'Of course you can come in but do we have to go out? Can't we just sit on my bed and talk?'

'No, we bleedin' well can't. We've done enough of that. You and Max are finished, it's past 'istory. Now go and do something with yerself, can't go for a drive with the chaps looking like a dog's dinner.'

A frown swept across Jessie's face. 'What chaps?'

'Tom's been driving me round the bend and up the wall.

He wants to see yer. Him and Ron 'ave bought a car between 'em, an old banger they've named Susie. They 'ave to get out and push it now and then, but it goes all right for a good few miles. They want us to go out together. Tonight. They're outside, waiting for an answer, but Tom wants to have a little chat with you first. Me and Ron'll go for stroll while you get on with it. Well, go on then. Move yerself!'

'You shouldn't have done this, Sally. You shouldn't have brought him round here. It's not clever.'

'Couldn't stop 'im. He'd found out where you lived anyway and you know how he feels about yer. Once I told him you was finished with Max,' she shrugged, 'well, there ain't no keeping him down now. His ol' green eyes lit up, they did.'

'You *shouldn't* have told him. I asked you *not* to! It's none of his business.'

'Oh, shut up and brush yer bloomin' hair. Fink yourself lucky that someone as 'andsome as Tom fancies yer. Mind you, he might not if he sees you looking like this, like something the cat dragged in.'

'Well, we'll see just how much he likes me for myself then, won't we?' Not caring about her long unbrushed hair or pale face with no rouge or lipstick, Jessie strode out of the house, leaving Sally to go inside and drive Rose mad with her incessant chatter.

Striding up to an old black car, Jessie wrenched the door open and sat on the badly worn and cracked leather seat, staring ahead, waiting to hear what Tom had to say for himself. Since Max, she trusted no man to be honest.

'What do you want, Jess?' The voice was familiar, but it wasn't Tom's. It was one of her childhood friends, Freddy Knight. 'I'm just off to pick up me girl,' he said, worried.

What could she say? There were two other motors parked further along the road. She cursed Sally. Why hadn't she described what Tom's car looked like?

'Sorry, Freddy. I've got in the wrong car,' she said. 'What's he gonna think of me, Freddy? That must be the one, that old thing along the road. Help me out, Freddy. Drive off or something, anything.'

'Don't be silly. Get out now and tell him you needed to have a word with me. Go on, make him jealous — us blokes love it.'

'Do you?' Jessie said. 'Well, us girls don't. I broke up with Max because of something like that.'

'Well, that's a typical woman for you. Jess? You're feeling all right, ain't you?'

'Of course I'm all right, why shouldn't I be?' She didn't move. 'I didn't mean to suggest that *your* car's an old banger, by the way. I just wasn't thinking when I got in.'

'Well, you'd best start now, before he pulls away, before that little bit of jealousy turns into something else. Go on. Don't get in the black car, that belongs to Mr Allen, the credit man. He's paying his weekly visit to Merry Widow Jackson. The next one along's got two blokes in it.'

'That'll be them.'

'Right. Good. So you'll be off then? Only I've got to pick up my bird now.' He looked at his wristwatch. 'I'm already late. We're meant to be going to Epping Forest ... for a picnic.' He grinned, winking at her.

Jessie managed a smile and climbed out.

'Have a good time,' said Freddy.

Waving him off, she saw that he was laughing to himself inside the car. She couldn't blame him, it must have looked funny from where he was sitting.

She walked the few steps to Tom and Ron's car and bent down to speak to Tom through the open window of the back seat. She felt a rush of that old familiar black magic as he looked into her eyes and smiled. 'Sally said you wanted to have a word with me. Well, here I am.'

Tom blew a smoke ring, 'What did you get in that car for?'

'Freddy's a mate, I was passing on a message from another friend,' Jessie lied smoothly. 'Why?'

'Just wondered, that's all.'

Ron was out of the car in a flash. 'I'll, er, I'll take a stroll with Sally and leave the pair of you to it. All right if I knock on your door, Jessie?'

'I suppose so. But don't go in. Mum's not up to it.'

Tom looked at Jessie. 'You gonna get in then or what?'

'No. What do you want?'

Laughing quietly at them, Ron walked away. 'Ten minutes and I'll be back with Sally,' he said.

Tom cleared his throat and Jessie could see she was annoying him.

'What does Hannah think of your car, then?' she asked. 'Or wouldn't your girlfriend be seen dead in it?'

Leaning back and stretching one arm, he groaned deliberately. 'She's not my girlfriend. I like your hair like that, Jessie, it suits you. All free and easy. Pity about your charm though, that seems to have vanished. I remember the first time I saw you, outside Stepney Green station, looking sad. Then there was the dockers' march when you were smiling and lovely. How would your dad feel, I wonder, if he could see you now, acting like this? He'd be gutted, I reckon,' Tom chattered on, 'knowing his accident had changed you. His Jessie, his lovely girl, all nasty and bad-tempered. Now get in the car and do as you're told.' He moved along the seat to make room for her.

'Bloody cheek. Who d'you think you are?' she said pulling at the door and bouncing down onto the badly sprung back seat. She slammed the door shut.

'Jessie, stop play-acting. It's not clever and it don't suit you.'

'I wasn't play-acting,' she said quietly. Any mention of her father still upset her.

'Yes you were. Right,' He drew on his cigarette. 'Let's start again. I'm sorry I let you down that time, all right? I wanted to see you but I couldn't. I just couldn't get there. Don't ask me why.'

'Why?'

'Very funny,' he said, trying not to smile. 'Anyway, we're together now, in this motor and I'll say it just once, and then it's up to you. You can laugh or listen. I've not been able to get you out of my mind. Simple as that. You drive me mad, always there, when I fall asleep and when I wake up. Thank Christ I don't dream or I'd never be free of you. I knew you was getting engaged so I kept away. But once Sally told me it was off, that was it. Now if you're not interested, fair enough, just say the word and you won't hear from me again.'

Jessie looked away from him, out of the window, and went quiet. 'Don't put up much of a fight, do you?'

'I've got my pride. Anyway, I think you feel the same whether you like it or not, but if, for some reason, you want to fight it, I won't stop you. Maybe you don't think I'm good enough to meet the rest of your family. Who knows? With someone like you it could be any daft thing. And you don't have to worry about Hannah being competition, if that's what's on your mind.' He looked straight at her. 'She's a very close friend, right?'

'I'm sure. I thought my last boyfriend was honest, but I found out different.'

He raised an eyebrow. 'So can I take it that you'll go out with me?'

'Hannah could come with us, you must have plenty of friends who would jump at the chance. We could go on a foursome, couldn't we? Or would that be too much for you to bear, seeing her in another bloke's arms?'

Tom pushed his chin forward defiantly and tried to keep calm. Jessie had, after all, been through two losses, her dad and her fiancé. She was bound to be bitter. 'No, he said, thoughtfully. 'It wouldn't work. She's too much like a sister, I'd feel uncomfortable.'

'I bet you would.'

'Best forget it altogether.' He leaned across her, pushed open the door and waited for her to get out.

'Who said I was going?' She raised her eyes and saw the stony expression on his face. She knew she was pushing her luck. 'I'm sorry. You were right. I *was* acting up.'

He pulled the door shut again. 'Why?'

'I don't know. I'm a bit confused and ... I can't be sure about you and Hannah. I don't want to barge in and break something that's good. You do get on really well and I like her a lot. I mean that, I'm not just saying it.'

'I can see that. Would you sooner I went away?'

'No.' She struggled to find the right words but it wasn't easy. 'Look,' she finally said, 'something did happen between us. I don't know if it was the first time we met or on the dockers' march, and I don't want you to think I'm saying this because I'm on the rebound ...'

'Go on.' His voice had changed, he sounded more serious, older.

'Well, I have thought about you, probably more than I should have. When I saw Hannah coming into the hospital when I was visiting you, well, I was jealous. I had no right to be, but I was.'

Tom's face lit up with both relief and joy. 'Jessie, Jessie, Jessie.' He pushed his hand through his fair hair. 'I'm crazy about you! I thought you didn't care.'

'Why else would I have agreed to go out with you in the first place? I was nearly engaged, don't forget. I'm not the sort that two-times. You can imagine how I felt when you didn't turn up.'

'Good. I'm glad you're not a two-timer, because I would hate to share you with anyone.' He gently pulled her close to him. 'I think I love you, Jessie Warner,' he said, crossing a bridge he had not crossed before. He had often said he was in love but had never declared it to the girl in question.

'I don't think I know what love is, Tom.' Jessie's heart was thumping as she spoke.

'I do, now.' He kissed her softly on the lips and very, very slowly, they moved closer together until his arms were holding her tight and their bodies were touching. Jessie responded in a way she had never responded to Max. This was different. Very different. She felt her body stir, come alive; every part of her seemed to be gently throbbing. Her breathing changed and her heart beat even faster.

Freeing his lips from hers, Tom gazed into her face. 'I'm putting my trust in you . . . I hope you don't leave me a broken man.' His voice was deep and husky.

'I won't hurt you, Tom. I'm not a heart-breaker.' There was a slight tremble to her voice which was nothing compared to the way she was trembling inside. 'I don't know what's happening to me,' she said. 'You make me feel different.'

Laughing at her, Tom stroked her face, her beautiful face. 'I don't know when it happened, Jess. Maybe the first time I saw you — who cares? Who cares when it was, how it was, what it was. I've never been this scared before. You frighten the life out of me. I suppose it's happened at last — you've bowled me over.' He narrowed his green eyes and grinned at her. 'You've made me love you.'

'I made *you* love *me*? And what have you done to me? Cast your spell over me, that's what.'

'Maybe. But I'll say this much, I won't hurt you, Jessie. I'll never hurt you. I'm yours for as long as you want me. I don't know how long that'll be, maybe for ever or maybe for a while, until you go off with someone else or back to your boyfriend. You might break my heart but I'm willing to take that risk.'

'You can stop thinking that way. I've never felt like this before. You make me angry, you make me laugh, I like quarrelling with you . . .'

'And I want to squeeze you to death,' he said. 'Squeeze the life out of you and keep it for ever.'

Tearing herself away from his embrace, Jessie kissed him on the cheek. 'I'd better go back inside. Sally's waiting and Mum'll be worried.'

'So shall we all meet up tonight then?'

'I don't think I can cope with it, Tom. You, me, Sally and Ron, I've been through a lot during the past couple of weeks. All I want to do is be alone and think about us. I suppose that sounds daft.'

'No. I know what you mean,' he said, taking a very deep breath. 'So, how about if I pick you up tomorrow? We can go for a drive – or we could go dancing. You name it.'

'Let's just wait and see how we feel. Come round tomorrow at seven, then we'll decide.'

'Whatever you say, Jess, whatever you say.'

They sat there for a few moments, neither saying anything, until Jessie broke the silence.

'But how would that look? Sally and Ron are expecting us to go out with them.'

'That was the idea,' he said, 'but actually I don't wanna share you with anyone right now. I wouldn't be able to take my eyes off you – or keep my hands off you, come to that. Go on, out you get. Too much too soon. And don't slam the door, it might fall off.'

Laughing, she got out and walked slowly away, knowing his eyes were on her and loving every second. *Now* she knew. Now she knew what love was.

'Is he your new boyfriend then?' She could hear Stephen's small voice but she was on another planet. 'I liked Max. He never 'ad a car but he brought us sweets and played cards with us. You never gonna go out with 'im again then? Jessie? *Jessie!*'

His penetrating voice brought her back to earth. Stephen was sitting on the front step, cupping his chin with both hands. 'Max is all right, Stephen,' she said. 'We'll still see him, he's a family friend, he's bound to come and visit ... and play cards.'

'But you won't kiss 'im on the doorstep no more?'

'No, I won't kiss him on the doorstep no more. Me and Max'll always be friends though, I hope. You know what I reckon? I reckon he's found something out. He kissed another girl and he found something out.' She was thinking about herself and Tom and what they had just discovered.

'So he won't be sad then?'

'No, he won't be sad.'

'What did he find out?'

'That even though he liked me a lot, I wasn't the right one for him.'

'And that man in the car. Is he the right one for you?' Stephen looked sideways at Jessie. 'You gonna marry 'im?'

Laughing, she put her arm around his shoulders. 'I don't know. We'll just have to wait and see, won't we? Now then, how about you running down to Riley's and buying some twisted cough candy for all of us?'

'I've gone off it. What about if we wait for the toffee apple man? He'll be round soon.'

'All right, but how about if you nip down to Riley's first and get me tuppenny worth of snowfruits.'

'Don't mind.'

'Well, go on then. Take a shilling out of my purse. It's in my handbag on my bed, and don't go pinching any of my sweets before you get back with them.'

'Course not,' he said, rushing into the house. When he got to the stairs, he turned round. 'Can I 'ave a ride in his car one day?'

'We'll 'ave to wait and see. See how well you do at school now that you've been moved down the front of the classroom. See if it really was poor eyesight or laziness that got you bad marks.'

'It was! I do try hard!'

It would have been nice if she could have believed him, but quietly, in her own way, Jessie had been testing Stephen, without him knowing. From what she could tell, there wasn't much wrong with his eyesight. Her brother had a way of winding people round his little finger to get what he wanted. But then no one was perfect.

Catching sight of her reflection in the oval mirror in the

hall, Jessie could see that Sally had a point; she looked terrible, her hair was too long and straggly and it was out of style. She placed her hands on either side of her face to see what she might look like with short hair. She liked what she imagined, and she knew exactly where her mother's sharp scissors were.

Wasting no time, Jessie went into the sitting room and to Rose's sewing box. Lifting the heavy steel scissors, she hid them between the folds of her cotton skirt and went to her room, closing the door behind her and wedging a chair under the handle, in case she was disturbed.

Holding the scissors just above her shoulders, she cut a straight line. As the thick chunk of wavy blonde hair slid down her front to the floor, she suddenly had second thoughts. She had had long hair since she was a small child. But it was too late for regrets, and she had to work quickly, before Dolly demanded to be let in.

Using her hand mirror to cut round the back, she concentrated and kept a keen eye as she snipped away, first one side and towards the back, and then the other. The crunching sound as the blades cut through her hair gave her goosebumps. What would Rose say? Facing front again she was mortified to see that one side was much shorter than the other. She carefully snipped the longer side but still it wasn't even. She snipped again. Now it was shorter than the other side. Panic set in.

She threw the scissors onto the bed, kicked all her thick hair underneath it, cleaned up the dressing table and put on her hat. She pulled the rim down as far as it would go.

She crept down the stairs and managed to get out of the house without being seen or heard and she walked very quickly, her head down, hiding her face until she arrived at the local salon. She looked furtively through the window. The hairdressers were all busy cutting or setting, and two more customers were waiting for curlers to be taken out.

Leaning on the wall between the salon and barber shop, she wished away the past hour. What had she been been thinking?

If only she hadn't picked up those scissors! How could she go on her first date with Tom the next day looking as if rats had been at her hair?

She covered her face with her hands as she felt tears sting her eyes.

'The hat pulled down is a dead give-away, young Jessie.' It was Maurice Simons, the barber.

'I cut my own hair,' she said tearfully. It's a mess.'

'You're not the first. Come on in. I'll call my wife down and she'll take you upstairs to our flat. Give me fifteen minutes and I'll come up. I'll give you a short back and sides,' he joked.

'Oh, Maurice, if you could get one of the hairdressers to—'

'You should be so lucky. On a Saturday she wants a hairdo on demand. Today you will have to settle for me.'

'But you're a barber, you cut men's hair and you use a razor. I don't want short back and sides, Maurice.' She shuddered at the thought of it.

'Come with me. Upstairs — before you draw a bloody crowd.'

Ignoring the cheeky asides from the male customers in his shop, Jessie followed Maurice through a small doorway and upstairs. 'I only meant to give it a trim,' she said.

'Sarah!' Maurice called to his wife who was in the kitchen preparing the evening meal. 'You remember when our Ruth got hold of my scissors?'

'Could I ever forget!' she yelled back. 'Why aren't you cutting hair? It's a holiday all of a sudden?'

'We have a private customer!' Flapping a hand and rolling his eyes, Maurice took off Jessie's hat. 'Well, at least you haven't shorn the lot. With this I can do something. Come and see, Sarah.'

'My God. What have you done?' Sarah stood in the entrance to their flat, a hand over her mouth. 'Does your mother know about this, Jessie?'

'Leave her alone, woman. Hasn't she got enough to worry about? Of course her mother doesn't know. Rose would go potty.'

'I was trying to give myself a new look.'

'Sit her in front of the mirror, Maurie. I'll fetch your scissors and a towel.' She went back into the kitchen, smiling to herself.

'So, madam,' he said, sitting her down and speaking to her reflection in the mirror, 'you want the new style, yes?'

She nodded and managed a faint smile. 'I'm not sure about a fringe though.'

He pushed his fingers through her hair and tousled it. 'No. Your face wouldn't suit a fringe. I think you should keep the side parting.'

'Oh, I thought the new style needed a middle parting.' She was disappointed and a touch worried. He was a barber, after all, and in his sixties. What could he know about the latest trends?

'*You* thought. Which one of us is the stylist here? I'll show you something.' He drew a comb through her hair to produce a straight right-sided parting, then combed it again to show a left-sided parting. 'As a matter of fact it would look wonderful with a left parting but then you'll say that's the boys' side, correct?'

Jessie nodded, her worry deepening.

'But you can see how the left suits you?'

She nodded again, half-heartedly.

'But you won't break the rules. What do you think, Sarah?' he said, taking the towel from her.

'For once in your life, you're right. Let him do what he wants, Jessie. You'll get the best cut and you'll start a a new rage. But I think you should have a fringe.'

'Why? Why should she be like everyone else? Look.' He combed Jessie's hair back and pushed it to the side. 'That doesn't suit her?'

'It'll fall across her eyes . . .'

'Do me a favour, woman, go away.' He flicked his fingers at her. 'Go cook the supper. You think I would give her a cut that would fall where it shouldn't? She's got good, thick, strong hair. It's a joy to work with. I've never come across natural blonde hair like this before, it's normally so fine you can't do a thing with it.'

'I suppose you could be right,' said Sarah, 'but then Jessie's got such a lovely face you couldn't go far wrong.'

'I never go anywhere wrong, thank you very much. Go away.'

Sarah threw up her hands and smiled at Jessie's reflection. 'He asks my advice, I give it, he takes no notice. Why ask in the first place?'

'I'm going to give her a fringe! I'm taking your advice! But it will be a long fringe, one she can brush away from her face, not one that sits there looking like a bloody pelmet!'

'Which is what I said in the first place!' she called, going back to the kitchen.

Maurice smiled at Jessie in the mirror. 'See what I mean? She wins whatever. Now then, I'm going to dampen it, then cut it, then wash it; finish off with the scissors, a little snip here and there, then almost dry it, and then use the curling tongs on the ends. What I would like you to do is put a smile on that face because you are going to walk out of here looking like a million dollars, a model out of one of those women's journals you young girls waste your money on.'

Jessie wasn't convinced but was relieved to be hidden away and in safe hands. 'Wake me up when it's over,' she said wryly.

'Tch. Anyone would think I was a surgeon.' He continued to talk while he dampened, combed and considered. Once he began to cut, not another word escaped his lips and Jessie kept her eyes closed throughout, too frightened to watch as her hair got shorter and shorter.

'OK, young lady,' he said at last, 'but before you examine this work of art, remember, it's still damp, it hasn't been washed or tonged.'

'I know,' she said. She opened her eyes and stared at the reflection of someone she hardly recognised. Her face broke into a broad smile, showing her lovely straight white teeth. It was a perfect cut and style, level with her chin. She gazed at her new self, speechless.

'Well?' There was laughter in the old man's voice.

'I love it. I love it, Maurice, you're a genius. A real genius.'

'I know.' He winked at her, pleased as punch. 'You wait until we've finished with you. Every head will turn as you walk along the street.' He called loudly to his wife, his face filled with pride. 'Sarah! Come and show Jessie to the bathroom, she can wash her own bloody hair.' Proud of his good deed, he went down to the barber shop.

Ten minutes later he was back. The last of his customers had gone and he had closed the shop. He put the finishing touches to Jessie's hair and then admired his work over a cup of tea with her and his wife. Thanking both him and Sarah, Jessie eventually got up to leave. As they took her through to the front of the shop, she asked for the fourth time if she could pay for the cut and style, but they wouldn't hear of it. 'I loved doing it,' said Maurice, 'and I owed your father a favour – he did one for me once. Besides, when they see you, maybe the ladies will be queuing up outside my door instead of the hairdressers'.'

'You steal my customers and I'll divorce you,' said Sarah in her droll way.

'Mum will love it and I expect Dolly'll be down first thing, sitting in one of those barber chairs. I wouldn't be surprised if the girls at work . . .' Her words trailed off as she followed Sarah and Maurice's gaze. They were staring at their shop window, their faces twisted with torment. Painted across their window, in large white letters, were just two words: JEWS! YIDS!

Sickened by it, Jessie felt ashamed. There was nothing she

could say or do to help. She left them to scrub away the abuse themselves, which is what they wanted. Each of them had been living in the East End since they were very small children, immigrants from Poland, and each of them, like a thousand or so others, considered England to be their home.

Jessie was scared to think what might follow now their shop had been marked. Her thoughts turned to Alfie and she prayed that he would be at home when she got there, that he had had nothing to do with it.

'Blimey!' Alfie was the first to react when Jessie walked in with her new hairstyle. 'You look like someone else, Jess!'

Jessie had never been so pleased to see him. He obviously hadn't just come in, he looked as if he'd been there, reading his comics, since when she went out.

'Oh. Thanks very much, Jessie!' said Dolly. 'I was gonna get mine done like that next week. Now everyone'll say I've copied you. Well, they can say it. I'm still getting mine cut in that style.' She went back to her paperback.

Stephen said nothing. He just sat there gazing at Jessie, wide-eyed.

'Do you like it, Mum?'

'I do, Jessie, I do like it . . . but it's a bit of a shock. Whatever made you decide to do it?'

'I don't know. You'll never guess who cut it.'

Rose stood up and circled her. 'It's a very good cut. Wherever did you go? Not up to the West End, I hope. That would have cost a week's pay.'

'No, Mum, not up to the West End. Down the road, to Maurie Simons.'

'Maurie Simons? The barber? You went to a men's barber shop? Well, I never did, what a dark horse that man is. I hope you thanked him, Jessie.'

'Of course I thanked him.' Jessie didn't mention what had happened afterwards because her mother was smiling for a change.

'You wanted to make yourself look nice for this new boyfriend, I suppose. The one Sally brought round here. Tom, wasn't it? The one you told Dad about a while ago.'

'Yeah, Tom,' she said, with stars in her eyes. 'Tom Smith.'

'It's a bit soon after Max,' Rose said cautiously. How on earth was she going to keep Jessie from meeting Hannah if Tom really was the new love of Jessie's life? 'Be careful, Jessie. People do strange things on the rebound.'

Jessie didn't want to get into an argument but she did want her mum to accept Tom. 'It's not on the rebound,' she said, calmly but firmly. 'To tell you the truth, I was smitten by him right from the beginning.'

'Out of the frying pan and into the fire, if you ask me,' said Dolly, green with envy, having seen Tom on her way home from shopping for a new pair of shoes. 'Still, we can't tell you anything, Jessie, can we? You always know best. So where does he live then, this Tom?'

'Mind your own business,' said Jessie lightly. 'I don't want you pinching him off me, do I?' The truth was, Jessie had no idea where he lived and didn't think her mother would be too pleased about that. Little did she know that her mother could have told her where he lived.

Rose kept her knowledge to herself. She would have to warn Emmie to keep quiet too. Rose sighed. She was beginning to see that creating new secrets as well as keeping old ones was dangerous.

Chapter Eight

'That was a lovely dinner, Emmie girl, smashing,' said Charlie, giving his wife one of his special winks. The old saying was certainly true where he was concerned – the way to a man's heart is through his stomach.

'I'm off out.' Johnnie, their eldest, looked across the dinner table at Tom. 'Fancy a pint?'

'Might do. I've just got to pop round and see Jessie first. Where you drinking?'

'Blind Beggar, but I won't bother to look out for you. If you're meeting this incredible Jessie of yours, we won't be seeing you.'

'Yes you will. I won't be there more than half an hour so if you go on from the pub, don't forget to leave a message behind the bar.'

'Will do. Don't wait up, Mum.'

Emmie snorted. 'As if I would. Keep your voice down and take your shoes off when you get in. Some of us need eight hours' sleep.'

'I'll tiptoe, promise.' Johnnie turned back to Tom. 'Why don't you bring Jessie along? You've been courting the girl for a good while now. Time we had a look at the goods.'

'All in good time, Johnnie boy, all in good time. She's the right one so you'll be seeing plenty of her in the future.' Tom grinned.

'Oh yeah. Like all the others that got the elbow – or gave you the boot. Do you know what I reckon, Dad?' said Johnnie, in a baiting mood.

'Go on, what?' Charlie liked joining in his sons' banter.

'I reckon he's frightened that me or Stanley'll pinch this one from him, so she must be a looker, eh?'

Laughing, Charlie waved him off. 'Tormenting fucker,' he said. 'Go on out. Pity Tom don't take a leaf out of your book, son. Don't love 'em – just leave 'em.'

'Too right, Dad, too bleeding right,' said Johnnie, laughing. 'I've got a million to make before I settle down. Ain't that right, Mum?'

'That's right, son, yeah. A million for you and a million for me and one for the pot.'

'You wait and see. I'm the only one in this room with a bank account, so what does that tell you?'

'That you're tight,' said Charlie, 'and stashing it all away. Come the war and you'll be lucky to see any of it. They'll bomb your bank first off. Spend it while you can, son, preferably on me.'

Tom looked thoughtful. 'So the football coupons are working out then?'

'Yep. I told you it would work, but oh no, you didn't wanna come in with me. I've got a few hundred in the bank which is better than being a hundred in debt, which is what I was eighteen months ago. But the bank manager had faith; yep, a stranger had faith in me. What with that little sideline and my regular job with all that lovely overtime—'

'Oh, sod off out,' said Charlie, used to his son going on about money. 'Just don't give up your proper job, that's all. At least that's reliable money.'

'I won't, Dad, don't you worry. If there's an hour to work, I'll work it. See you.' With that, Johnnie was gone.

'Mind you, he has got a point,' said Charlie, leaning back and looking at Tom. 'Money grows more money. What's with the black shirt then? New fashion, is it, or did your pet flea die?'

'Go to bed, Charlie,' said Emmie, 'or you'll be in a right mood first thing and blaming us for keeping you up.'

Standing up, Charlie made a business of having a good stretch. 'I was up at half past three this morning. Blooming fruit comes in from the farms earlier and earlier. Blackberries tomorrow, Em. That should please you, eh?'

Once Emmie and Tom were alone, she nodded at Tom's shirt and said, 'I hope you're not wearing that for the reason I think you're wearing it.'

'I'm going to the club, Mum, and that's all there is to it.'

'So you're not seeing Jessie then?'

'Yes I am. Before I meet up with Johnnie for a pint.'

'You're a bloody fool, getting involved with that lot. I knew this was coming. You've been thinking about joining for a long time, I know. Getting a hiding was just the excuse you'd been waiting for.'

Tom gave up the pretence. 'Dead right. I've been thinking about it long enough, now I'm doing it. They're not *all* bully boys. It's just a handful of spivs that 'ave wormed their way in, a small faction, not interested in politics. You'll always get that. We can wipe them out.'

'I won't be able to look some of my neighbours in the face if it gets out. You needn't have bought that shirt, they don't all walk around like that.'

'Course they don't. This style of shirt, in black, is all the rage. Besides, I never bought it, Johnnie gave it to me. Stop worrying. We're not all thugs. You'll be surprised to know that a lot of police officers are Blackshirts on the quiet. A hell of a lot.'

'Never! As if they'd have anything to do with it.' Emmie refused to consider it.

'It's got nothing to do with law and order, that's the point. It's politics.'

'Tell that to Hitler.'

'We're not talking about Hitler. We're not copying Germany or Italy. We just want what's best for our country. If things go on the way they are, by the time we reach the end of this century, England'll be bursting at the seams. There won't be enough houses or jobs for a quarter of the population by then unless it's controlled now. If we don't make noises now, Europe'll suck us in and you can forget what England stood for. What Britain stands for.'

'Yeah, and if we're daft enough to be taken in by Mosley, Hitler'll suck us in,' said Emmie.

'Forget Hitler', Tom said firmly. 'We'll blow him to bits in the next war – with Mosley leading the way.'

'I think you're getting your facts a bit mixed up, son. The papers say that Mosley doesn't want another war against Germany.'

'Maybe not but that's not to say he'll sit back if we're a target. I told you, he's for England, and we'll fight to keep this country the way it is, war or no war.'

'Well, it's all a bit much for me to fathom. How you know so much about it beats me. I think you've been a bit of a dark horse on the quiet. I shouldn't let your brothers hear you talk like this.'

'You'd be surprised. Ask Johnnie what he thinks about it. He's the clever one, after all, the one who's gonna be top dog living in a bloody mansion.'

'Johnnie? What's he got to do with this?'

'Take a look in his trunk. I did. He's never pushed his views but when I found out, 'cos I was nosy, he explained one or two things to me. You don't really think he's gonna spend the evening in a pub, do you? Johnnie? He's as tight as a bank manager. There's no bar in the social club that we're going to. Cups of tea only. Free cups of tea.' Smiling, Tom picked up his tobacco tin and left.

As Tom's words sunk in, Emmie could see how it all fitted. Johnnie had always been the secretive one, never too open about his comings and goings. She had to face the fact that she'd been living in a world of her own. She wondered about her other son Stanley. But Stanley was only just sixteen, and mad on girls and dancing. He wouldn't waste his time on such things. Not Stanley.

Blackshirts. Two of her sons were Blackshirts. She should have felt angry, or at the least very disappointed with the pair of them, but she didn't. Loath though she was to admit it, secretly Emmie felt quite proud of her boys, of their patriotism, and she imagined that Tom was probably right, it was only a handful who were anti-Semitic and uninterested in politics. She wondered about her husband, Charlie. Did he know what Johnnie and Tom had got themselves into?

When she had cleared the kitchen, Emmie went into the best room and put up her feet. Her sons were old enough to know what they were doing and by the sound of it Tom wasn't joining the Blackshirts because he wanted to see the Jews leave this country but because he didn't want to see millions more foreigners coming in. No doubt Johnnie was of the same mind. She couldn't argue with that, not really.

She picked up her knitting. She was making a pullover for Charlie's next birthday; it was a very tricky Fair Isle pattern with six colours, no easy task. When the door knocker sounded she cursed. She wasn't expecting anyone and all the men were out except for Charlie, who was in bed, snoring.

She was more than surprised to see Rose on her doorstep. 'Hello, Emmie. I'm taking a bit of your advice and getting out while the evenings are still nice. So I thought I'd pop round for a visit. I'm not disturbing you, am I?'

Emmie thought that her friend's little speech had been rehearsed and her heart went out to her. Rose was probably feeling the loneliness of widowhood. 'Course you're not disturbing me. It's lovely to see you. Charlie's in bed and the boys are out so I'm by myself.'

Rose didn't stop talking as she followed Emmie into the

living room, which was unusual for her. Emmie was only half listening at first, her mind on her knitting which she would have to put away, but not before marking which row and colour she was on. When Rose mentioned Ingrid, Emmie drew breath.

'I couldn't believe my ears, Emmie, when my mother mentioned your name . . .'

'Sit down, Rose, and I'll pour us both a drop of sherry. I've still got some left over from Christmas.'

'When my mother said you had been seeing her all these years, I was shocked. You never said a word about it, I felt as if I'd had my head in sand all this time.'

'I know what you mean, Rose, I've had my fair share of such feelings of late. Not very nice, I grant you.'

'Why didn't you write and tell me you'd seen her, Emmie? Why did you let me believe that my mother was dead? You'll never know the shock I had when she arrived out of the blue.'

'For a start, Rose, I was sworn to secrecy — once again. Secondly, you never believed she was dead and you know that's the truth. You might have thought she'd gone back to Germany, and I could see nothing wrong with you believing that. Had you ever shown the slightest interest in your mother, I would 'ave been in like a shot. To tell you the truth, I'm glad it's all come out.' Emmie handed Rose a glass of sherry and drank hers down in one before refilling her glass.

'She said you'd met up in Wickham's,' Rose murmured.

'That's right.' Emmie sank into her old feather-cushioned armchair. 'She came in after a hat — way back, when I was working in millinery. It was lovely to see her again. She asked me to not mention it. She spotted you once, you know, along Whitechapel, but ducked into a side street.'

'How could she recognise me after all this time, Emmie? That really is too much to believe.' Rose shook her head.

'I showed her photographs of us taken after the war,' Emmie admitted.

Rose laughed bitterly. 'Well, well. Whatever will you tell

me next? My mother knows all there is to know about me and my family while I knew nothing about her life.'

'No, and whose fault's that? Besides, there was nothing much to tell. Ingrid wanted to know how you'd fared and I told her. She invited me over to her little basement flat for coffee and I went. I love Victoria Park, you know I do. You remember us, years ago, on the boating lake? We used to shriek with laughter.'

Rose nodded. 'Of course I remember it. They were happier times.'

'Anyway, once we'd met again we kept it up, seeing each other every month or so and that way she got to hear about Hannah. I shouldn't have told her about the twins but I did, and only because she asked and I was trying to get her to go and see you. I do believe she's blamed herself all these years. In fact, I know she has. She thought that because she'd given you away, you'd done the same – history repeating itself. Silly woman. I thought it was a load of bunkum but I never said so. It wasn't my place to pass judgement, one way or the other.' Emmie looked at her friend. 'So there you have it, Rose. No more, no less. I bumped into an old family friend one day and we kept in touch.'

'But there's something else I've got to worry about isn't there?' Rose pointed out. 'Jessie and Tom. I did think you were going to have a word with your son. I would have come round sooner to broach you on the subject but I thought it had fizzled out. It seems to be going from strength to strength now.'

Emmie held up a hand. 'I did have a word when you first asked me to, Rose. And he listened. In fact, he stood Jessie up on that first date, you may remember. But once she split up with that Max feller, there was no stopping Tom – or Jessie, if you ask me.' She paused and then went on, 'And I'm afraid the girls have met up too, which was no fault of Tom's. He was out walking with Hannah and they bumped into Jessie. Apparently the girls got on like a house on fire – which is to be expected, in my opinion. It happened some time ago.' Emmie's expression was sympathetic as she looked at her friend's stricken face. 'I did think about coming to see you about it, but what was the point? They'd met, and that was that. I do believe they've become friends. I believe it might be for the best.'

Rose's knuckles were white. 'Have they now? Well, things seem to be going from bad to worse, Emmie, and your son, Tom, always at the centre of it.'

'I'll pretend I didn't hear that, Rose.'

'Knowing how delicate the situation is, I would have thought he'd have kept away. There are plenty more fish in the sea for the young men round these parts.'

With a smile on her face, Emmie leaned forward and patted her friend's hand. 'It's about time, Rose Warner. You've been bottling your anger for too long. Maybe you should go straight round to see Gerta now – while you're fired up?'

'I had every intention of doing so . . . but I came here instead. I can't face the woman, Emmie. I've news over the compensation claim but if I go round there – I might just slap her face. That face. I can still see her expression at the funeral even after all these months. She was gloating, I'm sure of it.'

'Well then, write to her instead. I take it you've something to tell her that she'll be pleased about?'

'Yes and no. Hannah will have a fair share but it's to go in a trust where Gerta won't be able to get her hands on the funds. It will go to Hannah when she's twenty-one, which is when I shall see her and when she'll learn the truth.'

Resting back in her armchair, Emmie was pleased. 'You've done well, Rose. That's the best news I've heard in a long time.'

'I've an excellent solicitor, I will say that. But yes, I have had to think on my feet over this. I dare say Hannah could do with the money.'

'Dead right. She's still looking for a flat but I'm afraid they don't come cheap. She doesn't earn that much at the

library. It would be lovely if she didn't have to wait that
long—'

Rose raised a hand. 'Enough said, Emmie. She'll *have* to wait.
Of course if Gerta gets nasty over it, then things will be forced
out into the open before then. I pray to God that isn't the case.
I'm in no fit state to fight her or to face Jessie or Hannah should
it all come out sooner than I would like. Now let's leave it there,
shall we?' There was a no-nonsense tone in her voice.

Rubbing her eyes, Emmie yawned. 'Whatever you say, Rose.
Whatever you say.'

'And you will have a word with Tom? I feel certain that if
he were to stay away from Jessie, she and Max would get back
together again, which would simplify things.'

Ignoring that, Emmie turned the conversation to Ingrid. 'I'm
pleased you and your mother have got together at last. It's a pity
it's taken so long. Too many wasted years, eh?'

Rose knew exactly what her friend was implying. 'Oh, I
don't know so much. What you don't have you don't miss.'

'If you say so, Rose,' smiled Emmie, 'if you say so . . .'

When Rose arrived home, she went into the kitchen where she
found Jessie by herself, drinking a glass of freshly pressed lemon
and water.

'I can hear those boys aren't asleep yet. I don't know where
they get their energy from,' said Rose, taking off her light blue
straw hat. 'I suppose Dolly's out dancing again.'

'No. But she's getting ready to go out,' said Jessie.

'Is she now?' Rose glanced at the clock. 'Not at this hour
she's not. It's gone nine. I'll have to have a word with her. She
goes too far.'

Jessie was only half listening. She was feeling nauseous. She
prayed the lemon drink would make it pass before Rose noticed.
Jessie's worst fear had been realised; she was pregnant. Pregnant
with Tom's baby. She hadn't told him yet; she hadn't had the
courage. He seemed preoccupied lately. Jessie had a strong

feeling that he had joined the Blackshirts but she couldn't think about that, she had far more important things to worry about.

The lemon drink wasn't working. Rose was going on about Dolly. Her voice sounded distorted to Jessie, as if it was coming from miles away. She recognised the sensation; it was similar to when she had passed out at work, the day after the accident at the docks. She wrapped her arms round herself. *Not now, Jessie, not now!*

'What's the matter, Jess?' said Rose suddenly. 'You've gone a terrible colour.' She placed an arm round her daughter and studied her pale face. 'What is it? Are you in pain?'

'Stars . . .' murmured Jessie weakly. She heard Rose call her name and the next thing she knew she was on the floor, her head between her knees, being propped up by Dolly.

'The . . . floor . . . hit . . . me . . . in . . . the . . . face.' She barely managed to get the words out. 'It came up . . . and hit me in the face.' Rose told her to save her strength, not to say another word, as she patted Jessie's sweat-beaded face with a wet sponge.

'She's as white as a ghost, Mum,' murmured Dolly. 'Should I run for the doctor?'

'I'm all right, Dolly,' said Jessie, recovering. 'I drank some milk earlier, the remains of the bottle, and I think it had curdled.'

Rose stroked away damp strands of hair from Jessie's face. 'Help me get your sister upstairs and into her bed, Dolly. It won't hurt you to stay with her and have an early night, you've been clocking in at work late far too many times recently.'

'I'm all right, Mum,' said Jessie, taking deep breaths of air. 'Honestly, I can manage. Let Dolly go out.' Her legs felt like jelly, but if she had to she would drag herself up those stairs.

'I'd rather not be clocking in at all,' Dolly said, helping Rose ease her sister up from the floor. 'The rest room reeks of old ashtrays.'

'Well, that's your own fault. If you'd stuck it out at the handbag factory until they put you on satin evening bags, which you would have loved, you wouldn't be working at the toy factory, would you? You would have been very good at sewing the satin handbags and it's good wages, piecework.'

'I'm leaving the factory soon anyway.' Dolly put her weight under Jessie's arm as they helped her up the stairs. 'I might apply for a position at the Bethnal Green Museum if it's not too boring.'

'Work is work, young lady, not a daily outing to find amusement.'

Once Jessie was in her bed, Rose folded and tucked in the sheet and then felt Jessie's forehead for a temperature, and stroked her hair, telling her she would be fine by the morning. Jessie felt as if she was a small child again, being watched over and cared for.

'I'll come up later to see how you are, Jessie,' said Rose. 'Try and get some sleep.'

Try and get some sleep? It was a job trying to stay awake. She heard the bedroom door close behind Rose and Dolly before she drifted into sleep. Tom appeared in her dreams; he was standing tall, smart and handsome at the altar, waiting for her. She was wearing a beautiful trailing satin dress and long veil, with Dolly and Sally as her bridesmaids, dressed in blue. Everyone was smiling as she walked along the aisle, holding her dad's arm. Her grandfather was there too. Happy and smiling, gliding along to the sound of the organ, Jessie glanced at Rose in the front row. There was a look of horror on her face; she was staring at her daughter's stomach, which was growing by the second, bigger and bigger, and she was screaming, telling everyone to keep away from her.

'Jess! Wake up! *Jessie!*'

'It's all right, Dolly,' Jessie murmured, half asleep. 'It was only a nightmare. Where's your bouquet?' Then she sank into a deep sleep.

The following weeks weren't easy for Jessie as she tried to hide her condition, but at least their lavatory was outside in the back garden, away from everyone. She could be sick without being heard. She still hadn't told Tom she was pregnant. She was afraid that the burden and responsibility of a baby would be too much for his free spirit. She couldn't face seeing his reaction, not yet.

Her mother would be furious, of that she had no doubt, furious and ashamed. And then there was the rest of the family, her aunts and uncles and, worst of all, Grandmother Blake. Jessie pictured her on hearing the news, a telling look on her face and that knowing smile. The neighbours would talk, and Emmie, Tom's mother, would likely think her a tramp. She and Tom had, after all, only been courting for a few months.

She had tried telling Sally on one occasion, leading up to break the news by saying that she couldn't describe the love she felt for Tom, but Sally had been in one of her frivolous moods and had ruined it by laughing at her. 'One word'll cover it, Jess. Fancy. You fancy Tom and he fancies you,' she said, 'just like me and Ron.'

So Jessie had decided to keep the secret to herself for as long as possible. Once it was out in the open, everyone would start making plans, plans that hundreds of other women who had conceived out of wedlock had made, and she didn't want that yet. She had feigned a period and would go on doing so until she could no longer hide her secret. She was eating good nutritious food but no bread or sweet pudding. She had just eaten an egg salad for lunch. She had to be healthy for the baby but she couldn't afford to put on weight too fast.

'You need fat on your bones, Jessie,' said Rose, before leaving the house to go shopping. 'It's bad enough when people are ill and lose weight through no fault of their own, without you going on a diet for the sake of vanity.' With that, she picked up her shopping bag and left the house.

Jessie asked Dolly why she hadn't gone into the factory that day. She usually worked Saturdays.

Ignoring the question, Dolly kept her back to Jessie – she was washing a blouse in the butler sink. 'You wouldn't think it, would you,' she said, 'but back in Saxon times they ate really well, beef, mutton, chicken and goose, and they ate oysters like they was peanuts. There's a girl who works in the office at the factory who's as skinny as a rake, all she ever eats is—'

'I'm not on a diet for my looks!' Jessie cut in. 'I'm just trying to stay healthy, that's all. One of the girls at work has studied nutrition and she says that we eat far too much fat – butter, lard and cheese. And it's not good for the heart ... or the blood.'

Dolly found this amusing. 'See if you say that when it's Sunday with roast beef and batter pudding for dinner, with apple pie and custard for afters.'

'You shouldn't just take a day off when you fancy,' Jessie continued, determined to get her sister's mind off food. 'You'll get the sack if—'

'I'm gonna give it up.' She gripped the sodden blouse with both hands and twisted it until she had squeezed most of the water out before she put it through the mangle. 'There's no jobs at the Bethnal Green Museum for the likes of me so I might try for a job in one of them Marks and Spencer branches that 'ave opened up.'

'You go from one job to another and if you're—'

'So?' interrupted Dolly sharply. 'What's wrong with that? Better than sticking in one boring job for nearly three years. I don't know how you can bear it, no wonder Max dumped you. Three years with having to listen to you go on about the same old people at work.'

'Max didn't dump me. Anyway, I've got Tom now and I wouldn't have him if I was still with Max.'

'Probably not, knowing you. Can't have *two* boyfriends – oh no! You're so bloody prim and proper. You want to break out of it.' Dolly twisted the mangle forcefully.

Jessie couldn't help smiling. Prim and proper. She was hardly that. If only she could have told Dolly there and then that she was pregnant, it would have given her the shock of her life. 'So why're you thinking of leaving? I thought you didn't mind the work?'

'It's all right,' said Dolly, 'but the women are boring, except for Cook in the canteen. I love Cook, she looks after me, piles up my plate when no one's looking. I sneak off the factory floor sometimes and go and give her a hand. She has to make up the fire in the snug where Management have their coffee, bloody cheek. They take right liberties there.'

Jessie was surprised at the way Dolly was opening up. She hardly ever talked about work, only boys. 'She'll miss you if you leave then, won't she?'

Dolly threw her blouse over the airing rack and scowled. 'That bossy cow . . .'

'Who?'

'The secretary. The chairman's secretary. I was stoking the fire yesterday afternoon to give Cook a five-minute sit-down and I was making the flames burn just right when she came in and shouted at me, asked what I was doing in there and not at my work bench. Smug cow. It's all her fault.'

'*What* is?' asked Jessie. Dolly seemed close to tears. 'What happened?'

'I laid the poker down for a second to try and make up an excuse why I was in there, one flipping second . . . She saw the smoke and smelt the singeing before I did.'

'It burnt the carpet?'

'Course it did. I was looking at her! Trying to look sorry while she barked at me. She saw the smoke and that was that, said it would cost me my job and it did, she saw to that. I wasn't even rude to 'er and only called her a bleeding cow once I knew I was out.'

'There'll be other jobs, other nice people to work with,' Jessie said sympathetically.

'I'm not bothered. I might learn shorthand and typing, keep Mum happy. Sitting in a warm comfortable office all day doing bugger all can't be bad.'

'Don't you believe it. I'll never forget when I first started work in that typing pool at the London Electric. The manageress used to walk up and down the aisles, keeping an eye on every one of us girls as we sat there typing. She made sure we were typing all the time. We weren't allowed to talk except at tea break, in the canteen. Fifteen minutes we got, and it took half that time to get there and back. By the time we got our cup of tea we had to swallow it down. You wouldn't put up with something like that, Dolly.'

'At least you've got a career. You could get a job anywhere now, in any office. Whereas I can only work in a factory, below stairs or in a tea shop. What kind of a career's that?'

Jess was surprised by Dolly's change of attitude; up until now she'd been adamant that she would never work in a stuffy office. 'A career's not everything,' she said. 'You'll be married by the time you're twenty, I bet. Married with babies. You're pretty enough.'

'I might even go abroad to find work,' said Dolly dreamily. 'America. Don't imagine that all I want is the butler sink and boiler. If that sort of life's not for you why should it be the life for me?'

'Maybe it is for me. A little one up, one down ... a small fire burning ... dinner in the oven for when my man comes home ...' It was Jessie's turn to sound dreamy now.

'Oh yeah? And what's come over you? What's changed *your* mind? The handsome Tom? He's done this to you, has he? Made you go all soppy?'

'Maybe. It was different with Max. I did sort of think about a future with him, but it was Max who brought up the subject of marriage – and Moira who smashed it down.' She smiled to herself, pleased now that Moira had stepped in. 'I'd marry Tom tomorrow if he asked me.'

'What're his brothers like?'

'I haven't met them yet. Why?' Jessie knew why she was asking. She was hoping there might be another at home like

Tom. Dolly always opened the door when she knew Tom was coming round and would chat to him while Jessie collected her things.

'Just wondered,' said Dolly. 'So, you haven't been invited round his house and Mum's not asked you to fetch Tom in yet even though you've been courting for months now. Max was in for a cup of tea on your first date.'

Dolly had touched a raw spot. It was true, Rose hadn't shown any interest in meeting Tom and whenever Jessie mentioned him she went quiet.

'Don't forget that Max's parents own the shop next door to ours,' Jessie said. 'Mum already knew Max. She's known the family for years.'

'What about Tom's then? I bet you don't even know what his address is.'

'Of course I do.'

'Well then, why don't we pop round there and see them? It's Saturday and I'm skint. I can't go out shopping, not even for a new lipstick. We could go for a stroll, pop in to see Tom.'

'I suppose we could.' Jessie cleared the table of cups and saucers. 'It's a lovely day. The boys won't be back from the boxing club for a few hours yet.'

'Our Stephen,' laughed Dolly, 'in a boxing ring, all white and skinny with gloves bigger than his own 'ead.'

'Don't be daft, Stephen never goes into the ring. He likes to watch Alfie winning his rounds. It's better than sitting at home doing nothing.' Jessie examined her face and hair in the mirror. Since she'd had her hair cut, it always looked good, even if she said so herself. Tom had been strange about it at first, sulking because he liked long hair, but he soon came round, admitting in the end that her chic new style suited her face. Lovely was the word he used, eventually.

'Come on then,' she said. 'I'll just put a bit of lipstick on and we'll go round there, see if we can fix you up with his brother Stanley.'

'Right,' said Dolly. 'I'll go and make myself look my best then – mustn't let the side down.'

Walking down the street arm in arm, talking and laughing, Jessie realised that she and Dolly hadn't been out together like this since they were very young.

'Mum seems a lot better since Granny German came onto the scene and they see more of each other,' said Dolly, 'and you're a lot different since Tom came along. It's funny how everyone seems to have changed.'

'So you think I did the right thing, then?'

'You know you did the right thing. Max was all right but Tom's a cracker and more like us, in a manner of speaking.'

'I think Mum would have preferred me to stay with Max.'

'She'll come round, Granny German'll soon pull her up. She's all right, I like 'er. I'm glad you went and found her, Jess,' Dolly said earnestly.

'What's come over you? You didn't care tuppence before. Or was that an act?'

'Course it was an act, I'm not made of stone, you know. I felt really sorry for Mum when she told me about it and I was sad but I'm not like you, I don't dwell on morbid things. You take life too seriously.'

What a dark horse she was turning out to be, thought Jessie. She'd kept her true feelings hidden all this time. 'We're nearly there,' she said. 'Don't get all huffy if we're not invited in or I'll die of shame.'

'Tch. Of course I won't. I've got manners. I just pick and choose when to use them, that's all.'

'Well, bite your tongue if your temper gets up.'

'Temper? What temper?' said Dolly with mock innocence. 'I'll be as quiet as a mouse. What number is it?'

'Eighteen.'

'Not far then.' Dolly stopped and looked around her. 'This is nicer than I thought it would be. A few trees as well. I thought the back streets of Bethnal Green were a dump and full of rubbish. This ain't bad, nice little corner shop ... no horse dung in the road ...'

At that moment a horse-drawn cart turned the corner. It was the fruit and veg man. The red-faced vendor tipped his cap to them as he passed and then turned into another street, leaving a pile of steaming horse manure in his wake.

Laughing, they linked arms again and walked on towards Tom's house. 'Bethnal Green's changed,' said Dolly. 'I was thinking of the old days instead of now. The Jago, near Shoreditch. That *was* the pits at one time, right up until the turn of the century. Fights went on there day and night and the women drank neat gin. Did you know that before Queen Victoria had—'

Jessie quickly cut her off before she could get into her stride. 'Dolly, please, not now. Tell me later. We're here.'

Outside Tom's front door, Jessie suddenly felt unsure of herself. Had Tom wanted her to see where he lived, he would have taken her back there by now. 'I've changed my mind, Dolly, let's go home.'

'Not likely!' Dolly pulled herself away and knocked three times before Jessie could stop her.

It was Emmie who answered the door. 'Is Tom in?' said Dolly, as bold as brass.

'He is.' Instead of a welcoming smile, there was concern on Emmie's face.

'We were just passing,' said Jessie, 'so ...'

'Ah.' Emmie had to think fast, Hannah was inside. 'Well, you'd best come in, the pair of you. I'll give him a shout.'

Dolly was the first in, eager and smiling. 'I've come to see if your other son, Stanley, is as handsome as your Tom.'

'Dolly!' hissed Jessie. She could kill her sister at times.

'Well, you're out of luck, madam, Stanley's at work, although he should be home soon. But that's not to say he won't be out again in a flash after filling his belly and having a quick spruce. You can wait in the front room and I'll—'

Laughter drifted into the passage, a girl's laughter, merging with Tom's. It was Hannah.

'Jessie! I can't believe you've called in at this very moment! I was just thinking about you. Tell her, Tom. Tell Jessie what I just said.' Hannah and Tom came out and joined them in the passage.

'Word for word?' asked Tom, sighing and slightly embarrassed by Jessie's unexpected appearance in his home.

'Word for word.' Hannah's eyes were sparkling.

'She said, "I've just had a vision of Jessie looking in at the window as if this was a baker's shop and she was choosing which cakes to buy."'

'It's true! I really did see it, and you were wearing *that* frock!'

'I wore it when I saw you in the hospital,' said Jessie, 'so you were bound to think of me in it.' She felt jealous that Hannah was here.

'But you must have lots of dresses, yet I imagined you in that one. Were you thinking about cakes, Jessie?' There was hope in her voice.

'Well, I wasn't thinking about this being a bakery or choosing cakes, but I thought I could smell a cake baking and it made me think of buns, which made me feel hungry.' Her jealousy disappeared as fast as it had come.

'You see! Thought transference.' It went very quiet as Emmie and Tom glanced at each other.

Hannah turned to Dolly, enjoying herself. 'I'd say that you are Jessie's younger sister. Now tell me I'm wrong. I bet I'm not.'

'You're right,' said Dolly dispassionately, 'we're sisters. We don't look much like each other though, so you *must* be a witch. Jessie looks more like you than she does me as—'

'I'll have no talk of witches, if you don't mind!' snapped Emmie, cutting her short. Collecting herself, she turned to Jessie. 'How are you, Jessie and how's your mother?'

'She's fine, thank you. We were just passing and—'

'You thought this was a railway station? Because that's what it looks like, everyone standing around waiting for the next train. If you'll all go into the front room I'll fetch a pot of tea and some buns, hot from the oven.' She turned to Tom. 'The cat might 'ave got your tongue but I'll have your hands. Come and take them buns out for me, my rheumatism's playing up.'

Following Hannah into the front room, Dolly said, 'Are you family then?'

'No. I'm Hannah. Tom's friend.' They all sat down.

'Oh? What's his brother like? Stanley? Only his mum's trying to fix us up.'

'What she means, Hannah,' said Jessie, 'is that she's hoping Emmie will fix them up. You have to take everything Dolly says with a pinch of salt.'

'Are *you* courting, Hannah?' asked Dolly, unfazed.

'No . . .' Hannah turned her face away. 'Actually, I've never been on a date. I have been asked but never had the courage to go. My mother always said that boys ask you out for one thing only. I've heard her say that so many times that I think I believe it.'

'So you should,' said Dolly, 'it's true. Let 'em kiss you goodnight and their hands are up your jumper or inside your blouse and in your knickers if you're not quick enough to stop 'em. Dirty sods. Are you a foreigner?'

'No. My mother's German but I was born in this country. My father's British born and bred.'

'I thought as much. Being German's all right, your lot were in the East End much earlier than most people like to think. After the collapse of Roman rule, German tribesmen took over the East End – I bet you didn't know that. *Stibba* people came to Stepney, *Bleda* to Bethnal Green and *Weappa* to Wapping. The country was re-Christianised and a small wooden church appeared in *Stibba*, that's when the church began its six-hundred-year rule in East London,' Dolly finished proudly.

'That's very interesting, Dolly.' Hannah went very quiet and then said, 'I didn't think I had an accent . . .'

'I never said you did. It's the *way* you talk. You can always tell.'

'Tom'll be in soon,' said Emmie, coming into the room. 'He's just having a quick shave and change of clothes. You took him by surprise, turning up like this, Jessie. Took us all by surprise.' She placed the tray on a small side table and told the girls to help themselves. Dolly was in like a shot.

'How many sugars, Jessie?' asked Hannah.

'Give her six to fatten her up a bit, she's too skinny.'

'Just *one*, thanks, Hannah.' Jessie scowled at Dolly. She wanted her support right now, not torment. Jessie was beginning to feel she'd done the wrong thing, barging in on Tom's family like this.

'Well, I'll leave you to it, girls,' said Emmie. She was worried her tense expression would give things away. 'I've work to do in the kitchen. Give my regards to your mother, Jessie.'

'How come you know Mum?' asked Dolly.

'She doesn't, Dolly. We were in the papers, don't forget. Most people around her know about Dad's accident. Isn't that right, Emmie?'

'Yes, that's right.' She sniffed the air. 'Ah, here he comes, his Brylcreem goes before 'im.' Sure enough, Tom came in a moment later, going straight to the tea table.

'It's funny you should come round, Jess, I was gonna pop round to you earlier than I said, as it happens. There's a meeting at my club that I can't miss.' He poured himself a cup of tea. 'If I do come round, I can only see you for an hour or so. Is that all right?'

'An hour? But it's Saturday night, Tom.' Jessie tried to hide her disappointment.

'I know. Can't be helped.' He sipped his tea and winked at her. 'I'll make it up to you tomorrow. We'll spend the day over

Victoria Park and I'll take you on a boat. I'll even let Mum make us a picnic up.'

'Sounds lovely to me,' said Dolly, stretching and showing her legs and leaning back in the armchair as if she was at home. 'What club is it?' she asked, thinking she might go and keep Tom company.

'Trade union. Stuff and nonsense but there you are, it's all to the good.'

'Speaking of which,' said Hannah, 'I'd best be going. I'll see you there, Tom. Try not to be late.'

'Oh, so you're going as well, are you, Hannah?' said Dolly.

'Yes. I help the secretary – take notes of the meeting, that kind of thing.' Hannah was covering up for Tom and Jessie sensed it, but she would say nothing, she could rely on Dolly to ask the questions.

'Are there many girls there then?'

'Not too many,' Hannah told her.

'So it's mostly men?'

'You could say that.'

'I wouldn't mind joining a club like that,' said Dolly, thinking about all the lads who might be there.

'You have to be a member of the union,' said Tom. 'The Workers Union.'

'Oh, that lets me out then. You must be popular, Hannah. Not much female competition.'

'Does that pot want refilling yet?' Emmie was back in the doorway, being mother.

'No more for me, thank you,' said Jessie, ready to leave. She wanted to go home, to have a chance to think things over. She did trust Tom, but she could tell he was lying about where he and Hannah were going, and she didn't like it.

'Are you a member of the trade union as well, Mrs Smith?' joked Dolly.

'Trade union? Ha, not likely.' She turned to Tom. 'Have you glanced at today's paper yet, Tom? Unemployment's set to rise again. The docks'll be the first to be hit, you won't find so much work down there if this goes on. That's why I think you should be casting your nets for back-up wages instead of wasting time on *union meetings*.' Emmie didn't believe his story about where he was going any more than Jessie did.

Emmie sat down and looked from Tom to Jessie. 'I've come up with an idea. A bloody marvellous idea. But to see it through we'll need a bit of capital. Property investment. It's just the right time to buy and rent out, I reckon. The houses round this way will never be as cheap as they are now.'

Tom looked astonished. 'You want to buy this house, Mother? Whatever for? I know the rent went up but—'

'Not this one, no, but the rent rise is exactly the point. I'm talking about four terraced houses, the two up, two downs in Grant Street. I got the word today and I think we should move ourselves, get in quick. The landlord, like a lot of other people, believes there'll be a war and if there is, this part of London'll be hit. Well, let 'em think that way, let 'em sell up cheap and go off to Dagenham to buy rows of houses there. It'll make way for the likes of us.'

'How much are the houses?' said Jessie, holding back on her enthusiasm. A two up, two down was the very thing that she and Tom would be needing, now a baby was on the way – not that Emmie and Tom knew that.

'Three hundred pounds for each one, I heard,' Emmie continued, 'but that's way over the top. I should think the man will take a lot less than that. He's got other property to sell and he wants the cash quick to reinvest.' She breathed in as if the air was fresh off the sea. 'I've always fancied owning a bit of property.' Tom's sudden reflective mood gave her hope. She could see he was listening. 'Your dad's got a bit put by in his post office account, Tom, and Johnnie's got a few bob in the bank. You should think about it too, Hannah,' she said, without thinking.

'But I don't have any money, Emmie, you know that,' said Hannah.

'Not now ... no,' said Emmie. Quickly checking herself, she added, 'Well you know your dad's been sending money for years. I should think it's mounted up by now.'

'Yes, but my mother wouldn't give me any of that. It's hers. It's definitely hers.'

'Well, maybe she'll come round one of these days, eh?'

Jessie had slipped into a world of her own as she thought of herself and Tom owning a house. A surge of excitement rushed through her. Her hand instinctively moved across her stomach to where her baby was growing and she smiled inwardly. This was turning out to be a visit and a half. 'I've got some money coming to me,' she murmured dreamily. 'If I have a word with Mum ... she might be interested in making an investment.'

Tom chuckled quietly, and Emmie glared at him. 'You think it's funny, do you?'

'I think that you talking like a property magnate is, Mother. Hilarious. You're living with the fairies again,' he said, adding to the insult, which made Jessie see red.

'I think your mother's right, Tom.' Relaxing into the armchair, Jessie felt a strange calm come over her. 'But if there is going to be a war, would it be wise to buy houses around here, Emmie?'

'It's a risk but I think it's one worth taking. We can take out insurance, don't forget, and war or no war, in a few years that row of houses'll be worth a damn sight more than the landlord'll accept right now.'

'Could we go and see inside them today?' asked Jessie, surprising everyone.

Tom's patronising chuckle riled Jessie but she held her tongue. 'I thought you had more sense than that, Jess,' he said, 'listening to the ramblings of an old woman.'

'I would like to see them!' snapped Jessie, furious with him for the way he was patronising both her and his mother. 'Because you see, Emmie' she went on impulsively, 'I'm having your son's baby.' There was a stunned silence in the room. 'So we'll be needing a little place of our own – or I will, at least.'

The silence continued to hang in the air.

'I hadn't meant to break the news like this,' Jessie added, 'but since those houses are coming up ...'

It was Dolly who broke the deathly hush. 'God, Jessie, Mum will do her *nut*. Phew. And you'll cop it, Tom.' Dolly sounded genuinely worried. Scared even.

'Well, well, well. There's one in the eye for all of us,' said Emmie, stunned.

'When our Jessie drops a bombshell she really drops one.' Dolly shook her head as if it was the end of the world. 'Mum'll blame you, Tom. She won't have you in our house now. You've done it now. She'll send Jess away, and once the baby's born, she'll get it adopted ... and she won't let Jessie ever see you—'

'That's enough, Dolly,' said Jessie. She looked across the room at Tom. There wasn't a flicker of movement in his face or his eyes. Then he licked his lips with his tongue, swallowed, then licked them again. He was well and truly knocked for six.

'What the bleeding hell's going on?' Charlie stood in the doorway. 'It's like a morgue in 'ere. What's 'appened? Em?'

'It's all right, Charlie,' said Emmie, as if in a trance. 'Tom's having a baby, that's all.'

There was a moment's pause while Charlie took this in. 'Fair enough,' he said, rubbing his chin. 'St Peter's. It'll have to be St Peter's. All my family have wedded there and been christened there.'

'St Dunstan's is my church,' said Jessie to Charlie. She had found an ally. A prop.

'Well, you please yourself, gel. We'd best 'ave your mother over for tea, though, to talk about it. I haven't seen Rose in years.'

'Go and check that tap in the back yard, would you, Charlie,' said Emmie, glaring at her husband. 'I think someone might have left it running.'

'You what? Tch. Wasting bloody water,' he grumbled, turning to leave.

'Do you know Mum then?' said Dolly, mystified. 'Jessie never said anything about—'

'No, I didn't. Because I never knew,' said Jessie, looking at Tom for an explanation.

Emmie flicked her hand at Charlie, a casual signal for him to leave. He made a hasty exit. 'That was donkey years ago,' she said, covering herself. 'It's a pity the silly old sod's short-term memory is not so good. He was the one who left the tap running. So,' she said, shaking her head gravely, 'we have a little problem then.'

Turning away from Emmie's chiding eyes, Jessie braced herself for what was to come, hoping that Tom might take the lead, but it was not to be.

Emmie finally spoke. 'You have shocked me, Jessie, taken the wind out of all our sails, I should think.'

'So, shall we all go and look at those two up, two downs then?' said Jessie, desperate to avoid any debate on the matter.

'I think you might have told me when we were on our own,' said Tom, his face drawn with worry.

'I was going to but ... it just came out. I'd said it before I knew.' She bit on her bottom lip. 'I'm sorry.'

He looked away from her and drew breath. 'It would have been nice to be the first to be told.'

Charlie came back into the doorway, easing the tension. 'I'll have to give the place a coat of emulsion, Em, if there's to be a wedding. We got any more of that green paint left?'

'You've been at that bloody whisky bottle, 'aven't you?' Emmie said, bemused by his casual handling of the situation. 'I marked the label so I'll know, Charlie.'

He flapped his hand and left, making for the street door. His voice once again cut through the awkward silence. He was on the doorstep outside, calling to a neighbour. 'Harry, mate!

Come and 'ave a drink. Our Tom's just got himself engaged. Fetch Winnie and the girls. I'll send one of my lads out for a crate of beer!'

'Charlie! Come inside! You bloody fool!' Emmie turned to Jessie, apologising. 'Showing us all up like that. I'll take the rolling pin to him, so help me. Charlie! Get in here!'

'Oh, don't be like that, Em,' said Charlie, back in the doorway. 'This is a proud moment for me. We're gonna 'ave a wedding at last ... and I'm gonna be a grandfather.'

'Go upstairs and have a wash and shave. And put on a clean shirt! We'll all go round the pub once Tom and Jessie get back from ... where they're going.' She didn't want to tell him about the houses and start him off again. 'Save your invites for the wedding day, you bloody fool.' She turned to Jessie and did her best to make things easier for her. 'Well, go on then, the pair of you. Go and take a look at what we were talking about. See what you think.'

Jessie caught on. She could see the sense in not letting on to Charlie just yet.

'And that's it, Mother?' said Tom, baffled. 'No angry lectures? No excitement? Nothing?' He sounded let down by the casualness of it all. He was, after all, going to be a dad.

'It's a bit late for lectures. Save the excitement for when you get back from Grant Street. And as for nothing, don't you ever call my grandchild a nothing!'

Tom's face broke into a smile and then quiet laughter. 'She's taking over already, Jess.'

Jessie looked back at him, smiling shyly as the happiness slowly returned.

Practically pushing Tom and Jessie out of the door, Emmie said goodbye to Dolly and asked her to pass on her best to their mother. 'You'd better not let on to your mother that it's out in the open,' she said. 'We don't want her thinking I wormed it out of Jessie first. Have a drop of brandy ready, though, for both your sister and your mother. They'll need it.

She's not going to be the least bit happy about this, make no mistake.'

Outside in the street, Jessie took Tom's arm and squeezed it, whispering in his ear that she loved him and wanted to have his baby more than anything. Before he could respond, his brother Stanley yelled to him from the end of the turning.

'Tom! Hang about. Where you going?' Stanley, looking rugged and handsome in his work clothes and boots, swaggered towards them, his eye on Dolly.

'We're just off to see a man about a dog, Stan. Catch you later, boy.'

'Hold your horses, Tom. Slow down.' Arriving at Dolly's side, he gave her the once over and then winked. 'Who's this then?'

'Jessie's sister, Dolly. Jessie, meet my kid brother, Stanley.'

'Hello, Stanley,' smiled Jessie, loving his style.

'All right, Jess?' He spoke as if he'd known her for an age. He turned back to Dolly. 'Fancy coming out for a beer tonight?'

'I don't drink beer,' she said. 'Mine's a port.'

'Whoooo, the girl's got taste, Tom. I'll call for you at eight. Be ready.' Giving them a quick nod, he slipped into the house, calling to Charlie, telling him to put the kettle on.

Dolly was over the moon. 'Well, it looks like I won't be going out with my mates tonight after all,' she said with a huge smile.

Having told Stanley off for shouting in the street, Emmie went back into the sitting room. Hannah was still there, alone and looking sad. 'You should have gone with them, love. Why didn't you?'

'They didn't ask me. I wasn't part of that happy scene.' She smiled bravely. 'It's all right, Emmie, I understand. I'm not really family . . .'

'Don't talk so daft. But what about this shocking news, eh?' How Emmie longed to sit down and tell her that she was going to be an aunt.

Hannah made no response. She sat gazing at the fireplace, miles away.

'Of course you're family, Hannah,' said Emmie, patting her hand. 'Don't be upset, they'll realise you've been left behind and be more the sorry for it. Excitement got the better of them, that's all.'

'No, I don't think so. My place is with my mother whether I like it or not – until I move away, that is.' Hannah raised her eyes to Emmie's. 'Do you know what she said to me the day after Tom was beaten up, when I was in bed crying over it? "You think that lying in bed will make your friend better, Hannah? No one, *no one*, feels sorry for those who feel sorry for themselves. Get up and open the windows, let the air in. All I can smell in here is stale air and stale clothes." Why does she hate me so much, Emmie? What did I do?'

Gutted, Emmie swallowed. 'There's always the attic room, Hannah. I've told you that before. We could clear it out and make space for a single bed and a cupboard. It wouldn't be the Grand but it's better than ... living with that woman.'

'That woman. She's my mother and yet I also think of her as that woman. Why? I just don't understand. Look how you are with your sons.' She turned back to the fireplace. 'But never mind, I'll find a room somewhere soon, further away from here. I can't take much more, Emmie. I can't bear it in that place, not even in my own room. And she's the one to blame for Tom joining the Blackshirts, not me.'

'You think I don't know that? I know your mother better than you think, Hannah.'

'She tells me over and over, "You have no pluck, no mettle. I spit on you." Tell me, Emmie, tell me the truth, do other mothers talk to their children like that? Am I too sensitive, like she says?'

'You are sensitive, love, and that's no bad thing. But no, a mother doesn't usually say such things.'

'I thought that Tom wouldn't want to see me again after

he was beaten up. I didn't think I would be welcome here, but I was wrong. You've been kind to me, all of you, but it's time I sorted out a life for myself.

'It's a very strange thing, but once my mother had finished going on at me that morning, a kind of feeling of freedom passed over me. I opened the curtains in my room to let in fresh air and sunshine, and as it flooded in, quite suddenly I was filled with a sensation that someone was there, giving me love and comfort and hope. I didn't hear a voice exactly but a message ran through my brain – the very gentle voice of a man. "It's all right, Hannah," he said. "Everything is going to be all right." Does that sound foolish?'

'No, Hannah, it doesn't.' Deeply moved by what she had said, Emmie took time to settle herself. Hannah could not know that on that morning her real father, Robert, had been killed. While she was lying on her bed, he was lying dead in the River Thames.

Shuddering, Emmie collected herself. 'It's a strange world we live in, Hannah, a very strange world.'

'Do you think it's possible that my father was picking up on my misery, from all those miles away in New Zealand?'

'It's possible, love, who are we to say?'

'Emmie . . .' Hannah's eyes moistened. 'Why didn't he come back for me?'

This was all a bit too much for Emmie, this conversation. What could she say to Hannah? What could she say to make her feel worthy of herself? She didn't know why Jack hadn't come back for her. She wasn't a mind reader.

'He will come for you, Hannah. He said he would and he will. I expect he's been saving for the fare all these years, his fare over here and both fares back. That's a lot of money, love, and it would take a long time for him to save that much.' She said this having decided that as soon as Hannah left to go home, she would write to Rose's brother Jack in New Zealand. Enough was enough. It was time he got over here and sorted things out. Rose would know his address, surely, or Grandmother Blake, if it came to that.

Once Hannah had gone home, Emmie made the most of the quiet to think about the eventful afternoon and wondered if outside forces were at work, herding Rose and herself together again and into pastures they'd visited before.

Chapter Nine

Jessie was pleased to find that Grant Street was only a five-minute walk from Tom's house. Had it been further they would have got into conversation about her condition and she didn't want that. That would come later when she and Tom were by themselves. Looking at him, she could see that he was in a daze, one minute a wry smile on his face and the next thoughtful.

'They must be the ones,' said Tom, looking across the narrow road at four houses in the terrace. There weren't any For Sale boards out but it was obvious that no one was living in any of them.

'Looks like someone's got here before you,' said Dolly, looking up at a window where a woman was staring out at them.

'Stroke of luck,' smiled Tom. 'Let's hope they've got keys to all four houses.'

They crossed the narrow cobbled road and while Jessie peered into the filthy downstairs windows, Tom knocked on the door. It wasn't long before they heard footsteps echoing on the floorboards. 'Let me do the talking, girls, all right?' he said.

'Ay ay, Captain,' said Dolly, giving a fine salute which Tom ignored. 'House ahoy!'

'Daft as a brush,' he said. 'Should go down well with Stanley.'

The door, after a couple of jerks from the inside and a nudge from Tom's foot, finally opened to reveal a man in his fifties, wearing a suit and tie.

'What can I do for yer?' he said, frowning, as if they had disturbed him.

Tom offered his hand. 'Sorry to bother you, mate, but we've just heard that these places are coming up for sale and I'm interested.'

'In all four of them?' The man eyed him suspiciously.

'Depends. Need a lot of work doing to 'em,' said Tom, stepping back and giving them the once over. 'Are you the owner or a contender?'

'I'm showing someone around. The couple's only interested in this one. I'm looking for three hundred and twenty for each one, but I'm a fair man and it's open to discussion.'

Hearing quiet conversation from the couple who had been viewing the upstairs, Tom gave Jessie and Dolly a sign to keep quiet.

'I think we've seen enough, thanks,' said the woman who looked to be in her thirties and down on her luck.

'More than enough,' said her husband, a short, squat man. 'If we can pay five shillings a week, we'll take it. Between us we can clean the rest of 'em up and caretake for yer, two years rent at five bob a week and you've got a deal.'

Ushering them out as quickly as possible, the owner told them he'd be in touch and then turned to Tom. 'Dreamers,' he said, rolling his eyes.

'All right to come in and have a butchers then?' Tom was behaving as if he had a wad of money burning a hole in his back pocket.

'Don't see why not. In you come. You as well, girls. Can't have you standing out there, can we? Someone might run off with yer. He's a lucky man, I'll say that for 'im, two women and looking to buy four houses. Can't be bad.'

'I'm his future sister-in-law, actually,' said Dolly, sweeping past him. 'Growing mushrooms, are you, or is that damp I can smell?'

Laughing at her, the man closed the door behind them. 'You'll smell more than damp by the time you've viewed these properties, my love. If you're looking for fresh paint and lace curtains, you'd best look elsewhere.'

'Take no notice of her,' said Tom. 'She was born with a silver spoon in her mouth. Be all right once I shove a scrubbing brush and bucket of hot soda water in her hands.' He patted the passage wall. 'Trouble is, she's right. The place is damp.'

'That's why they're cheap. Mind you, it's not as bad as—'

'Cheap?' said Tom, stopping his flow. 'Who're you kidding? I do read the papers, you know. A new three-bedroom semi with garden and garage costs as much as you're asking for these slums. I wasn't born yesterday so show a bit of respect.'

Tom's audacity paid off. The man sniffed and considered. 'True,' he said finally, 'you can get a new house for what I'm asking but that's in the suburbs. Add fares or petrol onto that and—'

'How much?' said Tom, halfway amused by the charade.

'And you're after all four? Well, we landlords have to scratch each other's backs, I suppose.'

'I'm not a landlord, but I've got brothers and we might be interested if the price is right.'

'Mmm.' He sucked his teeth and slowly shook his head. 'It's one price for the dealer and one for the public, you see. We have to be fair. A dealer's got to make a profit, whereas you—'

'Six hundred for the four of 'em – if I like what I see once I've had a butchers at the insides.'

'Six hundred? You out of your mind or what? Six hundred. Oh dear, oh dear, oh dear. You are a card. Well now, let's see, *might* let them go for a grand if it's cash in hand. Can't say fairer than that.'

'Six hundred but not all in cash. There aren't many who could come up with that kind of money. Make it six and you can have two hundred in notes.' Tom was thinking about Johnnie and his bank account.

'Well, you might as well take a look now that you've come. Rock-solid, these little houses. Built to last and only been standing for twenty-five years or so.'

'Is that right? So whoever had that date inscribed on the plaque outside was telling pork pies then.'

The man looked at Tom, his eyes narrowing. 'Outside, you say?'

'That's right. It's filthy but my eyes are good. Eighteen ninety.'

'Do you know, I've never noticed that. Well, that throws a different light on things. That was a very good year for building houses, and once you've got all the windows and the back door open, I reckons this damp'll dry out. It makes no odds to me anyway, these'll be gone by the end of next week at the price I'm asking. I hate to let them go but I've been made an offer I can't refuse – in Dagenham. Row of cottages, ten of 'em. They were gonna be demolished to make space for a factory, some kind of fashion industry.' He shrugged. 'I should get a good price for 'em once I've done them up a bit. They're more for your middle-class sort of person.'

'Is it all right if we look round then?' said Dolly, breaking up the chummy monologue.

'Course it is.' He looked at his wristwatch. 'Fifteen minutes and I'll be back. Here, take the keys so you can have a look at the others as well. One's much the same as the other but you'll still want to go over 'em. I can see you've got your wits about you. If you can raise the six hundred for all four, you'd be a fool not to grab 'em. If you are interested, I can arrange for electricity to be wired.' He tapped the side of his nose. 'You name it, I've got the contacts.'

'That's decent of you, trusting me with the keys.' Tom looked him straight in the eye and waited for the catch.

'Well, you're 'ardly gonna run off with 'em, are you? Ta ta, girls – for now.' With a wink and a grin, he strode off down the road.

'Tom? You didn't really expect him to come down that much in price, did you?' asked Jessie.

'I'm kicking myself, Jess, I should have said five hundred. Never mind, we'll send Mother round to see him, she'll get it down to five for us, you'll see. Right then.' Tom rubbed his hands together. 'You girls check this one out while I take a look at the others. Don't forget to look at the back yard – and the lav.' Tom went straight out and into the house next door.

'Well, this is all exciting, Jess. I wonder if there's a cellar.' Without another word, Dolly was gone, in search of treasure, leaving Jessie to herself.

She placed the flat of her hand on the passage wall and checked all along it and yes, it was damp here and there, and the place did smell of dirt, but there was something appealing about it. She hadn't seen any of the rooms, but she liked the house. Leaning on the passage wall she imagined it with fresh white paint on the woodwork and delicately flowered wallpaper. Plain white nets and curtains at the window, nice lino on the floor and a couple of rugs.

Dolly returned, wiping the dust from her hands onto the skirt of her frock. 'Why does this house seem much older than ours when it's not?'

'Because it's not lived in, Dolly. What would you expect?' Jessie was already being defensive about the house, as if it was her own.

'Maybe it's because it's got a cellar and the rooms are small, but it's got a good feel about it,' said Dolly. 'It reminds me of my local history teacher. He used to live down this road when he taught at our school. He wanted the class to go on a tour of his house, which hadn't been touched, other than cleaned, since it had been built. Even the wallpaper was original, so he said. He was posh but loved the East End,' Dolly prattled on, 'especially Bethnal Green which, according to him, was the nicest of the villages, surrounded by woods, with a small wooden church and cottages. He said the village was ruled by the Lord of the Manor in Chaucer's time. He'd go on for hours about Chaucer, where he lived, where he ate, what he did for entertainment. It is interesting, mind you,' she continued, opening a corner cupboard and flinching at the sight of a spider. 'Chaucer took lodgings in the Gate House, over the Ald Gate. The rooms had a cellar beneath and when the first bell of the day tolled, the great gates were swung open and—'

'Yeah, all right, Dolly. You do get carried away. Could you see anything in the cellar or is it too dark down there?'

'Too dark.' She turned and leaned on the wall, arms folded, still there, back in the days of Chaucer. 'Grain and dung carts would arrive from Essex, cattle being driven through, and pigs, herded onto Smith Fields.'

'You amaze me sometimes, Dolly. How you fitted so much information into your brain, I don't know. Maybe that's why you 'ave trouble taking things in now, it's all crammed with Chaucer.'

'Yeah, but just imagine it, Jess. The lowing of cattle, the creaking rattle of carts and the clip of hooves. Street vendors shouting, "*Rabbit and venison pie! Roast pork! Pheasant! Eels peppered! Saffron mackerel!*" Not to mention "*Strawberries, ripe! Strawberries ripe!*"'

'You'll end up being carted off yourself if you go on like that. Come on.'

'I've seen enough,' said Dolly. 'I'll go and find Tom and look at the others. Let's hope they haven't got rats in the back yard as well. I saw one run along the fence, just now.'

'Dolly, that's not funny!'

'It wasn't meant to be, don't get so aerated, Jessie, think of *the baby*.' Dolly grinned, pleased at the thought of becoming an auntie. 'Anyway, a single rat's nothing. One trap and it'll be dead. Clonk!'

'If it really was one then there'll be more,' said Jessie.

'I wish I hadn't mentioned it now, one single rat and you go white. There won't be another plague, don't worry. The plague bell won't toll, Jessie.'

'Dolly, stop it. Go and find Tom and drive *him* mad.'

Thankful to be in the house by herself, Jessie walked cautiously around, looking and listening for any signs of vermin. Her fears soon dissolved as she went from one small room to another and out into the back yard. She loved the place. When she caught sight of a mouse scampering around an old ruined shed, she shuddered and then smiled. At least Dolly was wrong about the rat. You won't find rats where there are mice, her mother had always insisted.

Standing in the middle of the downstairs room, Jessie admired the small old-fashioned cupboards and shelves. They gave the place a cottage feel. The scullery had an open fireplace which smelled of damp coal and there were antiquated brass oil lamps hanging in every room. In each of the fireplaces, there were gas pokers and on the windowsills burned down candles. Cobwebs were everywhere.

Above the street door there was an arched coloured-glass window, with just one small crack in one of the panes. The sun shining through cast a ray of yellow and pink light into the hallway. Jessie avoided the cellar which was small and pitch black. The two bedrooms upstairs were fine and once they had peeled off the layers of lino, she felt sure it would smell a lot better. The late afternoon sun seemed to be shining in through every window, as if it was welcoming her into this new home. She wondered what Tom was making of the other three and of Dolly's chatter.

'It's true, Tom, honest, Stepney *was* a village, with rich and poor, farmers and millers – a thriving village. And I'll tell you something else. Way back, the Duchess of Suffolk had a house in Stepenham and a marquis had a mansion just by the church.

Our part of the woods was seen as a *rural retreat*. London's back yard, more like. Still is.'

'Do me a favour, Doll, and pass me that old bit of curtain cane on the windowsill. I want to measure this room,' said Tom, paying not the slightest attention to her ramblings.

Sighing, Dolly handed him the curtain rod. 'I'm going next door, see what Jessie's up to.' She left him to it, wondering why he couldn't show just a bit of interest in the way things used to be.

'Tom's been in and out of all the other three, she said, joining Jessie in one of the bedrooms. 'I bet that brass bed'd come up a treat. Some of the bits of furniture want chucking on the bonfire but some of it's solid oak and sound. Did you see that bedside cabinet in the other bedroom? I should imagine that's an antique. Early Victorian.'

'I wouldn't want it.'

'I wasn't thinking of using any of it, Jessie. I'd clean it up, polish it, and put it in the auction rooms. My friend's dad does that – he earns out of it as well. Used to be a rag and bone man. Now he's gone upmarket.'

'You upstairs, girls?' called Tom from below.

'Yes. Come on up!'

'No need,' he called back. 'I've seen enough. I wanna get back and fetch Mum and the boys to have a look, while I've still got the keys.'

'Looks like someone's thinking of going into the property market,' said Dolly. 'We'd best get home, you've got some music to face.'

Not wishing to spoil her present carefree mood, Jessie ignored Dolly's reminder of the battle to come. 'So you like it then?' she said as they went down the stairs.

'I will once you've scrubbed it. Don't know what Mum'll think though.'

'I think she'll like it,' murmured Jessie, 'and she'll love the idea of a Warner owning their own house. It's what she and Dad always wanted.'

'Mmm,' smiled Dolly, 'but not quite as soon as this.'

Closing the front door behind them and linking arms with Tom, Jessie was touched to see that her sister was being thoughtful and strolling ahead, giving them a chance to talk privately about buying one of the houses. 'What do you think then?' she said, hoping Tom liked what he'd seen as much as she did.

'I think you'll make the best mum in the world, Jessie Warner.' He put his arm round her waist and gently squeezed her. 'The best mum and the best wife. I'm the luckiest man alive.'

'That's not what I meant, I was talking about the house. I daren't ask how you feel about . . . well, you know.'

'Shocked. Bloody shocked. But I keep seeing this tiny little version of you,' he said, his emotions stirred. 'Anyway, the house. If we can buy the four off him, we'd get a good deal. How we'll raise the money is something else but we've got to do it, it makes sense.' He grinned broadly. 'The Smiths owning property. That'll be one in the eye for some of the neighbours, I can tell you, and Mum deserves the thrill she'd get from it. She's been a grafter all her life, Jessie. So has Dad. There are four working men and one working woman at home and Johnnie's got enough cash in the bank to buy one for himself. He'll put in a word with the bank manager for the rest of us. I don't like to ask, Jess, but—'

'There'll be enough from my share of the compensation money for us to buy one. Mum says it should all be settled in a month or two.'

'No. I didn't mean that. I meant will you be able to manage? If I get one of these mortgages, well, we'd be a bit struck for cash for a while. I'll get two jobs, of course I will, but—'

'Tom I want to use the money to buy that house, there's no point in lining the bank's coffers with interest payments. If we use my money, we can use your wages to do the place up a bit and buy some furniture – second-hand furniture that we can paint nice light colours. We don't have to move in straightaway and we needn't get married for another two months – that's if you want to get married.'

'Nah, not me, you'll have to find someone else. Sod that for a lark,' he said, sounding serious. 'I'll still buy one of them houses though, in case I find someone I do want to marry.'

'Stop it, Tom. I've been worried sick in case you wanted to get rid of me.'

'Oh, thanks. You think I'd do a thing like that, do you?'

She squeezed his hand. 'Sorry. I was just checking. Anyway, can we use my money to buy it?'

'No. That's your money, Jessie. I'm not touching that.'

'Once we're married, it'll be *our* money, Tom. I'll tell you what, I'll do a deal with you. I'll say no more about you having joined the Blackshirts, because I know you have, if you let me do what I want to do with my own funds. If your brothers and your mum manage to buy the other three, all well and good, but don't bank on it. Let's just think about us.'

'Fair enough, Jess, but if you use your money, the house'll be in your name. It's your name that goes on the deeds or nothing.'

'That sounds fair,' she said, not caring one way or the other.

'If you're really sure it's what you want ... I'll work day and night to make it like a little palace for you. I can get a bit of work down the market as well as at the docks. I'll work my fingers to the bone. I will, Jessie. I'll work till I drop.' Taking her by surprise, he let go of her hand and lifted her high in the air. 'My Jessie, having my baby. What more could a man want?'

'A two up, two down?' she said, laughing. 'Put me down, Tom. You might drop me.'

'Never in a million years would I drop you, sweetheart.' He slowly lowered her until her feet touched the ground, and kissed her. 'I love you, Jess. I love you so much it hurts. I've driven the blokes down the docks mad, telling them how lovely my Jessie is.'

'I love you as well,' she said, brushing a kiss across his cheek, 'but I've got to get back home now, to face Mum. She's not gonna be as thrilled about this as we are.'

'Do you want me to come with you?' he said, but half-heartedly.

'No. That wouldn't go down very well. She'll want me to herself so she can vent her anger. I'm going to have to look a very sorry daughter, Tom, full of regret. No, I don't think your being there'll help, the opposite in fact.'

'Thank God for that.' He gave her a peck on the cheek. 'I was dreading you'd want me to be there. Go on then. Catch Dolly up. I've got a meeting to go to.'

A deep and worried sigh escaped from Jessie. 'I hope you haven't joined just to get your own back, Tom. It was a street brawl and you came off worse. Why can't you just leave it at that?'

'It's not revenge, Jessie. I believe in the cause. I love my country and I don't want to see it going down the pan with every Tom, Dick and Harry coming in from every bloody country. I'm not saying we should kick out all the foreigners, they're here now, but something's got to be done to stop them pouring in. Britain's not that big a place, and England's a lot smaller. It stands to reason, if you pour too much beer into a glass, what happens?'

'It spills over and makes a mess. Trust you to use beer as an example.'

'Now stop worrying over it and mind your own business.' He glanced at her stomach. 'You've got enough to think about now.'

'But they're Fascists, Tom.'

'Fascists. People say that as if it's the devil with horns they're talking about.' He shrugged. 'It's no more than a bunch of politicians trying to do what they think is right for their country. You can't blame 'em for that, Jess, and before you even think of asking, no, I won't be chalking insults on walls or throwing bricks through windows. But I will go to the meetings, and I will march with them, and I will beat the drum. I'll beat the drum for England. Our England, Jessie. Our children's England.' Smiling at her, he brushed loose strands of hair off her face. 'I promise you one thing, if war comes, Blackshirts and Jews will fight alongside each other, the same as we live alongside each other, the same as we love to have a good punch-up now and then, and the same as we fall in love with each other. You loved Max – he was a Jew. I once courted a girl who was Jewish and she adored me. Couldn't keep her hands off!' He kissed the tip of her nose and winked. 'Stop thinking about things that don't concern you. Think about what kind of wallpaper you'd like to see in the nursery instead. I think the back bedroom'd make a smashing little nursery.'

Quietly laughing at him, Jessie shrugged off her worry. 'I don't agree but I don't care, not right now.' She did care but that could wait until they were married, then she'd change his way of thinking. 'So you liked it then? The house I was looking at?'

'I preferred one of the others which had a little lean-to out the back. We could use that for a kitchen, once I'd fixed the broken panes and that.'

'We could let that second bedroom – until baby comes along,' said Jessie, thinking of Hannah.

'That's true.' He held each side of her face and kissed her. 'See you later. Good luck with your mother.'

Stepping up her pace to catch Dolly, Jessie was filled with thoughts of the future and the last person on her mind right then was Max, but there he was, standing outside the Bancroft Hospital, chatting to Dolly. She hadn't seen him since the day she threw his gifts back at him.

'Hello, Jessie,' he said, looking sheepishly at her. 'You look well.'

'Thanks. How are you – and the family?' She could feel herself blush. 'Your mum and dad all right?'

'So so.'

The awkward silence that followed was broken by Dolly who once again was being tactful. 'Nice to see you again, Max.' She turned to Jessie and winked. 'I'll see you back at the house.'

'Don't say anything, Dolly!' Jessie called after her. Dolly didn't look back but just raised a hand.

'She's growing up at last,' said Max, smiling. 'I suppose that's because of your dad. It takes shock and grief to pull us round sometimes.'

Jessie decided to get to the point. 'Seeing a photo of you kissing another girl gave me a jolt, I can tell you, but I can see now that Moira had a point, we weren't really right for each other, not for marriage, and I think you know that, Max, deep down.'

'My family don't rule my life, you know. They couldn't see it working but that doesn't mean to say that I felt the same. You did though,' he shrugged, 'so there we are. One little lecture from Moira and you ran. I think I had more of a shock than you, Jessie.'

'Are you seeing the girl in the photograph, Max?'

'Of course I see her, I've been seeing her since I was very small. Her family and mine are very close. I've taken her out a couple of times since we broke up, yes.'

'Well, there you are then. There must be something between you and there's no way I would have put up with that.'

Max looked sad. 'But I still love you, Jessie. I'll always love you. If anything goes wrong, promise you'll come and see me, or write. Promise?'

'Do things have to go wrong then? For us to stay friends?' Jessie smiled, trying to cheer him up.

'No, we don't have to wait for that.'

'Max ...' Jessie searched for the right words. 'Max, don't wait for me and Tom to break up. It's not going to happen.

I know it's all a bit sudden but,' she clenched her hands, her fingernails digging into her flesh, 'we're going to be married, quite soon.' She reeled off the last line very quickly.

'That's absurd, Jessie, and you know it. You know nothing about each other. How could you in so short a time?'

'I love him, Max,' she said, shrugging. 'We've been together a while now. I don't need longer than that.'

He looked from her face to her stomach. 'Well, I hope it all goes right for you. Dolly said something and I guessed the rest.'

'Oh. Well, it's not a case of *having* to, if that's what you think,' Jessie said hastily.

'No, it's not a case of having to because I would marry you tomorrow. I wouldn't mind about ...' He nodded at her stomach. 'I would bring it up as my own.' He took her hand and moved closer. 'Jessie, please don't marry that man. It's too quick. Marry me instead. Please, darling, I'm begging you. Don't do it. Please don't do it.'

That man. Max had referred to Tom as *that* man. Did he know already? Had he found out more about Tom than he was letting on? 'Tom's a decent bloke, Max.'

'No, Jessie. He's not. I know what I'm talking about. I know his brother, Johnnie.'

Jessie slowly withdrew her hand and smiled weakly. 'Maybe in another life, eh?'

'This *is* our life, Jessie. We should be together.'

She was beginning to feel trapped. 'Look, let me come round to see you now and then, or let's meet up for coffee. We don't have to cut each other off. You'll find someone else to love, a nice Jewish girl, someone who'll fit in. Let's stay friends.'

He looked down at the ground. 'If that's what you want. It's better than nothing. You can phone me at the office.' He slipped his hand inside his pocket and pulled out a small wad of business cards. 'I've been promoted,' he smiled. 'Junior accountant. I get to deal with the small uncomplicated clients.'

'You deserve it.' She took the card and nodded. 'I'll have to go. I've got to break the news to Mum. Don't say anything, will you, to Moira or your mum and dad or—'

'Of course I won't say anything. Besides, you're not married to him yet.' Choked, he turned and walked away, thinking that he would make it his business to keep in touch with her, married or not. Once she learned that Tom was a Fascist, she would be shocked, he thought.

When Jessie arrived home, she found Rose in the kitchen boiling the whites. Jessie signalled for Dolly to go upstairs, so that she and their mother could be by themselves. Searching for the right words, Jessie sat on the low windowsill and glanced out at the back garden. She thought about her dad and what he would have said. No matter how hard she tried to picture his reaction, she couldn't. She couldn't even picture herself telling him.

'Mum,' she said, her voice a dead give-away, 'I've got something to tell you, something that you're not going to be pleased about.'

'Go on then,' said Rose in a tone that suggested she was expecting a confession. 'Your sister hasn't said a word out of place but I could tell that something's happened.' She paused. 'Has it got something to do with your visit to Tom's house?'

'Not really. It had already happened before I went. But Tom did ask me to marry him while I was there and I said yes.' She kept her eyes lowered. Her mother's silence told her that she had guessed – there was no need to spell it out.

'I should have realised when you fainted that morning,' said Rose, her tone resigned and dispirited. 'I should have known then. Does Max know?'

'Max? Why do you ask that?'

'Well, he is the father, isn't he? He's got every right to know. He might well want to marry you himself, and I can't say I wouldn't prefer him for a son-in-law, even though he has taken liberties with you.'

'Max isn't the father,' said Jessie, closing her eyes and waiting for the explosion.

'What do you mean?' Rose sounded appalled.

'I'm carrying *Tom's* baby, Mum. We shouldn't have made love but—'

'Good gracious . . .' Rose grabbed the back of a kitchen chair and steadied herself. 'I've never heard such talk. Where do you think you are? In a *brothel*? You bring shame on our good name. I dread to think what your father would say . . . God rest his soul.' She lowered herself into the chair. 'That things should come to this,' she murmured, her voice breaking. 'You've not been with the scoundrel for five minutes.'

'I love him. Really love him. I thought I loved Max but I didn't, I mistook what we had for love. He realises that as well, deep down, that's why he never came round. He's a smashing feller, Mum, but if I married him it wouldn't last five minutes. Either that or we'd both regret it and stay together in a third-rate marriage to keep up appearances.'

'And you think that this fly-by-night will make you happy? Because I don't. I give it a year, if that, before he's off somewhere else.'

'How can you *say* that? You don't *know* him. I'm sorry it's not Max, I know that's what you wanted, to see me off with a solid, reliable husband, but what good is that without love?'

'Rubbish! Love. You don't know what you're talking about. You've a lot to learn yet, my girl. A lot.'

'I know. I've got to learn how to be a mother.'

'There's no "got to" about it! You can have an abortion. I know a decent midwife who'll do it and keep it under wraps. I'll shame myself by going to her over this but it'll be less of a disgrace than letting everyone watch your stomach grow, and you only knowing the father for a second. It'll be all round the streets. We've never had a scandal before, never. I'll thank you not to mention it to anyone, especially my sons.' Rose couldn't know how much she was hurting Jessie with her words.

'I want to have my baby,' she said.

'Out of the question.' Rose shook her head. 'Out of the question.'

'I'm not going to kill my own flesh and blood.'

'You *are* killing your own flesh and blood! You're killing *me*! Haven't I had enough heartache? Wasn't it enough that your father put pride before his fall? He got into that crane *knowing* it was dangerous. *Knowing* he was taking a risk. He left me a widow with *four* children to take care of. Wasn't that *enough*! Did you have to add to it by acting like a whore!'

'I'm sorry. I didn't want this to happen. But it has and I'm keeping it.' Tears were running down Jessie's face.

They made no difference to Rose, she would not allow emotions to rule the day. 'Either you get rid of it or you leave this house. I'll wash my hands of you. I'll have nothing to do with weddings, births or a blighted marriage.' She brought her hand down onto the table with a crashing blow. 'I'll have *nothing* more to do with you if you have this baby! And what's more, you can't marry that man!'

'Why not?'

'You just can't, that's all! That's all there is to it. You will not marry him or see him again! Now let that be an end to it!'

Pressing her hands against her face, Jessie tried to stop crying but it was hopeless; she loved her mother and couldn't bear to hear her saying such things. She loved her father and wanted him to be there, to make everything all right.

'If you go through with this,' said Rose more calmly, 'I mean what I say. You'll have to go. You can have your share of the compensation for the death of your father to set up home. There's to be no more discussion.'

'What if I went away and had it adopted?' said Jessie desperately. 'I would do that if you'd let me go on seeing Tom. If it all works out we could marry later on, in a year or so.'

Rose shuddered and turned her back on Jessie. 'I don't want

to talk about it any more. I can't think straight. I've had a shock. Leave me be.'

Dolly came into the kitchen. Rose straightened her shoulders and lifted her chin. 'Don't creep around like that, Dolly, there's a good girl,' she said. Jessie marvelled at how quickly she could pull herself together.

'I didn't mean to creep. Granny German's arrived. She's upstairs in the sitting room. I said that you and Jessie were having a few private words. Shall I tell her to come down or to go away?'

'Of course you won't tell her to go away, child. I didn't hear the door.'

'No. I was outside, sitting on the step. I saw her coming.'

Rose stood up and brushed her hands down her skirt and pushed her hair into place. 'Make a fresh pot of tea, Dolly, and bring a tray up to the parlour.' She checked her face and hair in the small mirror over the sink. Ignoring Jessie's eyes, she left the room.

Dolly let out a low whistle. 'Rather you than me.' She looked at Jessie's tear-stained face. 'That went down a bomb, didn't it?'

'Worse than I thought it would. She wants me to have an abortion, give up Tom, go back with Max. If I go against her wishes she'll cut me dead. I'll gain a husband and lose a mum. Not a bad day so far, is it?'

'I can't say I'm surprised, you did jump into bed a bit sharpish. I know Tom's irresistible but all the same . . .'

'I'm not ashamed of myself if that's what you think. I'm just angry for not making sure Tom had a Durex.'

'Oh, that's very nice. Speak your mind, don't you?'

'You can learn from my mistake. Don't let your boyfriend have his way unless he puts one on.' Jessie wasn't in the mood for niceties, she wanted to shock someone and Dolly was as good as anyone. 'You should use a Dr Rendall as well, just in case the rubber splits.'

'Stop being so *disgusting*. It's not clever. If Tom could hear you now ... I'm glad it's you getting married and not me. I'm not gonna put up with all that mucky business. It sounds revolting.'

'Why're you smiling then? I can tell you are, Dolly. Little Miss Innocent. Don't tell me that you and Fred didn't do anything naughty.'

'Course we did, but nothing like that! He used to slip his hand inside my knickers and massage me ... and that was lovely. But he never undid his flies when he rubbed against me, I would have punched him in the face if he'd tried that.'

When Dolly had gone upstairs with the tea tray, Jessie felt very low. Upstairs her fate was being discussed. She imagined her mother and Granny German discussing the best way to hide the disgrace – send her away to the country to have the baby and then give it away, or take her to a back street in Whitechapel where she would have it ripped from her. She started to cry again. It all seemed so unfair, what she and Tom had done had happened so naturally, they loved each other in a way that no one could understand and now they were being punished for it. She thought about the little house, her two up, two down with the lean-to that would have been turned into a proper kitchen. She glanced out of the window at the flowers in her dad's garden and imagined her own little house with vases and vases of flowers, picked from her own back yard.

'Mum said will you go up.' Dolly had returned.

'What does she want?'

'How am I s'posed to know?' she said, a touch indignant. 'I don't get talked to around here, I get told.'

'What kind of mood are they in?'

'Jumping for joy. What mood do you expect them to be in?'

Jessie gave her a look of contempt. 'I don't know why I bothered to ask, you're just a kid. What would you know?' She got out of the kitchen before Dolly could answer back – she had seen the flash of anger in her eyes.

'Miss High and Mighty!' Dolly yelled up the stairs after her. 'Not so *saintly* now, are you!' Her voice rang through the house; not only would her mother and grandmother hear, the tenants in the attic would too. 'They've got names for girls like you!'

Jessie ignored the insult and went into the sitting room, bracing herself to face both mother and grandmother.

'Pay no attention to Dolly,' said Rose quietly. 'It's reaction, shock. I dare say she's as shocked as I am.'

'Sit down, Jessie,' came Ingrid's quiet, controlled voice. 'Your sister has a lot to learn about people. You are not a whore – far from it.'

Jessie smiled weakly at her. 'I've got to get used to it. It's what everyone will say, in their own way.'

'You're not a bad girl, Jess,' said Rose. 'You've been feckless but you're not bad. Sit down now, we've something else to tell you.' Her voice was so low Jessie could hardly hear her.

'I think it might be better if you closed the door first,' suggested Ingrid.

'I don't want to talk about it,' said Jessie. 'I know what you're going to say and I'll just have to accept whatever you have in mind. So do what you want with me.' She turned to leave but Rose stopped her.

'Sit *down*, you silly girl. What I have to say has nothing to do with your condition. Besides, we've been talking. Your grandmother thinks you should marry your fiancé and have the baby.' Rose shuffled in her seat, embarrassed and uncomfortable.

'Fiancé? You mean ... Max?'

'No. I mean Tom. You can wear this for now,' she said, offering Jessie a ruby and diamond ring. 'You can keep it if you want. Don't thank me for it, thank your grandmother.'

Jessie looked from Rose to Ingrid, puzzled. Her grandmother gave a nod of approval, silently telling her to accept the gesture and to go easy on her mother. 'I haven't met this young man of yours,' she said, 'this Tom, but I have heard about him from time to time from his mother, Emmie. It would seem to me that he is a caring and thoughtful youth. Do you love him? This Tom?'

'Of course I do. But I don't understand ... you know Emmie as well?'

'Yes I do. She's a good friend.'

The memory of Ingrid's first-visit washed over her. She had mentioned Emmie then, but it hadn't occurred to Jessie that she was referring to Tom's mother. 'Everyone seems to know Emmie,' she said, miles away. She turned the ruby ring in her fingers. 'Thank you for this,' she said, 'it's lovely.' There was a moment of quiet as a more relaxed atmosphere took over the room. 'Was this the one that Grandfather gave to you when you got engaged?'

'Yes,' said Ingrid. 'Your mother would like you to wear it and I think you should have it. I know you were very dear to him – as I was, once.'

Bewildered, Jessie asked if she could go to her room for a while and talk again later on. All she wanted right then was to be by herself. To think and to cry by herself.

'No, Jessie.' Rose's tone was serious. 'I've something to tell you, something very important. Once you've taken in what I have to say, I'll call Dolly up. The boys can be told later, when they're in their beds.'

Worried as well as confused now, Jessie sat down. What could be more serious than her being pregnant?

'Now,' said Rose, 'what I have to say isn't going to be easy for me, Jess, and if it wasn't for your grandmother, I wouldn't be telling you at all.' Rose glanced at Ingrid and took a deep breath. 'I've just been told off, Jessie, by *my* mother.'

Thumbing her wedding ring, she began her story. She told Jessie that when she was in the same predicament, eighteen years ago, she and Robert had been courting for over two years before they broke the rules. She told her about Armistice and how overjoyed the women were when their men came home from war. Jessie wondered if she was telling her all of this to help make her feel better about her *condition*, but she was wrong.

'The thing is, Jessie, me and your dad were very hard up, struggling to make ends meet. We could hardly afford to feed ourselves and pay rent on our rooms, let alone feed two babies.'

'*Two* babies? But Dolly wasn't born then.'

'No, that's right, but you were and . . .' Rose swallowed and turned her face away, hiding the pain, 'so was your twin,' she whispered. 'I gave birth to twins, Jessie, non-identical twin girls.'

'You can't have,' said Jessie, a nervous smile on her face, 'you would have told me.' She looked to her grandmother, but Ingrid avoided her eyes.

'I should have told you . . . me and your dad should have explained when the time was right, which is what we'd promised ourselves, but the time was never right.'

Jessie felt very strange, her emotions mixed. She was a twin? She had a twin sister? That feeling of someone being missing all through her life came flooding back.

'She died . . .' murmured Jessie. 'I had a twin and she died. I think I knew.' She met Rose's troubled eyes. 'I always felt as if something was missing . . . missing from me. She didn't die straightaway, did she?' Then, like a flash of lightning, she remembered the photograph of the twins in a pram.

'She didn't die, Jessie. We just couldn't afford to clothe and take care of two babies . . . so we had to let someone else take care of one.'

'No!' An icy sensation swept across her, she shook her head, not wanting to hear it. 'No. You wouldn't do that. Dad wouldn't have done that. You wouldn't do that to us. We loved each other. She was part of me and I was part of her . . .'

Both Rose and Ingrid were stunned by what Jessie was saying. Could it be that they had somehow stirred a deep memory within her? They slowly turned to look at each other and then at Jessie, who had a strange, faraway expression. 'My twin,' she murmured, 'my twin, you took her away from me, you took her away and it was cold.'

Rose was too upset to speak. Ingrid moved across the room, sat on the arm of Jessie's chair and gently patted her back. 'It's the hardest thing of all, child, to give away your own flesh and blood. Like me, you mother did it for the very best of reasons, she had only you and your sister's welfare at heart.'

'Did you choose?' said Jessie, gazing into Rose's face. 'Did you pick and choose which one would go and which would stay?'

'No, it wasn't like that,' said Rose quietly.

'Where is she now?' asked Jessie, in a low, controlled voice.

'Not many miles away,' said Ingrid, lifting Jessie's chin and smiling at her. 'I think that once you have got over the shock, you are in for a nice surprise.'

'It's all right, Mum,' said Rose, 'I'll tell her.' She patted her face dry, cleared her throat and took a deep breath. 'There was a reason for my not wanting to entertain Tom, Jessie. And I have to confess that his mother, Emmie, tried her best to persuade me to tell you about Hannah before you found out from someone else. But I was so scared, Jessie . . .'

'Hannah? Did you say Hannah? Tom's Hannah?' A vision of Charlie standing in the doorway of Tom's living room swept across her mind, when he had said that he hadn't seen Rose in years. And Tom's mother, Emmie . . . who had brushed it off, saying she knew Rose from way back.

She wondered about Tom, about their first date when he stood her up. Had he been warned off? Jessie turned her attention to her grandmother. Hadn't she all but told her on *their* first meeting? Hadn't she said, *your mother gave away your sister*? More importantly, why had everyone kept the truth from her? From her and from Hannah? Or did she know too? Surely not? No . . . Hannah hadn't been told, of that she felt certain.

'Yes,' said Ingrid. 'Hannah is your twin sister. So you see, she was never gone for ever, *meine liebling*. It was destined that you would come together.'

'Of course she is,' murmured Jessie, trance-like, 'of course she's my twin. I knew that ... we both knew that ...' The tears were trickling down, a slow stream of tears. 'We felt something straightaway, I think, but we didn't know what it was.'

Rising from her seat, a little unsteady, Jessie went to the window and stared out. 'Why isn't she here? Didn't she want to come?'

Concerned over her fragile state of mind, Ingrid went to her. 'She hasn't been told. She doesn't know that Gerta's not her real mother or that your uncle Jack is not her father.'

Jessie laughed bitterly. 'I never even knew she was supposed to be my cousin, let alone my twin. You weren't taking any chances, were you? All of my life I've missed her. I know you won't believe that, but I did, I missed someone and all the time it was Hannah.' She blew her nose and looked at Ingrid. 'I want to see her.'

'And so you shall. Come and sit and make it easier for your poor mother,' said Ingrid.

Allowing her grandmother to lead her back to the armchair, close to Rose, Jessie remembered the baby growing inside her. 'Maybe I'll have twins,' she murmured through her tears. She looked across at Rose. 'It's all right, Mum, I don't blame you. I don't blame anyone. I know it must 'ave been hard for you, having to tell me now.' She smiled faintly. 'I think your mum's bossier than mine.' That spontaneous quip broke the tension and lightened the heavy mood.

'You could be right there,' said Rose, smiling. 'Your dad wanted to bring you together years ago, Jessie, but I was terrified you'd hate me for splitting you up, not to mention how Hannah would feel. It's only recently, after you'd met up with Tom and I started to see Emmie more often, that I learned how unhappy she's been, living with that wretched woman. I thought she was wanted.'

'She'll be all right,' said Jessie. 'She'll be fine ... we'll make up for it. We'll make up for everything. She can come and live with us now ...'

Rose cautioned her. 'Maybe, but we *must* tread carefully and not rush into anything. I know it'll be hard for you, but you've got to be patient ... and more importantly, you're to keep away from Hannah until we have a full family reunion.'

Jessie started. 'But why? Why can't I see her today? You've told *me* so—'

'Your uncle Jack is coming back to England and we have to wait until he's arrived. He especially requested, urged even, that we wait. Apparently he's been trying to get a transfer from the New Zealand office to London ever since he received the news that your dad had ... met with an accident. But his arrival is fairly imminent. He'll let us know once he's here and ready to face Hannah.'

'You make Hannah sound like a judge,' Jessie said.

'Well,' said Rose, 'in a way both my brother and myself will be on trial. Hannah is in for a shock and one she won't be too pleased about. We've all been lying to her since she was a baby in a pram. I don't expect her to fall into my arms — blood mother or not.'

Jessie could hardly take it in. 'Everything's happening at once.'

Ingrid nodded. 'Yes, and not before time where you and your twin are concerned, and where your mother and I are concerned. It would seem that this is the year for estranged mothers and daughters to come together.'

'Yes ... and estranged sisters ... and brothers.' Jessie imagined the expression on her brothers' faces when they learned there was another one of them. 'You can live here too ...' She spoke without looking at Ingrid. 'We can all live together.'

'There are tenants in your attic rooms who bring in rent for your mother and I have a nice flat all to myself, thank you.'

'The tenants could move into the rooms above the cobbler shop,' said Rose, tentatively. 'There's no reason for you not to come and live with us – unless you'd rather not.'

'I would rather not. I'm too set in my ways. I'll stay over by Victoria Park and you may visit me there. I don't know or care much for this part of the East End. And an invitation for Christmas would be nice. Christmas with grandchildren is how it should be. Pride has deprived me of that for too long.' Ingrid got up. 'Now I must make my way home.'

Showing Ingrid to the door, Rose thanked her, not just for the visit but for helping to sort out her mind and her life. 'Maybe now that we've cleared the air all round we can do some catching up,' she said.

'I would like that, Rose. I would like that very much. Do you know what my worst fear was? That one of us should die without us having repaired the bridge. That was my very worst fear. God does work in mysterious ways, doesn't He? The person responsible for bringing your family together is the very person who might have been the cause of pushing you and Jessie apart.'

'Tom?'

'Tom. *Auf wiedersehen.*'

Rose hugged her mother for the first time since their parting many years ago.

She went back into the sitting room filled with a sense of long-awaited relief, and was moved by the way her own child, Jessie, was curled up on the settee, still tearful but smiling. 'Well, things do have a way of working themselves out, don't they, Jess? We've got a long way to go yet. The gossips will have a good time denouncing the Warner family but, oh my Lord, how far along the road we've all come.'

Pulling her shoulders back, Rose suggested they call Dolly in to tell her about Hannah. 'Let's hope she won't be jealous,' she said, 'or fearful that Hannah will take you away from her. Dolly's more sensitive than you think.'

'I know, but before she comes in, will you do something special for me? Will you hold me close and rock me, the way you used to when I was little?'

'Oh Jessie, what are we to do with you? One minute you're a woman and the next a baby,' said Rose, smiling and sitting next to Jessie on the settee, drawing her close. 'You don't want me to sing a lullaby as well, do you?'

'No, you can save that for when your first grandchild comes along.'

Chapter Ten

Turning out some freshly baked tarts, Charlie's favourite, Emmie was doing her best to soften up her husband who had never like meddling in other people's affairs.

'I just don't think you should get involved, Em, that's all I'm saying.' He licked a finger and turned the page of the *Betting News*. 'Leave it to the Warner family, let them sort it out. You'll get no thanks if it goes wrong or if it comes right.'

Emmie smiled to herself; her Charlie could go on at times, repeating himself over and over.

'You're like a record on the blooming gramophone with the needle stuck, Charlie,' she said. 'If that's not the fifth time you've said it today, I'm a Dutch herring.' Of course he had a point and in other circumstances, she would be the first to say leave other people's family matters alone, but the Warners' business had become her business, firstly because of Hannah and secondly because of Tom. Tom and Jessie. 'Anyway, I'm not interfering, if that's what's worrying you,' she went on. 'Rose asked me to have a word with Gerta and that's all I'm going to do, have a word. Something I should have done a while back but as it's turned out, the timing would have been wrong. Jack Blake's ship came in first thing this morning and Tom's arranged to pick him up from his hotel this evening, to take him to Rose's house.'

'So why go to Gerta's?'

'Needs be, and I owe it to Rose. Once today is over, Charlie, I'll be able to wash my hands of it and we can concentrate on putting on a nice wedding reception here.' That was her trump card. Charlie couldn't wait to have all his friends round and the neighbours in for a good old knees-up. 'I do feel sorry for poor Jack though.'

'Poor? I doubt it,' said Charlie, his nose still in his paper, as if it held more interest than what was going on in his own back yard. 'He's probably made himself a fortune out there.'

'Selling encyclopaedias? Fat chance of that.'

'Don't you be so sure, Em. How else d'yer think he can afford to come all this way? I might 'ave a word with 'im once he's sorted out his commitments. Wouldn't mind emigrating myself. I bet the rents out there are a damn sight cheaper than they are in this country.'

He had played right into her hands over another bone of contention and she was quick to take advantage. 'Very true, Charlie,' she said earnestly, 'which is all the more reason why we should think seriously of taking that loan from Johnnie's bank to buy one of them houses. We could afford to pay it back between the two of us, and we wouldn't have rent to pay then, would we?'

Hoping that Charlie's sudden silence meant that he was thinking about it, she kept quiet and waited. Tom had almost talked the subject to death, going on and on about it since the day he visited the houses and had shaken hands on a very good deal if the four went at once. Johnnie the entrepreneur was going to pay cash for his one and take a loan for another, and Tom had already marked one for himself and Jessie. So that left one and Emmie wanted it for Charlie, herself and young Stanley.

'I'd rather go to New Zealand,' said Charlie. 'Johnnie should give us the money to go, see us safely over there, out of England when the war's on. If you was thinking straight,

Emmie, you'd want the same.' He shook his head despairingly. 'Getting in debt to buy a bloody 'ouse that's gonna get blown to smithereens. Fucking stupid.'

'Don't swear, Charlie. Now that young Jessie's coming into the family you're gonna have to give it up. If you swore in front of her mother, Rose, I would die. You know how strait-laced she is.'

'Well, don't blame me if it all goes wrong, that's all,' he said. 'Just remember that I was against it and all for going across the world and away from the bombs. Just you remember that.'

Emmie felt her heart lurch. Whether Charlie knew it or not, he had just agreed to the bank loan and house purchase. She would have to be very careful and go along with his game-playing.

'The day you get off your arse, Charlie Smith, to go anywhere further than Southend is the day I'll sing for my supper.'

'Now who's swearing.' He flicked another page of his paper. 'And as for your singing, you'd do better to say your prayers and ask Him where the money's coming from for this wedding, 'cos if you think it's gonna be a ham sandwich and trifle do, you're wrong. We're doing it properly and not on a bloody shoestring.'

Happier by the minute, Emmie forced back her laughter and kept a straight face. She wanted to be on her way but she would have to bide her time, let him think he was the boss for a bit longer. To have him on her side was a good deal better than having to live with his sulks, which had been known to go on for weeks sometimes. She still hadn't won him round over her visit to Gerta.

'England beats anywhere abroad any day,' said Emmie, knowing full well that that was Charlie's true sentiment; he was a King and Country man. Mention England and he almost stood up to sing the national anthem. 'Oh, yes,' she continued, 'England's a good place, so long as you know how to work with the system to make ends meet and pinch whatever else is needed to lighten the load.'

'Work with the system? Ha. Go and talk to all the bleeding foreigners, they'll tell you how to do that. Pouring in from every corner of the bloody world to take our jobs and 'ouses.'

'You're beginning to sound like Mosley, Charlie.'

'Give over, woman. That pompous bastard? A lot of good his claptrap's done. The man wants to try doing a full day's work. I'll have kippers for tea.' Charlie's tone made it clear that there was to be no more talk on that particular subject. 'Nice pair of kippers today instead of for Sunday breakfast.'

'So you will think about that house then? I've got my heart set on it, Charlie, a place of our own, something to leave to our grandchildren and a fresh start for us – a lovely new house.'

'New? You must be joking. It'll want a lot of bloody work done on it before it'll look halfway decent – God knows how many gallons of paint and rolls of wallpaper. Well, go on then. Sod off round to Gerta's, give me five minutes' peace.'

'What about your kippers?' she whispered, as she kissed his cheek.

'I'll have 'em when you get back, so don't be long. Tom's fetching Hannah back 'ere after the dog stadium, which should be in about an hour if I'm right ...'

'Then he'll pick up Jack from his little hotel in Aldgate and take him round Rose's place, but not before I get there with Hannah, right, Charlie?'

'Yeah, all right, I've got it. But what if I can't keep Hannah 'ere? What if she wants to go home, and walks in on you and Gerta going at it hammer and tong ...'

'That mustn't happen,' said Emmie quickly.

'Exactly. Which is why Rose and Jack are the ones who should handle this.'

'Well, you'll find a way to keep her 'ere for me, won't you, Charlie? We don't want to mess things up now.'

There was a rustle of newspaper and a grunt from Charlie.

'Good. That's that settled then,' said Emmie. She checked her face in the mirror above the fireplace and reached for her lipstick and powder, she didn't want Gerta to think she was going to seed.

'Don't let the German get the better of you,' said Charlie, as she headed for the door.

Smiling to herself, Emmie left the house. You're a funny chap, Charlie Smith, she told herself. Never show your true feelings. You're just as worried about Hannah as I am but you'd never let on.

Emmie knocked three times, on Gerta's front door, the copper's knock, as it was known in the East End. Three sharp raps. She could see then why they did it, there was a ring of authority and no-nonsense about it.

'Yes? What can I do for you?' Gerta peered from a crack between the door and the wall.

Giving the door a nudge Emmie wedged her foot between it and the door frame. 'I could tell you what I want right here if you like, Gerta, but the neighbours would have a field day because I don't intend to keep my voice down. It's up to you. Ask me in or let the world hear about your private, sordid business. Rose Warner has been to see me.'

She shrugged. 'You'd better come off the street before my neighbours think you've escaped from an asylum.' She stood to one side and jerked her head for Emmie to enter.

'This staircase could do with brightening up,' said Emmie, goading her. 'A pot of paint doesn't cost much. All these dark shades of paint and varnish . . .'

'I don't bother with fashions. Why pay good money just to make other people feel better? Besides, I don't encourage visitors and this is good enough for me.'

'And Hannah?'

'Hannah? Ha! She's plainer than anyone. She would be happy living in a cell in a convent.'

'Yes,' said Emmie, 'compared to living with someone like you I should think that would be an attraction.'

Gerta showed her into the sitting room and nodded towards the chair in which she was to sit – a tall-backed wooden chair. Emmie sat down on the sofa instead. 'I'll come straight to the point, Gerta, since neither of us wants to be in the other's company for longer than necessary. Rose has come clean with the girls and let them know that Hannah is not your daughter but Rose's.'

Gerta snorted in disbelief. 'That woman would die rather than let the scandalous truth come out. What would people think of her, giving away a baby? Separating twins. You are more foolish than I thought if you believe that Rose Warner has the guts to tell the truth.'

'So wheels have been set in motion,' said Emmie, 'and steps taken to ensure you don't get a penny of Hannah's share of the compensation.'

'You may set whatever you want in motion. The authorities will take my side. I have kept the unwanted child all these years, loving and caring for her, as a blood mother might. It was hard for me, since my own husband left, and I am entitled—'

'You won't get one penny, Gerta. I wrote to Jack and he tells me he divorced you. You kept that one close to your chest, didn't you?' Emmie was feeling very much on top of things. 'He's with Rose and his family right now.' He wasn't, but Gerta wasn't to know that, and he would be with them soon. 'He's coming to see you, tomorrow, to ask about the money he's been sending Hannah, which she hasn't seen a penny of.'

The colour had drained from Gerta's face, Emmie noted with satisfaction, and she seemed dumbstruck. But not for long.

'I spit on you,' she hissed. 'I spit on the Warner family and I spit on Jack Blake. I spit—'

'Spit where you like,' Emmie cut in. 'It doesn't change anything.'

'And soon my homeland will spit bombs all over your precious England. Hitler will take this country. Then he will clean it of *all* degenerates. Britain will become his domain, Emmie Smith, and people like you and Jack Blake will be swept into the gutter.'

'I don't think so, Gerta.' Emmie wished Charlie was here, he would be roaring with laughter by now. 'The British are stronger than you think, my dear. Hitler won't stand a chance against us British, trust in that.'

'This country is not prepared for another war. It is asleep,' Gerta sneered.

'Cat-napping, Gerta, cat-napping, and whether you believe it or not, most of us can read the newspapers and listen to the news on the wireless. It would seem that your favourite cause is on the wane.'

'Really?' said Gerta spitefully. 'And how will your sons cope with that?'

'Find another social club to join, because that's all they're in it for, Gerta. The free women and the tea dances. Not many take it quiet as seriously as you do, my dear. There are Blackshirts and there are Blackshirts.'

'Oh,' said Gerta, deflated. 'So you know. You surprise me.'

'We don't believe in secrets between family, which is why Hannah is being told the truth. I've stepped in now and there's no getting rid of me. You see, my son is going to marry Jessie Warner, Hannah's twin, so it really is my business now. Don't test me on this one, Gerta. Don't even think about bringing my sons down with your vicious tongue because if you do, I'll make you wish you'd never left Germany.'

Gerta stood up abruptly and asked Emmie to leave. 'Please pass on a message to your friend. Tell her that I will settle for less than I asked but I will not settle for nothing.'

'I'll do that with pleasure. I'm sure she'll be ready to make a small settlement ... for your troubles. She's not a greedy woman.' And with that, Emmie swept out.

At home, Emmie found Hannah in the best room enjoying a cup of tea with Charlie. The next step was to get themselves to Rose's house, before Tom arrived there with Jack. The plan was well laid but it could still go wrong.

'Charlie's been telling me about his time in the trenches during the war, Emmie. It's such a good story. What heroes he and all the other soldiers were.' There was a knowing smile on Hannah's face; she had heard the story many times and Emmie knew it.

'Well, up you get, Hannah. We've a visit to make.'

'A visit? To where?'

'It's a surprise, now be a good girl and don't spoil it for me. Come on, I may have found you a nice room with a good family.'

'A room? With a family? But I was thinking about a flat, a small place of my own.'

'I know, but you haven't found anything you like after all this time and I think this would suit you nicely. It's only a fifteen-minute walk or so, and it's a lovely evening. At least come and see it, Hannah. I've gone to a lot of trouble.'

'Well, I suppose there's no harm in looking ...'

'Course there ain't, gal,' said Charlie, his timing perfect. 'If Em's given it the thumbs-up, it can't be bad. Go on, the pair of you, and don't take too long about it. The boys'll be in soon and I'm blowed if I'm gonna start frying kippers for that lot.'

Hannah was quieter than usual as they walked through the back streets, listening more than talking. Emmie thought she had probably picked up that something was afoot, but Hannah asked no questions. What she was thinking was anyone's guess. As far as Emmie was concerned, once she'd delivered her into Rose's hands, her job was done and she would slip away.

When they turned into Rose's street, Emmie began to panic a little. How would Hannah react to suddenly finding out the truth and being thrust into the Warner family? Her insides fluttered with worry, but there was no turning back now.

'The family you're about to meet are not exactly strangers, Hannah,' she said as they reached the front door. 'This is Jessie's home. She'll be waiting to welcome you.'

'Jessie? Jessie lives here?'

'That's right. Jessie, her mother, her sister Dolly, and their two young brothers, Alfie and Stephen.' Saying no more, Emmie knocked on the door.

Hannah craned her neck. 'I can see there are attic rooms. Are they the ones to let?' Now she was smiling.

'Let's wait and see, shall we?'

It was Rose who answered the door, looking apprehensive. 'Hello, Emmie,' she said, and then turned to Hannah. 'You look in fine fettle, Hannah. Come in.'

Ignoring Hannah's quizzical look, Emmie motioned for her to go first and she did, without a word.

Jessie appeared in the hall and stood looking at her twin, not moving a muscle, hardly breathing. It all seemed to fit, the way she looked, the way they had got on when they first met. Walking slowly towards her, Jessie's instincts were to go against all that she'd been told to do, which was to stay passive. Excitement rose within her and she just wanted to lead Hannah away from everyone else and hold her tight. She gripped her arm instead and brushed a kiss across her cheek, whispering, 'Hello, Hannah. You're in for a surprise.'

Hannah looked over Jessie's shoulder at Emmie, her eyes full of questions. Jessie was still clinging to her and Hannah had the strange feeling that she was smelling her skin.

'That's enough now, Jessie,' said Rose quietly. 'You'll frighten her off.'

'Into the sitting room, is it, Rose?' prompted Emmie. Now that it came to it, she found she couldn't just slip away as she'd intended. She had to see this thing through, she had to be there for Hannah.

'Yes. Dolly's waiting to welcome you too, Hannah. The boys are upstairs, we'll call them down once we've explained a few things.'

'I don't want to sound ungrateful,' Hannah was at a loss for words, 'but this is all a bit overwhelming. I don't understand.'

'I'm sure,' said Rose, guiding her in, 'but everything will become clear.' Rose sat down on the sofa and patted the space next to her. 'Come and sit down.'

Hannah did as Rose asked, looking very uncomfortable. Jessie and Emmie sat on chairs. Dolly was in the armchair.

'Now ...' said Rose, 'this is all going to come as a shock to you and once I've said what I've got to say, you'll no doubt wonder why I've left it so long to tell you.'

Hannah looked to Emmie for some sort explanation, but Emmie just nodded encouragingly.

'Has something happened to Tom?' she finally asked.

That one small question touched Emmie to the core, Hannah's thoughts had gone straight to her Tom.

'Tom's fine, Hannah,' she said. 'In fact, he'll be here shortly.'

Another silence followed. This time it was Dolly who stepped in.

'You're not gonna believe this, Hannah,' she said, leaning back, arms folded, 'but all that you said that day at Tom's house about you and Jessie thinking the same thing and at the same time – well, you would wouldn't you, being twins.'

The room went still, no one seemed to breathe even.

Hannah stared at Dolly. 'Say that again?'

'I know.' Dolly grinned. 'I was shocked as well when they told me. Mum and Dad had you adopted 'cos they couldn't afford to feed two babies. We're your family and we want you to come and live with us. We've got some catching up to do.' Dolly was the only one smiling. 'They picked a right one, though, didn't they, with that bleeding German woman. From what I've heard of it, she's a bit of a loony.'

'That's enough, Dolly,' said Rose, secretly grateful for her daughter's straightforward manner. She took Hannah's hand and squeezed it. 'Dolly certainly doesn't beat about the bush, does she?'

'What did she mean? I'm nobody's twin. I don't have any brothers or sisters.' Again Hannah turned to Emmie. 'Why are they doing this? Is it some kind of a parlour game?'

Emmie, who knew her better than anyone, realised that Hannah was waiting for a simple explanation. She wasn't shocked, she wasn't upset; she was slightly indignant, that was all. Rose was going to have to open up and stop beating about the bush herself soon, before Hannah got totally confused.

'I'm sure Dolly didn't mean what she said about your foster mother, Hannah,' said Emmie, giving Rose a sharp look to prod her into speech; this was her job, after all. 'Gerta might have her strange ways but she's hardly a loony.'

'Foster mother? You mean this is serious? You think I'm Jessie's twin sister?'

Rose laid a hand on Hannah's shoulder and squeezed it. 'I know you are, my dear. It pains me to think about it, but I let Jack and his wife Gerta have one of my babies to bring up as their own. At the time, Robert and I were very, very poor and didn't have enough money to look after you, but they did, and they wanted you very much.'

'She took me in,' murmured Hannah, her eyes now fixed on the floor, 'when my own mother turned me out ... is that what you're saying? If so ... that means a great deal, doesn't it?' Again she looked to Emmie for answers. 'She saved me from Dr Barnardo's ... from going into a children's home.'

'No, Hannah!' Startling everyone, Rose stood up. 'She did no such thing. I would *never* have placed you in a home. Gerta was my sister-in-law. I trusted her. She and my brother begged me to let them have one of my girls. I didn't want to give you up, of *course* I didn't! But we were living in one room which only just had a roof. We thought it was the best thing all round, and so it was, at the time. My brother loved you like a father would love his own child.' A strangled cry escaped from Rose. 'He cherished you.'

'So my father is not my father, he's ... my uncle? Is that what you're saying? And when he tired of me, he left me there ... with her?'

There was a heavy silence, and once again it was Dolly who broke it

'That's all over now,' she said brightly. 'You can live here with us. I think you look more like me than Jessie – except for the blonde hair.'

Hannah looked across at Jessie but did not return her twin's weak smile. 'How long have you know about this?'

'Not long. I wanted to come straight round to tell you but I was told I had to wait until now. Mind you,' she said, her cheeks flushed, 'I think I've always known something. It was as if I missed you without knowing who you were. I know that sounds daft but—'

'It doesn't. I've lived with that feeling too and it made me feel very lonely, I would rather not have had it. I know I was once very close to someone ... someone who wasn't there any more.' She turned to Rose, still no smile to light up her pretty face. 'How old was I when you did this thing?'

'Almost a year old,' said Rose, her voice heavy with remorse.

'So we would remember something, of course we would. No doubt we shared the same pram and the same cot.'

'Yes,' Rose managed to smile through her tears, 'you did.'

'Well,' said Hannah, 'I feel very sorry for myself as that baby. I think it was a cruel thing to do to a baby. I don't think that my mother, Gerta, is the wickedest one of all.'

She stood up, tall and erect, rendering them all speechless. 'If you will excuse me, I think it's time I left. Don't bother to show me out, and Emmie, don't bother to walk me home. I'd prefer to be alone.' She looked from Dolly to Rose and then to Jessie. 'And as for welcoming me into your home, I'm afraid it's too late for that. I don't belong in this family. I don't have any brothers or sisters and you are not my mother!'

This was more than Emmie could take. She stood up and faced Hannah. 'You just stay right where you are, Hannah! How *can* you condemn Rose out of hand like this? You have no idea what she has been through! You owe your mother an apology!'

'*Apology?*' Hannah's anger was frightening. Emmie hadn't bargained for this. 'I'm not bloody *apologising* for what *she* did to *me!*

'Calm down, Hannah,' said Emmie. 'Listen to what—'

'No! I've heard *enough*. Who do they think they *are?*' She turned on all of them. 'You lure me here under false pretences and then tell me that I am one of you! Strangers! That's what you are to me, *strangers!* So prim and *proper*, living in your nice big house with this fine furniture. One big happy family. You shun me for nearly eighteen years and then expect me to come smiling and grateful? Well, I don't want to be one of you. I hate the sight of everyone in this room! You can go to bloody hell! *All of you!*'

The knock on the front door was a relief; Tom had timed it perfectly.

'Do you want to tell Hannah who's at the door, Rose, or shall I?' asked Emmie.

Rose, pale and drawn, shook her head. 'I'll tell her myself, then I'll go to my bedroom. Don't be so hard on my brother, Hannah. He's come a very long way to help you through this.'

'What did you say?' Hannah's voice and expression changed

271

instantly. Her face and neck became taut and her soft blue eyes filled with tears. 'My father ... is *here*? At the door?'

'Yes,' said Rose, 'he's here. I'll leave you to your reunion. I'll be in my room if I'm wanted.' A broken woman, Rose was grateful for Jessie and Dolly either side of her.

'It'll be all right, Mum,' whispered Dolly.

'It was shock, that's all,' added Jessie as they went upstairs together.

Downstairs, Emmie wearily pulled herself to her feet. 'Well, I suppose I'd better open the door. Tom can walk me home. We'll leave you alone with your father, Hannah.'

'No, Emmie! No! Please don't leave me. Please, Emmie! I'm sorry for what I said! I'm sorry, Emmie! Don't go! He might hate me too!'

'Hate you? You think they asked you here because they hate you? Is that what you think?'

'Well, perhaps not, but they do now. Stay with me!'

'All right, Hannah. I'll stay with you.'

She opened the street door.

'Hello, Emmie,' smiled Jack. 'It's good to see you again.'

Emmie did her best to return his smile. He looked older, his face lined and tanned, his hair sprinkled with grey, but he was still handsome Jack Blake. 'Hannah's in the parlour, Jack. I'm afraid it's all gone badly wrong. Maybe you can talk to her. Rose is too upset to see you, she's in her room and no doubt crying her eyes out.' She looked from him to Tom and he did exactly what any mother would want her son to do, he put his arms round her and held her close, shushing her and telling her not to be upset.

'Did you really expect Hannah to fall into their arms?' he said gently. 'I suppose she shouted the odds.'

'She was a very wicked girl, Tom. The things she said to poor Rose, and in front of those girls. I blush at the thought of it. I wish I'd let you have your way. She wouldn't have behaved like that if you'd been here. I'm sure of it.' She looked at Jack.

'Oh Jack, I am sorry. I thought it was going to be so lovely. It's what I've always dreamed might happen and it all went wrong. What *have* I done?'

Jack touched her arm comfortingly. 'Started the ball rolling, my friend. We've a long way to go but look how far we've come. Now you go on upstairs to comfort my sister, and Tom, you go and see to your sweetheart. I want to see my Hannah alone. I've waited a very long time for this moment.'

Jack went into the sitting room and closed the door behind him. He gazed at Hannah for a moment and then held out his arms to her. 'Come here, sweetheart. Come and give your old dad a hug.'

Crying, Hannah fell into his arms. 'I've missed you,' she said. 'I missed you so much it hurt.'

'I know, I know.' He stroked her lovely soft hair. 'I'm here now and I promise I'll never leave you again. Never.'

'But you'll have to go back surely,' she said, her head buried in his shoulder. 'How can you stay in England?'

'Very easily, my pet,' he said. 'I have no intention of going back. This is the day I've been saving for.' He pulled himself away from her and looked into her face. 'Now then, I know you've had a shock. A real shock. But there is more, sweetheart, and I think it's right that we get it all out of the way now. It's to do with your mother.'

'Which one?'

'Gerta.'

'I want you to know before the others, and if you don't want to tell the others, we won't. I think we should sit down.'

Jack explained briefly that Gerta wasn't all she seemed. Her role as an ardent Blackshirt was a clever double-edged cover for the fact that she was a German agent, a spy, who had been under surveillance for quite a while. He told Hannah that Gerta had insisted she get a position in the local library because the books that she brought to and fro contained coded information for another agent to collect.

The fact that Gerta was an agent did not shock Hannah; on the contrary, it came as no surprise. If anything, it threw light on things she had often found puzzling. 'But how could you know all this?' she asked, sitting closely by Jack's side on the sofa. 'I feel as if I'll wake up soon and find myself in that room, with her reading into the small hours, if reading is what she was doing. She doesn't look like a spy.'

'Agents are usually very ordinary-looking people who don't draw attention to themselves. Gerta, in her own way, was an ordinary German, living in England, who loved the Führer.'

'Why are you telling me now? Because they're going to arrest her?'

'Yes. So you must come and stay with me in the hotel or stay here with ... with your family. You mustn't go back to the flat for a few days. Then we can return to collect your things.'

Hannah let out a low whistle. 'I can't believe all this is happening. Does Tom know about it?'

'No. But I will have a word with him in private. He and his brother have got to stop attending meetings and burn any evidence of a uniform or anything to do with the Fascist movement. It's very possible that there will be a war, Hannah. If there is, Oswald Mosley and his officers will be interned.'

'Well,' said Hannah, all self-pity gone, 'what will I find out next? Maybe they'll want to arrest me?' She looked at Jack, suddenly frightened. 'Will they?' Her hand flew to her chest as the implications sank in. 'I was passing messages in the library books I took out. Why haven't they interrogated me?'

'No need, Hannah,' he said, quietly laughing at her. 'You've been under surveillance too, and they checked you out, believe me, right down to the rubbish you throw away in the dustbin.'

'But how do you *know* all this?'

'I just do. Don't ask questions I can't answer. Just accept it, Hannah, if you can. It will take strength—'

'Oh, I think I've got that. I've had to have it. It was only the thought of you coming back for me one day that kept me going at times. You, Tom and Emmie, and dear, lovable, Charlie.'

'Shall we ask my sister Rose to come downstairs now?'

'Is she really my mother? And Jessie my twin sister?'

'Yes, Hannah, she really is. Now I suggest that we don't say a word this evening about Gerta and what's about to happen to her. There won't be a fuss, nothing in the papers about her in particular — several agents will be arrested over the next few days in and around London. My arrival in England today and not last week or next week was deliberate. I wanted to be here when it happened and I wanted you out of the flat when they took her.'

The waiting seemed like an age to Jessie as she sat with Tom and Dolly in their bedroom. She went into Rose's room to ask if it was time yet for them to go down and was pleased to see that her mother looked better for having had a chat with her close friend, Emmie.

'I should think we're all ready for a good strong cup of tea,' said Rose, smiling at Jessie. 'It's been a long day and it's not over yet.'

'I'll go and tell Dolly, Tom and the boys to come down, shall I?'

'Yes, I should think they've had enough time together now. Let's hope he's managed to bring Hannah around.'

When they all went back into the sitting room, Jessie pushed the boys in ahead of her. She thought they would be enough to bring a smile to Hannah's face if she was still upset.

'Well,' said Emmie when they were all settled and it was clear that Hannah was more like her old self, 'now that we're in the one room together, I would like to say something. Getting everyone together like this, and giving poor Hannah not one shock of her life but two was *my* idea. I was prepared to take full blame if it had all gone wrong, as it looked as if it had at one point, but since all seems fairly well, I'll take the credit instead.' Emmie's smile was broad. She focused on Alfie who was yawning. 'So if you don't mind, I'd like a little thanks. Well, Alfie?'

'What you looking at me for?'

'You're the eldest son, head of the family.'

His expression changed instantly. 'Oh, yeah ... well, I suppose I am. Um ... thanks very much ... from all of us.' Alfie looked across at Dolly and flapped his hand. 'Pour out the tea now, will you, Dolly?'

'Cheeky bugger.'

'Will you be moving in then, Hannah?' asked Stephen, a touch nervous.

'No. I won't be moving in. It was very nice to be asked, but I'm going ahead with plans I had already made.' She looked at Jack and smiled. 'My father isn't going back to New Zealand.'

'Is that right, Jack?' Rose's face lit up.

'Yes it is. When I received Emmie's letter, I decided then that England was where I belonged and, well, what with one thing and another, the time was right. So I asked for a transfer to London and the head of department agreed. I bought a one-way ticket.'

'Well, I'm very very pleased to hear it,' said Rose. 'If you should ever want to take up my eldest son's offer, I would love to have you here. We all would. I'm sure our tenants would understand, provided we give them fair notice to leave.'

'It's a lovely offer,' said Jack, 'but one I won't take up. No disrespect. It's just that I'm not really cut out to live in attics, although I'm sure it's a great flat.' He glanced at Hannah and smiled. 'I'm happy to stay in the small hotel with my daughter and look for a nice comfortable house which suits us both.'

'In the East End?' asked Rose hopefully.

'No, my dear, I'm too used to space around me now. Epping Forest perhaps.' He checked his wristwatch, 'We should be leaving soon, Hannah. I want to pay a visit to my mother and my brothers, who you may or may not remember.'

'I don't,' said Hannah, 'not really.'

Jack's easy manner had banished all shyness from the boys and before he could leave he had to answer all their questions about his life in the bush. Dolly and Hannah took their tea to a corner of the room and sat on the low stool, chatting. Emmie and Rose sat quietly, sipping their tea, too tired to talk.

'Come on, Jess,' whispered Tom. 'Let's get out of here.'

'I'll just say goodbye to Hannah in case they've gone by the time we get back.' Weaving her way round chairs and the table, Jessie touched her twin's elbow. 'I'm just going out for a walk with Tom. You will come and see me soon, won't you?'

'What about tomorrow? I don't think I'll be going into the library,' she said. 'I'll be taking a week off – Dad said it would be good to do that.'

Jessie kissed her on the cheek, squeezed her arm and whispered, 'I'm really pleased we've found out about each other.'

Outside in the street, Jessie and Tom put their arms round each other and strolled along, happy to be alone. They talked about Hannah, Jack, and their own future. Rose had listened when Jessie told her about the house she and Tom wanted to buy and after hearing all the details, she agreed to let Jessie use her part of the compensation money to buy it.

When Jessie talked about the baby, Tom became thoughtful. 'Jess, I've got something to ask you. I want an honest answer because it's your future, our future . . . or maybe just yours . . . that we're planning.'

His serious tone worried her and she wondered if he was about to suggest something horrible. 'Go on then, Tom, get if off your chest.'

'I know you bumped into Max the other day,' he said,

'Dolly mentioned it. And I know you're bound to bump into him again, so I want you to be absolutely sure that it is me you want as your husband and not Max. It's best you say now, Jessie, to save messing up both our lives – and his.'

'Of course it's you I want to marry. You know I love you, and in case you've forgotten it's your baby I'm having, not Max's. I've not been seeing him while I've been seeing you, if that's what you think. Is that what you think?'

'Oh, thank Christ for that.'

She couldn't believe her ears. 'You mean you *did* think the baby might be Max's? Surely not. You wouldn't think I'd trick you over something that important?'

'No, of course not, silly. I just thought you might want a back door to slip through, that's all. I was just checking, in case you were still in love with Max ... and felt stuck with me.'

'Well, now you know. I've never been this happy, so don't spoil it. I loved you before I even knew that you'd been looking after my twin for me.' She picked a small wild rose from a hedge growing in a neighbour's front garden and pushed it into the buttonhole in his jacket. 'I don't want anything to change ... ever.'

He cupped her face and kissed her lightly on the mouth. 'You'll be all right now, Jess. You've got me to look after you.' He slipped his arm round her waist and they walked on, passing a newspaper seller. He was shouting to draw attention to his placard which read: 'Advice from Minister of Defence, *"JOIN THE TERRITORIAL ARMY – BE PREPARED FOR A SECOND WORLD WAR!"'*

'Warmongers,' said Tom, smiling. 'What they'll do to sell a newspaper.'

'I hope you're right. Some are saying that they'll be calling men up before next summer. They wouldn't do that if they weren't expecting a war, would they?'

'Stop *worrying*. Everything's on the up. Anyway, our baby's due in April. Wild horses wouldn't drag me away from my family, neither king nor country will take me away from my Jessie and my baby girl.'

'How come you're so sure it's a girl?'

'I just know. Don't ask me how. I just do. I can see her now, long white hair, running towards her daddy, arms outstretched. My daughter. My little Emma-Rose.'

'Oh, so you've chosen a name already, have you? Don't I get a say in it?'

'You can pick the name if it's a boy.'

'Fair enough.' That suited Jessie; she couldn't lose either way, Emma-Rose was perfect.

'In April nineteen thirty-nine I'll be the proudest father of the most beautiful baby girl, you'll see.'

'And our little family of three will be living in Grant Street.'

'In our little two up, two down. So no more talk of me going off to fight the Germans. It's not gonna happen. Trust me. There won't be a World War Two.'

That night, before turning off her bedside lamp, Jessie wrote in her notebook: '13 August 1938 – Our Prime Minister, Neville Chamberlain, is to visit Hitler for a crisis talk. It's more frightening than the *The War of the Worlds* on the wireless. Mum's secretly looking forward to being a grandmother. Tom says there won't be a war. Hannah has been told she's my twin and I think – I hope – she's pleased.'

SALLY WORBOYES

OVER BETHNAL GREEN

Coming soon from Hodder & Stoughton

Sally Worboyes' fantastic East End trilogy continues . . .

Jessie Warner has married Tom Smith and their baby Billy has been born. But the newfound joy in Jessie's life is not reflected in the outside world, as the threat of war finally becomes a reality. Tom is called up almost at once, leaving Jessie to cope with the new baby alone. The Blitz over the East End begins, bringing panic and despair to the Londoners, as well as courage and hope in the face of danger. Then Tom goes AWOL and Jessie finds herself in a desperate situation. Meanwhile, Hannah, Jessie's clever twin sister, has been recruited to Bletchley Park to help crack the German communication codes . . .

Vivid and atmospheric, OVER BETHNAL GREEN captures the spirit of the East End and its indomitable people during some of the darkest days of the Second World War. Don't miss this wonderful novel in Sally Worboyes' East End trilogy, beginning with DOWN STEPNEY WAY.

Read this exclusive extract from Sally Worboyes' next book, OVER BETHNAL GREEN, continuing the story of the lives and loves of the characters in DOWN STEPNEY WAY, as they face the trials and tribulations of war time . . .

Chapter One

On a sunny September morning in 1938, a group of workmen turned up in Bethnal Green Gardens and started to dig trenches. There was such an air of high spirits and so many onlookers that the mood was more comparable to children playing with their spades and buckets at a seaside beach than to preparations for the potential horrors of war. The gravity of the situation soon became clear when just a few days later the fitting and issuing of gas masks began.

Cupping her hands round her warm drink in her tiny living room, Jessie Smith, although tired and looking the worse for wear, was at least thankful that at last her six-month-old son Billy was sleeping soundly after a fretful night of teething trouble. Like most people in Britain, she and her twin sister Hannah, who was on a one-day home leave, were waiting to hear what the Prime Minister, Neville Chamberlain, had to say. In their hearts each of them knew what was coming and the room seemed to have filled with doom and gloom even though in their own way they had been willing the news not to be bad. They had deliberately avoided any talk of what might be and fantasised instead about the type of house that Hannah might one day live in should she end up married to the wealthy but boring man who had set his sights on her at Station X.

'The trouble is,' said Hannah, 'there only seem to be two types of men, rich and boring or poor and interesting.'

Jessie found it strange that her twin had not mentioned qualities which she would have named – magnetic, exciting, irresistible. 'What about my Tom? Where does he fit into your ideas about men?'

'A bastard but you can't help loving him?'

Quietly laughing at her sister's honesty, Jessie had to agree. 'Especially when he's been on a drinking binge with 'is dad and brothers.'

'Ah,' said Hannah, all-knowing. 'I remember those nights out. They were always getting up to some kind of no good, sailing on the wrong side of the law. Emmie used to wait for them with a rolling pin. She really did. And she hit them with it too. Across the bottom. She would tell me about it the next day, with a crafty smile on her face. "They pulled it off, love," she would whisper, slipping me a pound note. I hardly knew whether to take it or not.'

Recoiling from Hannah's familiarity towards Tom and his family, Jessie tried to rise above her jealousy. Her sister had, after all, known Tom for years before she herself had ever spoken to him. 'He never tells me where he gets the money to drink,' she said. 'He just winks. I don't need to know more.'

'Of course,' said Hannah, laughing. 'Another parcel falls off the back of a lorry at the dock gates and he and his dad and brothers go on the town to celebrate.'

Their diversion from reality ended when from the wireless came a hushed silence broken only by a quiet crackling. The stillness seemed deliberate, as if the BBC was preparing listeners for the worst kind of news. It was 3 September 1939.

With a ghastly dread in her stomach, Jessie quietly prayed that the country's biggest fear had not been realised. Head bowed and wishing that Tom, her husband of one year, was there by her side, she listened earnestly to Chamberlain's slow and grave delivery.

I am speaking to you from the Cabinet Room, 10 Downing Street. This morning, the British Ambassador in Berlin handed the German government the final note, stating that unless he heard from them by eleven o'clock, and they were prepared at once to withdraw their troops from Poland, a state of war would exist between us. I have to tell you now that no such undertaking has been received, and that consequently this country is at war with Germany.

Stricken by the announcement, Jessie switched off the wireless. Her mind went back to a dark day in the spring of this year, in April, two weeks before Billy was due. Tom had received his call-up papers ordering him to report to the Tower of London where he would be conscripted into the army. They had been married for just six months at the time. Until that morning post had arrived, Jessie believed that nothing could spoil her and Tom's perfect world.

'I can't say I'm all that shocked,' murmured Hannah. 'This war was on the cards.'

'I s'pose so,' replied Jessie, half wishing her twin wasn't there right then and saying such things. It made it too real too soon.

'Life is about to change, Jessie. For all of us. No more thinking the best.'

'I know. I think it hit me really when Tom's call-up papers came in April. I shook like a leaf. Couldn't stop. That poor bloody postman. I feel sorry for 'im now. He was only doing his job but he must've sensed the resentment us wives and mothers felt when he delivered them brown envelopes. Poor sod. You should 'ave seen the look on 'is face.' Jessie covered her face with her hands. She wanted Hannah to go. To explain why would be impossible. She and her twin were very close but for some strange reason she needed to be alone right now. Wanted to be by herself to think for herself.

'Thank God for Tom's mum next door. Good old Emmie,'

she said finally, trying her best. 'I expect she'll be listening in with the other women at work. Three sons to go to war. I don't know what's worse, seeing your husband go off and wondering if you'll ever see 'im again, or watching three sons walk away.'

'Well, aren't you the light at the end of a dark tunnel,' said Hannah, smiling, trying to lift her sister's spirits. 'We Brits have more backbone than that, Jessie. And Emmie's got guts for two strong women. And as for Hitler, let him try to take England. Just let him try.'

'Britain,' said Jessie. 'He won't settle for less.'

'Well then, he's in for a surprise, isn't he?'

'Let's hope so.'

'Oh, you can take it from me. If—'

'Hannah, please! I don't want to talk about it.' Jessie's tone was anguished. She glanced across the room at Billy and sighed. 'I don't really want to talk about anything. It's all too much for me.'

'Sorry, Jess. I wasn't thinking.'

With Billy asleep and the wireless switched off, the only sound in that room was the ticking of the clock and the hissing of the fire. Staring into the glowing coals, Jessie glanced at the wedding photograph of her and Tom on the mantel shelf, radiant and in love. Next to it was a group wedding picture showing her mother standing proudly between Jessie and Hannah, and their sister Dolly, with her younger brothers, Stephen, in his Boy Scout uniform, and Alfie in his very first suit. The smile on their mother Rose's face hid the disappointment she had felt. There had been no white satin lace dress for her daughter, no bridesmaids and, worst of all, Jessie had been carrying Tom's child when she went to the altar.

But Jessie had made a beautiful bride and looked radiant in her oyster satin coat with tiny coloured glass buttons and matching skirt, which now hung in the wardrobe upstairs, waiting for another occasion when she might have the chance to wear it.

Jessie couldn't blame her mother for being cheerless at her wedding; she did, after all, have to stand alone to see her daughter married, without her late husband by her side. It had pained Jessie that her dad had not been there on her special day. She knew that her mother had not really taken to Tom and, well-mannered though she was, Rose hadn't been able to hide her feelings. His easy-go-lucky approach to life worried her.

Rose had made her views known to Jessie about her son-in-law's attitude towards the possibility of war. In her opinion, he liked the idea of being paid to train as a soldier, with board and lodging provided, while Jessie received an army pension. Jessie told her mother she was wrong and that once she got to know Tom properly she would realise he had been innocently baiting her. Rose had not been convinced.

Before his conscription in April, Tom had given up his job at the docks and taken an offer of freelance work as painter and decorator, which Rose considered reckless of him. The work had been spasmodic and he and Jessie, during those late winter months, had struggled to make ends meet.

Hannah pushed Chamberlain's speech from her mind and went into the kitchen to make them both a cup of tea while Jessie enjoyed the memory of one particular weekend when Tom had been home on leave. Standing by the butler sink, stringing some runner beans, she had been admiring the bluey-pink hydrangea bush in the garden when Tom had crept into the house and sneaked up behind her, giving her the biggest surprise of her life. It was little things like that that kept their love burning. During his periods of leave from the army, they had spent much of the time making love or fussing over their baby, Billy. On that leave Tom had seemed more worried than usual. He'd dropped hints about her being in London with all the French sailors on the lookout for a bit of romance.

'Actually they're called matelots,' she'd said innocently and in fun. It hadn't gone down well. Tom was a jealous man by nature and it was beginning to show. He had related tales he'd heard about the generosity of the French sailors who lavished presents of silk stockings, chocolates and brandy.

'Just don't go leaving our Billy and going out with 'em, that's all,' was his usual parting remark when his leave ended.

'You know,' said Hannah, coming into the room with their tea, 'Tom's very nervous about losing you.' Once again, as had happened before, the twin sisters seemed to have been thinking the same thing at the same time even though they had been in different rooms.

'What makes you say that?'

'Well,' said Hannah, sitting down, 'that time when I had a day off and came to see you when Tom was on home leave, he quizzed me on the goings-on around town.'

'Did he now?'

'It's all right. I was quick off the mark. Gave him a look that said don't even think about using me to spy on my own sister. I had, after all, come especially to tell you *my* good news.'

'That you'd been summoned for war work.'

'Yes.'

'And are you still chuffed over it, now that you're there?'

'Yep. I love my work. It's such a fantastic place. The hours are long and it's hard work, but I love being there. And you know how I enjoyed working in the library. I don't even miss being around books.'

Jessie's curiosity was piqued. 'Come on then, tell us what goes on there – or where it is at least. Don't be mean. You know I won't say anything.'

'I can't. I'm sworn to secrecy. Tom tried and failed and you know how persistent he can be,' Hannah said, smiling, hoping that would be the end of it.

'Please yourself. I just wondered what your room was like, that's all. I'm not bothered one way or the other.'

'Oh, I can tell you that. It's small but it's mine and the sun streams in through the window which looks out over the grounds. That's why I like it so much. It's heaven compared to that miserable flat over that dusty shop in Bethnal Green.'

'With a tyrant for a mother.' Jessie remembered Gerta, the woman who had made Hannah's childhood a misery.

'*Foster* mother,' Hannah corrected. 'And it's all buried in the past where it should be.'

Jessie turned the conversation back to her sister's work. 'What do you do there then? Just tell me that bit. Office work? Filing?'

'I mustn't tell you, Jess! I can't tell you what I do or where I work and live. It's secret stuff to do with the government and it was made clear that my lips must be sealed. I could get into a lot of trouble for even talking this much about it.'

The room went quiet again. Jessie didn't like the sound of it and didn't like her sister having to be away from the area, especially now. 'So now that war's been declared, will you still be able to come back now and then?'

'I hope so.' The tone of Hannah's voice made the message she was giving clear: no more talk of it. So Jessie pushed it from her mind. Very soon Emmie would be home from work and straight in to commiserate over the announcement on the wireless. They had things to discuss, that was for sure. Emmie would want to make plans straightaway, marking out every single air-raid shelter in the borough and advising Jessie to only shop close by those shelters for the sake of safety. After all, she had her grandson to think of as well as her daughter-in-law.

'I wonder how Tom's taking the news,' said Jessie, feeling worse by the minute.

'He's with men, don't forget. Soldiers. Their instincts will be to protect their territory. Knowing Tom, he'll be in a fighting mood.'

Maybe Hannah was right but on his last visit home, just a few weeks previously, Tom had still been adamant that Britain would not go to war. He had never believed that the day would come when the Prime Minister would make the announcement that Jessie had just listened to on the wireless.

'I think,' said Hannah, 'that Tom plays his cards close to his chest. All that talk about war never coming was a cover. He's not daft, Jessie. He knew.'

'Maybe.' It was becoming clear to Jessie that her twin sister knew Tom better than she did. And there was no denying that Tom knew Hannah better than all of them. But that was understandable. Jessie had only discovered the existence of her twin a year ago and Hannah had been a close friend of Tom since early schooldays. And now Jessie hardly saw anything of Hannah since she'd been posted to Buckinghamshire. What with her sister's absence and Tom having been stationed at Thetford, Jessie wanted to get out of the house sometimes and bring some fun into her life. Every other woman she knew, it seemed, was working in a factory preparing for a war and going out with friends in the evenings for a lively time. If she was honest with herself, she would have had to admit that she did sometimes feel envious. Jealous of her twin Hannah and jealous of her other sister, lively, carefree Dolly. Her own life seemed dull and lonely by comparison to theirs, even if she did have the beautiful son she adored.

'I'm going to have to go now, Jess,' said Hannah, checking the time. 'I don't want to miss my train.'

'No, you don't want to do that,' Jessie said with a touch of bitterness. They hugged and Hannah promised to come and see Jessie as soon as she could.

'It'll work out, Jess, you'll see. This time next year we'll be looking back with relief and smiling.'

Once Hannah had gone back to the centre at Bletchley Park, where enemy codes were deciphered and where Hannah's adoptive father, Jack Blake, had also been stationed months before her, as a code breaker, Jessie felt very much alone in her two-up, two-down in Bethnal Green, which she loved. It was true that she regularly saw her in-laws who lived in the same street, and her own mother, Rose, twice a week, and sometimes her younger brother Stephen stayed overnight, but for all of that nothing filled the empty gap she felt. She missed Tom's strong arms holding her close in bed and she missed the times when she and her twin sister had sat and chatted for hours on end about everything and nothing.

Jessie's other sister Dolly, true to form, had been having a whale of a time and making the most of the pre-wartime spirit. She was always going out on dates and was very popular with the Dutch marines whose ships sometimes docked in London. The East End, it seemed, was as popular as the West End when it came to night life, the pubs and taverns full of laughter, cheerful music, and song.

On the way to the bus stop to see Tom off on his last leave home, Jessie had been mortified when he said he had thoughts of not going back. The conversation immediately changed into an argument with her telling him not to dare to do anything stupid. She told him to stick it out like the rest of the conscripts and that was when he revealed his true worry to her. He asked if she'd been seeing her old boyfriend while he was away, Max Cohen, whom she had courted for three years before meeting Tom.

The unexpected question had thrown her. Of course she hadn't been seeing Max but more importantly, why had Tom even asked? She had been faithful, unlike some other married women, and hadn't even gone out for one evening, and there he had stood, accusing her. She had refused to answer him at first, which had caused him to be even more testy. She wouldn't deny it and that, in Tom's eyes, made her look guilty. When Tom had demanded to know why she wasn't denying it, she had yelled, 'I shouldn't need to!' not caring who heard. 'Of course I haven't seen him! He's in the bloody army as well, isn't he!'

His reply had shaken her. 'No he's not! As if you didn't know! Got out of it and all because he's got two left feet. Did you know he 'ad two left feet, Jess?'

If she had not been so livid with him she would have found his remark funny. She hadn't thought about Max in a while but Tom had obviously been worrying about leaving her in London with the man she had once given herself to and said she would marry living close by. Now with the likelihood of being posted abroad, Tom would be even more anxious as to what she might be getting up to. She hadn't realised until then just how damaging jealousy could be. It had all started with a light joke from Tom but had grown and was still spreading, affecting them both for different reasons.

With Billy in her arms, awake and contented, Jessie went out into the back garden and picked a dahlia for him to play with before letting Harry out of his hutch for a run-around, which would please her son more than anything. He loved the rabbit and chuckled whenever it ran or hopped or deliberately turned its back on them. Able to crawl about now, Billy struggled to get down from Jessie's firm grip but the last thing she was going to do was let him loose in the back yard. 'You'll have to wait, Billy, till you can walk. Then you and Harry can chase each other.' From the expression on his face, she almost believed he understood every word and had a feeling that he'd do his utmost to pull himself up on to his feet when he was in the old playpen a neighbour had recently given her.

Walking around the garden, pointing out different leaves and flowers, Jessie felt as if she was in a strange kind of dream. Here she was with her adorable baby boy, her rabbit frisking around in the afternoon sun, the roses still in bloom and autumn flowers all around, and yet war had been declared. *War.* It didn't seem possible that it could happen in her country.

She recalled the day in April when Tom had been summoned into the army. It came flooding back as clear as if it was happening right then. Jessie had wept when she saw the letter. She was in bed when Tom let himself into the house and she heard him knocking into furniture and singing, badly and out of tune, obviously very drunk.

'You were meant for me ... I was meant for you ...' he sang. 'Nature patterned you and when she was done ... Jess was all the good things rolled into one ... You're like a plaintive ... melody ...' There was a pause, then he sang loudly, 'Jessie — I've had no tea ... I ... 'm so hungry I could eat ... a horse ...'

When he found the letter propped on the table, telling him to report to the Tower, he staggered up the stairs, drunk and flabbergasted, as if it had arrived without any warning whatsoever. 'Jess. Jess ... they can't do this to me ...' he said, hardly able to end a sentence. 'I can't leave you, Jess.'

His performance irritated her. 'Tom, you'd better sober up. An' didn't you once say, you'd fight to the bitter end to keep Hitler's hands off Britain?' She tried to hold in her anger. 'Stop play-actin' and go to bed — in the box room, where you can snore as loud as you like. I need my sleep.'

But Tom had been in no mood to be quietened. 'I wasn't looking forward to going away to fight Hitler, Jess ... and I *don't* snore.' He did and he knew it.

'When you're this drunk you do. Where'd the money come from for your night out?' She wasn't going to let him off the hook.

Winking, hoping to soften her, Tom smiled and then hiccuped. 'Perks. Perks of life. A parcel fell off a lorry as it was coming out of the dock gates ... and the driver pulled away without realising.' Hunching his shoulders he sported that look of innocence he often used. 'What could I do but pick up that parcel? I've had a few beers, Jess, that's all. I was celebrating with my brother, Stanley. We sold most of the stuff.'

'And the rest?'

'We've, er, we've stored it,' he said, telling what he would call a white lie. 'Round a mate's house.' Play-acting or not, he suddenly looked like a man in the depths of a despair as he sat on the edge of their bed. 'Not much to celebrate though, is there? I've got to leave you, Jessie, and I don't wanna do that.' Watching him waving the call-up papers in the air, she knew very well that he was deliberately being melodramatic. 'They can't mean it. I'm not a bloody soldier, I'm a decorator!' He slumped down on to their bedroom chair, a sorry sight. Looking like a frightened child, head lowered, he sobered up and became more serious and more honest. He said haltingly, 'This has really upset me.'

That got Jessie's back up. 'Upset *you*?' she snapped. 'Well, how do you think *I* felt? I saw those papers and went crying to your mother and *you* went down the pub.'

'Yeah, but . . . I hadn't seen the letter, *had* I?' he said, trying to get her sympathy. 'I wouldn't have gone out if I *had* seen it, Jess. You know that.'

It all seemed so trivial now, looking back. But Jessie still believed that it was the stress of Tom's antics and his call-up that had brought on her birth pains the very next day, two weeks before her time. For a while, it had been touch and go if she and the baby would live. Thank God it had been all right.

Pushing all of that from her mind, Jessie left her baby in his pushchair, happily watching Harry the rabbit, and went inside to make herself another cup of tea. After all, there was worse to come now. Bloodshed and killing of innocent people, men, women and children, with bombs dropping all over the world. She feared for Tom who underneath it all was a real softie at heart. He had cried his eyes out on the night Billy was born when they had very nearly lost him. It had been a close thing and they were lucky that their baby had an excellent midwife to watch out for him and Jessie. Not only had he arrived early and unexpected but when she finally gave birth, the house had gone dark. The electric meter had run out of coins. Worse still, the umbilical cord was caught round Billy's neck and the midwife had only the light of a torch to work by.

'Never mind, Billy,' Jessie whispered, 'I won't let anything 'appen to you. No. It would 'ave to be over my dead body.' She looked up at the sky. 'Please, dear sweet Jesus, keep me safe so I can take care of my baby.'

To Jessie's surprise and joy, Tom was allowed home for an overnight visit the day after war had been declared and before he was posted abroad. When he turned up on the doorstep, she simply couldn't believe it. He was the best sight for sore eyes anyone could wish for and she didn't want to let him out of her sight. They made the most of every minute together, hardly apart, always in the same room, always with Billy – and for the first time since she had known him, Tom helped her in the kitchen, preparing food, washing up, anything so long as he was by her side and touching her. In bed, they made love for most of the night, clinging to each other as if they might never see each other again.

At the breakfast table, Tom looked terrible. His eyes red and his face drawn. 'I don't want to go, Jess,' he said, choked. 'I want to stay here with you and Billy.'

'You can't, Tom, you know that. Try not to think about it.' She was finding it all too much and her voice gave her away. Of course she didn't want him to go but what choice had they?

'Why am I going?' he said, looking like a child about to be abandoned. 'I don't wanna murder people and I don't want a bullet through my 'ead. All I want is to stay back 'ere in Bethnal Green, go to work, and come home to my family. That's not too much to ask, is it?'

'No, but you 'ave to go for the same reason as every other man. If you don't go out there and stop Hitler, he'll take this country and who knows what kind of a life we'll be facing. This is a free country, Tom. Fight to keep it that way. For Billy, if not for us. Think of 'is future and our grandchildren.'

'I s'pose you're right,' he said, sipping his tea. 'Greedy bastard wants to own and rule the world. Territorial rights. That's what this is all about. The twentieth century and we're still thinking like cavemen.'

Jessie glanced at the clock. 'We'll 'ave to get a move on soon. You don't wanna miss your train back.'

'I won't miss it, Jess, 'cos I've no intention of catching it. I'll go back in a few days' time. Say I 'ad the flu. Doctor'll give me a sick note. He's all right. We 'ad a chat last time I was back when I met 'im in the street. He didn't know it but I was checking up on what his views were.'

Jessie laughed out loud. 'Silly bugger, Tom. Course he knew what you was up to. Don't you think that scores of other men'll be trying it on? There'll be a mile-long queue outside 'is surgery, you see if I'm wrong.'

'Well, there you are, then,' said Tom, easing a cigarette into the corner of his mouth. 'There's my excuse. I couldn't get an appointment.'

The banter continued until Jessie realised that he really had made up his mind. He wasn't going back that day and relief began to take over from worry. She would have him around for a couple more days and where was the harm in that?

They made the most of their two extra days together. Instead of Tom going down to the pub, Jessie fetched home ale in a jug and she couldn't remember a time when they had been more in love and happier.

But fate had something up its sleeve. The very morning that he had intended going back, there was a knock on the door and it had the same sound to it as what was commonly known as the 'copper's knock' in the East End. Tom was playing with Billy, jumping him up and down on his lap, his uniform ready and waiting on the back of the kitchen door. Jessie was in the kitchen frying bacon and poaching eggs. Coming into the living room, she paled. 'Tom.' Her voice was no more than a whisper. 'Tom, I think it's the red caps.'

His mood now sombre, Tom slowly nodded, showing that he was thinking the same thing. 'Take Billy. I'll open the door.'

Dressed only in his trousers with braces dangling, Tom faced them. Neither of the two men on the doorstep said a word, they just stared into his face. 'Fair enough,' said Tom. 'I was going back today anyway.' He waved them in and closed the door. 'Fancy a bacon sandwich? I'm just frying breakfast for the wife while she feeds the baby.'

The delicious smell and sound of the sizzling bacon was tantalising and something that no ordinary man could resist and, duties aside, these two were ordinary men.

'Take a seat,' Tom offered. He winked at Jessie and went into the kitchen to take up where she had left off. They would have to do without eggs – the bacon was ready and he didn't want to keep them waiting longer in case they had second thoughts and resisted the sandwich.

'Them bloody barracks,' said Tom cheerfully, coming into the room, 'damp as you like. Thought I was in for pneumonia.' He handed each of them a sandwich. 'Felt all right when I woke up this morning though – apart from a splitting headache. I was gonna send in a sick note but you know what it's like when you're in bed sweating it out. And the doctor was too busy to come out.'

'I'm sure he was,' said one of the men, chuckling. 'You'd be surprised how many of you have gone down with this sudden epidemic which only seems to have affected blokes ready for war. Strange, that.'

Enjoying a short break from work and the unexpected pleasure of hot, crisp bacon between two slabs of baker's bread, the men kept their thoughts to themselves. And when Tom asked if there was time for him to have a quick wash and shave, they shrugged and told him to be quick about it. He left

Jessie telling the officers about baby Billy and how she feared he might have caught Tom's heavy cold on top of having just got over a chesty cough. They only half listened to her; they kept one ear on the movements of Tom upstairs.

Ten minutes later one of the men said, 'Sorry, Mrs Smith, but I'll have to ask you to fetch your husband. It's time to go.'

'Tom!' she called up the stairs but deep down she had a sickening sense he was not there. The creaking floorboards from Billy's nursery had been a dead giveaway as far as she was concerned. There was no reason for Tom to go in there unless he had decided to slip out of the upstairs back window.

Her instincts were right. Tom had gone and a neighbour hanging washing on the line had helped him by opening her yard door which led into another neighbour's garden and then to a narrow alleyway. All of this Jessie learned from her neighbour once the military police, furious and red-faced, had gone. The woman was pleased with herself and Jessie had to smile, though she really would have liked to scream.

'It was good of you to help out,' she said, 'but he'll get into more trouble for it. He should have known better.'

Laughing, the woman left Jessie to herself. She and the other women in the street knew Tom Smith quite well and it didn't surprise them one bit that he'd managed to dodge away. To them it was funny but then they didn't have to rely on him to stay put and ensure that the army paid Jessie her pension to feed and clothe herself and Billy.

Tom made his own way to Thetford, unescorted. Once again, he somehow managed to talk his way out of trouble. He wrote to Jessie, telling her that being on the run from the army and dodging the red caps was not only stimulating but easy. His casual joking about it worried her. To Tom this was no more than a prank; to Jessie it spelled trouble.

Soon after war with Germany was declared, air raid sirens

were heard all around Britain but thankfully it was a false alarm – a false alarm, but a grim reminder that during this war ordinary people, young and old, would be a target. But Britain was prepared this time, unlike during the First World War. Prepared and as ready as they could be to face the ordeal ahead.

Gas masks were issued to adults and children and trenches had been dug in readiness. Important buildings were sandbagged and public air-raid shelters, built earlier that summer, were ready and waiting. Air-raid wardens had been well trained and knew what to do when the bombs began to fall. Auxiliary firemen, too, had been drilled and tested and knew how to tackle a growing fire as well as how to extinguish an incendiary bomb with a stirrup pump. The stamp of active war was present everywhere and the atmosphere, strangely enough, was not of depression but camaraderie as people of differing class and religion were drawn together, by the threat they all faced.

Before the month of September was out, communities began to break up as women and children were evacuated and men went off to fight for king and country. Over a million Britons were evacuated from the cities but Jessie had no intention of leaving the East End and neither did her family or several of her neighbours. They, like many others, chose to stay at home and rely on the government's offer of protection to every household in the big cities – an Anderson shelter, to be erected in the garden. The corrugated iron hut was to be sunk halfway into the ground and covered with earth and sandbags as a means of shelter from the bombing.

It was a strange time for everyone. Women took their responsibilities seriously and were strong in the face of having to begin new lives without their men and keep their heads above water and hold their families together. It wasn't really until January 1940, when the government issued millions of ration books, that the grim reality of what was to come truly hit home.

Four ounces of butter and four ounces of bacon or uncooked ham a week, with just twelve ounces of sugar per adult, was a joke as far as Jessie's mother-in-law, Emmie, was concerned. She was known for her cooking abilities and she did not want to let the side down. With just herself and Charlie at home to feed, she had volunteered to prepare meals for five old folk in her turning, who would find it impossible to fend for themselves under the circumstances. She wasted no time in rooting out extra provisions via the black market. Her husband, Charlie, too old to be called up, had joined the million other men who had signed up with the Local Defence Volunteers, which proved to be an excellent grapevine as to where those extra provisions might be found or swapped.

Jessie's mother, Rose, continued to run her cobbler shop with her youngest son, Stephen. Stephen's love for the stage had led him to join a local drama group; he found his vocation early in life – and his sexual preference. His mother's inner worry over the years that there might be something different about her son was becoming a reality. Stephen was destined to remain a bachelor boy. Jessie's other brother, the rebellious Alfie who was just seventeen, had secured work in the metal foundry, hoping this would release him from having to defend his king and country should the war drag on. Alfie had other fights to fight when fledgling mobsters crossed the territorial line of his gang's patch in Stepney, where he now lived by himself in two rooms above an Italian café.

As for Jessie, she worried about her sometimes irresponsible husband and was kept on her toes by her lively baby. The happy family life that she had been looking forward to was now overtaken by the war and the restrictions it brought, including the blackout. Even the tiniest hint of light from the edge of a window at night prompted an angry shout of 'Put that light out!' And, beneath the blackout curtains, like every other household, the windows were heavily taped to prevent flying glass, and so by day as well as by night there was a constant reminder of the country being at war.

But Jessie took the war in good heart and like others began to grow food in every part of her garden. It was the same all over the country. Allotments, gardens, back yards, even window boxes were now being used solely to grow vegetables or fruit.

There were other changes too. Trees, kerbs and lamp posts had been marked with white to help in the blackout and women were doing the work of men in factories, shipyards and railway sheds. Ironically, the war was doing far more for the women's movement than the Suffragettes had managed in earlier years.

Jessie's sister Dolly had applied for a job as a bus conductor, which she loved, it being more sociable than any other occupation she could find. Petrol rationing had been introduced with a severity that forced many people take their cars off the roads and use public transport. Men from all walks of life now came into Dolly's happy orbit and she was always full of it when visiting her sister and nephew, baby Billy.

While Dolly chatted about the latest and most handsome sailor she'd met, Jessie hid her envy. To her, it seemed an age since she had enjoyed an evening out. To walk arm in arm with one of the tall blond Dutch sailors Dolly spoke of was a dream that often comforted Jessie when she was feeling at her lowest.

'I don't know why you don't come out with us, Jess,' said Dolly, carefully repainting her fingernails. 'Mum would come and sit with Billy, you know she would. You can't stay in forever.'

'It won't be forever, Dolly,' said Jessie. 'The war'll be over soon and my Tom'll be back where he belongs.' She strapped her son into his highchair and went into the kitchen. 'Watch him for me, Doll. He's worked out how to undo the buckle on his straps. It's spam sandwich with a bit of mustard for lunch.'

'That'll do me.' Dolly cupped Billy's double chin and kissed his smiling face, finding some of his dribble. 'Erghh, you messy little sod!'

'What's he done now?' called Jessie, pleased to have him off her hands for five minutes.

'Messed up my lipstick!' Undoing his buckle, Dolly lifted her nephew out of his highchair to squeals of laughter. 'He weighs a blooming ton, Jessie! What you been feeding him on?' She tickled Billy under the arm and chuckled with him. 'Little fat sod, ain't yer?' she said, cuddling him. 'Handsome devil. Got your dad's lovely green eyes and your mum's blonde hair. Them little girls are gonna love you.'

Billy babbled on, talking in his own language.

'Gibberish,' said Dolly, laughing at him, 'that's all you can do. Talk a load of gibberish.'

'Juish,' said Billy, demanding more attention. 'Dirsty.'

Dolly pushed her face closer to his. '*Juice* not juish. And *thirsty* not dirsty. Billy try. *Thirsty*. Go on then . . . *th-th-th-thirsty!*'

'Dirsty!' The fourteenth-month-old laughed out loud and clapped his podgy hands together. 'Juish!'

'You little tyke. *You* know. Yes you *do. You* know 'ow to say it.' She tickled him again. 'I can't wait to get one of these little bundles of trouble, Jess.'

Coming into the sitting room, Jessie sighed. 'You, a mother? Tied down to the kitchen sink?'

'I'm talking about later on once the war's over and I'm ready to settle down. Have you heard from Tom this week?'

'A postcard came this morning. He's getting on all right with the French now. His landlady's come round at last.'

'Blooming cheek they've got, them frogs. I wouldn't mind, our men are out there in France for their bloody benefit, you'd think they'd be grateful.'

'Anyway, he seems all right.' Jessie took Billy from her for his afternoon nap. 'I hope he's behaving himself with all them mademoiselles, that's all.'

'That's doubtful,' said Dolly, biting into her sandwich.

'Oh, thanks! What a ray of sunshine you are,' said Jessie, taking Billy upstairs.

'Trouble with you, Jess, is that you go through life thinking nothing'll change! It's about time you livened up a bit. Come dancing with me and my mates tonight. You won't look back!'

'I'm a married woman, Dolly,' said Jessie, coming back into the room.

'So? Loads of married women whose men have gone to war go out. You can't sit in all the blooming time. Silly cow.'

Jessie dropped into an armchair, fed up. 'I don't sit in *all* the time. Once we've finished this bit of lunch I've got every intention of going out for a walk. You can wheel Billy in the pushchair for me.'

Dolly sipped her tea. 'A nice trip over the park, I s'pose.'

'Yep. And then on to visit Mum and Stephen. It's better than sitting in all day.'

'Yeah, I grant you that. It is better than that. Tch. I don't know. You're getting old before you've stopped being young.'

'And you're getting on my nerves. Be quiet for five minutes.'

That said, Jessie and Dolly sat in silence. Dolly wondered what she would wear to go out that evening and Jessie wondered whether she should hang the washing on the line or dry it by the fire. It was a crisp, bright January day but it could change to cloud and rain within minutes. 'Did you catch the weather forecast today?' she asked, miles away.

'No, funnily enough I missed it, Jess.' The last thing Dolly thought to do was listen to a weather forecast. 'If it rains we'll put our umbrella up. If it don't, we won't. It's risky but sod it, let's live dangerously on our walk, eh?'

Amused by her sister's sense of humour, Jessie snapped out of her mood. A couple of hours later she went upstairs to brush her hair and put on some lipstick and powder. Staring at her reflection in the dressing-table mirror, she could see that Dolly had a point. She *had* turned into a dowdy housewife.

Wrapped up against the cold air, hats pulled down over their ears, with Dolly pushing the pram and Jessie by her side, they enjoyed the early January sunshine as they strolled along the Mile End Road to take Billy to visit his grandmother Rose. Turning into Whitehorse Road, they heard someone give a wolf whistle. Glancing over her shoulder to see if the admirer was worth a smile, Dolly was amused to see that it was Max, dressed smartly in a suit and unbuttoned dark overcoat.

'Well, well, well,' said Dolly, loving it, 'look who's come out of the woodwork.'

'Who?' said Jessie. 'One of your old flames?' She kept her eyes firmly fixed in front. She didn't want to be tarred with the same brush as her wayward sister. 'Or one of your new boyfriends?'

'No,' said Dolly, cockier than ever, 'one of yours.'

Max reached their side and tipped his hat. He had eyes only for Jessie. 'Mind if I walk with you?' he said, showing his row of perfect white teeth.

'Max, it's you!' Jessie, without thinking, kissed him on the cheek. She was pleased to see him and didn't mind who saw. 'Tom said you'd managed to stay in civvi street. Lucky devil.'

'It wasn't good luck, Jessie, it was bad luck. Wouldn't have me because ... apparently ... my feet wouldn't be up to all that marching.' He turned away from those blue eyes of Jessie's, which he had once adored, and paid attention to Billy who was sitting up, enjoying a Farley's rusk biscuit. 'He's a mixture of both of you, Jess,' he said, his regret showing.

'Right, well, if you'll excuse me and my nephew,' grinned Dolly, 'we'll be on our way.' Grabbing the handle of the pram again, Dolly strode off, wiggling her buttocks for Max's benefit. 'I'll see you at Mum's, Jessie!' she called back over her shoulder.

'She's a gem,' said Max with a smile. 'Come on, Jess,' he laid a hand on her arm, 'I've got masses to tell you and I want to hear how you've been coping.'

'I'm not sure, Max ... you know what people are like. If Tom should get to hear—'

'That you walked along the street with me in broad daylight? Come on, Jessie, this isn't like you. What's happened to your self-confidence?'

'I don't know about that ... but yeah, it's not as if it's nighttime, is it?'

'No. But then again, that didn't both us much once upon a time. So long as we were alone.'

'Don't, Max. Don't stir up all the memories. I'm married now and a mother as well.' She couldn't believe how shy and embarrassed she now felt in his company. 'Not that anyone would take me for anything else but a married woman. Dolly reminded me today how dowdy I was looking.' Jessie would be the first to admit that she was begging for a compliment. Max was right, her self-esteem was on the low side.

'Trust Dolly,' he said, quietly laughing. He remembered Jessie's exuberant, loud-mouthed sister well. 'She never was one for being tactful.'

'So you do think I look drab then?'

He squeezed her arm and an old familiar feeling swept through her. Nothing physical, just a nice friendly feeling. 'You look lovely, Jessie. Although your hair could do with styling. You should go and see the barber again.'

She laughed to be reminded of when she had once had her hair chopped off. Chatting about old times, they soon arrived at Joe Lyons, their previous regular meeting place. 'How's your mum and dad?' she asked, slipping on to a chair at their favoured table by the window.

'More relaxed than they were. At least the war's stopped all the other troubles. They had another brick through their shop window, you know. Blackshirts. I know what I'd like to do if I came face to face with one.' Max looked murderous thinking of the racist attacks his family had suffered.

'Tom and his brother Johnnie walked out, you know, as soon as they realised—'

'That Mosley was likely to be interned?' Max cut in.

'No, it was before all that. They didn't know—'

'Jessie, please. Don't start making excuses for them. They were Blackshirts no matter what. I'll never forgive them. Never. No Jew would.'

Thankful when the waitress arrived with tea and cakes, Jessie took the opportunity to steer the subject back to Max's family. She hadn't heard from Mrs Cohen since she'd married and in a strange way Jessie had missed her. Only once or twice had Mrs Cohen been to visit her mother at the cobbler shop, next door to the Cohens' delicatessen. Having discussed Max's mother and father, Jessie took the bit between her teeth and mentioned Moira, his sister, the one who had been responsible for them breaking off their engagement.

'Moira's fine,' said Max soberly.

'But?'

'But she's been told she'll never have children and it's devastated her.' Max looked serious. 'She and Nathan will adopt children but not until the war's over.'

Breaking off a piece of her fruit bread and popping into her mouth, Jessie shrugged. 'Let's hope they don't adopt someone's twin.'

Max looked bemused by her off-the-cuff remark. 'What makes you say that?'

'You mean you haven't heard?'

'Heard what, Jessie?' He leaned back in his chair and listened intently as she told the incredible story. Her parents, Rose and Robert, had been young newlyweds just after the First World War and very poor, unable to feed and clothe one baby, let alone two. Rose's half-brother Jack Blake and his German wife Gerta had pleaded to adopt one of the twins since

Gerta could not herself have children. It had been a well-kept secret and had it not been for Tom introducing the twin girls much later in life, neither Hannah nor Jessie would have known anything about each other. Hannah would have continued to live in Bethnal Green with her adopted mother, Gerta, who had turned out to be a tyrant – a cold, uncaring woman and a strong supporter of the Blackshirts. Hitler was Gerta's hero and Mosley her heartthrob. Since the day the girls had discovered they were twins they had become closer than very best friends. Closer than ordinary sisters. Ending her story, Jessie said, 'I always knew something was wrong. I thought I was losing my mind at times. Missing someone who didn't exist. That I *thought* didn't exist. And then, wham bang, it's out in the open.'

'You've lost me, Jess . . .' He chuckled. 'My loss, not yours. But there we are – you chose Tom.'

'Max, please. Don't.'

'I can't help it. We would have been married by now. I would have married you, Jess. I *should* have married you.'

'No. Billy wasn't your baby.'

'That wouldn't have mattered. It doesn't matter now even.'

'Maybe not but what *does* matter is that I love Tom. I love him and I'll wait for him.' She sipped her tea and looked at him over the cup. 'You're not shocked then at my having a twin sister?'

'I *am* shocked. You've shocked me. You've really shocked me, Jessie.'

'I know,' she said, enjoying the thrill of shaking the one person she thought was unshakable. 'Mum's been more relaxed since it came out. She's been wonderful, Max. She bought most of the things for the baby – the pram, pillows, blankets . . .'

'Jessie,' said Max, a faraway look in his eyes, 'I can't believe you've got a twin.'

'You will once you meet her. She's more attractive than me.'

'I don't know what to say.'

'I know what you mean. It came as a shock to me as well.'

'*Your* twin. I can't wait to meet her.'

'Well, once she's back for good, I'll introduce you.'

'Back? You mean she went off again?'

'War work. For the government. Can't talk about it though.'

'Why not?'

'Because I haven't got a clue what she does. I suppose you've heard about our Alfie?'

'Alfie.' Max chuckled. 'He surprised us all, didn't he? Who would have thought that little wayward sod would have turned out to be so independent and quick off the mark.'

This attitude from Max surprised her. 'What are you talking about?'

'Well, he's employed, at the ammunition factory, he's got himself a nice little flat and he's involved in good work – selling tickets for charity in Mile End. He even helped by selling dance tickets in aid of the Boys Jewish Club. Made two pounds for us, Jessie.'

Yes, thought Jessie, two pounds for your club and four pounds for Alfie, more like. 'Oh, good. He is keeping up the good work then.' There seemed little point in spoiling her brother's good if false reputation. Maybe he would grow into it.

'Speaking of which, I should be off soon, Jess,' said Max, checking his watch. 'I'm due at the under-eighteens' boxing club. I've joined the board.' Pausing for a few seconds, he looked into her face. 'Can we do this again? Or maybe go to the pictures instead?'

'I don't know, Max. Let me have a think about it.'

Of course. Listen, I've just got to pop next door to the

tobacconist.' He stood up and Jessie felt sure he'd grown taller. 'Wait here for me. I'll be two minutes,' and he rushed out of the tearooms.

'Did you want some more tea?' The waitress's voice drifted through Jessie's thoughts.

'No thanks. I'm just waiting for my friend to come back from the shop next door and then we'll be off.'

The girl broke into a smile and looked relieved. 'I thought he'd walked out on yer.'

'No . . . and he's just a friend. An old mate. Not a boyfriend. I'm already married. He's gone to buy some cigarettes.' At that moment, Max returned, carrying a large box of chocolates which brought a different expression to the waitress's face. Jessie saw it as a smile of condemnation. She wondered if she and Max had looked like lovers sitting there, talking together as if the time in between seeing each other had never passed.

'These are for you, Jess,' said Max, offering her the pretty floral box of chocolates. 'A treat.'

'Max, I can't take those.' Jessie was aghast.

'Why not?'

'Well, my mother for a start. I'm just going round there, don't forget. She'll think we're up to something.'

'Don't be silly,' he said, pushing them into her hands. 'I don't know what things are coming to if I can't buy an old flame a small gift.'

'Small? It must have been the biggest box in the shop.'

'Maybe. Anyway, take them to your mother's and tell her they're for you, her and Dolly, if that makes you feel better.'

'It does, Max. Thanks.' Jessie stood up to leave with him and was embarrassed when he took her arm. She could feel the eyes of the young waitress on her and felt guilt creeping in again. She imagined Tom looking in on the scene – he would be angry and jealous, hurt and scared. Frightened that he might be losing his wife.

'Thanks for the tea, and the chocolates. I'll see you . . . some time. When Tom's back on leave, maybe we could go for a drink together. In a foursome?'

'Maybe,' he said, tipping his hat. 'See you around.'

'Max, don't go.' Embarrassed, she smiled and shrugged. 'Well, not with that look on your face anyway.'

'What look?'

'Doom and gloom.'

Relaxing into his usual easy-going manner, he smiled. 'Jessie, listen. If anything should happen ... I mean if you need me, well, you know where I am.'

'Thanks. I'll remember that.' Exchanging a look that required no spoken word, they turned and walked away from one another.

OVER BETHNAL GREEN will be available from July 2000. Don't miss it.